A Line of Cutting Women

A Line of Cutting Women

EDITED BY

BEVERLY MCFARLAND

MARGARITA DONNELLY

MICKI REAMAN

TERI MAE RUTLEDGE

ET AL.

CALYX BOOKS • CORVALLIS, OREGON

The publication of this book was made possible in part through grant support from the Lannan Foundation, the Oregon Arts Commission, and the Meyer Memorial Trust. With grateful appreciation, CALYX acknowledges the following "Immortal" who provided substantial support for this book: Nancy Dennis.

Cover design by Cheryl McLean. Book design by Cheryl McLean and Micki Reaman.

CALYX Books are distributed to the trade through Consortium Book Sales and Distribution, Inc., St. Paul, MN, 1-800-283-3572.

CALYX Books are also available through major library distributors, jobbers, and most small press distributors including: Airlift, Baker & Taylor, Banyan Tree, Bookpeople, Ingram, and Small Press Distribution. For personal orders or other information write: CALYX Books, PO Box B, Corvallis, OR 97339, (541) 753-9384, FAX (541) 753-0515.

Library of Congress Cataloging-in-Publication Data

A line of cutting women / edited by Beverly McFarland . . . [et al.].
     p. cm.
     ISBN 0-934971-63-3 (alk. paper) : $32 —ISBN 0-934971-62-5 (pbk : alk. paper) : $16.95
     1. Short stories, American—Women authors. 2. Women—social life and customs—Fiction. 3. American prose literature—Women authors. I. McFarland, Beverly.
PS647.W6L56   1998
813'.540809287—dc21

98-42510
CIP

Alternative Cataloging-in-Publication Data

A line of cutting women. Edited by Beverly McFarland, Margarita Donnelly, Micki Reaman, Teri Mae Rutledge, et al.
     "Anthology of collected prose from 22 years of *CALYX, A Journal of Art and Literature by Women.*"
     Includes 37 short stories by Cherríe Moraga, Linda Hogan, Shirley Geok-lin Lim, Tahira Naqvi, Ruthann Robson, and others.
     1. Women's fiction. 2. Women—Fiction. 3. Feminist fiction. 4. Short stories, American—20th century. I. CALYX, A Journal of Art and Literature by Women. II. CALYX Books. III. McFarland, Beverly. IV. Title: Cutting women.
Fiction or 813.5408

Printed in the U.S.A.
9 8 7 6 5 4 3 2 1

Acknowledgments

Since their first publication (except where noted) in *CALYX Journal*, these stories have been published in the following publications: "The Transforming Eye" by Kathleen Alcalá: *Mrs. Vargas and the Dead Naturalist* (CALYX Books, 1992). "Luisa in Realityland (excerpts) " by Claribel Alegría: *Luisa in Realityland*, translated by Darwin J. Flakoll (Curbstone Press, 1987). "New World" by Julia Alvarez: Appeared in a slightly different form in *The Other Side/El Otro Lado: Poems* (Dutton, 1995). Reprinted by permission of Susan Bergholz Literary Services, New York. All rights reserved. "River" by Dee Axelrod: Originally published in *CATALYST, A Magazine of Heart and Mind,* issue no. 4, Fall/Winter 1994. "Nighthawks" by Carolyn Barbier: *Between the Heartbeats: Poetry and Prose by Nurses,* ed. Cortney Davis and Judy Schaefer (University of Iowa Press, 1995). "Sheets" by Beth Bosworth: *The Whole Story: Editors on Fiction* (Bench Press, 1995); *A Burden of Earth* (Hanging Loose Press, 1995). "Her Wild American Self" by M. Evelina Galang: *Her Wild American Self* (Coffee House Press, 1996). "The Doe" by Molly Gloss: *The World Begins Here: An Anthology of Oregon Short Fiction,* ed. Glen A. Love (The Oregon State University Press, 1993). "The Wings" by Kristin King: *1998 Pushcart Prize XXII: Best of the Small Presses* (Pushcart Press, 1998). "Two Deserts" by Valerie Matsumoto: *Making Waves: An Anthology of Writings by and about Asian American Women,* ed. Asian Women United of California (Beacon Press, 1989); *Walking the Twilight II: Women Writers of the Southwest* (Northland Publishing, 1996); *The Woman I Am: The Literature and Culture of Contemporary Women of Color,* ed. D. Soyini Madison (St. Martin's, 1994). "It Is You, My Sister, Who Must Be Protected" by Cherríe Moraga: excerpted from *Loving in the War Years* (South End Press, 1983) © 1983 Cherríe Moraga. Reprinted by permission of the publisher. "Paths Upon Water" by Tahira Naqvi: *Hear My Voice: A Multicultural Anthology of American Literature,* edited by Laurie King (Addison-Wesley, 1993); *Immigrant Women,* ed. Maxine S. Seller (State University of New York Press, 1994); *Intercultural Journeys Through Reading and Writing* (HarperCollins, 1991); *The Woman I Am: The Literature and Culture of Contemporary Women of Color,* ed. D. Soyini Madison (St. Martin's, 1994). "A Line of Cutting Women" by Rita Marie Nibasa: a three-page monologue has been performed on the stage by the author and published in *More Monologues for Women by Women,* edited by Tony Haring-Smith (Heinemann, 1996). "Esther, or The World Turned Upside Down" by Alicia Ostriker: A different version was originally published in *The Kenyon Review,* 1990, vol. 12, no. 2, 1990; *The Nakedness of the Fathers: Biblical Visions and Revisions* (Rutgers University Press, 1994). "Young Mother" by Maria Luisa Puga, translated by Julie Albertson: Originally published in Spanish in *Accidentes* (Martin Casillos Editions, Mexico, 1981) © 1981 Maria Luisa Puga. Reprinted in English translation by permission of the author. "Lives of a Long-Haired Lesbian" by Ruthann Robson: *Eye of a Hurricane* (Firebrand Books, 1989). "Killing Color" by Charlotte Watson Sherman: Originally published in *Memories and Visions* (Crossing Press, 1989); *Killing Color* (CALYX Books, 1992); *Spooks, Spies and Private Eyes,* ed Paula L. Woods (Doubleday, 1996). "Siko" by Marianne Villanueva: *Contemporary Literature of Asia,* ed. Arthur W. Biddle, Gloria Bien, and Vinay Dharwadker (Prentice Hall, 1996); *Ginseng and Other Tales from Manila* (CALYX Books, 1991). "White-Out" by Phyllis Wolf: *Talking Leaves,* ed. by Craig Lesley (Dell, 1994).

Table of Contents

Introduction

W hen four women friends with little publishing experience and no funding decided to found *CALYX, A Journal of Art and Literature by Women,* they had no idea that *CALYX* would blossom into a nationally respected journal of fine literature and art. They were passionate about women's literature and intended to provide a needed forum for women's artistic work, stressing excellence with a feminist sensibility. The first issue of *CALYX Journal,* released in June 1976, received immediate national attention and quickly outgrew its original subtitle—*A Northwest Feminist Review.* Over time the journal has gained a reputation for introducing emerging writers. Literary journals, always the champions of risky, edgy, and unknown work, play an important role in the development of American writers. While many small journals collapse after a few years, some, like *CALYX,* are able to endure. Among the twenty-four hundred writers *CALYX* has published, an impressive number are now well known.

The prose gathered in *A Line of Cutting Women* reflects *CALYX*'s history as well as the impact women writers are making on contemporary literature, cutting into a literary canon that continues to be dominated by men even in 1998, as The Modern Library's recent list of "100 Best English-Language Novels of the 20th Century"—which includes only eight woman authors—demonstrates.

In *A Line of Cutting Women,* famous writers share the pages with emerging writers, exposing connections between cultures and generations. Through *A Line of Cutting Women* flow voices from many walks of life, voices that don't always agree, voices that create a conversation about the concerns of a gender too often invisible in the literary landscape. Voices that—when provided in the context of other women's work—tell a distinct and eloquent story.

There's young Jenny—from "Apple and Stone," a story set in an ambiguous time—who realizes her revenge the night before she is forced to marry her rapist. Julia Alvarez writes about Tía Ana and Tía Fofi, two women from the Dominican Republic who never quite acculturate to life in the USA. Grandma, in Linda Hogan's "Crow," a fiercely independent, gritty grandmother, finds comfort in a crow's companionship. Charlotte Watson Sherman dedicates her story, "Killing Color," to Beulah Mae Donald, who won a judgement against the Ku Klux Klan for the murder of her son

Michael. Siko haunts his mother Saturnina in Marianne Villanueva's fiction set in the Philippines. And a young Mormon wife is drawn to the angel on her roof in Kristin King's story "The Wings."

Stories of young girlhood, of the choice between death and life sustained by a machine, of unwed mothers, of older women coming into their own, of struggles for individual identity, of sexual abuse, of racism, of independence, humor, adventure—the complexity and diversity of women's lives and realities are reflected in the prose of *A Line of Cutting Women,* and *A Line of Cutting Women* reflects back the unique contribution and editorial vision of *CALYX Journal.*

Editing at *CALYX Journal* has never been done traditionally. From the beginning we strived for diversity among the editors selecting work for publication and operated with an open and nonhierarchical collective editorial board, which has included over fifty fiction editors during our twenty-two-year history.

A remarkably energetic and committed group of editors has volunteered to read the thousands of manuscripts received annually. Currently seven editors select work for publication in *CALYX Journal* at lively editorial meetings. Because the *CALYX* collective often functions like a good writing group, offering suggestions to writers who appreciate the careful attention and respect for their work, *CALYX Journal* is able to publish work by writers whose craft is developing—and to discover writers early in their careers.

For special theme issues we have reached out to editors of different communities. Mary Tallmountain, Diane Glancy, and Ada Medina assisted in editing *Bearing Witness/Sobreviviendo: the Chicana/Hispanic/Native American Issue* (Volume 8:2); Shirley Geok-lin Lim and Mayumi Tsutakawa helped edit *The Forbidden Stitch: An Asian American Women's Anthology* (Volume 11:2&3); and Amy Agnello, Sonia Gomez, Laura McFarland, Zola Mumford, and Mira Chieko Shimabukuro joined Micki Reaman and Teri Mae Rutledge in editing *Present Tense, CALYX*'s twentieth anniversary anthology of young writers (Volume 16:3).

In a recent review of *CALYX Journal, Library Journal* Editor in Chief John Berry paid *CALYX Journal* a great compliment, praising both the editors and the long line of cutting women, the writers of *CALYX.*

"CALYX has survived two decades of struggle in a society that only grudgingly pays for excellence, especially in challenged genre like the short story or poem. Yet here in CALYX such works thrive, and move, and command your attention…. [CALYX is a] paragon of the literary arts, [an] exemplar of what great writing and editing can create. From here will come our literary heritage."

As always special thanks are due to the student interns who assisted with this anthology: Neela Banerjee (Oberlin College), Megan Fairbank (Whitman College), Kate Lamont (Linfield College), Jill Leininger (University of Oregon), Joanne Mueller (Western Oregon University), and Jill Salahub (Oregon State University). We also extend our gratitude to all the editors who read and selected this fiction over the past two decades: *Founding Editors*: Barbara Baldwin, Margarita Donnelly, Meredith Jenkins, Beth McLagan. *Fiction Editors*: Amy Agnello, Jo Alexander, Debbie Berrow, Jan Caday, Yolanda Calvillo, Jo Cochran, Lois Cranston, Luz Delgado, Lisa Domitrovich, Valerie Eames, Bettina Escudero, Diane Glancy, Sonia Gomez, Rebecca Gordon, Barbara Hadley, Catherine Holdorf, Anne Krosby, Barbara Lewis, Shirley Geok-lin Lim, Susan Lisser, Dorothy Mack, Ruth Malone, Beverly McFarland, Laura McFarland, Cheryl McLean, Naomi Littlebear Morena, Linda Morgan, Zola M. Mumford, Carol Pennock, Emily Ransdell, Karen Ratté, Micki Reaman, Kathleen Reyes, Christine Rhea, Barbara Rohde, Beth Rosania, Teri Mae Rutledge, Carolyn Sawtelle, Mira Chieko Shimabukuro, Vicki Shuck, Linda Varsell Smith, Sara Swanberg Spiegel, Ann Staley, Mary Tallmountain, Mayumi Tsutakawa, and Sarah Williams.

The Editors

Katherine Sturtevant

APPLE AND STONE

A llhallow Even, time of omens and auguries. The mir-
ror forecasts marriage, the bonfire predicts death.
Thomas rose that morning thinking of tasks: wood to be hauled, fodder
piled up, the house to be made ready for winter. But his wife Kate was
worrying about Jenny, their eldest.

It was her thirteenth birthday, but as Jenny woke it was her pain she
thought of, needing to take its measure. Though the room was chilled with
night, she felt the sleepy heat of her brothers and sisters surrounding her
and thought: *they don't know yet.* She turned her head, and her cheek
touched cold glass. It was then that she remembered her birthday and realized
gladly that Mother had won the argument. Father shouted that she had
enough of vanity, but Mother said to break it would bring a curse upon all
her daughters and sons, too, for seven years. During Father's silence Jenny
imagined the bad luck rising vaporous from the glittering shards of glass,
like the sweet-smelling evil of poison herbs, perhaps, from a tea or soup.

In two weeks I am to be married. What would the children think when
they were told, she wondered. Already they were bewildered by Father's
wrath and Mother's grieved uncertainty. Thinking of Mother's doubt plunged
a pain through Jenny beside the first—did Mother blame her too? But the
hurt subsided as she touched the icy glass of the mirror with her sleep-
warmed fingers. Toward her father she felt bitter, but it was the old bitter-
ness. Always he found fault with her. With Mother it was different. Jenny
was the favorite, the first of all the babies to live, her strength built from
infant corpses and winter burials. Proudly she lifted the mirror to her face.
A weak dawn light entered through the papered window, not yet shuttered
for winter. In the glass she saw the marks that matched her pain: a yellow

ditch beneath her left eye, the arc of her swollen cheek, the blood-dark cut on her lip. The mirror didn't show the trails of purple thumb marks on her new breasts, or the pain that wound like a river through her womb and clenched like a fist as she rose. It was a week since Jonathan Pearson had seized her crossing the woods between her uncle's house and her father's, homeward bound at dusk. He slapped her, he crushed her with his weight, he entered her like a stone. He bloodied and bruised her, with his knees made long yellow ovals of flesh on the insides of her thighs. He tore her clothes, her skin, her maidenhead. As his punishment, he must marry her.

Jenny lowered the mirror, breathing deep to quell her guilt and her rage. She wished she knew charms; she wished she knew secrets. Or if Lydia still lived, she could slip into the woods and ask her aid—for surely, Jenny thought, remembering Lydia's clever, wrinkled eyes, surely Lydia could have saved her. But she was dead, her cottage burnt, six cats killed in her spirit's wake.

Allhallow Even. Would Lydia ride tonight?

In the kitchen Kate, too, thought of Lydia.

"Oh, don't! Your back!" Jenny cried out when she found her mother leaning low over the kitchen fire.

Kate turned, thinking eagerly of her gift to Jenny, but her daughter's words made her aware of the ache that rose hot in her back.

Jenny dipped her head in quick remembrance. "Thank you, Mother, for the looking glass."

"My love with it, Jenny," Kate said, and held her daughter close, gentle of her bruises.

It was a morning swift with work. The children did their tasks eagerly instead of lagging about, for they knew that after dinner they would be freed to gather fuel for the bonfire, and to seek out stones. Their gaiety made a sullen flame inside Jenny; what had she to anticipate? More cleaning after dinner, and taking care of Baby. "Good practice," Grandma said, as Jenny ran to still his crying. But hurrying woke her pain and Grandma's words woke her rage, until, picking up the fat, screaming child, she wanted to dash his downy head against the stone hearth, as if all were his fault. Father had come home early to dinner so as to shutter the windows, and the blows of his hammer rang in Jenny's head, while her arms trembled under their live burden.

"Jenny!" Kate called out. The squalling continued, the hammering continued, but something in Jenny quieted when she heard her mother's voice.

"Let Grandma take him," Kate said. "I need some apples before dinner." And at the gladness on Jenny's face she felt her own strength settle and harden, like clay under a summer sun.

What freedom! Jenny had little time before dinner, yet she went slowly out of doors, pulling her shawl close. The day was sunny but chill. There was a flavor of summer sorrowed after, winter promised merrily. Snowballs, roasted crabapples—promises for children. At the apple tree she stooped to gather fallen fruit into her apron. She had often climbed this tree. She wanted to climb it again, but thought she must not, now that she was thirteen and sore limbed. And then she *did* climb it, because she wanted to, because she was angry and sullen, and to celebrate having been so recently a child. She sat on a thick bough with her legs dangling, smarting from having stressed her bruised body, and chomping a yellow apple in its bright jacket with the good side of her mouth. Thus she was sitting when she heard Jonathan's whistling and saw his blondness shining among the colored leaves not yet fallen from the trees that hid her from his path.

She swallowed her terror, her breath. She was perfectly still, apple wrapped in her palm. Though she had been easy on the bough the moment before, suddenly she feared that she might lose balance and fall.

For some moments after he passed Jenny remained motionless. Then she dropped her apple to the earth below and saw it roll, gathering dirt to its white flesh. She climbed down. Quietly she filled her apron with apples and took them to her mother, saving one out for the mirror at midnight. A girl eating an apple would see her future husband's face in the glass, Jenny knew, at midnight Allhallow Even. Or if she saw only her reflection, she'd stay a spinster the year to come. Jenny wondered: would Jonathan's face smirk back at her?

After dinner Jenny and Kate swept the kitchen and scrubbed it, making welcome the spirits. Grandpa and Aunt Fay, perhaps, would come glow like moonlit clouds in the kitchen chairs. When done they sat at the table to rest for a moment, while Grandma rocked Baby in the other room.

"We will have much to talk of these coming two weeks," Kate said, breathing deep and steadily as she settled into her chair. "There is much a wife must know." She regarded her daughter closely and curiously.

Jenny could not hide her aversion and looked away from the young lines in her mother's face. "How old did you marry?" she asked.

Kate shook her head, slowly. "That is not the way," she said. "Let me tell you about my third child, baptized Marguerite. She was born without arms or legs, and her skull also was misshapen. This may happen to you, to any woman. You must be prepared." Jenny nodded uncertainly. "I prayed that the Lord would heal her," Kate went on. "Prayer is always the first choice. Do you pray, Jenny? Have you prayed?"

"Of course, Mother."

"Of course. I prayed as well. And I consulted midwives, but they did not help. Then, Lydia. You remember Lydia?" Jenny's head bobbed quickly, breathlessly. "With special preparations I bathed and fed my child. I prayed for her healthy life, but it was the Lord's will that she die rather than live deformed. She was not yet two months old. Do you understand?"

Jenny shook her head, confused.

Kate laid her palms over her eyes.

"I'm sorry—" Jenny began timidly.

"No, listen," Kate said quickly as she lifted her hands. "The Lord does his will in many ways. Some are very old." She paused for a moment. Jenny plucked at her skirt, wishing they would go back to work. She was beginning to be frightened. "You remember your Aunt Fay?" Kate began again.

"Yes."

"Her husband, Edward, died the year you were born. He was not a good man. He drank, he neglected his work, he beat your aunt and their children, your cousins. Fay turned to God. She prayed for release or for endurance, she prayed that the Lord's will be done. He sent her a dream, a dream of Lydia. She went to see Lydia, and they—they prayed together. A few weeks later, Edward died. Do you understand?" Her voice was low, almost a whisper. "Think! Think!" she said sharply. "Do you understand?"

And Jenny saw! But she was terrified.

Kate began to cry. "I will help you all I can," she said. "I can show you how to make soups and stews and medicines. I can teach you much— enough. But *you* must choose how to apply what you learn."

I, Jenny thought wildly, *I must choose!*

"Go, gather some cones for the bonfire," Kate said urgently. "Go, find a stone."

Jenny ran far into the woods; her anger and pain rose in her like a building fire. She did not want to choose, *why* had she to choose? But she felt the new blood healthy beneath her bruises and thought: *I am healing! I will be strong again!* Then she saw Richard, her youngest brother but one, wandering unminded, and saw Harriet's red shawl through the trees. She caught him up, and the sticks he grasped poked into her swollen cheek. How she loved him! He wriggled and yelled, protesting, while she bellowed at Harriet for letting him stray. Harriet ran guiltily back, thrashing through the litter of dead branches on the forest floor, and Jenny looked at her flushed face and loved her too. She set Richard down and together they carried sticks and cones to the little rise of bare earth near the house, already piled with earth's brittle decay. Here three families would gather round the fire and cast their stones, and if any stones were gone the next morning that soul would surely die within the year. Omens and auguries. *Let the mirror decide,* thought Jenny.

How the bonfires blazed! Jonathan's family, Uncle William's, and Jenny's own stood grandfather to toddler in a circle, with their marked stones in their hands. Across the village and over the bare, harvested fields, the fires billowed against the black sky, and the smoke sailed off the feathery tips of flames. In heathen times, Jenny knew, people danced around such fires and made human sacrifices. She slipped into the ring next to Jonathan.

"Have you your stones?" Jonathan's grandfather cried above the fire's hot wind. His face looked red and twisted as Jenny stared through the heat-glazed air. She looked hard at her mother, but Kate would not look back. Jenny's hip touched Jonathan's and her shoulder his arm, and he looked down at her in surprise. She lowered her eyes and saw the gray rock sloped like a turtle's shell in his palm. "Make sure they are marked well!" his grandfather commanded, "and cast them into the fire! He who cannot find his stone the morrow will not live to see another Allhallow Even!"

They cast their stones and prayed long by the fire. When they were done Jenny slipped quickly away, for it was nearly midnight.

Softly she passed through the kitchen and saw the settling of wind about a chair. Was it Grandpa sitting there, or Aunt Fay? The fire burned low and red. Hurriedly she entered the bedroom and there dragged the mirror and apple from beneath her blanket. But not a star's light shone through the covered window, so she crept carefully back to the kitchen and by the fire held the rosy glass to her face. She watched her broken lip slide over the apple's skin, her teeth tear into sweet meat. One bite after another, and still her image did not fade. How had she known it would not?

She saw that she would have a long night, cold and sleepless, with risk of death if she were caught. Whose spirit would find her at the bonfire's ashes? Might Uncle Edward attack or betray her? Might Lydia protect her?

And in the morning, when Jonathan could not find his stone, would he then be afraid? But that did not matter. It was not his fear she sought.

Marisha Chamberlain

Firewood

E venings, Gran sat on the side porch of the farm-house, reading and watching the sky. She liked doing two things at once and had rigged an extra-long cord on the floor lamp, so she could take it out of the bedroom onto the porch with her. She'd switch it on as soon as it began to get dark. The lamp had a huge red shade, cracked and curled in places, blotched with dew from the evenings when she'd forgotten to take it back in the house. From where I swung on the gate by the road, it lit her face in a strange way—half her chin, one side of her nose, and her eyelashes; half a face lit up against the tall, dark corn that grew right up to the house.

She'd look up from her book and lean out of the lamp's glow to check on the stars coming out. The electric light would travel over her head as she leaned, through her wispy grey hair with its little curls at her nape, across her wide shoulders and down her back. As she leaned, I'd study the patch of sweater illuminated at the small of her back—its black and silver strands running off into the dark.

Sometimes I got curious about what she was reading. Then I'd sneak into the house through the front door, tiptoe up to the windows in the bedroom, and look over her shoulder. She read Shakespeare and *Prevention Magazine*, books of philosophy and religion, though she was definitely not religious—an atheist in fact. The only time I read over her shoulder for long was when she was reading a mystery story, which wasn't very often.

That particular night in October, I remember, she looked out at the sky more than she read. In fact, when it got dark, she never even turned on the lamp. Though a book lay open on her lap, she studied the sky the whole time, while the sun set purple. Out of the dark she called suddenly, distinctly. By the time I climbed down from the gate and reached the porch, she'd vanished inside, taking the lamp with her.

When Grandfather died, she'd decided to stay put right there in Wisconsin, so she rented out the land. But because the renter had insisted on the full acre, she had to get used to the wall of corn where her backyard had been. There'd been other changes, such as the windows. She'd torn out the wall between the bedroom and the porch and in its place, bolted together a bunch of storm windows to make a crude glass wall facing the hayfield, so she could see outdoors from her bed. Her habits had become even more pronounced, especially her porch time. We chattered and argued through most of the days of the weekends my parents let me visit her, but when the sun began to sink and she picked up her book, I knew I had to leave her alone. There'd be no dinner, either, till the sun had set and the stars were shining. Then, stirring mushroom sauce into rice, or sneaking a little of her vegetarian goulash into my hamburger, she'd begin to talk to me again, as abruptly as she'd left off.

The local people knew of this habit—that she sat out on the porch of an evening with a book. Luvern, driving by in the creamery truck, would call out hello to her on the porch. She wouldn't answer. If I was there, he'd stop a minute. He'd wish me a good evening and in an especially loud voice, would remind me to call on him across the valley, if any of us two women needed a hand. She wouldn't answer and I was proud of that. She was like a queen in her silence. So that strange night I hurried in, curious to know why she'd left the porch so abruptly.

She was standing at the stove, cutting red onions into the beans. When I asked her why she'd called me, she looked surprised and shrugged. I put my arms around her and felt her relax. Then she laughed, shoved me away with her butt, and opened the refrigerator.

"I don't know why, but I was going to tell you to come in out of the dark. Go back on out if you like, stay out all goddam night. You're twelve, it's your life."

"If you don't mind, Gran, I'll eat dinner. It's nine o'clock."

We ate the main course and then argued over whole wheat or white flour to go into the brownies. We both liked to make a dessert and then eat it right away. By the time we climbed into bed, it would always be late. The jazz show would come on the public radio station, the only station Gran allowed, and she'd insist that we sing along as we brushed our hair, humming and la-la-laing over the unfamiliar music. Sometimes we'd eat apples, too, singing with our mouths full, then putting the cores in a bowl by the bedside table. Gran called it vice. She brushed her hair in short jerks, while I languorously undid my pigtail and stroked and stroked my wavy hair. It was the only time I can remember being allowed to brush as long as I liked. I watched us in the windows, brushing and brushing, and the outline of the woodpile like a faint double exposure beyond us, and the lush alfalfa, edged by the cornfield, and finally the woods. Above the woods was a thin stripe of starry sky cut off by the peaked roof. When Gran turned the light out, the night would invade the room. The glass wall made me feel half out of doors. I pulled the sheet immediately over my head, and we'd snuggle down under the covers, five layers of blankets in October for when the fire went dead later on in the night.

Later that night, I stirred in my sleep. I felt Gran curled beside me, smelling of onions and talc. It gradually dawned on me that her breathing was quiet and much too regular. She was awake. I opened my eyes and noticed, then, the strange shadow on the wall. Then I saw the man standing by the bed. He had a thick stick of stove wood in his hands and was raising it slowly over his head. I drew in my breath to scream and Gran reached over and put her hand on my arm.

"I'm glad you found the firewood," she said clearly. "We left the door open for you, and now, if you'll build up the fire, I'll cook your dinner. There's a place for you to sleep here." She sat up in bed.

He lowered the stick of wood and stood for a minute. "But I'm dirty," he mumbled.

"Would you like to wash?"

"No, ma'am."

"You don't have to then. Susan, will you fill the kettle please. And we'll need more firewood, so if you'd bring in eight or nine more sticks."

The man walked out the porch door toward the woodpile. We hadn't even seen his face yet.

"Gran," I whispered, "do you know him?"

"Put the kettle on," she said.

She turned the light on in the kitchen, the little light under its copper shade that lit the table just enough for a midnight snack. She relit the burner under the leftover beans. The man came back into the house with his arms full of wood. I heard his boots clunk heavily across the floor, though I hadn't dared look at him yet. I filled the kettle and reached down the jars of instant coffee and Creamora. Over my shoulder I heard the rustle of newspaper and a match striking against the top of the cast iron heat stove.

Gran appeared beside me at the cookstove, rummaging around the pan shelf for the leftover brownies.

"Why don't you sit down," she said to the man.

"Maybe," he said. And in a minute he drew a chair out from the table and sat down.

"You remind me something of my grandson, Johnny. Susan here, her brother. I never get to see enough of him. Are you from someplace around here?"

I had no brother named Johnny, no brother at all. I turned to look at the man, then. His dark hair was messed and his ears stuck out oddly through his hair. He looked nothing like me. He was hot now that the fire was going, and I watched him take off his hunting jacket, noticing that when he lifted his hands from the table, he'd left smudges on the cloth. His hands were dark and greasy. I saw a stripe of red across his palm under the light.

"You've cut yourself," Gran said, and she put a bowl of bean soup in front of him, with the pan of brownies. I watched incredulously as she sat down with him at the table. She leaned her chin on her elbows and when he reached for a brownie, their arms nearly touched.

"I hope you like that kind of whole flour they mill in town, because Susan and I had an argument. She favors the white stuff from Milwaukee, but I overruled her."

He took a brownie and dipped it into his soup, pushing a piece of celery into the spoon and then cramming the brownie into his mouth after the spoonful of soup. I watched his face to see if he'd realize what he'd done— the sweet brownie with the salty, oniony soup. He looked nervously at Gran. I heard my own voice, thin, reedy.

"I don't know," I began.

"Susan," Gran said, "give the man his coffee."

"Gran, you know what Mother would say."

"Oh, young lady, chatter, chatter. I think it's time to get you back to bed."

"Your sink is dripping," he said, suddenly.

"Yeah, I told Johnny a dozen times, but he doesn't seem to find the time. Maybe he doesn't know how."

"A wrench," he said.

"Let me see what I can find." Gran crossed the kitchen and opened the cupboard under the sink. "You handy at this sort of thing?"

He shrugged, pushed the bowl away from him, half full, and opened and closed his hands. Gran found a box of rubber washers and pulled them out. He poured them out into the sink. Gran found grandfather's big wrench. It took her two hands to lift it. For a second I thought she'd hit him with it. I hoped and prayed she'd hit him. But she only set the wrench on the sideboard.

Gesturing at the sink, she said, "I think it just naturally drips. I'll make the bed up for you. Go on, Susan, I'll tuck you in, in a minute."

"Tuck me in!" I said. She raised her eyebrows. I looked longingly at the wall phone over the table.

"Can I call Mom?" I said.

"No, honey, it's the middle of the night."

"But, Gran," I said.

"Susan," she said sharply, "go right to bed now and no more annoying us." I searched her face for some sort of signal. She must've been afraid, but I saw nothing but annoyance, more annoyance than I'd ever seen before in my grandmother.

"All right!" I said, annoyed myself, and I stomped out of the room.

"Teenagers these days," she said to him.

"That girl a teenager?"

"Oh, she's twelve, she's a teenager," Gran said. I pulled the covers tight around me and turned on the red lamp overhead. I heard Gran moving farther away in the house; then the sound of metal on metal as he put the wrench on the faucet. The dripping got faster, then stopped. I heard Gran call out across the house, "You tired?"

"Tired," he said. "I'll tell the world."

I heard their footsteps moving away. Gran said, "Good night now, Johnny," and she came back into the bedroom. She turned the switch off over my head and picked up a book and the lamp and stepped toward the door.

"Gran," I hissed from bed, "I want you."

"Susan, you just mind yourself. This is my porch time and I want to see the sun rise in peace." And she put on socks and pulled her sweater over her nightgown, and then curled up in her reading chair beyond the windows and switched on the lamp. I lay in the dark, watching her from the window, her hair tousled into little cowlicks, lit red by the lamp, and the soft skin of her cheek, powdered red. She looked smaller, somehow, sitting in the middle of the Wisconsin night with her lamp. I crept to the glass and looked over her shoulder. She was reading the Bible! Gran, who hardly believed in God, was reading the Old Testament.

"Mark the doorposts," I read with her. "And none of you shall go out of the house until morning. For the Lord will pass over the door. And when your children say, what do you mean by this, you shall say that the Lord passed over the houses of the people of Israel in Egypt and did them no harm. But

Pharoah rose up in the night, with his firstborn dead in his arms, and called Moses and Aaron to take their people out of slavery and be gone."

I tapped the window. Gran turned the page. I got back into bed. If she could stay up, so could I. I gripped the bedpost to keep awake, but the house was uncommonly warm from the firewood and I slid down the pillow. I woke up to see the man stepping out the door onto the porch. I saw Gran turn to him. The sky behind them was a glory of light purple; the stars, gorgeous, prickly; and a stripe of orange was widening above the woods. She put her finger to her lips. He gave a nod, then crashed off through the corn. I drifted off again.

But the morning came on brightly. There was a knock at the door and I got up to answer it, seeing Gran slumped snoring into her book. The sheriff stood there and Luvern was with him. I brought them in and made them coffee, roused Gran and she came in, smoothing her hair with her hand.

The sheriff cleared his throat a couple times, but it was Luvern who finally spoke. "I guess I should tell you, Rose Ellen . . ." He stopped a minute, then began speaking again. "It's just that I'm surprised to be talking to you. Somebody . . . killed a lot of the neighbors last night. You've got empty houses on three sides."

Then Gran phoned my mother. She asked her to come out and get me right away. She hung up the phone and sat down. Her face wobbled. She sobbed and shook a long time, while Luvern knelt beside her and the sheriff leaned against the sink, cracking his knuckles.

I thought Gran would move away, but she didn't. She told them all she felt safer at her place than she would in a cement fortress. As time went on, the empty farms around her were bought up by people from out of the county, people who weren't so susceptible to the story. I was never allowed to stay over alone at Gran's again, though it wasn't because she told my parents about our visitor. I was the one who couldn't stop talking about him, even when my parents said it made them nervous.

Sometimes, at least, there'd be family reunions out at Gran's place. When her porch time came around, the family would joke among themselves about how she was alone in all this quiet most of the time anyway. As for me, I'd go quietly to stand at the glass and read over her shoulder as the night fell. I don't think Gran slept straight through the night much anymore. In the morning, more often than not, when we awoke, she'd be out in her reading chair again, asleep under the glow of the red lamp.

THE DOE

K ate took the river highway to Astoria and then went slowly down the coast searching for a vacancy in that long strand of villages facing the sea. The weather was poor, and because of that she'd hoped to find the weekend crowd diminished a little. Instead, it was encamped. Where the highway curved up the seaward face of Neakahne Mountain, there were oyster-colored clouds breaking like surf against the cliffs, and below, at Garibaldi, the rain hung like a beaded curtain in a door-way. But everywhere, for fifty miles along the coast, the decent rooms were taken. Finally, in twilight the color of pewter, she doubled back to Nehalem and turned inland into the knobs of the coast range—the slow road home. The fourth annual Kate-needs-some-time-alone weekend was now officially a washout. And by this time she was almost too stale to care.

The road sliced a clean, curving furrow through the timber. There were no other cars and the margins of the road were black and wet and feature-less and Kate didn't see the doe until afterward. There was a pale water-color of movement against the near trees, only that, and the sound when it struck the car, a padded sound like the one you'd make smacking your open hand on a seat cushion, and there was a jumbled minute, or part of a minute, getting the car in hand, skating on the wet pavement, and then she was sitting still in the darkness beneath the eaves of the trees. Under the palms of her hands, through the steering wheel, she could feel the car still quak-ing, or her hands quaking, and she managed after a while a sort of pro-test—"God *damn!*"

In the pulse of the emergency parking lights she walked back along the edge of the road. The doe lay flat against the gravel shoulder, waiting, watch-ing Kate with dark, brittle-bright eyes. The rain beaded in the wooly hairs of Kate's coat, on the lenses of her glasses, on the smooth khaki-colored hide of the deer. She stood back a little beneath the trees, staring, hunching her shoulders against the wetness, and in a little while, when she could, she said, "I've never killed anything in my life," offering the words out loud so they seemed an explanation, and an apology. The doe's eyes, watching her, were flat, depthless, shining. In a bit Kate stooped to touch one smooth brown shoulder. Beneath the tips of her fingers the life sign was a soundless and simple tremble.

"I won't hurt you," Kate said, and didn't hear the irony until afterward. She sent the flat of her hand sliding across the big curve of belly where, *ah God,* the unborn fawn's timid heartbeat released the first of her tears. She squatted where she was, scrunched up small with her hands drawn back to her lap, rocking a little on her heels, staring out to the curve of the road and the ditch running brown and fast with the rain and the trees climbing up the hillside behind in a black palisade. Damn. Ah, damn. Swearing without focus or purpose. Damn. Damn. Damn.

She sorted through the possibilities. The first, the worst one, unspeakable and horrifying, she cast out. The rest seemed vaguely melodramatic, wagging not-quite-real happy endings, but she squeezed her eyes shut and grabbed one: If there was someone else here, one of them could stay beside the doe, protect her, with road flares and blinking taillights, while the other went for help. For a vet. Or someone. She had simply to be patient and wait for a car to stop. She had simply to wait.

So she set flares along the road, spurting their red jets into the darkness, and she pulled the soccer blanket from the trunk and put it carefully over the doe until only the heartbreakingly patient face and the long brittle ankles showed above and below the fringe. Then she stood beneath the trees with her hands pushed in the pockets of her coat and her face turned out to the road shining in the rain. The doe lay quiet, indifferent or resigned, and no one came. She's in shock, Kate decided. There's no pain when you're in shock, is there? So she waited.

It was only when headlights struck the far trees that she remembered her own vulnerability, and she went quickly back along the edge of the gravel to the car, locked herself in, and then rolled the window down enough to wave one hand out, signalling.

The car slowed cautiously at the flares and then finally stopped beside Kate. In the light thrown from the dashboard there were two very young faces, the boy showing brushy stripe of eyebrows and wide mouth and the girl a round face, honey-colored hair. The girl cranked her window down but it was the boy, leaning across, who said, "Broke down?"

Kate leaned her chin toward the open space in the window. "No, my car is fine, I guess. But I *could* use some help. I've struck a deer. Would you know if there's a vet back in Nehalem?" She gestured vaguely toward the doe. "I think she's in shock. Maybe if one of us could get help for her . . . ," turning up the last word to make the whole thing a question. To leave room for other options. Or refusals.

The girl made a quick, splintered little sound of grief, fluttered one hand toward the doe. "Oh Jake, look, a deer." The boy turned his face to where she pointed.

In a moment, with his wide mouth pulled out stiff now, he said, "She's not dead?" and at Kate's dismal shake of head he flipped on his own emergency lights and left the car, bunching his thin shoulders as he crossed through the rain to the doe.

Kate spoke to the girl across the wet space between the cars. "I'm sorry if I've ruined your evening," offering, too, an apologetic half-smile.

The girl's round face was solemn, forgiving, faintly inattentive. "It's okay," she said, while her eyes followed the boy.

Kate watched him, too, twisting to peer through the smeared rear window. His hands, reaching to touch the doe, were slender and tentative and, watching him, Kate betrayed herself with a despairing thought: *He is too young.*

The boy stayed with the doe quite a while, touching her carefully, thoroughly, and then for a moment simply squatting as Kate had done, staring out to the trees with the rain beading shiny in his hair. Finally he came back to Kate. He ducked his chin slightly before he said, "I think she's carrying a fawn." The girl made a wordless outrushing sound, pain or dismay, and the boy glanced briefly round to her with a helpless shrugging of his eyebrows.

In a moment Kate pushed out the little plea she had readied. "I don't know how badly she's hurt, but maybe she can be helped, or at least maybe the fawn could be saved."

In her own head the words whined with a childish and thin sound of urban naivete, and now she began to feel the first prickly edges of a kind of embarrassment. The boy ducked his chin slightly, as he had before, with that look of shyness or discomfort, and fixed his eyes on a point in the trees somewhere behind her.

"I hate to say it but I don't think there's much chance. You'd never get anybody out tonight, not for something like this," with a slight gesture of his head toward the doe. "And I think she must be in a pretty bad way or she'd be moving more, maybe trying to get up or something."

In the red light between the cars he displayed a smooth and very young face, but Kate had lost that earlier sense of his helplessness, of his beardless innocence. She didn't feel, what, twenty years older than him? Instead, simply on the strength of his one forthright statement (or maybe just on the strength of his masculinity), she found she was sliding toward a feeling of dependence—and deliverance. It was easy to give up the tidy little happy ending now that someone else had come.

For the moment he seemed to wait, as if Kate, having struck the deer, should be the one to say out loud the one thing that seemed unavoidable. And finally, past a closed throat, she managed: "I guess the poor thing should be put out of her suffering," tacking around at the end to leave a faint and rueful question mark.

The boy made a wordless sound, pained, agreeing, then nothing more; in the silence Kate began to feel fresh despair. Something else, too, leaking in under the edges. Impatience?

"Do you have a gun or anything like that?" the boy asked finally.

Kate shook her head. And watching his grave eyes beneath their ledge of brows, found she could not bring herself to suggest a stone. The silence seemed thick and cottony and dingy with gloom. I can't, she said with her silence. I'm sorry but I just wouldn't be able to do it. It will have to be you. I'm sorry. Seeing now, in a sudden wash of anguish and guilt, that this had been the reason for waiting. Someone else will have to do it.

"Well, I've never had to do anything like this before," the boy said, glancing gingerly toward the doe and then toward the girl, with that characteristic ducking of his chin. "But I can't see letting her lay there and suffer." He lifted both hands in a sudden sharp-edged gesture of resolve. "I'll get your blanket," he said, "and then you can just go on if you want. I'll take care of it."

His face had become very pale and hard, all of its adolescent smoothness gone jagged. He ducked his chin again and walked very stiffly through the rain to the place where the doe waited. Kate watched him retrieve the blanket. He bunched it against his chest with both arms so his shoulders were a bow, a long turned-in curve. He came and stood beside her a moment, looking out at the trees from his stiffened face, and into the silence made a sound of sour amusement. "My mom just bought me a 'Save the Whales' tee shirt," he said, and managed to make his words say something else, something complex and only dimly relevant. He pushed the blanket to her through the window and where he brushed her hand the touch was chill and wet. He went through the rain to his car and said something to the girl and then went to stand looking at the doe with his hands fisted in his pockets, working nervously against the sacs. He stood with his shoulders tucked in tight and protective.

Kate looked away, looked out at the indifferent darkness of the trees. At the edge of her view she could see the girl in the other car holding herself very stiffly, her pale round face staring straight out through the windshield, straight out to the road while she waited for the boy. Kate began to shake again, thought, *Someone else will have to do it,* and remembered with not much surprise that she'd said that once already, with a different intent.

She unlocked the car and walked back through the rain, through the cool and unburdening rain, to stand beside the boy.

"She doesn't act as though she's in pain," Kate said, offering him one of her own earlier self-deceptions.

There were down-turned puckers at the corner of his mouth, as though weights hung there dragging. "No," he said. "She doesn't."

She said, "I'd feel so much better about this if we at least tried to get her some help." She had already begun to feel cool and controlled, floating detached from her earlier feelings as if they had happened to someone else, as if she'd heard the story second-hand. It was unexpectedly easy to get the right tone of voice, imploring, apologetic. "Since she doesn't seem to be suffering, I just hate to give up without making an effort to save her."

The boy's thin shirt was dark across the shoulders where the rain had soaked through. The ends of his hair dribbled wet down inside the collar. "I don't think there's a vet in Nehalem," he said in a moment, but she thought she could hear a softness, a loosening there at the edge of his voice.

"Then we could call the State Police," Kate said. "Or the Fish and Wildlife people, or the Humane Society, or the SPCA." Her whole list of happy endings. Then she waited for the boy, who stood watching the doe from that frighteningly young, frighteningly splintered face. Finally he made a sound of surrender or relief, a sigh.

"I guess it wouldn't hurt to try a couple of people," he said. And then, with his face turned carefully toward the trees, "If worse comes to worst, we can get my girlfriend's dad to come out," adding in a moment, "He goes elk hunting every year," as a clear little footnote.

Kate said, "Yes, if worse comes to worst," while her eyes watched the doe.

The boy shifted his weight, patted his pockets. "Have you got a piece of paper? I'll draw you a little map to get to my girlfriend's house."

She made a slight gesture of dismissal. "You know where you're going. I'd only get lost and you'd be waiting here. I want you to go."

He gave her a doubtful look of objection. "I don't know if you should wait here alone."

"I'll lock myself in the car."

He looked from her to the doe, shifted his feet again, uncomfortable. "She lives between Nehalem and Manzanita," he said. "I might be an hour, maybe more, if I have to go get her dad. That's kind of a long time for you to wait. Kind of a long time to leave the doe like that too."

"It's all right," Kate said. "It will be all right."

He looked at the doe again and then down the sloping curve of asphalt running red-beaded in the shine of taillights. Finally his shoulders moved indistinctly, a shrug, or a shrugging off. "Okay," he said, with another sound, a faint sigh. "I'll be back as quick as I can," and he crossed the road to his car.

The windows were black and wet and lustrous, like facets of gems. The girl showed her face within one, a pale image smiling a melancholy encouragement, and then the boy stirred the car. Inside the cones of headlights each rain bead seemed to fall singly, with a solitary glare. And Kate, watching the two of them out of sight behind the bending of the road, watching through melting scald of tears, felt at once as encapsulated as those separate drops of rain.

Still, she did not wait. She went a little way into the trees to find a rock, a big flat slab, lying wet among leaves, and pried it from the earth with scrabbling fingernails, pried it out silently, with a sort of fierce impatience. Then she held it against her hips with both hands and went back down the slope to the place where the doe waited, put the rock carefully on the ground and then went back to the car for the blanket, shaking it out smooth over the doe again, and after a moment drawing the edge up over the doe's face, over those pleading eyes, those bright and dying eyes.

She knelt carefully beside the rock. It was bright and slick with rain, hard and cold and wet against the inner curve of her hands.

You'd better not wait. You'd better do it right now. Don't think about it any more.

She wiped her palms against her thighs, one harsh downward stroke, and touched the stone again.

"You'll be better off this way," she said, for the doe and for herself, pushing the words out loudly to the edges of the trees, shaping the words carefully and clearly with her stiff pleated mouth.

She lifted the great stone, swinging it up in a shivering arc to her chin and then quick, blind, fierce down, *ah God, God,* rocking back sightless with a wordless outcry of agony and release and completion.

CALYX Journal, Vol. 6:1, 1981

Carol Orlock

THERE ARE COLORS

The river is where we go sometimes. When the air is wet, it rains. When there is more, that makes the river. Sometimes clouds. If they lose a part, my mother says seagull.

Colors have names. Seagull is a cloud that sleeps on the river. White is seagull, cloud. The colors all have names.

My father goes in a boat. He comes back. The boat goes under the water, he says. We stand by the river. He is down beside me and loosens a rock and throws it. "Like that," he says. A seagull goes screaming there to look. "Then we come back up."

The rock is hidden. I cannot find the color.

I am taken places. There is school now. She is tall and plays the piano. I said my name and my favorite color was red. She showed me to draw the letters.

My brother takes me to a movie. I could not hold the money. He is eight.

Then that time I thought it would be a movie, but we went in a car, our family, all four. My brother said he could make a boat. My mother wore a dress. We saw my father's water and his boat. It is gray and shaped like a seagull sleeping on the water. It had gray colors inside.

We got on. I wore new shoes and they made noise like my brother and I jumping up and down. We jump on the couch. Everything for the boat was gray with some red. It smelled like the river. That was green, and some brown like under the porch. The gray spot on the floor of the garage too.

My brother saw the periscope. I saw clocks with numbers wrong. They had only the little hands, red, and they did not go around. They shivered like the little leaves on the Christmas tree. I could touch cold steel. Then my hand smelled like it.

We went down round ladders. My mother pushed down her dress, but wind came and picked it up. My father laughed. I had on overalls.

There are men here. Some are white, some are brown, some are yellow. The brown ones are called colored. My father told me once at a store.

The men are afraid of my father. They are afraid of me. It is a small place, down in here, after the stairs. It is hot, but all the steel is cold. The men call my father Sir, but his first name is Jake. When we go back up the stairs my mother holds her dress better.

Sometimes when I eat I pretend I can be the food, falling all the way down to my stomach. After the boat I felt like I have been in a gray stomach. I can still smell it on my hands in the car.

He wears a uniform. It is one color except for ribbons. The ribbons are striped and shiny with green, red, white, yellow going up and down. Once when his coat was on a chair, I looked in back of them. I thought there would be something else there.

They have gold colored pins in back, like the one my aunt sent me for Christmas. My mother keeps it so I don't stick myself.

The ribbons are for places he went in a war. At the movies we saw pictures of it. War pictures are black and white with a crackly gray voice talking over. Ships slept on the water, then smoke.

Maps are colored like the ribbons. Yellow states, red ones, green Connecticut. I live in Connecticut. Blue lines are rivers and all blue for oceans. The tops of mountains are white because of snow.

I got tired looking at the ribbons. The movie pictures of war are black and white, but ribbons are colors. They are flat. The world in school by the blackboard is round. It turns. Usually when I close my eyes and spin the world, then I point and look, I land in water. My brother laughs. He can swim.

Water is blue. I look for blue but there is no blue stripe on the ribbons. No crackly gray like the talking voice at the movie. There are gold pins holding them, no smoke back there. But he says they are for places he went in a war.

His uniform is navy blue. That is black, but not really. I thought it was at first. He held it in the light and showed me I was wrong.

I looked in the old book about colors—red apple, yellow flower, green tree, blue sky. The black hat in the book could be navy blue. But the word says black.

His uniform is navy blue, they said. I ask about the hat. The hat is navy blue. "If I forgot my hat, I would not be in uniform."

I say the sky is blue, but he says not always. Not really either. "It has no real color," he says. "The dust in the air makes it look blue."

I look for blue dust. He finds gray dust on his uniform and rubs it off. I ask why can't I see the dust in the air.

"It's there. It's too small to see." I am afraid for a while. Then I learn to see dust in the sunlight, only not the blue kind.

Then I forgot my book on the table. It got dust, but no new colors on top. I think dust might be like water, clear in a glass, blue in the ocean. I am happy.

Days go by, blue like dust, gray like dust. Everything is all right so I ask about water. They say it has no color. I was right.

In the summer he wears a white uniform. Still the ribbons are on it. In the summer I go swimming. The water is blue.

I ask again about water. It is clear, they say. It has no color.

"Is it white then?"

No, white is not a color. White is the empty place where there is no color. In my book, a cloud is white. Snow is white. Snow White had lips as red as rubies. A hat is black.

Black, they say, is all colors mixed together. I do it at school, spreading wet paints until they went past navy blue.

Wash my hands off in colorless water. Black is all colors mixed together. White is no color. They are opposites. The uniforms for summer and winter are opposites. The ribbons are the same, gold pin in the back.

Water has no color and no taste. Paper is white, but tastes like dust. And old chewing gum. I put off spitting it out. Then it tastes like a scab.

Black can taste like licorice. Before I wash my hands I tasted black. It was salty in fingerpaint. The teacher took a brown paper towel, wet it, and scrubbed my face. A brown paper towel is really khaki, another uniform.

Khaki is almost flesh, not quite. In my book the baby is flesh colored. A crayon is marked FLESH. I use it, but I cannot draw a baby. Mine is too thin.

Some of the men on the ship were khaki. Some were BURNT SIENNA. I broke the BURNT SIENNA drawing a tree trunk. When I put it back in the box, it looked like the rainbow had a tooth missing.

Once we went, all four, in another boat. It was on the river and we took a picnic. We rented a rowboat, which was painted gray but had a khaki smell. We rolled along the water, my father moving the oars.

Green river, burnt sienna trees, yellow flowers, blue sky. The wind was pink, then it turned yellow. First we stopped and had our picnic, even with a white tablecloth on a grassy place.

Then it was time to go. The wind had been turning yellow, and then it felt green. In the boat going back, he rowed and was angry.

Then we lost part of the sky. First blue fell asleep to gray, then the clouds floated and landed some birds on top of the trees. Green trees turned gray, then their trunks were lost. Then the mud brown riverbank was gone and we were lost. The cloud came close to us like dust, or shadow and cave and a mouth closing. We were inside of a stomach.

We are inside of my father's boat then, and he is angry. I can tell because the oars sound like his footsteps on the ladder. The fog makes us seem like inside of a television set. The sound is turned down. The air tickles like spider webs, and somewhere far, animals are moaning.

My brother says he thinks he sees the dock. We rented the boat at a dock. My father rows where my brother says, but then he has to push away from a tree log with the oar. He pushes, whack. Tree fingers scrape their nails around the boat.

I think I cried. He is angry now. Are we lost. I want to know. He says no, stop it. She holds me but her dress is damp. I hear her heart inside her body, and she sounds afraid.

He makes the oars slap the water, snap, slap, like cap guns. We are not lost, he says. We will be at the dock in a minute. We could be there sooner, but my brother told him the wrong way to go.

Then we went on, going more, slap, snap. Moaning near us. I may have become fog somewhere. I was afraid for my colors. They would not come back. I was bad and gray punished. But then gray must have been sorry. Colors came back.

Maybe a year went by. Summer sifted sunny days and dust. Winter sifted snow and sleeping. My brother was ten. I remember because he got in trouble at school. His homework always got scribbled with drawings of planes and ships on the water. The ships had flags of flames going up, and smoke.

Then one night my father got home late and dinner was almost cold. He set his briefcase by the door. He hung his uniform jacket on the back of his dinner chair.

My mother said bless. We had meat with gravy to go on it. We had white baked potatoes freckled with pepper. We did not talk. When my brother was in trouble at school we ate inside a fog of no noise. I remember the colors. My father's jacket hung on the back of the chair. There were ribbons on it. No one spoke. Forks tinked on china, sharp like bright stripes on dark navy blue.

My brother liked to look at the jacket. He was in trouble at school then, but he did not cry. Not anymore. Boys aren't supposed to. But he kept looking at the jacket.

Maybe he wanted to find out if my father was mad at him. When he is angry, my father's voice has a color that has no name. My brother asked a question to try to hear it.

"In the war, how many planes did you shoot down?"

My father put down his fork. The butter in my potato was golden, but I could not taste it.

"I personally did not shoot anyone. I was part of a crew." My father moved his tongue around his lips. "It's not like baseball, where you get your batting average."

He picked up his fork and took a bite of potato. "It's like tug-o'-war. The whole team pulls."

My brother's voice wanted to cry, but he told a lie instead. "It's for my homework." How many, he wanted to know. "When it's over, don't they tell you something like how many were yours?"

My mother finishes putting gravy on her meat. She slaps the ladle into the gravy boat. Three brown spots come to the white tablecloth, going yellow and clear at the edges.

My father says to stop asking questions. "This is not a topic for the dinner table." His voice does not want to cry.

I was afraid then. But I had to know how he felt. I was afraid to see his eyes. I looked as high as I dared. His lips were the color of dust.

CALYX Journal, Vol. 7:3, 1983

Julia Alvarez

NEW WORLD

I

Tía Ana and Tía Fofi worked at *la factoría*. Tía Fofi attached sleeves to the gaping shoulders. Her specialty was sleeves. But if the Jewish boss, through the Puerto Rican gringa, ordered collars, she did collars, she did buttonholes and panels, stitched darts and pleated gathers. She was a tender-hearted old maid with the sentiments of the married and a sweetheart's pet name, Fofi, for Josefina. She cried often, homesick, *pobrecita* . . . Tía Ana was the serious sister. Her dark eyebrows knotted up like beginner's embroidery. Her hands when she wasn't sewing lay in her lap, praying, one finger capped with a thimble. Tía Ana did the fine needlework, lace collars, shirred bodices, blind stitches only she saw, squinting at the spit-moistened end of the thread she directed into the eye of the needle. They had all come through that eye from Havana, Santiago, San Juan to this United States paradise: old-world seamstresses stitching sleeves to shoulders, yokes to collars, seams holding, skirts flaring like flags unfolding.

II

Tía Ana led Tía Fofi through a maze of subways, three changes and a transfer to the Jamaica Avenue bus station where Mami and I picked them up Saturdays to sew school clothes. We drove the long way home through our nice neighborhood; each lot had a maple blazing in October, a hedge of azaleas blooming in late April. We passed house after house after house that looked like ours. Tía Fofi cried, *¡Ya llegamos!* half a dozen times. Tía Ana packed the instructions Mami had written out with a P.S. in English, asking anyone reading this to kindly help our lost aunts. A second P.S. thanked them. At home the aunts pulled doors to be pushed in, reached to the wrong walls for light switches, answered the door when the phone rang. They were dazed with journeys. But their cutting hand was unerring, their stitching strict as a border, their foot steady on the Singer.

III

Tía Ana knew before anyone else that my breasts had come, that my waist curved in like an hourglass. Tía Ana knew that the blood had come with ghastly stains on the cotton pants she had made me. But she did not disclose the roundness of my buttocks, did not whisper to Mami, *This one is ready to know our secrets.* Did not expose with a wink or a pat the embarrassing inching out under my thin undershirt. No, she pinned in at the waist, out at the hips, stitched secretive darts, altered old seams, and silently, she let the new woman in.

IV

Tía Fofi was another story, tattling as she cut, stitched, seamed, and let in hand-me-downs. Sometimes, pins between pinched lips, she hemmed in silence. But once gossip got going, she unpinned her mouth and put in her part, *Fulano had been seen stepping out with Fulana. Fulanito would come to no good with Fulanita.* As she gabbed, the odd cutouts slid under the babbling Singer and came out cotton jumpers, Sacred Heart blazers, wash-and-wear blouses. I wondered how after decades without a visit to the island, Tía Fofi knew what wickedness was going on in her absence. She never told about the man who had nicknamed her Fofi, left her waiting at the altar in a gown which had a stitch from every woman in her hometown. Sometimes she fell silent as she lifted off her black-corded glasses and dabbed each watery eye with one of my practice handkerchiefs.

V

Papi was the only man around and so it fell to him to keep up flagging spirits with old world compliments. Dimpling, Tía Fofi giggled, fiddling with her hair, the wispy feminine kind, her bun always unraveling in helpless black and white waves down her back. Tía Ana pinned it back up. Her thin hair behaved itself, the gray strands packed in a knot and bobbypinned to her skull. She was partial towards Papi, could recite how big around was his chest, how many inches from his shoulders to his wrists. She had mended his pants, fixed his stuck zipper, darned his undergarments intimately. Papi steered wide of her plain horse face and instead praised her good health, hard work, and the fact that America hadn't changed her, she was still Ana García Morales Perelló Fernández Alfau Pérez Rochet González.

VI

Mami wanted to invite them to my graduation. *We're their only family here, and they dressed you all through school.* It was bad enough having Papi bowing like the janitor at all my girlfriends' fathers, his fedora at his chest, and bad enough when Mami looked my girlfriends over, inventorying missing buttons, unravelled hems, torn seams, dirty American habits—without also having to bear Tía Ana and Tía Fofi in their best, old-fashioned, matched outfits, trying out the few words they knew for American politeness. On the stage my teachers sat. Each one had taught me something that would have shocked my old aunts: Freud and the unconscious, the gassy origins of the galaxy. The stars and stripes hung on a pole that was lifted out of its bracket at the end of our commencement as all of us stood to sing, *Oh say can you see,* and Tía Ana and Tía Fofi rose as if they also agreed with what had become of me.

CALYX Journal, Vol. 8:2, 1984

Cherríe Moraga

IT IS YOU, MY SISTER, WHO MUST BE PROTECTED

1.

Maybe you'll understand this. My mother was not the queer one, but my father.

Something got beat out of that man. I don't know what. I don't have any stories of him much to speak of, only a memory as tame and uneventful as his movement through the house. You *do* remember the man with skin white as a baby's and that is how we thought of him: a battered child. Yeah, something hit him down so deep and so for sure, there seems to be no calling him back now.

But it is this queer I run from. This white man in me. This man settling into the pockets of woman's vicious pride and conviction to make a life for herself and her children.

The year he was left to his own devices, we came back to find our home in shambles. My mother climbed up onto a stool in the kitchen, stuck her head into the cupboard, and started throwing onto the floor boxes and boxes of cereal, seasons-old and opened, now crawling with ants and roaches.

Do you remember that? . . . and how so often during those days my mom would interrogate Dad, asking him about religion and god and didn't he believe *anything.* He would nod back nervously, sure honey sure I believe, he'd say, I just don't know how to talk about it. And I'd stare across the top of my glass of milk and the small yellow kitchen table, and as far back as I could imagine into that wide rolling forehead, I saw nothing stirring. For the life of me, there wasn't a damn thing happening in that head of his.

It is this queer I run from. A pain that turns us to quiet surrender. No, surrender is too active a term. There *was* no fight. Resignation.

I'm afraid of ever being that stuck. Stuck back in a story of myself as a six-year-old blond-haired boy, very quiet. I guess he was probably very quiet, even then, watching his father leave.

When Dad told me the story of his father's return, the restaurant visit sixteen years later, the three hours together after a lifetime of abandonment, I asked him, "Were you angry with him, Dad? How did you feel?"

"I was very nervous," he answered, sighing. That's all I could get out of the man, how nervous he was.

I thought of the old man sleeping in his grave somewhere in Canada, blameless as an English saint. In our children's imagination, he was so unlike the other one, the dark one, who died a young and defiant death. We had seen that grandfather's grave with our own eyes, touched with our own hands the dry and broken earth which held the stone. I remember during those visits to Tijuana how you and I would stand so reverently at the sides of the tombstone. Our eyes following my mother carrying water in small coffee cans back and forth in silent ritual to wash the face of the grave. Then, Grandma would brush it off carefully with the crumpled Kleenexes she drew from her purse, until the letters of his name shone through as vividly as the man they chose to remember at that moment.

This is the portrait of a father whose memory you could live with, kicking and screaming. But the saint? I vaguely recall only one picture of my Dad's dad in a double-breasted grey suit. He was standing alone. Palm trees in the background. Hat dipped.

After Dad had finished the story, I sat with him watching his face slowly curl up into a squint, his eyes fluttering to a close. You know the expression where the vertical crease along the side of his forehead deepens into a kind of scar. I realized then that he was going fast—to the place past and beyond the pain where he had laid his face in the lap of a woman and like a boy begging, promised never to ask for much, if only she would keep him there.

I wanted to shake the man from his grave! Bring him back to life for a reckoning! But it's hard, I'm sure you feel this too, to sustain any passion, really, for my father.

Daddy, you did not beat me, but every blow I took from the hand of my mother came from the caress you could not give her.

The hole burning through her belly had nothing to do with my lack of loving. I loved her through and through, alive and in the flesh.

We women settle for dead men with cold or absent touches. We carry the weight of your deaths, and yet we bore you as the first life you knew.

You have your father to thank, father, for his leaving you. Not your mother nor mine who fed you all the days of your life.

2.

The only time I ever saw my father cry, sober, was about six months after his mother's death. Do you remember? We must've been only about five and six and we had gone to see a movie, a famous one I don't recall the name of. But a woman dies at the end in a hospital bed. And my dad, later, driving the family home, suddenly out of nowhere begins to cry. I don't, at first, understand that he is crying, only that he is making these strange blurting noises, his head falling down onto his chest. Then I hear my mom in the front seat snap, "Pull over, Jim! Pull over!" Like she were talking to a child. And my dad does. Draping his arms over the steering wheel, he starts bawling like a baby.

There seemed to be no tears. I don't remember seeing any. I only knew that I had never seen a person, a grown man, look so out of his body. Lost. Awkward. Trying to reach for a cry so much deeper than the one he was hitting on.

3.

My mother tells me that it is you, my sister, who must be protected. That this will hurt you too much. But I can understand these things. I am wordly and full of knowledge when something goes queer.

Splitting a beer between us, she says, *"Cecilia, mi'jita,* your father, he has no feeling left in him." I think, *this is no news.* "It's in a certain place in his body," she explains. The absence.

She asks me, have I noticed how he's "so soft, not very manly?"

"Yeah, *Mamá,* I've noticed," I say too eagerly, hungry for the first time to speak of my father with *some* kind of compassion. A real feeling.

"I think he's different like you. *¿Entiendes? Pero, no digas nada a tu hermana.*"

"No, *Mamá,*" I say, "but Daddy seems to love men. It's true. You know how he always gets so excited with any ole new friend he makes at the plant. Like a kid. How he goes overboard when my brother or cousins come around. Not like the way he is around women, just part of the scenery." I regret these last words, seeing her face flinch.

I bite my tongue down hard, holding it. I must not say too much. I must not know too much. But I am so excited, thinking of the possibility of my father awakened to the touch. Imagining my father feeling *something* deep and profound and alive.

Alive.

She knows the difference, she says, she knows what it's like to have a "real" man touch her. "If it hadn't been for Baker, the first one," she says, "maybe I wouldn't of known, maybe it wouldn't of mattered, but . . . forty years, *mi'jita,* forty years."

Grabbing my hand across the table, "Honey, I know what it's like to be touched by a man who wants a woman. I don't feel this with your father," squeezing me, *"¿Entiendes?"*

The room falls silent then, as if the walls themselves begged for a minute to swallow back the secret that had just leaked out from them. And it takes every muscle in me *not* to leave my chair, *not* to climb through the silence, *not* to clamber toward her, *not* to touch her the way I know she wants to be touched.

"Yeah, *Mamá,* I understand."

Pulling her hand back, she pours the last few drops left in the bottle into my glass. "Talk to your father," she says. "He listens to you. Don't let him know you know. *Tiene vergüenza.*"

Phyllis Wolf

WHITE-OUT

In the penny postcard she sent home, she was pictured standing in a white high-collared waist. Twenty-five buttons could be counted down the front. The rest were lost in a voluminous skirt that skimmed her ankles.

—Do you remember this?

—No.

—This was taken when you were at school.

—Was it?

—Do you remember knitting dishrags?

—Oh, hell, I do. That's all we ever did was knit dishrags. That's why I don't like to knit. Go to school to knit dishrags.

She looked out the window and saw something no one else could see. She held her stomach delicately as young women hold theirs when it is first filled with life, smoothing hands over rounded curves. Her stomach wasn't gently rounded but protruded sharply to one side, yet she smoothed it with her hands. She held the contorted stomach as she stood to move toward the window. It was heavy and pulled at the intestines. The pain had made her cheeks hollow and she stood bent, waiting.

—Do you want to go outside?

—It's cold out.

There were only a few inches of snow on the ground but clouds the same color of snow had come. In the distance, she could not see where the earth ended and the sky began. Her hands moved over the stomach gently and caught it up from underneath. She thought of the babies, the bastard babies she buried. Her daughter was looking through a box of old letters.

—Who's this you're with?

—I don't remember.

—You're not even looking.

She turned toward the picture her daughter held up. It was a man in an ill-fitting suit two sizes too small. His hair was split down the center and greased flat to his head. His ears stood out.

—I don't remember.

She turned toward the window. She could hear cries being muffled. Infant cries muffled by dirt. She stood in front of the window and wiped her hands against her dress. Her stomach pulled. She looked down at it. Her cheeks had become even more hollow. No, she didn't remember and what she did she didn't want to remember. Small mouths filled with hard dirt. And the days would be like this where the sky was indistinguishable from the earth that she would pour dirt into those mouths. The mouths would be open and they would cry, but the crying would stop after a while. She only heard the cries now when her stomach pulled at intestines and then she would have to cradle the stomach in her hands to make the crying stop. She cradled the stomach now but cries still came from outside the window. Infant cries that pierced the stomach where she stood looking out to swirling white clouds that rose up from earth.

CALYX Journal, Vol. 8:2, 1984

Beth Brant

THE FIFTH FLOOR—1967

for Mary Moran

The mental ward is on the fifth floor of the county hospital. Inmates joke that it is put there to make escape difficult. They built this very new and scrubbed wing to accomodate the suddenly realized phenomenon of people going crazy. Or the suddenly realized income generated from Blue Cross, Social Services, and other agents. As soon as I arrive I am given Thorazine in a tiny pleated paper cup. Orange juice is supposed to mask the taste, but the sharp chemical burn breaks through. I make my first mistake by asking what it is that I am swallowing. Pencil eyebrows rising into brown bangs, the nurse tells me it will calm me down. But I am already calm. I walked here myself, my husband holding my arm. Why I am here has something to do with losing myself. I used to be there—a young wife and mother—in my house—washing dishes, bleaching diapers, reading a book, watching TV. Then I lost me. My husband tells me I am not myself. He tells the nurse that and she scrutinizes me, then takes me to a room which is to be mine for the duration. I am to share it with another woman who is not there. This room has a window. The window has bars growing from the cement sill. When I look out, I see the roof of the hospital. It is summer and the roof is wet from the air conditioning units used in administration and operating rooms. The nurse sweats from the heat. I do not sweat. Inside me there is salt. Drying up fluid. I begin to get out my cigarettes and am told that I may carry cigarettes with me, but only nurses and orderlies are allowed to carry matches and lighters. I realize I will have to begin to chain smoke. To light one cigarette from another, to avoid asking for anything. I am told—"You are free to move from your room to the game room." The game room has TV, Monopoly, Clue but no books. It is something to do with too much stimulation. And if we wish to write letters, paper and pen will be supplied by nurse, and our writing activity will be supervised. I am a piece of cloth—useless, with no pattern. "Say good-bye to your husband." I say good-bye to this man I thought I recognized, but no longer do. He brought me here, and signed a white piece of paper. After that I belonged to them—not him. But I am free to roam the halls. Until night.

In one week I have adjusted well. Each morning at 6:00 A.M. we are awakened. I am allowed to take a shower. I am allowed to wash my hair once a week. I keep it braided and it hangs on my back—oily—each strand separated by comb marks. My head looks like a wet clay pot, designs ringed around the outside. We get to wear our own clothes. This is a new age in caretaking crazy people. "The wearing of their own clothes will give a sense of being in familiar surroundings." For this trip I have brought cotton shorts and blouses. A mini dress in blue plaid. Sneakers and flats. No nylons, but knee socks. My summer nightgown. Underwear from Sears in white cotton. Since it is hot, I wear my shorts continuously. Until I am told I will have to change. It upsets the male Patients to see me wearing shorts. "They are only a hair's breadth away from violence." In one week I haven't eaten. This seems to disturb the nurses who have to write it down in their charts. At first they cajoled me with milk. The perfect food. Then they tell me that Doctor says I will have to be force-fed or fed intravenously. Then it is said I will have to begin shock treatments if I don't eat. I have seen the Patients who come from shock. Their faces are smooth and shiny. It's as if the electric wires have brushed over their skin leaving an area like a healed burn. Flat and glossy. Their eyes don't focus. I even saw a woman's eyes turn from brown to blue. After shock. Their bodies jerk. They have to be reminded over and over and over who they are. And where they are. One of the orderlies brings me a Coke from the machine. I take a drink and there is relief and triumph in the nurse's face. "That's a good girl." It looks like I will be here for a while. My husband comes twice a week. I don't want to talk, but have to find out how my children are. He says they are staying at my mother's. He sees them at night when he gets off work. I never think to ask why he can't take them home so they can sleep in their own beds. It is assumed he is helpless. He has enough on his mind with me. Next week, if I'm good, I will be allowed phone privileges, once a day. I will be allowed to go to occupational therapy. I will be allowed to help the other women clean the game room. I drink my Thorazine-laced orange juice twice a day. If I'm good, it will be cut to once a day. Thorazine is not addictive. It turns your brain into cheese cloth. Nothing sticks. My eyes are veiled in dotted swiss. I have not spoken yet with the other Patients who walk the halls with me. I feel the salt inside my body moving through my veins. I am surprised I am not dead. Dried like a fish. Salted and ready to eat. I sit in the game room. Watching TV.

At night I look for myself. Between each bed check and the flashlight in my face, I feel my body seeking a relationship with myself. I wish to know this woman. During the day I pass the mirror hung high on the wall. I try to look for me, but see instead a skinny woman with eyes that have no lids. Her hair will not stay tied up. It falls out of the rubber band and moves down her back like a ripple or a tidal wave. At home, this woman was a crybaby, but the tears never came out of her eyes. They spilled inside her skin, soaking her brain, trickling down the shelves of bones, coming out of her cunt and hands. She left trails of wet salt on her chair, in her bed. Her husband was not allowed to fuck her, or his penis would shrivel. Often he didn't listen to her protests and climbed on her shoving his cock against her face, coming in her mouth. She wiped the semen away—rinsing her head under the bathroom faucet. She dared not touch her daughters or their skin would stain. Their beautiful faces would scar from the wet salt. So she sat in her rocker, listening to her daughters chatter. Telling them not to climb on her lap, she would hurt them with hot salt. Her mother came to see what was wrong. She has heard from the son-in-law that something is wrong. Her mother sees a clean house—everything washed and starched. The children look afraid. The baby has dirty diapers, the middle one is wringing her hands, the eldest is heating a bottle for the youngest. Her mother asks the young wife what is wrong. She answers: "Inside me there are holes where the salt has eaten through. I feel I am turning into The Great Salt Lake. Or a glacier. White and cold." The mother calls the father. As he comes through the doorway, he instinctively holds up his hands when he sees her. Warding off a spirit. He says: "We must take her home, bring the babies, see if we can help." His face tears over. This is his favorite daughter. The one who understands his Indian ways, his talk, his lapse into alcohol. She is the one who knows who she is. They take her home. She is a piece of cloth, ready to be folded in fours, tucked away in a drawer. She was brought here. There are experts who know about such things. I explore the body of this woman. Hastily. Her breasts are flaccid and numb. I pinch her nipples, feel them rise. I place my hands at her waist, feel her ribs. Her rib cage is wide and round—like staves in a basket. Her thighs are cold and thin. I stroke the soft place of her inner thighs with both hands. Her skin gets warmer, she trembles with each brush of my fingers. The hair of her cunt is straight and heavy and thick. I touch the slit, the opening of her cunt, the inside of her. Her clitoris pulses under my finger. I touch her there. Try to find her. She is wet and open. I taste her juice off my finger. She is tart like sweat and medicine. Both hands attempt to enter her, to go up inside her hole, to touch a place in her that will tell me who I am. I rub her clitoris, she spasms and comes on my hand, the syrup from her coating my fingers. I bring my hand to my mouth and suck myself to sleep. I have dreams about her. She looks in the mirror and I see with her eyes.

In occupational therapy I am told I have a choice of making a trivet or an ashtray. The therapist is young and white. Her face is filled with school optimism—she will do her best and maybe she will get through to some of us. What she doesn't know is that others have already gone through us. We drip water, blood, and salt on the clean white floor. We are uncooperative and strange. But she knows how to handle that—talk in a perky, determined manner and ignore our strangeness. The O.T. room is a fairly large room with cupboards lining the walls. Everything seems to be Formica. The speckled surfaces gleam from polish. There are boxes of materials here and there on the floor. Scraps of cloth, chenille pipe cleaners in fuschia and chartreuse, plastic reeds for weaving baskets, hanks of acrylic for the loom. But the loom is silent. We are not taught to use it. It is something about our brains not being able to comprehend the instruction. Next to the loom is a small kitchenette. We wonder at its use. There are never signs of anyone having been there. Never an apron hung by the sink, a teakettle resting on a burner. We assume it is put there to remind us of what is normal—therefore unattainable for us. Some of the Patients have been here before. I sit quietly. Waiting my turn. "Do you want to make an ashtray or a trivet?" I am overwhelmed by choice. And watch the others create their escape routes out of the fifth floor. I grab the box of plastic tiles. Begin to sort through the colors. I pick out blue and green. I will make a trivet. Hang it on my kitchen wall at home. The sun will strike the tiles at a certain time of day. For a moment, the kitchen will look like how I imagine the ocean to be. The colors will amuse my daughters. The baby will laugh and reach out her hand to touch the colors. I will make a trivet.

At night I look for myself. Beneath the covers, underneath the bed. In the extra drawer. I touch her body, anxious for the darkness to cover my hands. The flashlights in my face have ceased to bother me. I pretend to be asleep, to have my hands primly on top of the sheets. The woman waits underneath to feel my delicate fingers probing her holes. She opens herself to me. There is no sound between us, except once—a sigh. She is always open. Open and wet, she is wet and opening up to me. My fingers go deeper. I have touched her insides. Her insides were soft and uncovered, and gave up secrets. Her breasts are no longer passive. Her thighs are not cool—she is open to me. Inside there is a magic place of wetness and a fiery house. I touch her. She opens.

I will be released in one week. I have begun to eat mashed potatoes, red meat, white bread, and to drink lots of black coffee. The Thorazine has been cut completely. They give me something else—in a capsule. I have behaved myself well. I pretend to smile at the nurses and orderlies. I have not found me—but the psychiatrist looked at my chart and at my good behavior. And besides, my insurance will not pay beyond six weeks of treat-ment. And we do not have the resources to let me stay longer. But I am taking the woman with me. I am smuggling her out. She will go with me—as my secret. During these six weeks, her face has begun to take on my features. My face has begun to take on lines and my skin is toughening. Her hair has one thread of silver. My hair is getting darker and thinner. Her body is round and when my fingers press her thighs, white marks appear which quickly fill up with blood, leaving her skin soft and brown and beau-tiful. My breasts feel everything. In my dreams, I remember my first-born suckling from me. I wake up to wet spots on my nightgown. They ache—I touch them often. Inside me there is salt. At times it seeps out of my eyes, dropping on my hand. Her body is not salted. Inside her is blood and muscle and electric pulses. Her fingers send currents through mine. Her fingers are long and rough and there are cracks in her nails. Mine are rough and my palms are lined. I am taking the woman home with me. It is our secret. She keeps me alive.

Linda Hogan

CROW

Even though she always has peppermint in her apron pockets, nobody much visits Grandma any more. Once in a while my brother, Buster, stops by to pick me up and we go out to the flats to see her. Or someone who has moved away returns to town on their summer vacation to look over their old homeplace, trying to pick up the lost pieces of their lives, wanting stories about their kin. They stop by to ask my grandmother where old so-and-so has gone. More often than not, she directs them to the cemetery, peppermint candy in their hands.

"That bag goes out to the car." I point at the brown paper sack. Buster moves the coleus plants and the clay sheep that has grass sprouting from its back like green wool. He snoops in the bag. "The cookies are in the cupboard," I tell him.

He opens the cupboard and rummages around for the Oreos. I have just enamelled the kitchen and the cabinet doors stick. "Leave them open," I say to Buster. I inspect the kitchen before leaving for Grandma's. It passes my scrutiny, the clean blue paint and the new tablecloth I made of white strawberry-printed cotton.

We pack up Buster's Chevy with my clothes, the groceries, my dog Teddy, and the radio I bought for Grandma. We drive past the Dunkard Brethren Church. There are some people, perhaps the choir, standing outside in dark robes. I think we look pretty flashy, passing by in the gold Chevrolet with shining chrome and bumperstickers saying *Indian Affairs are the Best* and *Pilgrim, Go Home*. I sit very straight with my eyelids lowered even though inside my body I am exhilarated, enjoying this ride in my brother's car. We drive past the stand of scrub oak and then turn off the paved road into the silence that exists between towns. The crows fly up off the road, cursing at us. Since his wife isn't along, Buster accelerates and lets the car go almost as fast as it will, "tying on the tachs." We speed along. "I clocked her at one ten," he says. He slows down by the cornfields, and paces himself on out through the flatlands where Grandma lives. It has been raining and everything is moist and bright, the outlines of the buildings cleaner than usual. When we pull off the road at Grandma's, I stay in the car a few minutes to look at the morning glories she has planted. They are blooming, the blue flowers on a vined arch over the old front door. The Heaven Blue circles nod in the ozone-smelling breeze.

Teddy is anxious to get out and go searching for moles. He whines and paces across the back seat. "Let that damn dog out," Buster says, but he opens the door before I can turn around and get to it. Teddy runs out barking, his tail pulling him sideways with joy. Grandma hears. She comes to the door and stands waiting in the shade, surrounded by the morning glories on her front steps. She already has her hand in her apron pocket, ready to lure us with peppermint, when Teddy turns and circles back viciously, barking at a car that has pulled up silently behind us. I didn't hear the limousine drive up, and now Teddy is all around it, barking and raging at the waxed, shining dark metal of the car and at its tires that remain, miraculously, clean, even driving through the mud.

"Theodore!" I yell out his proper name, reserved for reprimands and orders. Teddy continues to bark, his golden tail down between his short Dingo legs, his claws digging into the wet red clay. The chauffeur ignores him and goes around stiffly to open the back car door.

Grandma is taking it all in, looking proud and pompous. She respects money but she hates those people who have it. All money is dirty, she has said. It all started with the Rockefellers and their ilk. Now she remains standing very straight and tall, her hand still in the blue-flowered pocket, while a woman is let out of the car and begins walking across the chicken yard. The white woman's shoes are expensive. They are rich beige leather and I feel tense watching her heels dig into the clay soil and the chicken droppings. The muddy clay tries to suck the woman down. The chickens make a path for her, scurrying off and clucking. A copper hen that has been roosting in a tree falls out and screeches, scurries off muddy, and waddling.

I recognize the lady. She stopped in once for a meal at the Hamburger Heaven where Buster used to work. She was out of place and the customers and employees all stared at her. She made them uneasy and they alternately talked too much and too loud, or they were silent. When the order was ready, Buster took several plates around the room and stopped at the woman's table, flustered. He was overly serious in his discomfort, his face tense. Like an accusation, he said, "You're the Hamburger." I tried to hide my laughter, but it floated up into the entire room.

I step close to hear the conversation between Grandma and the woman. Grandma's jaw is tight like trouble is in the air. While they talk, I pull a stamen from a morning glory and suck it.

"I'd like to buy two dozen eggs," says the beige shoe lady, opening her pocketbook and releasing the odor of French perfume and money.

"We're all out of eggs." Grandma still has her hand in her pocket. She avoids looking at the woman's face. She looks past her at the horizon. It is the way she looks through city people, or people with money, as though they aren't there.

"I'll take a bag of feed then." The woman is thin and wispy. Her hair falls forward as she opens her wallet. The bills are neatly ordered. I can't help but notice Grandma's eyes on them.

"Haven't had any feed delivered from the co-op as late," says Grandma, nonchalantly. Grandma is the local distributor of feed grain and Watkins products, including the cherry-flavored drink mix. She keeps an entire room neatly stocked with bags of grains and bottles of vanilla, aspirin, vitamins, and linament. And she sells eggs. It is how she supports all those chickens, she claims.

Grandma offers the woman a mint, but the woman refuses it and grows huffy. "Probably the diet type," I hear Buster say under his breath and I'm sure the woman overheard him because she is clearly put out, and says to Grandma, "Why don't you close all the way down or put a sign out?"

"I'm fixing to, once you leave." I can feel a smile under Grandma's words even though her face has no expression and her eyes are blank, staring off into Kansas or some other distant state. The woman does not know she is being made fun of, and she wants something else, I can tell. She wants to help Grandma out, to be good to the poor, or something. It is often that way with the rich. But it seems to me that there are some barriers in life that can't be passed through by good deeds or money. Like the time I found a five dollar bill on the floor of the movie theater and felt guilty for picking it up, felt like a thief. It was a fire in my pocket. On the way home I saw a man going through the trash, collecting cans to cash in. I took out the bill and handed it to him. I said I just found it and maybe it was his. He took it, but there was a dreadful and shameful look on his face and I knew then that everyone ought to stay in their own place, wherever that may be, without trespassing on other people's lives. Maybe money just goes where it wants and leaves the rest of us alone.

But Grandma will not be shamed, even though the house looks dilapidated in contrast to the woman and her car. Grandma is proud enough still to plant the flowers and water them with the blue plastic pitcher.

The woman returns to the limousine and they drive away. If it weren't for the recent rain, the car would have covered the morning glories in a great cloud of dust. I wonder what it is that made the chauffeur so anxious to leave.

"Last week she wanted to buy the house," Grandma says, and takes out two lint-covered peppermint kisses and gives one each to me and Buster.

"This old place?" Buster has no tact. I give him one of my looks which he has said could kill, but he goes on talking. "How much did she offer you? You should have taken it." His cheek is swollen with the peppermint. "You are probably sitting on an oil well."

But Grandma loves her home and will never leave it as long as she lives. Now and then she is in a bad mood and this is going to be one of those times. Her eyes are sullen. I remind myself of her better moments. Out loud I say to Buster, "Remember the day we took Grandma to town? When she was in such a good humor that she went up to that tall policeman and asked, 'Do you know where any trouble is?'"

Buster's smile begins on the left side of his face, but Grandma ignores what I say. She hands me the egg basket. "Sis, why don't you go out and gather up the eggs?"

Teddy is overjoyed to go with me, looking in the corners of the barn, the storage shed, under old tires on the ground. I find a few eggs in new places, in a batch of damp grass, under the morning glories. Teddy runs in circles and the crows fly up around us. They remind me of stories, like how Old Crow Raven used to be white, white snowy feathers, marble white beak and claws, until one day he got too sure of himself and offered to go to an island of fire and bring back a coal for the two-legged, unwinged people. As he descended to the island, following the orange flames and black smoke billowing up from a hollow tree, he was overcome with the heat and blinded by a thick dark cloud of smoke. Disoriented, he flew straight into the flames and was scorched. That is the reason, people say, why the crows are black. Grandma's theory is that the bird went for the wrong reasons. He didn't really care about the people at all. He just wanted to prove his worth.

When I go inside and set the eggs on the table, Grandma is on one of her lectures about how people are just like black birds except they are paling. "Money is turning everybody to white," she says. "All the Indians are going white. Oh, I suppose they still care about their little ones and go to church on Sunday, but all they've got their minds on is the almighty dollar." She stops abruptly while I recount the eggs. There are thirty-one of them, and what with yesterday's eggs around the house, she could have sold the woman four dozen or so. She fixes her gaze on me and the whites around her dark pupils startle me. Even the eggs seem to wobble on the unlevel table. "How come you never come to visit any more? I have a hundred grandchildren and no one ever comes out here." It's no use arguing, so I don't answer.

"They're all trying to make a buck, Grandma," Buster says.

Most of the time Grandma doesn't have anyone to talk to and she gets lonely. All of my cousins have been breaking away like spiders, going to cities, to California, marrying and moving. That's why I brought her the radio.

"I don't want to hear anything about money or bucks." Her jaw is tight. She looks straight at Buster.

I turn on the water in the sink and the sound of it running drowns out Grandma's voice. She is still talking about all the Indians out here acting like white people, and about how no one comes to see her. "Those men bullying their sons," she says. "They shoot the birds right out of the air. And money, I wouldn't touch that stuff if you paid me to." And then she notices the radio and becomes quiet. "What's this?"

I dry my hands and plug it in. "I brought it for you. I thought you might like some music." I turn the station selector. Buster says, "You can talk to *that* thing all you want."

I put it on a gospel station, because that is her favorite music. But it's only a man talking and he has a bad voice. *I know my mother went to heaven, harumph, and I had a brother who died and I know he went to heaven.* The man clears his throat. *One by one, we, uh, proceed, our candles lighted. We, you, you, I, I think that maybe some of those Europeans haven't reached the height of Christianity, harumph, that we have, but maybe we have really gone below them and maybe we have, uh, wronged them.*

Buster imitates a rooster, his fists in his armpits. "Bock, Bock, Begaw," he says. I give him a dirty look.

"Don't you make fun," Grandma says. "The first time I ever heard a radio, don't you know, was Coolidge's inaugural address."

And she starts in again, right over the voice of the radio, about how no one comes to talk to her and how we don't even call her on the telephone. Buster gets angry. He says she's getting senile and he walks out the door and slams it. Grandma and I are silent because he walked out stiff and angry, and the radio says, *I got saved from the sermons you preach, uh, that's what he said, and from the sermons on your pages in the mail.*

I'm still thinking about going to heaven with a candle, but I hear Buster outside, scurrying around. I look out the window but can't tell what he's doing.

When he returns, he is carrying a crow and tracking in red mud. "How did you catch that?" I ask. Its eyes are wild but it is beautiful with black feathers shining like silk and velvet. I go closer to look at it. "Can I touch it?" I put my hand over the bird. "Is it hurt?"

Buster pulls back and looks me in the eye. His look scares me. He is too intense and his eyes are darker than usual. He takes hold of the wing. "Don't," I say, but he grabs that glorious coal-colored wing and twists it.

"Buster!" I yell at him and the crow cries out too.

He throws it down on the floor. I'm too afraid to move. "Now, don't say no one comes to see you. This damn crow won't leave. You can tell him all you want how nobody comes to see you." Buster stalks out and we hear the car engine start. I am standing, still unable to move, looking at the bird turning circles on the floor, and beginning to cry. "Oh, Grandma, how could Buster be so awful?" I go down to pick up the injured bird, but it tries to get away. I don't blame it. There's no reason to be trusting. Grandma is sad too, but she just sits at the table and I know we are both thinking of Buster's cruelty and we are women together for the first time.

I turn off the radio and I am thinking of all the poor earthly creatures.

There is a cardboard box in the Watkins room, so I go in to get it for the bird and notice that the room is full of the feed Grandma refused to sell the beige shoe lady.

Grandma has already broken a stick and is fitting it to the bird's wing. It is quiet in her hands. I strip off a piece of red calico cotton from her quilting cloth. She takes it in her wrinkled hand and wraps the smooth wing.

"I hate him," I say. "He's always been mean." But Grandma doesn't say anything. She is busy with the crow and has placed it in the box on a nest of paper towels.

"I guess that's what happens to people who think about money all the time," she says. "They forget about the rest of life. They don't pay mind to the hurts of each other or the animals. But the Bible teaches me not to judge them." Still, she says nothing else about money or visitors.

The crow listens when Grandma talks. For several days it has been nodding its head at her and following her with its eyes. It listens to the gospel radio too. "That crow is a heartbreaker," she says. "Just look at him." I hope it isn't true. It is a lovely bird and sometimes cries out weakly. He has warm black wings and eyes made of stolen corn. I am not a crow reverencer, but I swear that one night I heard it talking to Grandma and it was saying that no one comes to visit.

Grandma is telling it a story about the crows. "They were people and used to speak our tongues," she tells him and he listens. It is raining outside and the rain is hitting windows. The earth outside is full of red puddles and they are moving. Somewhere outside, a door is slamming open and closed in the wind.

"You'd like that rainwater," she tells the crow. "Make your feathers soft."

Though I am mad at Buster, I can see that he was right. This bird and Grandma are becoming friends. She feeds it grain and corn. It rides on her shoulder and is the color her hair used to be. Crow pulls at the strands of her gray hair. It is like Grandma has shed a skin. She is new and soft, a candlelight inside her.

"Bird bones heal pretty fast," she tells me. "Not like ours."

"Can we listen to something besides gospel for a while?" I ask her. She ignores the question so I go into the bedroom to read a magazine and take a nap. The phone rings and I hear Grandma talking and then the radio goes off and the front door opens and closes. I get up and go out into the kitchen but it is silent, except for the bird picking at the cardboard box.

For a moment I consider putting him out in the rain, splint and all, he looks so forlorn. But Grandma would never forgive me. I ask him, "Have you heard that money is evil?"

Teddy is barking at the front door. It's Buster. Even the dog is unkind to him, growling back in his throat. Buster wants to see if we need anything or if I am ready to go home. I don't speak to him and he sits down on the sofa to read the paper. I stay in the kitchen with Crow.

A house without its tenant is a strange place. I notice for the first time that without Grandma's presence, the house smells of Vicks and old wool. Her things look strange and messy; even the doilies on the couch and end tables are soiled. The walls are sweating and the plaster is stained. I can see Buster sitting on the sofa reading the paper and I decide to tell him I think he is beyond forgiveness.

"Leave me alone." He stands up. His pants ride low and he puts his hands in his pockets and pushes the pants down lower. It is a gesture of intimidation. "She's got company, hasn't she? And maybe that crow will teach her how to behave." He says he is bringing a cage and I say a cage is no place for a wild bird that longs to be outside in the free air. We are about to get into it when Grandma returns. She is crying. "I ought to kill myself," she says.

We grow quiet and both look down at the floor. I have never seen her cry except at funerals, and I sneak glances up at her now and then while she is crying, until she tells me, "Quit gawking. I just lost all my money."

"Your money?" I am struck stupid. I am surprised. I know she never believed in banks and I thought she didn't believe much in money either. I didn't know she had any. I worry about how much she lost. By her tears, I can tell it wasn't just the egg money.

"I hid it in the umbrella because I was scared of robbers, and I lost it in the rain. When I went back looking for it, it wasn't there." She checks inside the wet umbrella, opening and closing it as if she couldn't believe its absence, running her hand around the spokes. "I forgot I hid it there. I just plain forgot," she wails. "I used to keep it in the cupboard until I heard about the burglars."

There is a circle of water around her on the floor and her face is broken, but she takes two pieces of peppermint from her pocket and absently hands one to each of us, the old habit overpowering grief. "I think I should have sold that woman the eggs."

She has a lot of sorrow bending her back. "I walked up the road as fast as I could, but it was already gone."

She became as quiet as the air between towns. I turn on the radio and it sounds like a funeral with "We Shall Gather at the River." Grandma picks up Crow and he seems to leap right to her chest and balance there on one of the old ivory buttons. She reaches into her left pocket and takes out grains of corn.

Grandma's shoes are ruined. She puts them on the stove to dry but they are already curling upward at the toes and the leather soles are coming apart.

"How's your kids, Buster?"

"Pretty good," but he looks glum. He's probably worried about his lost inheritance.

"How's Flora?"

Buster has his ready-made answers. "Well," he drawls, "by the time I met her I knew what happiness was." I chime in, mocking, "But it was too late to do anything about it." I finish the sentence with him. Grandma looks at me, startled, and is silent a moment, and then she begins to laugh.

There's nothing else to do, so I get up. "Grandma, you want some eggs?" I turn on the stove. "I'll cook up some eggs and cornmeal pancakes." I wonder how much money she had hidden away.

"I'm all out of molasses," she says. "Plum out."

"Buster will go to the store and get some. Won't you Buster?"

"In this rain?" But he looks at me and I look stern. "Oh sure, yeah, I'll be right back." And he carefully folds the paper and picks up his keys and goes to the door. He is swallowed up by the blowing torrents of water.

I take Grandma's shoes off the stove and put them by the back door.

"Edna fell down the stairs last night," Grandma says, an explanation of where she has been. "Broke her hip."

"How is she?"

"I didn't get to see her. Because of the money. Maybe Buster will take me."

I put some batter in the pan and it sizzles. Crow chatters back at it and it sounds like he is saying how hard it is to be old. I want to put my hand on Grandma's shoulder, but I don't. Instead I go to the window and look out. Crow's lovers or cousins are bathing in the puddles of rainwater, washing under their wings and shaking their feathers. I think Crow is the one who went to that island after fire, and now, even though his body is so much like the night sky, he is doomed to live another life. I figure he's going to stay here with Grandma to make up for his past mistakes. I think Grandma is right about almost everything. I feel lonely. I go over and touch her. She clasps my hand tightly and then lets go and pats it. "Your pancakes are burning," she says.

CALYX Journal, Vol. 8:2, 1984

Sandra Scofield

LOVING LEO

Age is a desert of time . . . one has ample time
to face everything one has had, been, done;
gather them all in. We have time to make
them truly ours.
Florida Scott Maxwell, *The Measure of My Days*

Mrs. Boll built her house on Porter Street in 1953. It was at that time the last house on the street, only blocks from the city limits. She already owned and lived in a one-bedroom stucco bungalow at the opposite end of town on an unpaved street that flooded every spring. There had seldom been a season she had lived alone. In 1953 she was housing her daughter Laura and granddaughter Lucy, Laura's husband Charlie, and their daughter Faith, who had none of her mother's features whatsoever. Mrs. Boll would have been satisfied with the house she had—she had fine neighbors on the right and an open field on the left, with wild berries and mint—but she built a new one to make a better life for her family. She had thought three grown and married children would not depend on her for much of anything anymore, but she had been proved wrong too many times to count.

Mrs. Boll and her granddaughter Lucy went to watch the house's progress on a long series of consecutive Saturdays. They planted rose bushes that had been shipped from Jackson & Perkins in Oregon, a sycamore for shade, two apricot trees, and a pecan tree later on. Mrs. Boll's parents and grandparents had been farmers (wheat, pigs, and the miscellany of self-sustenance in harder times) and had always had such trees, though never roses.

Mrs. Boll bought the house (plan and construction) at a discount, and one cost to her of the bargain was that she could make no changes. The house was a little over nine hundred square feet with two small bedrooms. She had hoped for a long sleeping porch in the back, because she knew there would always be family there in good months (if not in bad), but the contractor told her she would have to take care of it later. This she never did; there were always other matters, greater needs. Her children and their children, her brothers and their wives, her oldest daughter's husband when he could not avoid it (or when he could not himself provide), all managed, on camp cots, the three twin beds in the larger bedroom, an extra mattress that was stored against the wall behind her bed when not in use; all made do and never tempered their visits with concerns about space.

On an early summer day Mrs. Boll goes outside to pick apricots. It is her lifelong habit, kindled by spring, to scan the sky, one hand shading her eyes. Beyond her to the south the city sprawls with miles of houses, a shopping center, drive-throughs for movies or food. The sky is a clean bleached blue, the blue of a Panhandle summer.

There is so much fruit at once. The branches bow toward the ground. They are golden, sweet this year, and bigger than she remembered. She barely touches them and they drop into her upturned hat. She empties the hat into a basket and fills it again. Her idle day is suddenly full; she will pit and freeze, make jam and syrup, stew a bowlful for her dinner tonight. In twenty years, there have been only a few seasons when the apricots failed her. Once it was bugs, another time a drenching spring. It is the nuts that have been unreliable; some years the meat was dry and bitter inside, and there were others when the clinging hulls lost their grip in high wind.

The year the house was built, Lucy was with Mrs. Boll all the time Mrs. Boll wasn't at the mill. Lucy was a quiet, dreamy nine-year-old who liked to read and to follow Mrs. Boll into the garden behind the old house. Mrs. Boll thought a child needed more than silent companionship, so she often talked of family, especially her beloved grandparents. They had been kind German immigrants who never raised a voice, let alone a switch—Mrs. Boll's mother was inclined toward willow branches—and sometimes Mrs. Boll would get lost in reverie. Lucy stood nearby with her bonnet upside down, collecting the beans or okra her grandmother picked with her fingers while her heart wafted away. Mrs. Boll told Lucy how her grandfather wouldn't let any of the children kill a bird. He said that farmers know birds look after the land. He taught her to fish, in the quiet cool hours of night or early morning, and he taught her songs in German, away from her mother who forbade her to speak a word of the old tongue. It was her grandmother who braided

her hair and taught her to make bread—Mrs. Boll's mother had been wid-
owed young and was slow to venture out again—and it was her grand-
mother who taught her the sweetness of love between the young and old.
Solemn Lucy took it in and touched her grandmother often, especially on
the soft flesh of the upper arm and along the jaw where it came up under
the earlobes. Mrs. Boll was a skinny woman until she was past sixty, but she
had that German dapple of cushion in odd places, like fat stored for hard
winters.

Mrs. Boll has more to do this day than apricots. She knows she must try
to make up her mind about her life.

She never thought there'd be another man, but Leo Clark has worn her
down. She has told him she'll think about his proposal, not because it isn't
fair to put him off, but because she doesn't know what she truly feels. He
says he'll call every few days, to see how he's doing. His smart-alecky confi-
dence makes her mouth twitch, where once it was annoying. He has been
talking marriage for half a year, since he left the rest home where Mrs. Boll
works, part-time, when they need her. He was recovering from glaucoma
surgery that had not gone well. He wrote her a note in a wild hand, *I can't
keep my eyes off you.* The silly old coot. "What a silly thing to say, Mr.
Clark," she said; her voice was high and reedy. "I know you can hardly see at
all!" He said, "I can see the girl under your belly fat." She was so angry, so
humiliated, she wouldn't go in his room for days. It was awkward, getting
what he needed to him, with the lazy help she had. He was sweet as sugar
when she finally went into his room with her lips pressed tight. "We're not
too old, Greta," he dared to say.

It is a very long time since Mrs. Boll has talked about the past. Lucy calls
from Seattle on a whim to ask some small detail that troubles her. "Re-
member that time we lived with you and then moved out?" she says. "And
there was this quarrel, and Daddy pushed you off the running board, back-
ing out?" Mrs. Boll's breath turns leaden in her chest. "What was it made
everyone so angry?" Lucy wants to know. Mrs. Boll doesn't remember, and
says so. She doesn't say she doesn't care for Lucy's asking; she lets her
silence take care of that. Another time Lucy calls to ask if it was true, as she
remembered it, that her great-grandmother always made three pies on
Sundays? Mrs. Boll can reply to that. It wasn't three pies, but three *kinds* of
pies. One was always custard for Daddy Luke whose farm it was. One was

apple, or some other fruit in season, and one was lemon with a frothy meringue. They told the story a hundred times about the time they all went to the farm for dinner and Lucy ran straight to the counter to check the pies. She lifted the soft worn feedsack towels that lay across the pastries. "Custard!" she called out; it was this caught their attention. Then, "Apple!" The grownups turned back to their talk and left the children to one another. Lucy wailed. "No lemon! What did we come over for?" Mrs. Boll knows, when Lucy calls, that Lucy wants to hear the story again. But Lucy calls long-distance. She hasn't been to Texas in over two years. Stories are for telling over stringing beans or kneading bread; stories aren't for blessing absence from one's home.

Now, at sixty-five, Mrs. Boll sees the past more firmly, with a clearer eye, and in it, unchanging, her scattered and lost menfolk, ungrateful children, and at work and large, despots, bumblers, liars, and thieves. She remembers the names of those long dead, some the others have all forgotten, and those that knock against her skull, desperate to be named. She remembers catastrophes and plays them late at night, watching Johnny Carson with the sound down low: tornadoes like the one that laid her husband Ira's head against a silo, or a later one that wrapped a pickup around a pole like putty; all the early deaths; the flood that took the Red River bridge out and two buggies full of churchfolk with it. She has built her memory on a scaffold of regrets. She no longer mourns the loss of unreliable men; grief is for her abandoned painting and the roses she had to leave at the other house, for not seeing Laura's madness for what it was.

She wonders if she and Leo would ever speak of death, being the same age. She feels sure she would lose too much in marriage. She needs her privacy and the company of ghosts. Leo would use the soap bar and leave it gummy. He would stumble, getting used to a crowded house, and knock the pictures haywire on the wall.

Mrs. Boll's daughter Opal wants her to move to Lubbock. Opal is still reeling from her divorce. She wants the company, and Mrs. Boll's small income wouldn't hurt either. Mrs. Boll tells Opal she can come to her, the way she did when she came home from Florida with a fourteen-month-old baby and said her husband was a devil. Opal expects her mother to understand that Opal's life is in Lubbock. As if Mrs. Boll's life is lint in the wind.

The house is paid for now. Nobody seems to understand what that means to her. Paid for, and taxes forgiven for age and low income. She can't be put out. You would think Opal would remember what it was like after her papa died. They lived in an old settlers' cabin on the farm of Mrs. Boll's parents. Like itinerant pickers or tenants. Like white trash.

Mrs. Boll's mother remembered about the pies. She said, "She really loved her lemon pie, didn't she?" Her soft, floury face was plumped by remembering. "Where is she?" she asked. She meant Laura. She thought Opal and Laura were girls. She had lost twenty-five years in a clutch of blocked blood. She died in Mrs. Boll's house, waking in the early morning to mew like a kitten, then curling like a baby back toward God, who begins things, and ends them. Mrs. Boll's mother was a harsh woman, badly treated by fate and abandoned, after her first stroke, by Mrs. Boll's stepfather, who went to live with *his* daughter. He sold the farm and stole it all. Mrs. Boll's mother was like a baby. Mrs. Boll forgave her everything and took her in. For almost two years, she was her mother's whole life. And in this house.

Leo always has something to show her. Once he gave her a rock he had polished for days on his pajama sleeve, and then a photograph of himself as a boy in overalls. She saw how his hand, quiet on his thigh, caressed. He admitted that he could not really see the features of her face. He said it was something in her stoop that smote him, that her shoulders sloped like a girl's, poised for touch. He'd been a farmer too, but he'd always read.

Before, only Ira had called her "sweet." Ira had called her "twig" and "my lovely," phrases their families would have never thought could pass between them. He had plucked her from her hard girl's life and made her tender. Then he died.

She washes the apricots one by one. It is a luxury of old age to have no hurry. It isn't being done, but doing, that matters; who says an old woman won't drop dead with her spoon in her soup?

Whenever anyone comes, they take jars away with them, but they take apricots for granted, and her time. Once she found a jar of jam, crusted by half an inch of mold, in Opal's refrigerator. The waste made her feel sick. Opal has forgotten all the years they lived like beggars. She needs two closets for her clothes. She wants Mrs. Boll to live in a trailer in back of her house, if she won't just live inside. Mrs. Boll says she won't leave her roses and her fruit. Already she wonders who will care, when she is dead.

Leo says she'll have more income married to him. She'll get her own check from Social Security, only more, on his record. He sold his farm early, then sold hardware, and made more than she ever did. He doesn't understand how this wounds her. She has worked fifty years, on farms, in railroad cars as cook, packing flour in a mill, and lately as an old lady looking after folks in worse shape than she for now. She wants what she has earned; she'd never let it disappear like smoke, to get a better deal.

Leo says he'll put a trailer on his lake lot and she can fish to her heart's content. He is divorced. He says his wife took everyone with her, two generations of kin, all blaming him for wanting a little chance at life before he died. He says he'll teach her to like football and he'll listen to her soaps. Already he's started, turning on "As the World Turns," just to show his intentions. "Look at that," he says. He is legally quite blind.

None of these things matter. What matters is what they have become inside her. Vanity and discontent. Her heart has been diminished by so much loss, it isn't heart that rises to his song. It's something wilder, young, long ago given up for dead. It has a cloak of laughter, an apron of shame. It's this that wears her down.

She imagines lying awake in her bed in the dark and listening to Leo moving around. She imagines herself thinking, *it's my house, he ought to go to bed*. He will annoy her and want things changed. He will think he has something to show her, because he is a man.

Dozens of washed apricots lie on towels on the cabinets. Mrs. Boll scoops up the last handful from her basket. Suddenly she fears she is going to be dizzy. She goes in to sit on her couch, hardly aware that she still carries the apricots in her hands. As soon as she sits down she knows there is nothing wrong, nothing at all, except that she is getting old. After all these decades on her feet, her legs are crisscrossed by heavy mottled veins. It is hard to remember that she once played basketball on a team that went all the way to state.

She drops the apricots into the space her sitting makes. On one she finds a brown spot. She looks at it more closely. The mark is only a discoloration and not a bruise. She decides to eat it. All morning she has moved in a cloud of fragrance and not eaten even one.

The apricot, opened by her teeth, exudes a warm sweet odor. She saves the dark spot until last and eats it deliberately, thinking there is some slight difference in texture, a kind of brownness, after all. She eats the flesh of the fruit and drops the pit into her lap, onto the mounds of apricots in the apron cupped between her spread thighs.

There is nothing to compare to the sweetness of apricots, nothing to stir her like that sweetness, their fur and pulp, the way they have come, year after year.

CALYX Journal, Vol. 9:2&3, 1986

Claribel Alegría
translated by Darwin J. Flakoll

LUISA IN REALITYLAND (excerpts)

First Communion

Everything was ready for the party the night before. Chabela, Luisa's *nana*, had just finished ironing the pleated organdy dress that reached to the girl's ankles and the wide, vaporous veil. Her mother gave the final touches to the table. It was covered with several damask tablecloths, and it extended the entire length of the patio corridor. The cake, surmounted by a tiny doll dressed just like Luisa, was going to occupy the very center.

"Off to bed now," Chabe told her, "and remember to drink a glass of water, because tomorrow morning you can't—not so much as a drop."

Luisa knew that even if she drank tons of water that night, she would wake up horribly thirsty, but there was no help for it. Her mother, Chabe, her aunts, had all told her it was to be the most important day of her life, and she had to make some sacrifice for it.

"Come along," Chabe told her. "Let's get to bed."

Luisa followed her obediently.

When Chabe turned off the light, Luisa called her to her side.

"Is it true that tomorrow I can ask for anything I want and I'll get whatever I ask for?"

"That depends. You can ask for one thing—something that's very important to you."

"What should I ask for, Chabe?"

"How should I know? That God keeps your parents safe and sound for many years, that you remain pure and healthy and good. You're the one who has to decide."

Luisa lay for a long time with her eyes wide open in the darkness. The next morning, both Chabe and her mother helped her get dressed. She was dying of thirst, her new shoes pinched her feet, and the cap that sustained her veil was terribly hot, but she didn't complain, not even once. What she was going to ask for was very important, and she had to make some sacrifice so it would be granted her.

Her father honked impatiently from the street, and Luisa went running out and climbed into the front seat so her dress wouldn't get wrinkled. Two nuns from Assumption College, dressed in heavy purple habits and cream-colored veils, were at the entrance to receive her, and they accompanied her into the chapel, which was already filled with schoolgirls. When Luisa entered, the choir up in the chapel loft began singing, and she felt her eyes filling with tears. The nuns escorted her to her prayer bench, which was covered with satin. Father Agapito, dressed in a white chasuble embroidered in gold thread and accompanied by a sacristan, gave the benediction and began to say mass.

Luisa opened her small mother-of-pearl missal and followed the mass attentively. After a long time the nuns came for her and accompanied her to the altar. Luisa knelt, opened her mouth discreetly, and received the host. With her head lowered and her hands clasped against her breast, she returned to her prayer pew, feeling slightly dizzy.

"It's now, right now that you have to make your wish," her internal voice told her.

"Dear Little Jesus," Luisa said under her breath, "I don't want to be married; I don't like the way men treat women, but I do want to have a baby, Dear Jesus, and Chabe says that only married women can have babies. So that's why I ask you with all my heart to let me get married, and as soon as I have my baby, to let my husband die."

The host dissolved in her mouth, and Luisa lifted her gaze, a beatific smile illuminating her features.

Roque's Via Crucis

"You can see death reflected in that boy's face," Aurora told Luisa, referring to Roque Dalton.

"Nonsense!" Luisa exclaimed. "He has as many lives as a cat. He's always escaping death by the skin of his teeth. The first time he was saved by an earthquake. He was in the prison of Cojutepeque when an earthquake brought down a wall and he was able to wriggle out. The second time, he was only two days away from a firing squad when a coup d'etat overthrew Lemus, who was the dictator at that moment."

Roque and Luisa never knew each other personally, but they corresponded between Prague and Paris and delighted in writing each other about Salvadoran *pupusas*, rooster in *chicha*, bread with *chumpe*, and all the other exquisite flavors and aromas that were unavailable to them in Europe.

Once Luisa travelled to Cuba where Roque was awaiting her in the airport with a bunch of flowers, but her plane was delayed two days, and he had to travel to the interior of the island. From there he would send her notes, which were invariably delivered at lunchtime.

They never so much as embraced each other, but a mutual friend assured her that, according to Roque, Luisa taught him to dance the rumba.

Years later, that same friend called Luisa to announce Roque's death. The news was confused, imprecise, and nobody yet knew who had assassinated him.

Luisa was deeply touched, and that same evening, in order to feel a bit closer to him, she had the urge to read aloud some of his poems. She opened his book at random, and the first verses her eyes encountered were:

When you learn I have died,
don't pronounce my name.

Farabundo Marti

"Didn't Farabundo Marti enter this house about twenty minutes ago?" Colonel Salinas asked Luisa's father.

"No," he replied. "I've known Farabundo ever since we were at the University together. The only person who has knocked on the door in the past half hour was a beggar."

"Precisely. We have information that he has disguised himself as a beggar."

"Don't worry, Colonel," Luisa's father laughed. "I'd have recognized him."

"I'll take your word, Doctor, that you are telling me the truth," the Colonel said as he went out the door.

Farabundo, in fact, was hiding in her father's clinic. General Martinez, who was defense minister at the time, had issued an order for his arrest.

Luisa's father went out to make his routine visits to his patients so as not to attract the attention of the Guards across the street. The only one with whom he shared the secret was Luisa's mother, who took some sweet rolls and coffee to the fugitive and remained conversing with him for a while. About six in the afternoon, Luisa's father returned home and sat down to read the newspaper as usual, so as not to arouse suspicions among the servants. Half an hour later, he slipped Farabundo into the garage, helped him into the trunk, and drove him to the Guatemalan border.

The Blue Theatre

"I haven't been able to sleep for nights," Alejandra told Luisa. "I don't know what's wrong with me."

"Are you worried about something?"

"No, but there's a blue neon light in the street that keeps me awake. Blue," she mused. "The Blue Theatre."

Luisa and Alejandra had been friends for many years. Alejandra was Chilean, and on a number of occasions she had told Luisa about her experiences in prison after the army coup and the death of Allende, but she had never mentioned the Blue Theatre.

"What's that?" Luisa asked.

Alejandra fixed her gaze on the wall.

"It's true, I never told you about it." Her voice was expressionless. "One day while I was in prison, a guard wearing a hood came to my cell and told me to accompany him—that he was taking me to the Blue Theatre.

"'Nothing is going to happen to you,' he told me, 'all you have to do is say yes or no.'

"I began trembling," Alejandra turned her gaze to Luisa, "without knowing why. He took me into a small windowless room, illuminated with blue neon lights. Another guard, also wearing a hood, was waiting for me.

"'There is nothing to be afraid of,' he said, 'all you have to do is say yes or no when I ask you a question. Bring him in,' he ordered the first man.

"There were only two chairs covered in blue plastic. The guard sat down in one, and I was left standing. A few seconds later, two more guards in hoods entered, dragging a young man between them. At first I didn't recognize him, because his face was disfigured. Then I realized it was Sergio, a university schoolmate. He raised his eyes to look at me and shook his head imperceptibly.

"'Seat him there,' the guard indicated the empty chair. 'Do you know him?' he asked me.

"'No,' I said.

"'It would be better not to lie,' the guard said. 'If he's a friend of yours, I'd advise you to tell the truth. Do you know him?'

"'No,' I repeated.

"'Cut off an ear,' the interrogator ordered.

"And right there, Luisa, right before my eyes, they cut off one of his ears. I almost screamed, 'Yes, I know him,' but he raised his head again and shook it almost imperceptibly. They cut off his other ear, cut off his fingers, his hands, and he bore it without screaming. I stood there watching, looking at all that blood, looking at him. At some point I fainted and awoke in my cell. The guard told me Sergio had died, and it was my fault, because if I had said the truth they might have let him go."

Appointment in Zinica

For Maria Gertrudis

"The body was already rotting when they brought it by truck to Zinica," Maria Gertrudis told Luisa. "The boy had been dead for seventeen days. The family opened the coffin and recognized by the teeth that it was not their son, but they didn't say anything. Their own son had gold inlays. They gave the boy a funeral with military honors, because he had died a hero's death. A group of us students who were harvesting coffee attended the funeral.

"The next day the news arrived that their own son had fallen in battle at Cua, and the *compas* had to bury him on the battlefield at four in the afternoon: the same day and the same hour we had held the funeral in Zinica."

CALYX Journal, Vol. 11:1, 1987/88

Shirley Sikes

FALLING OFF THE MATTERHORN

My son dreams I am dying. No. He dreams I am dead. But I am still there, he says, and he doesn't feel sad. Why should he?

I've dreamed I was dying. I've felt I was. But in the end I, too, found it was only a dream. I'm out of the hospital. I'm still alive.

I'm climbing the Matterhorn. There's no one else to rely on, yet I am steadily making my way to the top. Nothing discourages me. A minute ago, for example, I lost a glove. In this cold, at this height, that could be fatal. But I laugh. What is "fatal"?

In the village, below the mountain, people regard me as crazy.
Why are you climbing? they ask.
Why not? I ask.
In the cafe, the odor of raclette stings the air. I hate raclette. No one seems able to melt the cheese without burning it. Have you ever smelled burnt cheese?

I came to Zermatt alone. After the treatment, I wanted to sort things out.
What things? my friends ask.
What things? my son asks.
Isn't the sickness enough? they all ask.
Oh yes. It's enough.

You should rest, the doctors said.
You should rest, my acquaintances said.

But I said no, I haven't time for rest.
What matters is the Matterhorn.

When I was young, Time seemed endless. To wait to run flying from school at the end of the day, to wait until *he* deigned to look at me, to wait was impossible. Time wouldn't pass.

Now Time is impossible too, but it's different. I no longer wait for it. I have to run to catch up. I try to seize it, force it to slow down, hold it still for a moment, but I cannot. Now I am like the child traveling in a car who tires of looking forward and begins to stare out the back window at the road unrolling behind her. "Slow down," she shouts. "I *saw* something!"

But she is not in control and the car has hurtled ahead. The vision is lost.

We are always children.

"If it's cancer," the doctor said, "I'll take out the nodes. We have to see if it's spread."

And the nodes are gone. There's an incision, like a bleak smile, under my arm. The incision hurts.

"A carcinoma," the doctor says. "Infiltrating. It's like a terrorist—it sneaks up on you."

I imagine my breast like a grenade. I imagine it exploding. I imagine myself blowing apart, arms, legs, head flying in different directions, like a five-pointed star.

Okay, I'll level with you. I'm not on the side of the mountain, I'm in Zermatt. You can't drive here—you have to ride the little cog railroad train. It claws its way up the mountainside. You see houses with roofs of slate and hay in humps almost like the giant tooth of the Matterhorn. Wood for the winter is piled in triangular stacks like tepees.

Where have they learned this? Am I back on the Plains?

No one yodels. Yet I expect it. I seem to be in a dream again. This country—Switzerland—is a dreamland.

Isn't it?

People fall off the Matterhorn. Edward Whymper did. Or rather some people in his party.

The mountain was scaled from the Swiss arête. It's easier there. The party looked out over the great valley and the tiny village of Zermatt. They saw the worm of the Rhône. They saw what I will see when I reach the topmost peak.

Descending, four of them fell to their deaths.

Could it be the view was enough?

When I was irradiated, a giant machine opened its shutter like a malevolent eye. Suspended above me, it seemed to wink closed. It seemed to have an enormous secret.

When the technicians came back into the room (no danger they said, yet they always returned to their lead-filled walls), they turned me to another position. I felt like a doll being placed on a sill.

The Cyclops eye rolled open, rolled shut.

Someone once said, "In the great acts of life, we are alone."

When I took all the drugs, my hair fell out. I awoke one day and tried to comb it. As I moved the comb through my hair, huge chunks fell out. The comb became clogged. Hairs fell over my face and settled on my lips as though they were leaves falling from a tree.

My head looked like the top of the great, bald mountain.

My head looked like the plucked dome of that abandoned doll.

My head looked like a skull.

Last winter, I caught a mouse in a trap. The trap did not break the poor creature's neck. Strong, the mouse struggled to free himself, managed to break free of an upturned basket in which the trap got entangled. But it did not die.

I was lying on my bed trying to sleep. The chemicals were whimsical: one moment I felt tired, the next I felt seized by a gigantic energy. Mostly, I felt I was sinking into the bed, into the earth.

It was bleakly cold in the studio where the trap was. I listened, horrified, as the mouse struggled, grew still, struggled, grew still. I told myself it was the balance of Nature. One did not let mice run free in the house. There were predators and there was prey. The mouse was prey. It was the balance of Nature.

But it did not die.

I could not keep from thinking that the mouse represented a great Intelligence.

At last I decided that sudden death would be more merciful than expiring by inches. I went to kill the mouse.

But when the tiny bright eyes rolled up to me (faking death so I would not strike), I could not act.

I don't care for the balance of Nature.

Then I set the small thing free. Its body began to convulse.

In the end, it died.
Why did it die when I'd set it free?

When my hair fell out, I bought a wig. I was terrified the wig would fall off. People complimented me on my hair. At night, when I took the wig off, my head was cold. I covered my baldness with a scarf. I looked like a robot.

There are many tourists in this cafe. Germans, Scandinavians, English, a few Americans. Some of the Germans have dogs with them. Though the Swiss are immaculate, they don't mind dogs in cafes. Of course the animals have to be well trained.

The Scandinavians seem very gay. They like to ride the lake boats. When they ride them, they take off their shirts to sun themselves. The women have beautiful breasts.

The English are aloof and the Germans absorbed with their dogs.

The Americans like to talk loudly.

The Swiss workers do not seem to like any of us.

Today I study the mountain. I can put myself anywhere on it. I can even straddle the summit (I picture it like the back of a horse). Perhaps I could erect a flag when I reach the top; I could leave the family crest.

I met my son on one of the lake boats. How odd, I thought. I didn't know he was here. Switzerland, full of coincidences, has put us together again. We are drinking *café au lait*. My son is telling me he likes to travel alone. "I can do what I want to do," he says. "I don't have to ask anyone."

I, too, can do what I want to do. If I've learned nothing else, I've learned this.

We're not caught by the neck.
Are we?

Now, on the mountain, I've slipped. I not only have lost a glove, my hold on the pick is weak. Why did I try this alone?

You know I'm lying.

One of my dreams was strange.
There was a large train rumbling through the countryside. It curved back on itself. When I studied it closely, as though from above, I saw that it was not a train at all, but a giant caterpillar. The enormous maw was eating everything in sight.

"I'm going to Gruyères," my son tells me. "I want to try their raspberries with cream."
"I want to see Chiffon again," I say. "I want to see Lord Byron's name, carved on the walls. He was a prisoner there. I *think.*"

Once, when I was young, I took pencil and paper and made what I called "Rules for Life." I was going to read certain books, do certain things, taste, feel whatever there was in the world. There was nothing that would be forbidden to me or that I could not do. Where others failed, I would succeed.
I kept the list for a very long time.

When I took the chemo, I made more Rules.
But when I studied them, I saw they were only a grocery list.

I don't think it's the cold so much that's a threat up here. It's dying by inches. It's knowing that if I slip, no one will hear my cry and no one will care.
I could be buried in a crevasse for all Eternity.

"They tell me they pile on the cream so it's so thick you can hardly eat it," my son tells me. He smacks his lips. "I can just see my teeth sinking into the berries, slowly sucking the rich, rich cream through them. Can you believe it?"
Somehow he looks like a caterpillar. I see him eating everything in sight.
Why is he here?

Once I took a picture of the Jungfrau. From the window of my little third-class hotel room, I took the picture. It looked perfect.

When the film came back, the Jungfrau was not on it. There were pictures of Japanese tourists swarming over Interlaken, of Americans pointing their cameras back at me, of the train station, but there was no Jungfrau.

It was as if something in Switzerland erased it, as though if I'd taken the picture, I'd captured its soul.

I remember the Jungfrau resembled a breast.

Finding a new vein was the hard thing. After so many weeks, and with only one arm (you shouldn't put needles in the arm where the nodes are gone) you find fresh veins are extremely dear. If the technician is not good with the butterfly (the smallest needle they can find), it is going to be tough. Poking and probing and no blood is what will happen.

You find yourself reverting to childhood. You want to run and hide when you see the wrong technician is coming to take your blood.

They don't want to see you either. "I hope it's not _____," they say, naming you. "It's too hard to get blood out of her."

In a way, I'm pleased. I've been singled out somehow.

My son and I decide to go to Gruyères together. After all, who can resist that supreme taste and sensation? It is part of my Rules of Life.

Of course, I first have to get off the Matterhorn.

When I was in college, ready to assault the world, I was taken into a society with a ritual. The ritual was supposed to stimulate the best in young women.

We were taken up to the top of the administration building and allowed to look at the view.

I will never forget how different it is when you are looking down from above.

You just have to find the highest point, that's all.

My son tells me he will meet me in Gruyères. "We don't even have to make plans," he says. "Something in Switzerland is putting us together."

"It is," I say.

When he leaves, I look out the window of this small cafe. Inserting itself on the foreground of the Matterhorn is the blue carriage from the first-class hotel. It is drawn by horses. It is a coach really, and it looks as if Cinderella will be stepping down at any minute.

Somehow I have the sensation I get when, in a dream, I am in a play but I can't remember the lines.

Of course, one has to concentrate. One doesn't get anywhere in this world if one doesn't concentrate, and mountain climbing is no exception. It's hard to explain to people why you climb the mountain but I've heard it said it's to get to the top.

Somehow that doesn't please me. Neither does the saying, "Because it's there."

It's so ordinary.

Maybe that's the point.

If one would shout here, she might start an avalanche. I have seen the reflections of the barriers they put on the mountain side to stop avalanches. They wink when the sun strikes them. Like the Cyclops eye, they seem to have a great secret.

After the radiation, I stared at my breast—the "sickly" one. I thought of how I would have looked if the breast were gone: lopsided, with another grinning scar. It would have mocked me with its smug smile. It would have looked like a giant crevasse.

Here on the Matterhorn, the air is pure. Thin, but pure. One has to conserve it; it offers something missing at lesser heights.

Edward Whymper was here before me. I sense him.

In youth, I felt optimistic, as I do now on the days when I have a good climb. In spite of the bad things, there was hope one would still win out. Now middle-aged, with the view a bit grim, there is little optimism. Good days, like veins, are so hard to come by.

Yet I don't want to give up. Edward Whymper climbed the Matterhorn. Why can't I?

I've lost the pick. It slipped over the side. I've nothing to help me in the descent. I do not want to go down like the others, sliding helplessly, hurtling over the edge.

My son says he no longer understands me. "You've changed," he says in Gruyères. "I don't know you anymore."

Who do you suppose Edward Whymper could talk to?

In the hospital, we were all concentrating on this one breast—my son, my doctors, myself. It was as if it lived a life of its own. I imagined it with arms and feet, running away from me.

"Come back," I called. "You've got to come back."

In Gruyères, my son and I eat raspberries with cream. They are delicious. The juice runs down my chin. The juice resembles blood.

I think of the Swiss. They were not always so placid. Even Gruyères is a fortified city. Beneath its stone streets, one senses a pulse. It seems to be racing.

I'm not in Gruyères. I'm not on the Matterhorn. I'm in the hospital. Aren't I?

My son pats my hand. "You will recover," he says. "You'll beat this thing." "Oh, yes," I say, "I'll beat it."

But I think: are there armies within—marching against me?

The wind on the summit is fierce. I cling to the rock, digging my frozen fingers into it.

I look out over the Rhône and the mountains behind. I can see Italy, France. Night is coming and it's getting cold. I have to descend.

If I fall, I think, no one will know I've been here.

If I fall, I think, will *I* know I've been here?

CALYX Journal, Vol. 11:1, 1987/88

Valerie Matsumoto

TWO DESERTS

E miko Oyama thought the Imperial Valley of California
was the loneliest place she had ever seen. It was just
like the Topaz Relocation Camp, she told her husband Kiyo, but without
the barbed wire fence and crowded barracks. Miles of bleached desert punc-
tuated sparsely by creosote bush and abandoned debris faced her from al-
most every window in their small house. Only the living room had a view of
the dirt road which ended in front of their home, and across it, a row of
squat faded houses where other farmers' families lived. They waved to her
and Kiyo in passing, and Jenny played with the Garcia children, but Emiko's
Spanish and their English were too limited for more than casual greetings.

Emiko felt a tug of anticipation on the day the moving van pulled up at
the Ishikawas' place across the road—the house which in her mind had
become inextricably linked with friendship. She had felt its emptiness as
her own when Sats, Yuki, and their three children gave up farming and
departed for a life which came to her in delicious fragments in Yuki's hast-
ily scrawled letters. Yuki, who made the best sushi rice in the world and
had given her the recipe, who could draw shy Kiyo into happy banter. Yuki,
whose loud warm laugh made the desert seem less drab, less engulfing.

She had been thinking about Yuki that morning as she weeded the yard
and vegetable plot in preparation for planting. Sats and Yuki had advised
her to plant marigolds around the vegetables to draw away nematodes, and
she liked the idea of a bold orange border. Emiko liked bright colors, espe-
cially the flaming scarlet of the bougainvillea which rose above the front
door where Kiki their cat lay sunning himself. There was a proud look in
the amber eyes, for Kiki the hunter had slain three scorpions and laid them
in a row on the porch, their backs crushed and deadly stingers limp, win-
ning extravagant praise from Jenny and Emiko. The scorpions still lay there,

at Jenny's insistence, awaiting Kiyo's return that evening. Emiko shuddered every time she entered the house, glancing at the curved stingers and thinking of Jenny's sandaled feet.

Emiko had finished weeding the front border and was about to go inside to escape the heat when she saw the new neighbor woman plodding across the sand toward her. A cotton shift could not conceal her thinness, nor a straw hat her tousled gray curls. Her eyes were fragile lilac glass above the wide smile.

"Hello, I'm Mattie Barnes. I just thought I'd come over and introduce myself while Roy is finishing up with the movers. Your bougainvillea caught my eye first thing and I thought, 'Those are some folks who know what will grow in the desert.' I hope you'll give me some advice about what to plant in my yard once we get settled in."

They talked about adjusting to desert life and Emiko learned that Mattie's husband Roy had recently retired. "We decided to move here because the doctor said it would be better for my lungs," Mattie explained, wiping her brow.

"Would you like a glass of lemonade?" Emiko offered. "Or maybe later, after you've finished moving?"

"Oh, I'd love something cold," Mattie said, adding vaguely, "Roy will take care of everything—he's more particular about those things than I am."

Emiko preceded Mattie into the house, hoping that Jenny was not lying on the cool linoleum, stripped to her underwear. As she crossed the threshold Mattie gave a shriek and stopped abruptly, eyeing the scorpions lined up neatly on the porch.

"What on earth are those things doing here?"

"Our cat killed them," Emiko said, feeling too foolish to admit her pride in Kiki's prowess. "Jenny wants me to leave them to show her father when he comes home from the field."

"Awful creatures," Mattie shuddered. "Roy can't stand them, but then, he can't abide insects. He said to me this morning, 'Of all the places we could have moved to, we had to choose the buggiest.'"

There was no buggier place than the Imperial Valley, Emiko agreed, especially in the summer. In the evening the air was thick with mosquitoes, gnats, and moths. The cicadas buzzed in deafening chorus from every tree. They danced in frenzied legions around the porch light and did kamikaze dives into the bath water. All of them came in dusty gray hordes, as though the desert had sapped the color from them, but not their energy. Late at night, long after Kiyo had fallen into exhausted sleep, Emiko would lie awake, perspiring, listening to the tinny scrabble of insects trapped between the window glass and screen.

". . . but I like the desert," Mattie was saying, dreamily clinking the ice cubes in her glass. "It's so open and peaceful. As long as I can have a garden, I'll be happy."

Within a few weeks after their arrival, the Barnes had settled into a routine: Roy making daily trips to the local store and the Roadside Cafe, Mattie tending her garden and walking to church once a week with Emiko and Jenny. By the end of June Mattie had been enlisted with Emiko to make crepe paper flowers for a church bazaar.

"My, your flowers turned out beautifully," Mattie exclaimed one morning, looking wistfully at the cardboard box filled with pink, yellow, scarlet, and lavender blossoms set on wire stems. "They'll make lovely corsages." She sighed. "I seem to be all thumbs—my flowers hardly look like flowers. I don't know how you do it. You Japanese are just very artistic people."

Emiko smiled and shook her head with a polite disclaimer, but the bright blur of flowers suddenly dissolved into another mass of paper blooms, carrying her more than a decade into the past. She was a teenager in a flannel shirt and denim pants with rolled cuffs, seated on a cot in a cramped barrack room helping her mother fashion flowers from paper. Her own hands had been clumsy at first, striving to imitate her mother's precise fingers which gave each fragile petal lifelike curves, the look of artless grace. The only flowers in Topaz when elderly Mr. Wakasa was shot by a guard were those that bloomed from the fingertips of *Issei* and *Nisei* women, working late into the night to complete the exquisite wreaths for his funeral. Each flower a silent voice crying with color, each flower a tear.

"I did a little flower-making as a teenager," Emiko said.

"Will you come over and show me how?" Mattie asked. "I'm too embarrassed to take these awful things, and I've still got lots of crepe paper spread all over the kitchen."

"Sure," Emiko nodded. "I'll help you get started and you'll be a whiz in no time. It isn't too hard; it just takes patience."

Mattie smiled, a slight wheeze in her voice when she said, "I've got plenty of that too."

They were seated at the Barnes' small table surrounded by bright masses of petals like fallen butterflies, their fingers sticky with florist's tape, when Roy returned from shopping. When he saw Emiko, he straightened and pulled his belt up over his paunch.

"A sight for sore eyes!" he boomed, giving her a broad wink. "What mischief are you ladies up to?"

"Emi's teaching me how to make flowers," Mattie explained, holding up a wobbly rose.

"Always flowers! I tell you," he leaned over Emiko's chair and said in a mock conspiratorial voice, "all my wife thinks about is flowers. I keep telling her there are other things in life. Gardening is for old folks."

"And what's wrong with that?" Mattie protested, waving her flower at him. "We *are* old folks."

"Speak for yourself," he winked at Emiko again. "What's so great about gardens, anyway?"

"I hold with the poem that says you're closest to God's heart in a garden," said Mattie.

"Well, I'm not ready to get that close to God's heart yet." There was defiance in Roy's voice. "What do you think about that, Emi?"

"I like working in the yard before it gets too hot," she said carefully. Her words felt tight and deliberate, like the unfurled petals on the yellow rose in her hands. "I don't have Mattie's talent with real flowers, though—aside from the bougainvillea and Jenny's petunias, nothing ever seems to bloom. The soil is too dry and saline for the things I used to grow. Now I've got my hopes pinned on the vegetable garden."

"Vegetables—hmph!" Roy snorted, stomping off to read the paper.

"Oh, that Roy is just like a boy sometimes," Mattie said. "I tell you, don't ever let your husband retire or you'll find him underfoot all day long."

"Doesn't Roy have any hobbies?" Emiko thought of her father and his books, his Japanese brush painting, his meetings.

"He used to play golf," Mattie said, "but there's no golf course here. He says this town is one giant sand trap."

"There have been times when I felt that way too," Emiko admitted lightly.

"Well, don't let Roy hear you say that or you'll never get him off the topic," Mattie chuckled. "The fact is, Roy doesn't much know how to be by himself. I've had forty years to learn, and I've gotten to like it. And I suppose maybe he will too."

Her voice trailed off, and Emiko suddenly realized that Mattie didn't much care whether he did or not.

One day while Emiko was engrossed in pinning a dress pattern for Jenny she suddenly heard a tapping on the screen, like the scrabbling of a large beetle. She half-turned and felt a jolt of alarm at the sight of a grinning gargoyle hunched before the glass, hands splayed open on either side of his face, the caricature of a boy peering covetously into a toy store.

"Hey there! I caught you daydreaming!" he chortled. "Looks to me like you need some company to wake you up."

"I'm not daydreaming; I'm trying to figure out how to make a two-and-a-half yard dress out of two yards," she said. "Jenny is growing so fast, I can hardly keep up with her."

Roy walked into the house unbidden, confident of a welcome, and drew a chair up to the table. He fingered the bright cotton print spread over the table and gazed at Emiko, his head cocked to one side.

"You must get pretty lonesome here by yourself all day. No wonder you're sitting here dreaming."

"No," she said, her fingers moving the pattern pieces. "There's so much to do I don't have time to be lonesome. Besides, Jenny is here, and Kiyo comes home for lunch."

"But still—cooped up with a kiddie all day . . ." Roy shook his head. He chose to disregard Kiyo, who had no place in his imagined scenarios, and was hard at work miles away.

Emiko delicately edged the cotton fabric away from Roy's damp, restless fingers. I'll be darned if I offer him something to drink, she thought as he mopped his brow and cast an impatient glance at the kitchen. "I haven't seen Mattie outside this week. How is she feeling?"

"Oh, 'bout the same, 'bout the same," he said, his irritation subsiding into brave resignation. "She has her good days and her bad days. The doctor told her to stay in bed for a while and take it easy."

"It must be hard on Mattie, having to stay indoors," Emiko said, thinking of her peering out through the pale curtains at the wilting zinnias and the new weeds in the backyard.

"I suppose so—usually you can't tear Mattie away from her garden." Roy shook his head. "Mattie and me are real different. Now, I like people—I've always been the sociable type—but Mattie! All she cares about are plants."

"Well, Kiyo and I have different interests," Emiko said, "but it works out well that way. Maybe you could learn a few things from Mattie about plants."

Even as the suggestion passed her lips, she regretted it. Roy viewed the garden as the site of onerous labor. To Mattie, it was the true world of the heart, with no room for ungentle or impatient hands. It was a place of deeply sown hopes, lovingly nurtured, and its colors were the colors of unspoken dreams.

"Plants!" Roy threw up his hands. "Give me people any time. I always liked people and had a knack for working with them—that's how I moved up in the business."

"Why don't you look into some of the clubs here?" Emiko tried again. "The Elks always need people with experience and time . . . "

"Sweetheart, I'm going to spend my time the way I want. I'm finished with work—it's time to enjoy life! Besides, how much fun can I have with a bunch of old geezers? That's not for me, Emily, my dear." She stiffened as he repeated the name, savoring the syllables. "Emily . . . Emily . . . Yes, I like the sound of that—Emily."

"My name is Emiko," she said quietly, her eyes as hard as agate. "I was named after my grandmother." That unfaltering voice had spoken the same words in first, second, third, fourth, fifth, and sixth grades. All the grammar school teachers had sought to change her name, to make her into an Emily: "Emily is so much easier to pronounce, dear, and it's a nice American name." She was such a well-mannered child, the teachers were always amazed at her stubbornness on this one point. Sometimes she was tempted to relent, to give in, but something inside her resisted. "My name is Emiko," she would insist politely. I am an American named Emiko. I was named for my grandmother who was beautiful and loved to swim. When she emerged from the sea, her long black hair would glitter white with salt. I never met her, but she was beautiful and she would laugh when she rose from the waves. "My name is Emiko, Emi for short."

"But Emily is such a pretty name," Roy protested. "It fits you."

"It's not my name," she said, swallowing a hard knot of anger. "I don't like to be called Emily!"

"Temper, temper!" He shook his finger at her, gleeful at having provoked her.

"Well, I guess I'll be in a better temper when I can get some work done," she said, folding up the cloth with tense, deliberate hands. She raised her voice. "Jenny! Let's go out and water the vegetable garden now."

If Jenny thought this a strange task in the heat of the afternoon, it did not show in her face when she skipped out of her room, swinging her straw hat. It still sported a flimsy, rainbow-hued scarf which had been the subject of much pleading in an El Centro dime store. At that moment, Emiko found it an oddly reassuring sight. She smiled and felt her composure return.

"Tell Mattie to let me know if there's anything I can do to help," she told Roy, as he unwillingly followed them out of the house and trudged away across the sand. After they went back inside, Emiko locked the door behind them for the first time. When Kiyo returned home, his face taut with fatigue, she told him it was because of the hoboes who came around.

Emiko went to see Mattie less and less frequently, preferring instead to call her on the phone, even though they lived so close. Roy, however, continued to drop by despite Emiko's aloofness. His unseemly yearning tugged at her with undignified hands, but what he craved most was beyond her power to give. She took to darning and mending in the bedroom with the curtains drawn, ignoring his insistent knock; she tried to do her gardening in the evening after dinner when her husband was home, though it was hard to weed in the dusk. She was beginning to feel caged, pent up, restless. Jenny and Kiyo trod quietly, puzzled by her edginess, but their solicitude only made her feel worse.

Finally, one morning Emiko decided to weed the vegetables, sprouting new and tender. Surely the mid-morning heat would discourage any interference. Although the perspiration soon trickled down her face, she began to enjoy the weeding, pulled into the satisfying rhythm of the work. She was so engrossed that she did not notice when Roy Barnes unlatched the gate and stepped into the yard, a determined twinkle in his faded eye.

"Howdy, Emi! I saw you working away out here by your lonesome and thought maybe you could use some help."

"Thanks, but I'm doing all right," she said, wrenching a clump of puncture vine from the soil and laying it in the weed box carefully to avoid scattering the sharp stickers. Jenny was close by, digging at her petunias and marigolds, ignoring Mr. Barnes, who had no place in the colorful jungle she was imagining.

"If I had a pretty little wife, I sure wouldn't let her burn up out here, no sir," his voice nudged at her as she squatted on the border of the vegetable plot. If Mattie looked out of the window she would see only a pleasant tableau: Roy nodding in neighborly fashion as Emiko pointed out young rows of zucchini and yellow squash, watermelon, cantaloupe, eggplant, and tomatoes. Mattie would not see the strain on Emiko's face, turned away from Roy, when he leaned over and mumbled, "Say, you know what I like best in this garden?"

Emiko grabbed the handle of the shovel and stood up before he could tell her, moving away from him to pluck a weed. "I know Mattie likes cantaloupe," she said. "So do I. Kiyo prefers Crenshaws, but I couldn't find any seeds this year. What do you and Mattie have in your garden?"

"Just grass," he said, undeterred. "Mattie's always fussing over her flowers—you know what she's like," he chuckled indulgently, "but I'd rather spend my time doing other things than slaving in the yard."

Emiko hacked away at the stubborn clumps of grass roots and the persistent runners with myriad finer roots, thread-thin but tough as wire. She worked with desperate energy, flustered, her gloved hands sweating on the shovel handle, forehead damp. She was groping for the language to make him understand, to make him leave her in peace, but he was bent on not understanding, not seeing, not leaving until he got what he wanted.

"You know what, Emi?" He moistened his dry lips, beginning to grin reminiscently. "You remind me of somebody I met in Tokyo. Have you ever been to Tokyo?"

"No," she said, digging hard. "Never."

"You'd like it, it's a wonderful place, so clean and neat, and the people so friendly. When I was in Tokyo, I met up with the cutest *geisha* girl you ever saw—just like a little doll. She'd never seen anybody with blue eyes before, and couldn't get over it." He chuckled. "I couldn't think who you reminded me of at first, and then it just hit me that you are the spitting image of her."

"Did Mattie like Tokyo too?" Emiko said, continuing to spade vigorously as his eyes slid over her, imagining a doll in exotic robes.

"She didn't go—it was a business trip," he said impatiently. Then his voice relaxed into a drawl, heavy with insinuation. "After all, I like to do some things on my own." He was moving closer again.

Then she saw it. Emiko had just turned over a rock, and as she raised the shovel, it darted from its refuge, pincers up, the deadly tail curved menacingly over the carapaced back. It moved a little to the left and then the right, beginning the poison dance. Emiko glanced to see where Jenny was and saw Roy jump back hastily; the scorpion, startled by his movement, scuttled sideways toward Jenny, lying on her stomach, still dreaming of her jungle.

The blood pounded in Emiko's head. She brought down the shovel hard with one quick breath, all her rage shooting down the thick handle into the heavy crushing iron. She wielded the shovel like a *samurai* in battle, swinging it down with all her force, battering her enemy to dust. Once had been enough but she struck again and again, until her anger was spent and she leaned on the rough handle, breathing hard.

"Mommy! What did you do?" Jenny had scrambled to Emiko's side, fear in her eyes, gazing at the unrecognizable fragments in the dirt.

"I killed a scorpion," Emiko said. She scornfully tossed the remains into the weed box, and wiped her brow on her arm, like a farmer, or a warrior. "I don't like to kill anything," she said aloud, "but sometimes you have to."

Roy Barnes recoiled from the pitiless knowledge in her eyes. He saw her clearly now but it was too late. His mouth opened and closed but the gush of words had gone dry. He seemed to age before her eyes, like Urashima-taro who opened the precious box of youth and was instantly wrinkled and broken by the unleashed tides of years.

"You'll have to leave now, Mr. Barnes. I'm going in to fix lunch." Emiko's smile was as quiet as unsheathed steel. "Tell Mattie I hope she's feeling better."

She watched him pick his way across the dirt, avoiding the puncture vine and rusted tin cans, looking as gray as the rags that bleached beneath the fierce sun. Jenny stared past him and the small houses of their neighborhood to the desert sand beyond, glittering like an ocean with shards of glass and mica.

"Do you think we might ever find gold?" she asked.

They gazed together over the desert, full of unknown perils and ancient secrets, the dust of dreams and battles.

"Maybe." Emiko stood tall, shading her eyes from the deceptive shimmer. "Maybe."

CALYX Journal, Vol. 11:2&3, 1988

Marianne Villanueva

SIKO

T he village of Bagong Silang is an untidy assortment of
half a dozen palm-thatched houses, about a hundred
kilometers north of Manila. It falls under the jurisdiction of the municipal-
ity of San Pablo, a town of a few hundred people, a day's walk away. The
people of Bagong Silang have lived for generations along a narrow strip of
mud road that borders the rice paddies. They are, as a rule, thrifty and
industrious folk. When not toiling in the rice fields, they tend vegetable
gardens. They own a few pigs, a few chickens—nothing much else of value.

Aling Saturnina used to live in the last house on the left, the one behind
the *santol* tree. But last year, she and her married daughter were taken to
San Pablo in a military jeep, and since then no one has seen or heard from
them. The villagers don't like to talk about the events that led to Aling
Saturnina's disappearance. When asked, they cross themselves and their
eyes slide sideways and perhaps one or two invoke the name of the town's
patron saint, as though the saying of it had the power to protect them from
all harm. If the questioner becomes too persistent—as lately some of these
newspapermen from San Pablo have been—they escape to the rice fields,
and wait there till nightfall before returning to their homes. They are simple
folk and don't bother with things they cannot understand.

Everyone remembers Aling Saturnina because of her temper. She had
eight children and was always cursing and beating one or the other with
the back of her wooden slippers. She was fond of *tuba*, the potent drink
made from fermented palm sap. Whether or not she had money for the
children's supper, she would send one of her sons to the *tiyanggi* for a
bottle. The eldest son, Lando, ran away when he was fourteen. A few years
later, Isagani left. Then, in quick succession, Prospero, Lina, Catherine,
and Rey, too, disappeared.

Siko stayed until he was nearly full-grown. When he finally left, he took the last of his mother's savings with him—a few crumpled *pesos,* which she had kept in a tin tucked away under the eaves of the house. When Aling Saturnina discovered the loss, her curses could be heard all over the village. Now there was no money for *tuba,* and the youngest child, Ana, was a skinny, sickly girl, not much use out in the rice fields. The villagers avoided Aling Saturnina then because she would pace the street restlessly with feverish, yellow eyes, like a bitch in heat. They felt sorry for Ana, but what could they do? Sometimes they would press a few eggs into her hands, a few clumps of spinach. No one was surprised when, soon after Siko's departure, Ana took Poldo as a husband. There was no money for a church wedding, so Poldo simply moved in. Poldo proved to be a good son-in-law, a hard worker. He and Ana lived peacefully together in Aling Saturnina's house for many years.

One day, Aling Saturnina learned that Siko had been killed. It was Ana who brought her the news, Ana who came stumbling down the narrow street, crying and blowing her nose into her skirt. At first, Aling Saturnina was confused. Hands knotting her dress in anxiety, she ordered Ana to compose herself.

"Ah, Ina!" Ana cried. "Siko has been shot! He was caught breaking into a colonel's house in San Pablo."

Aling Saturnina sighed. She was not sad, no. She had not seen him in such a long time, and sometimes it pleased her to think that she could no longer remember his face, not even when, in those moments when she was without *tuba,* she wrinkled her forehead and tried hard to concentrate. He had hurt her, how he had hurt her! The memory of that bitter day when, with trembling fingers, she had reached up to the roof and lifted down the old tin can where she had ten, perhaps fifteen *pesos* lovingly stored, and, prying open the cover with her anxious fingers, had seen only emptiness staring back at her—ah! That memory rushed over her once again with overwhelming clarity. She remembered the helpless feeling—as though she had been hit in the belly—that had accompanied her discovery. She had not had *tuba* all that day, and the next, and her body had been wracked by chills, she had been in a fever of want. Over and over again, on those sleepless nights when she found herself pacing the village like a restless animal, she asked herself, "How could he do this to me?" She thought, for a time, that of all her children, Siko loved her the most. She had kept him warm beside her on cold nights. She had taken care never to beat him—not even when he had done something that angered her—preferring instead to beat Lando, because Lando was the eldest and should have been responsible for the behavior of his younger brothers and sisters. She had never suspected Siko of stealing, though after he had gone she began to hear stories from the neighbors, stories of how he had been caught more than once filching tomatoes from their vegetable gardens, and how when baby chickens disappeared, they all thought instinctively of Siko. How was it that she had never known? A son of hers a thief! Aling Saturnina was ashamed. And now this horrifying deed—breaking into someone's home, and that someone no less than a colonel! It was beyond Aling Saturnina's comprehension. She should have known, she berated herself, she should have known all along. Her heart was thudding painfully. The ingrate! She wanted to curse, to beat the air with her fists.

She looked at Ana crying helplessly in a corner.

"That's enough!" she cried. "You'll make yourself sick. Your brother was a fool, may lightning strike me, but he was. I would have beaten any of you with my *tsinelas* if I had caught you stealing so much as a twig from a neighbor's garden!"

Then she went to the shelf where she had kept a bottle of *tuba*, and took it with her to the rice fields.

As her feet trod the worn paths threading the rice paddies, Aling Saturnina's spirit remained cold and unforgiving. Her mind gnawed ceaselessly at the fact of Siko's betrayal. That fact had assumed the hardness and blackness of a kernel, lodged at the front of her forehead, between her eyes. On this she focused all her attention. She was oblivious to the fresh green of the rice saplings that blanketed the wet earth, the brilliant, blue arch of the sky, the birds gliding soundlessly overhead. The silence wrapped itself around her like a cloak. The village dropped farther and farther behind until it was no more than an indistinct blur on the horizon.

Aling Saturnina grew tired. She decided to sit and rest for a while in one of the bamboo thickets that sprouted up here and there, forming pockets of dry land among the paddies. As she stretched out on the hard, packed earth and looked around her, her eyes beheld the great, blue bulk of The Mountain, rising straight up out of the plain. The Mountain made her think contemptuously of the legend the villagers told their young children, the legend of the enchantress, Maria Cacao, who was said to live in a palace of gold on The Mountain's highest peak. Now and then, the villagers said, she ventured down to the lowlands and lured men away from their homes and families. Aling Saturnina had stopped believing this story a long time ago. She knew now that when sons and husbands disappeared from the village, as her own had done, they had been lured away by more dangerous enchantments, such as were to be found in the big city of Manila, not far to the south. Her husband had left her after one such trip to the city, never to return. And the rest of her sons, the ones who were still living—they were probably there too, probably living in the shantytown of Tondo, which she had heard was twice as large as the municipality of San Pablo. Some day, Aling Saturnina thought, some day I'll go after those bastards.

She sat in the fields, letting the wind riffle through her long, gray hair and calm her aching nerves. Now and then she took deep, long gulps of the *tuba*. She sat there a long time, until it grew dark and the rice paddies, filled with water, began to reflect the light of the moon. A cold wind rose and parted the bamboo thickets. Still she sat and stared. After a while, she thought she could hear a great clamor of barking dogs arising from the village, and she rose, suddenly expectant. She looked toward the village, ears straining. The clamor increased in ferocity. She could imagine the village dogs, twisting and straining on their hind legs, jaws agape. She had seen them bark in unison like this many other times, and always, always, the sleepy villagers, rushing to their windows in the dead of night, had seen, coming down the street, strange, pale figures—ghosts, spirits, goblins. The last time, they had seen the ghost of Aling Corazon's daughter. She had drowned herself in the Agno River after her husband left her. Her ghost had walked slowly down the middle of the street, crying silently and wringing her hands. At intervals she would stop and look around her with imploring eyes. The villagers had watched Aling Corazon, to see what she would do, but she remained dry-eyed at her window, and, after the wraith had passed, she closed her shutters and went to bed, like all the rest.

In a little while, Aling Saturnina thought she could hear Siko's voice, breaking through a gust of wind. The clumps of bamboo trembled and swayed. Aling Saturnina wondered what form her son would take in coming to her. Would he come as a huge black dog or a pig? She had heard that spirits liked to assume such disguises. Would he appear as one of those bat-like creatures that fly through the air with only the upper halves of their bodies? Several of the villagers had sworn they had seen such things hovering over the rice fields.

Just then, something dark dropped from the sky and landed before her with a soft thud. Aling Saturnina saw that it was a man squatting on his haunches, head lowered, palms pressed against the earth. He raised his head, revealing a blood-spattered face. It was Siko.

Even with his face so disfigured by blood, there was no mistaking the gap between his two front teeth, almost exactly like the one her husband had. Siko squatted, grinning, in the moonlight. He was wearing blue jeans and a white cotton T-shirt, and there were dark, purplish patches of clotted blood across his chest. After she recovered from her initial surprise, Aling Saturnina wanted to hit him. But what is the use of hitting a ghost? Instead she cried: *"Walang hiya ka!* How dare you take my money, leave me and your sister to starve to death!"

As soon as she said those words, she felt her limbs stiffen and become curiously immobile. She wanted to cry out but her tongue lay leaden in her mouth. She could not even reach for the bottle of *tuba* at her feet. Siko stopped grinning. He stood up and approached her, scrutinizing her face. He came so close that she could distinctly smell the odor from his rotting gums.

"Kumusta ka, Ina?" he said in a teasing tone of voice, a tone he might have used if he had seen her once a week all his life. "I am very pleased to see you again. It's good to see you looking so well."

He laughed soundlessly and Aling Saturnina shuddered. She wondered if he had returned to do her harm. She had nothing to defend herself with, not even one of those pictures of the Holy Family which the other old women of the village wore on cords around their necks, not even a bit of ginger pinned to her dress.

"Don't be alarmed, Ina," Siko continued. "I've forgiven you everything, even for the fact that you seemed to care more about the *tuba* than any of your children. Perhaps you couldn't help it. No one wants to be poor—mud between your toes all your life, *nipa* hut blown down with every typhoon. What a life!"

You bastard, Aling Saturnina thought. Who told you to go and kill that man?

"Let me tell you about that man," Siko went on. "He was rich. You know how it is. After years in the army you become a *padrón*. People come to you for special favors, and of course you would not be so stupid as to help without getting anything in return. It's why everyone wants to enter the army in the first place. Take any poor boy from the provinces, give him twenty years in the army, and at the end of that time, he ought to have enough to retire comfortably in a mansion—two, if he's any kind of operator."

But you did not have to kill him, Aling Saturnina thought.

It became quiet—so quiet that Aling Saturnina could hear the dogs of the village barking again. Far off she could make out one or two lights against the darkness of the rice paddies. There were a few people awake, but they would not venture outside on a night like this, not with the dogs warning them away.

Siko was squatting on the ground again, staring morosely at his wounds. He seemed to be remembering something. When he spoke again, his voice was sad.

"You remember Ate Lina? Little, snot-nosed Lina who was always falling into a pile of *carabao* dung when she was young?"

Ah, Aling Saturnina thought. Lina.

"You're frowning," Siko continued. "You look uncertain. Perhaps you don't remember? No matter. She'd changed her name so many times. At one time she was 'Fleur-de-lis', a waitress at the Fishnet in Manila. Later, when she became a taxi dancer, she changed her name to 'Pepsi.' Pepsi Perez. When I met her again last year, she was working the bars in Olongapo. She had gone back to using her own name because it didn't seem to matter to her anymore what she did. She had a regular customer, this colonel. 'In a little while,' she told me, 'this life will be over for me. I'll be a straight woman.'"

No, Aling Saturnina thought. No, that doesn't sound like Lina.

"Let me tell you, let me tell you, Ina," Siko said. "The colonel was not the first man I killed. There was another one in Aliaga. But he was only a minor official with the Bureau of Land Transportation. After a few days, the case was closed. His wife and two children lived way out in Cagayan de Oro. What could they do? No one worth anything comes from Cagayan de Oro."

Ah, how evil! Aling Saturnina thought.

"I admit that I felt sorry about that man afterward," Siko went on. "He was only doing his duty and not even getting rich by it. But this lousy colonel . . ."

Siko paused. His face became momentarily indistinct. Then he said, "I'll tell you how it was. This colonel was a dog, a real dog. I don't know what gutter he crawled out from. I could have killed him when I first saw him touch my sister. But Lina begged me not to. She said she had a plan, that I should be patient. 'One day,' she said, 'we'll come into our own.'

"So I waited. I was patient. Lina became the colonel's mistress. He took her up with him to San Pablo and I did not even try to follow. Now and then, I heard things. I heard that this colonel had a wife, a real shrew. She was used to her husband bringing home girls and she was not fooled when the colonel introduced Lina as his masseuse. Later I heard that she had threatened to go after Lina with a knife. Things were getting bad for Lina but every time I wanted to go and get her she said, 'Wait.' Well, the day came when she said, 'Come.' And when I saw her, she had a broken nose and bruises all over her chest and back. The colonel had gotten tired of her and stood by while his wife did this. Lina was crying and saying, 'Let's get out of here.' I said, 'Not before getting what's our due.' So that night I went up to the colonel's house. It was a mansion right at the edge of town, with tennis courts in the back and a swimming pool a mile long. You see how these dogs live!

"I had just gotten over the garden wall when—bang!—I heard a shot and part of my right ear flew off. A fat woman with hair all done up in curlers was standing a little way off. I guessed she must be the colonel's wife. She was very angry. 'Get him, you fool!' she kept shouting. I turned and saw the colonel behind me, preparing to shoot again. But he was having trouble— his gun had jammed. I started laughing then, because he was cowering in front of me like a frightened rat. I took his gun and cracked his skull with it. The next thing I knew, I was lying on the ground, and the last thing I saw before the world went black was the ugly face of the colonel's wife, leering over me with a knife."

Siko stopped, took a deep breath, and shuddered. Aling Saturnina moaned and closed her eyes. She was crying. She had not cried for years—not even when her husband had left her, not even when her parents had died, not even when, right after Siko left, the days of going without *tuba* left her weak and silly as a child. When she opened her eyes a few moments later, she was alone. Siko had disappeared.

Aling Saturnina got up slowly. Her legs were stiff. Her back ached. The thought struck her that she was already very old, that she would not have long to live. She hurried back to the village. How long had the dogs been silent? It was dark and peaceful in the little hut she shared with Ana, Poldo, and their two children. In the corner of the one room, a votive candle cast its reddish light on the painting of Christ which Ana had propped up on a table. Garlands of dried flowers hung from the painting's upper corners. Carefully, so as not to wake the sleepers, Aling Saturnina groped her way forward. Kneeling before the makeshift altar, Aling Saturnina gazed long and hard at the face, so foreign in its whiteness, staring back at her. The nose was long and sharp, the lips thin and straight. The long, brown hair fell in fantastic curls past the white-robed shoulders. Aling Saturnina clasped her hands. She wanted to pray for Siko and Lina, and for the rest of her children, who she imagined must be suffering, just as Siko and Lina had suffered.

"*Ama namin,*" she prayed. "*Ama namin . . .*"

But that was as far as she went, for she had forgotten the rest of the words to the Lord's Prayer. She gazed, helpless and mute, at the painting before her. Ah, she was unworthy, she had not been taught the proper words with which to couch her requests. For a little donation, perhaps the priest in San Pablo could be induced to say a mass for her children. How had she dared to raise her voice to God—she, who had proven to be such an unfit mother! For such impertinence she should be struck by lightning! Filled with remorse, she cowered for a few moments before the amiable glance of the Christ in the painting.

Slowly, before she realized it, her eyelids began to droop. Then she gave a tired sigh and her shoulders sagged. Aling Saturnina was fast asleep.

Early the next morning, a cloud of dust could be seen rolling at high speed down the narrow road that led to the village. The cloud would stop suddenly before a particularly deep pothole, the dust would subside, and the outlines of an army jeep could be briefly seen before being swallowed up again in a fresh cloud of dust. Just before the village, the jeep stopped, and four men in tight-fitting military uniforms stepped out. The villagers remained in their homes, peering watchfully from the windows. The four men paused at the first house they came to, the home of Mang Tomas. After briefly stopping to ask for directions, they continued down the street until they arrived at the house of Aling Saturnina. One of the men approached the ladder leading up to the house. The other three remained standing near the road. Before the man near the ladder could ascend, Aling Saturnina's face, stiff with suspicion, appeared at a window.

"What do you want?" she said.

"Are you the mother of Francisco Dawang?" the man by the ladder inquired.

"I have no son by that name," Aling Saturnina said angrily, and made to shut the window.

"Wait, Ale! Don't be so impatient. We know that Francisco Dawang, also known as Siko, was indeed your son. We just need you to answer a few questions."

"I have not seen Siko in over ten years," Aling Saturnina said. "And I curse the day I bore him."

"He was shot breaking into someone's house last night in San Pablo. We have another one of your children, Lina, in the jail. Won't you please come along quietly now?"

At the mention of Lina's name, Aling Saturnina seemed to waver. She disappeared from the window a moment and the men could hear her speaking to someone inside the house. Finally she reappeared at the door, tying a worn bandanna around her head.

"All right," she said. "I'll come. But I have to be back by nightfall, you hear?"

"Of course, Ale," one of the men said. "It's only a formality."

They tried to help her down the stairs, but she waved them away angrily. Then she walked quickly away from the house, not bothering to glance at any of the neighbors, who were peering from their windows.

When they had almost reached the jeep, they heard a voice calling, "Wait! Wait!" They all turned and looked. It was Ana, running down the road with her youngest child balanced on her hip.

"I'm coming too!" Ana cried. "I can't let my mother go alone."

"Stupida!" Aling Saturnina shouted. "Go home and wait for Poldo to get back from the fields."

Ana paused only long enough to hand her child to the astonished wife of Mang Tomas, who had been watching from her front gate.

"Ale, tell Poldo I've accompanied Ina to town. Tell him not to worry about me, I'll be back this evening."

Aling Saturnina continued to protest. "Idiot!" she berated her daughter. "You'd leave your own children!"

"Quiet!" one of the soldiers said. "We'll bring her along too."

Aling Saturnina grew dazed and silent. She and Ana got into the jeep, the engine roared to life, the soldiers leaped in, and soon they were far away; there was nothing to see along the narrow road but the dust steaming up from the potholes. It was quiet in the village again. Mang Tomas's wife cradled Ana's baby in her arms. "Shush, shush," she whispered, for it was crying.

The next morning, when Aling Saturnina and Ana had not returned, Poldo went into town to make inquiries. That night he returned alone, looking like a much older man than the one who had set out in the morning. He had been directed to various military offices, and at each one was told that the two had been turned over to the National Bureau of Investigation "for further questioning." The time for harvesting rice came and went, and still Aling Saturnina and her daughter did not return.

Poldo and his two children live alone now in the house behind the *santol* tree. The children, seven and four, are very thin and are always crying for their mother. Poldo continues to go into town to make inquiries, but his trips are becoming more infrequent.

Poldo himself is gaunt and quiet, not at all like his former self. The villagers can remember a time when he could plant more rice seedlings in a day than any other man in the village. Now they look sadly at him as he toils alone in the fields and note how, when he presses against the heavy wooden plow, his ribs create ridges on his chest and back. He is too thin, almost tubercular. Who will take care of his children if he goes?

In the meantime, Siko's ghost continues to roam the village. Several times the villagers have begged the parish priest from San Pablo to come and exorcise him, but each time the parish priest replies that he is too busy. The ghost can sometimes be seen dancing across the rice paddies on nights when there is a full moon, or sitting on the roof of someone's house, glaring with reddish eyes. In the beginning, the villagers tried to chase him away with holy water and crucifixes. He would disappear for a few days and then return. Now they merely shrug their shoulders. He has been absorbed into the pattern of their everyday existence. He is as familiar to them now as the air they breathe or the water they drink. They tell their children that he is a *tikbalang*, a creature who makes his home in the forest and who likes to play tricks on people. They avert their eyes from the shadows when walking alone at night. They have learned to live with the ghost, as they have learned to live with everything else, as they have learned to smile, to shrug, when pigs or chickens disappear, saying only, "It is Siko."

CALYX Journal, Vol. 11:2&3, 1988

Shirley Geok-lin Lim

NATIVE DAUGHTER

Ta´malu!"

Mei Sim wriggled at her mother's words.

"You no shame! Close your legs."

Mother was standing five steps below the landing, the soft straw broom in one hand and her head on a level with Mei Sim's shoulders.

Mei Sim stared down at her legs, which she had spread apart the better to balance her body, as she half-lay on the smooth wooden landing and thought her thoughts to herself.

Up came the broom and thumped against her knees. She pulled them together and tugged at her short skirt.

"What you do here all day? Go ask Ah Kim to give you a bath." Her mother's round pretty face was troubled. She had had a perm just last week and the fat curls sat like waxed waves over her brow, wrinkled with vexation. "We're going to visit Tua Ee. And don't sit with your legs open there. She think I bring you up with no shame."

"Ya, Ma." Mei Sim sidled past her mother's solid body down the stairs, glad for something to do. Every day was a problem for her until her brothers came home from school at three when they would shout at her to go away but could still be persuaded to give her a piggy-back ride or to let her hold their legs in a wheel-barrow run. The house was empty and dull until then, containing only chairs, tables, beds, cupboards, photographs, and such like, but no one to play with.

Ah Kim was scrubbing her brother's uniform on the ridged washboard. Drub, drub, drub, slosh, slosh. Mei Sim squatted beside her. Ah Kim's stool was only a few inches high and she had her legs thrust straight in front with the wooden board held firmly between. Her *samfoo* sleeves were rolled up high and the pale arms were wet and soapy up to the elbows. Taking the chunk of yellow laundry soap in her right hand, Ah Kim scrubbed it over a soiled collar. Then, seizing the collar in a fist, she pushed the cloth vigorously up and down the ridges. Her knuckles were red and swollen, but her face was peaceful. "You wait," she said, not turning away from the washboard. "I wash you next."

Bath-time was directly under the tall tap in the corner of the open-roofed bathroom. Mei Sim was just short enough to stand under the full flow of water pouring in a steady stream from the greenish brass tap while Ah Kim scrubbed her chest, legs, and armpits with LifeBuoy. She was six and soon would be too tall for this manoeuvre. Soon, Ah Kim said, she would have to bathe herself with scoops of water from the clay jar in the other corner of the bathroom. Dodging in and out of the water, Mei Sim thought she would not like to have to work at her bath.

Mother dressed her in her New Year's party frock, an organdy material of pink and purple tuberoses with frills down the bib and four stiff layers gathered in descending tiers for a skirt. She picked a red and green plaid ribbon which Ah Kim threaded through her plaits and, her face and neck powdered with Johnson Talc, she waited for the trishaw, pleased with herself and her appearance.

Mother had put on her gold bangles, gold earrings, and a long heavy chain of platinum with a cross as a pendant. Her *kebaya* was a pale blue, starched and ironed to a gleaming transparency under which her white lace chemise showed clearly. Gold and diamond *kerosang* pinned the *kebaya* tightly together, and the brown-gold sarong was wrapped tightly around her plump hips and stomach. She had to hitch herself up onto the trishaw and, once seated, carefully smoothed the sarong over her knees. When Mei Sim climbed in, Mother gave her a push to keep her from crushing her sarong.

Grand-aunty's house was all the way in Klebang. Usually father took them there for visits in the evening after their meal. It was enough of a long way off for Mei Sim to always fall asleep in the car before they reached home.

The trishaw man pedalled vigorously for the first part, ringing his bell smartly at slow crossing pedestrians and hardly pausing to look before turning a corner into another narrow road. At Tranquerah he began to slow down. There was much less motor traffic, a few bicycles, and now and again a hawker's cart got in his way. Mei Sim watched his brown legs pedal up and down. Green snaky veins zig-zagged up his calves. His shaven coconut-round head was dripping with sweat. He didn't stop to wipe it, so the sweat ran down his forehead and got into his eyes, which were deep-set and empty, staring vaguely down the long road.

Mei Sim grew bored with watching the trishaw man pump the pedals after a while. She leaned forward to stare at the houses on both sides of the road. What interesting things to see that she had missed on their evening car rides! Here was a small stall with bottles of *chinchaloh* and *blachan* neatly mounded on shelves. She glimpsed through an open door a red and gold altar cloth and bowls of oranges and apples before a dim sepia portrait. Two *neneks* in shabby sarong and *kebaya* sat on a long bench by the covered front of another house. Each woman had a leg pulled up under her sarong, like one-legged idols set for worship. Here was a pushcart with a tall dark *mamak* frying red-brown noodles in a heavy *kwali*. How good it smelled. Mei Sim's stomach gave a little grumble.

Now they were passing the Baptist Gospel Hall where on Sunday evenings she had seen many people standing in rows singing sweetly. In the morning glare the shuttered windows were peeling paint and a crack showed clearly on the closed front door which had a huge chain and lock on it.

"*Hoy!*" the trishaw man shouted. The wheels swerved suddenly and bumped over something uneven. Mei Sim hadn't seen anything.

Her mother gripped her arm and said aloud, "You *bodoh*. Almost fall off the trishaw. Sit inside all the way."

"What was that, *Ma?*"

"A puppy dog."

She turned her head to peer behind but the canvas flaps were down.

The trishaw man was talking to himself in Hokkien. A small trail of saliva was trickling down the side of his mouth. Mei Sim could only hear mumbles like "*hey . . . yau soo . . . chei. . . .*"

"What is he saying, *Ma?*" she whispered, alarmed.

"Never mind what he say. He angry at puppy dog, bring him bad luck."

Mei Sim looked at the bare brown legs again. They were moving much more slowly and the mumbles continued, sometimes louder, sometimes quieting to a slippery whisper. Her mother didn't seem to mind the trishaw's pace or the man's crazy talk. She had been frowning to herself all this time and turning the three thick bangles round and round her right wrist. Her agitated motions made a gentle jingle as the bangles fell against each other, like chimes accompanying the slow movements of the trishaw pedals.

They were on a deserted stretch of Klebang before the sandy rutted path on the left that led to Grand-aunty's house and the shallow sloping beach facing the Malacca Straits. Wood-planked shacks roofed with rusty galvanized iron alternated with common lots on which grew a wild profusion of morning glory, *lallang,* mimosa, and sea-grape. A few coconut and areca palms leaned in jumbled lines away from the hot tarmac. The sky was a blinding blue, barren of clouds, and arching in a vast depth of heat under which the dripping trishaw man mumbled and cursed. The bicycle lurched forward and the attached carriage, on which Mei Sim crouched as if to make herself lighter, moved forward with it jerkily.

"Aiyah! Sini boleh," her mother said sharply, and almost at the same moment the man's legs stopped and dangled over the wheels. She pushed Mei Sim off the sticky plastic seat and stepped down carefully so as not to disarrange the elaborately folded pleats of her skirt.

The man had finally taken a ragged face towel from his pocket and was mopping his face without looking at them. Mrs. Chung clicked the metal snap of her black handbag, zipped open an inner compartment, extracted a beaded purse from it, unbuttoned a flap and counted some coins which she clinked impatiently in one hand, waiting for the man to take the change. Pouring the different coins into his calloused palm, she walked up the path without a word. Mei Sim stood for a moment watching him count the coins, then, at her mother's annoyed call, ran up the narrow lane just wide enough for a car to go through.

Waddling ahead of her, her mother was singing out, *"Tua Ee, Tua Ee."* A wooden fence, newly whitewashed, separated Grand-aunty's house from the lane which suddenly petered out into a littered common compound shared with some Malay houses on low stilts. Beneath the houses and through the spaces between the concrete blocks on which the wood stilts were anchored, Mei Sim could see the grey coarse sand grading to a chalky white for yards ahead clumped by tough beach grass and outlined at stages by the dark, uneven markings of tidal remains, broken driftwood, crab shells, splinters of glass, red-rust cans, and black hair of seaweed.

Grand-aunty came out through the gap in the fence in a flurry of *kebaya* lace. Her gleaming hair was coiffed in a twist, and a long, gold pin sat on top of her head, like the nail on the fearsome *pontianak,* Mei Sim thought.

"What's this?" she said in fluent Malay. "Why are you here so early without informing me? You must stay for lunch. I have told that prostitute daughter of mine to boil the rice already, so we have to cook another pot."

Grand-aunty had four sons, of whom she loved only the youngest, and a daughter whom she treated as a bought slave. She was not a woman for young girls and showed Mei Sim no attention, but she tolerated Jeng Chung as the niece whose successful marriage to a rich *towkay*'s son she had arranged ten years before.

Mei Sim's mother visited her at least once a week with gifts of fruits, *pulot* and *ang-pows,* and consulted her on every matter in the Chung family's life. At six, Mei Sim was allowed to listen to all their discussions; she was, after all, too young to understand.

It was in this way she learned what men liked their women to do in bed, how babies were made and how awful giving birth was. She knew the fluctuations in the price of gold and what herbs to boil and drink to protect oneself from colds, rheumatism, overheat, smallpox, diarrhea, or female exhaustion. It was in this way she found out that women were different from men who were *bodoh* and had to be trained to be what women wanted them to be, like *kerbau* hitched to their carts.

This morning she settled on the kitchen bench behind the cane chairs on which her mother and grand-aunt were sitting close to each other sharing the *sireh* box between them, chatting and scolding in Malay and snatches of English, and she listened and listened without saying a word to remind them of her presence.

". . . and Bee Lian saw Hin at the cloth shop . . . she told me he's been going there every afternoon when he's supposed to be at the bank . . . that slut is probably taking all his money, but I haven't said a word to him, I thought maybe you can help me. What should I say to him, oh, that swine, useless good-for-nothing, I scratch his eyes out. Better still if I take a knife and cut her heart. These men always walking with legs apart, what does he want from me? Three children not enough, but she is a bitch—black as a Tamil and hairy all over. I keep myself clean and sweet-smelling, a wife he can be proud of. So itchified, never enough, always wanting more, more. That's why now he won't give me more money, say business bad. Ha, bad! We know what's bad. I'll get some poison and put it in her food, and all my friends talking behind my back. She's making a fool of me, but what can I do? I tell them better than a second wife, not even a mistress, just loose woman smelling like a bitch any man can take, so why not my Peng Ho."

It was Father Mother was complaining about! Mei Sim scrubbed her ears hard to clear them of wax, but quick tears had risen and clogged her nostrils, so her ears were filled with a thick air of sorrow. She knew all about second wives. Hadn't Second Uncle left his family to live in Ipoh because their Cantonese servant bewitched him, and now he has three boys with her and Second Aunty is always coming to their house to borrow money and to beg for the clothes they've outgrown for her own children? And little

Gek Yeo's mother had gone mad because her father had taken another wife, and she is now in Tanjong Rambutan where Mother says she screams and tears her clothes off and has no hair left. Poor Gek Yeo had to go to her grandmother's house and her grandmother refuses to let her see her father.

Mei Sim wiped her nose on the gathered puff sleeve of her dress. Grand-aunty had risen from her chair and was shaking the folds of her thickly flowered sarong. Her Malay speech was loud and decisive. "All this scolding will do you no good. Men are all alike, itchy and hot. You cannot stop him by showing a dirty face or talking bad all the time. You will drive him away. The only thing women have is their cunning. You must think hard. What do you want, a faithful man or a man who will support you and your children? Why should you care if he plays around with this or that woman? Better for you, he won't ask so much from you in bed. No, you must be as sweet to him as when you were first courting. Talk to him sweet-sweet every time he comes home late. This will make him feel guilty, and he will be nicer to you. Make him open the purse strings. Tell him you need money for prayers at Hoon Temple to bring luck to his business. He will appreciate you for your efforts. Some men have to be bullied, like your grand uncle, but . . ."

She stopped to take a breath, and Siew Eng, her skinny dark daughter, crept up beside and whispered, *"Na´ makan, emak?"*

"Sundal!" Grand-aunty shouted and slapped her sharply on her thin bare arm. "Who asked you to startle me? You know how bad my heart is. You want me to die?"

Siew Eng hung her head. Her *samfoo* was faded and worn at the trouser bottoms, and the thin cotton print didn't hide her strange absence of breasts. She was already sixteen, had never been sent to school but had worked at home washing, cleaning, and cooking since she was seven. All her strength seemed to have gone into her work, because her body itself was emaciated, her smile frail, and her face peaked and shrivelled like a *chiku* picked before its season and incapable of ripening, drying up to a small brown hardness.

Mei Sim had never heard her cousin laugh, had never seen her eat at the table. She served the food, cleaned the kitchen, and ate standing up by the woodstove when everyone had finished.

Mother said Siew Eng was cursed. The fortune-teller had told Grand-aunty after her birth that the girl would eat her blood, so she wouldn't nurse or hold the baby, had sent her to a foster mother and taken her back at seven to send her to the kitchen where she slept on a camp bed. Mei Sim was glad she wasn't cursed! Her father loved her best, and Mother bought her the prettiest dresses and even let her use her lipstick.

"Now your uncle . . ." Grand-aunty stopped and her face reddened. "What are you waiting for, you stupid girl? Go serve the rice. We are coming to the table right away. Make sure there are no flies on the food."

Her daughter's scrawny chest seemed to shiver under the loose blouse.

"Ya, emak," she mumbled and slipped off silently to the kitchen.

"Come, let's eat. I have *sambal blachan* just the way you like it, with sweet lime. The soy pork is fresh, steaming all morning and delicious."

Grand-aunty gobbled the heap of hot white rice which was served on her best blue china plates. She talked as she ate, pinching balls of rice flavoured with chilies and soy with her right hand and throwing the balls into her large wet mouth with a flick of her wrist and thumb. Mother ate more slowly, unaccustomed to manipulating such hot rice with her hand, while Mei Sim used a soup spoon on her tin plate.

"Your uncle," Grand-aunty said in between swallows of food and water, "is a timid man, a mouse. I used to think how to get male children with a man like that! I had to put fire into him, every day must push him. Otherwise he cannot be a man."

"Huh, huh," Mother said, picking a succulent piece of the stewed pork and popping it into her mouth whole.

"But Peng Ho, he is an educated man, and he cannot be pushed. You must lead him gently, gently so he doesn't know what you are doing. Three children, you cannot expect him to stay by your side all the time. Let him have fun. "

"Wha . . ." Mother said, chewing the meat hard.

"Yes. We women must accept our fate. If we want to have some fun also, stomach will explode. Where can we hide our shame? But men, they think they are *datoks* because they can do things without being punished. But we must control them, and to do that we must control their money."

Mei Sim thought Grand-aunty was very experienced. She was so old, yet her hair was still black, and her sons and husband did everything she told them. She was rich; the knitted purse looped to her string belt under her *kebaya* was always bulging with money. Father had to borrow money from her once when some people didn't pay for his goods, and she charged him a lot for it. He still complained about it to Mother each time they drove home from Grand-aunty's house.

"But how?" protested Mother, a faint gleam of sweat appearing on her forehead and upper lip as she ate more and more of the pork.

Grand-aunty began to whisper and Mei Sim didn't dare ask her to speak up nor could she move from her seat for she hadn't finished her lunch.

Mother kept nodding and nodding her head. She was no longer interested in the food but continued to put it in her mouth without paying any attention to it until her plate was clear. *"Yah, yah. Huh huh. Yah, yah,"* she repeated like a trance-medium, while Grand-aunty talked softly about accounts and ton-tins and rubber lands in Jasin. Mei Sim burped and began to feel sleepy.

"Eng!" Grand-aunty called harshly. "Clear up the table, you lazy girl. Sleeping in the kitchen, nothing to do. Come here."

Siew Eng walked slowly towards her mother, pulling at her blouse nervously.

"Come here quickly, I say." Grand-aunty's mouth was dribbling with saliva. She appeared enraged, her fleshy nose quivering under narrowed eyes. As Siew Eng stood quietly beside her chair, she took the sparse flesh above her elbow between thumb and forefinger and twisted it viciously, breathing hard. A purple bruise bloomed on the arm. "I'll punish you for walking so slowly when I call you," she huffed. "You think you can be so proud in my house."

Siew Eng said nothing. A slight twitch of her mouth quickly pressed down was the only sign that the pinch had hurt.

"What do you say? What do you say, you prostitute?" Grand-aunty raised her handsome head and yelled, spraying saliva around her.

"Sorry, *emak,*" Siew Eng whispered, hanging her head lower and twisting the cloth of her blouse.

Only then did Grand-aunty get up from the table. The two women returned to the chairs beside the *sireh* table, where two neat green packages of *sireh* rested. Sighing happily, Grand-aunty put the large wad in her mouth and began to chew. Mother followed suit, but she had a harder time with the generous size of the *sireh* and had to keep pushing it in her mouth as parts popped out from the corners.

Mei Sim sat on her stool, but her head was growing heavier, her eyes kept dropping as if they wanted to fall to the floor. She could hear the women chewing and grunting; it seemed as if she could feel the bitter green leaves tearing in her own mouth and dissolving with the tart lime and sharp crunchy betel nut and sweet-smelling cinnamon. Her mouth was dissolving into an aromatic dream when she heard chimes ringing sharply in the heavy noon air.

For the briefest moment Mei Sim saw her father smiling beside her, one hand in his pocket jingling the loose change, and the other hand gently steering an ice cream bicycle from whose opened ice box delicious vapours were floating. "Vanilla!" she heard herself cry out, at the same moment that Grand-aunty called out, *"Aiyoh!* What you want?" and she woke up.

A very dark man with close-cropped hair was carefully leaning an old bicycle against the open door jamb. Two shiny brown hens, legs tied with rope and hanging upside down by the bicycle handles, blinked nervously, and standing shyly behind the man was an equally dark and shiny boy dressed in starched white shirt and pressed khaki shorts.

"*'Nya,"* the man said respectfully, bowing a little and scraping his rubber thongs on the cement floor as if to ask permission to come in.

"*Aiyah,* Uncle Muti, *apa buat?* You come for business or just for visit?"

"*Ha,* I bring two hens. My wife say must give to *puan,* this year we have many chickens."

"Also, you bring the rent?" Grand-aunty was smiling broadly, the *sireh* tucked to one side of her mouth like a girlish pucker. "Come, come and sit down. Eng, Eng!" Her voice raised to a shriek till Eng came running from behind the garden. "Bring tea for Uncle Muti. Also, take the hens into the kitchen. Stupid girl! Must tell you everything."

The boy stayed by the bicycle, staring at the women inside with bright frank eyes.

Curious, Mei Sim went out. He was clean, his hair still wet from a bath. "What school you?" she asked. He was older, she knew, because he was in a school uniform.

He gave her a blank stare.

"You speak English?" she asked.

He nodded.

"You want to play a game?" She ran out into the compound, motioning for him to follow.

Mei Sim had no idea what she wanted to play, but she was oh so tired of sitting still, and the white sand and brown seanuts and blue flowers on the leafy green creepers on the fence seemed so delicious after the crunch, crunch, crunch of Grand-aunty's lunch that she spread her arms and flew through the sky. "Whee, whee," she laughed.

But the boy wouldn't play. He stood by the sweet-smelling *tanjong bunga* and stared at her.

"What you stare at?" she asked huffily. "Something wrong with me?"

"Your dress," he answered without the least bit of annoyance.

"What to stare?" Mei Sim was suddenly uncomfortable and bent down to look for snails.

"So pretty. *Macham bungah.*"

She looked up quickly to see if he was making fun of her, but his brown round face was earnestly staring at the tiers of ruffles on her skirt.

"Want to play a game?" she asked again.

But he said, "My sister no got such nice dress."

Mei Sim laughed. "You *orang jakun,*" she said, "but never mind. You want to feel my dress? Go on. I never mind."

He went nearer to her and stretched out his hand. He clutched at the frills around the bib, staring at the pink and purple tuberoses painted on the thin organdy.

"Mei Si-i-m!" Her mother's voice brayed across the compound. There was a confusion as the boy rushed away and the woman came running, panting in the sun, and pulled at her arm. "What you do? Why you let the boy touch you? You no shame?"

Grand-aunty stood by the door, while the dark man had seized his son by the shoulder and was talking to him in furious low tones.

Mei Sim felt tears in her mouth, and wondered why she was crying, why her mother was shaking her. Then she saw the man pushing his rusty old Raleigh through the gate, without the hens, still holding the boy by his shoulder. She saw the look of hate which the boy threw at her, and suddenly she felt a hot pain in her chest as if she knew why he must hate her. A huge shame filled her and she was just about to burst into noisy weeping when she saw her mother's red, red eyes. "He did it, he pulled at my dress," she screamed, stretching her body straight as an arrow, confronting her lie.

CALYX Journal, Vol. 11:2&3, 1988

Tahira   Naqvi

PATHS UPON WATER

There had been little warning, actually none at all to prepare her for her first encounter with the sea. At breakfast that morning, her son Raza said, *"Ama*, we're going to the seaside today. Jamil and Hameeda are coming with us." She had been turning a *paratha* in the frying pan, an onerous task since she had always fried *parathas* on a flat pan with open sides, and as the familiar aroma of dough cooking in butter filled the air around her, she smiled happily and thought, I've only been here a week and already he wants to show me the sea.

Sakina Bano had never seen the sea. Having lived practically all her life in a town which was a good thousand miles from the nearest shoreline, her experience of the sea was limited to what she had chanced to observe in pictures. One picture, in which greenish-blue waves heaved toward a gray sky, she could recollect clearly; it was from a calendar Raza brought home the year he started college in Lahore. The calendar had hung on a wall of her room for many years only to be removed when the interior of the house was whitewashed for her daughter's wedding, and in the ensuing confusion it was misplaced and never found. The nail on which the calendar hung had stayed in the wall since the painter, too lazy to bother with detailed preparation, had simply painted around the nail and over it; whenever Sakina Bano happened to glance at the forgotten nail she remembered the picture. Also distinct in her memory was a scene from a silly Urdu film she had seen with her cousin's wife Zohra and her nieces Zenab and Amina during a rare visit to Lahore several years ago. For some reason she hadn't been able to put it out of her mind. On a brown and white beach, the actor Waheed Murad, now dead but then affectedly handsome and boyish, pursued the actress Zeba, who skipped awkwardly before him—it isn't at all proper for a woman to be skipping in a public place. Small foam-crested waves lapped up to her, making her *shalwar* stick to her skinny legs, exposing the outline of her thin calves. Why, it was just as bad as baring her legs, for what cover could the wet, gossamer-like fabric of the *shalwar* provide?

The two frolicked by an expanse of water that extended to the horizon and which, even though it was only in a film, had seemed to Sakina Bano frightening in its immensity.

"Will Jamal and his wife have lunch here?" she asked, depositing the dark, glistening *paratha* gently on Raza's plate. She would have to take out a packet of meat from the freezer if she was to give them lunch, she told herself while she poured tea in her son's cup.

"No, I don't think so. I think we'll leave before lunch. We can stop somewhere along the way and have a bite to eat."

"They'll have tea then." She was glad Raza had remembered to pick up a cake at the store the night before (she didn't know why he called it a pound cake), and she would make some rice *kheer.*

If she had anything to do with it, she would avoid long trips and spend most of her time in Raza's apartment cooking his meals and watching him eat. The apartment pleased her. The most she would want to do would be to go out on the lawn once in a while and examine her surroundings.

Bordering each window on the outside were narrow white shutters; these had reminded her of the stiffened icing on a cake served at her niece Amina's birthday once. And on the face of the building the white paint seemed impervious to the effects of the elements. Discolorations or cracks were visible, and she had indeed craned her neck until it hurt while she scrutinized it.

The apartment building was set against a lawn edged with freshly green, sculptured bushes, evenly thick with grass that looked more like a thick carpet than just grass. Located in a quiet section of town, the apartments overlooked a dark, thickly wooded area, a park, Raza had told her. Although tired and groggy on the evening of her arrival from Pakistan, she had not failed to take note of the surroundings in which she found herself. Her first thought was, 'Where is everybody?' while to her son she said, "How nice everything is."

Looking out the window of his sitting room the next morning, she was gladdened at the thought of her son's good fortune. The morning sky was clear like a pale blue, unwrinkled *dupatta* that has been strung out on a line to dry. Everything looked clean, so clean. Was it not as if an unseen hand had polished the sidewalks and swept the road? They now glistened like new metal. 'Where do people throw their trash?' she wondered when she went down to the lawn again, this time with Raza, and gazed out at the shiny road, the rows and rows of neat houses hedged in by such neat white wooden fences. In hasty answer to her own query, she told herself not to be foolish; this was *Amreeka*. Here trash was in its proper place, hidden from view and no doubt disposed of in an appropriate manner. No blackened banana peels redolent with the odor of neglect here, or rotting orange skins, or worse, excrement and refuse to pollute the surroundings and endanger human habitation.

She had sighed in contentment. Happiness descended upon her tangibly like a heavy blanket affording warmth on a chilly morning. Once again, she thanked her Maker. Was He not good to her son?

"Is the sea far from here?" she asked casually, brushing imaginary crumbs from the edges of her plate. Raza must never feel she didn't value his eagerness to show off his new environment. This was his new world after all. If he wanted to take her to the seaside, then seaside it would be. Certainly she was not about to be fussy and upset him.

"No, *Ama*, not too far. An hour-and-a-half's drive, that's all. Do you feel well?" His eyes crinkled in concern as he put aside the newspaper he had been reading to look at her.

She impatiently waved a hand in the air, secretly pleased at his solicitude. "Yes, yes, I'm fine, son. Just a little cough, that's all. Now finish your tea and I'll make you another cup." She knew how much he liked tea. Before she came, he must have had to make it for himself. Such a chore for a man if he must make his own tea.

The subject of the sea didn't come up again until Jamil and his new bride arrived. Jamil, an old college friend of Raza's, angular like him, affable and solicitous, was no stranger to Sakina Bano. But she was meeting his wife Hameeda for the first time. Like herself, the girl was also a newcomer to this country.

"*Khalaji*, the sea's so pretty here, the beaches are so-o-o-o large, nothing like the beaches in Karachi," Hameeda informed Sakina Bano over tea, her young, shrill voice rising and falling excitedly, her lips, dark and fleshy with lipstick, wide open in a little girl's grin. There's wanderlust in her eyes already, Sakina Bano mused, trying to guess her age. Twenty-one or twenty-two. She thought of the girl in Sialkot she and her daughter had been considering for Raza. Was there really a resemblance? Perhaps it was only the youth.

"Well, child, for me it will be all the same. I've never been to Karachi. Here, have another slice of cake, you too, Jamil, and try the *kheer*."

For some reason Sakina Bano couldn't fathom, sitting next to the young girl whose excitement at the prospect of a visit to the seaside was as undisguised as a child's preoccupation with a new toy, she was suddenly reminded of the actress Zeba. The image of waves lapping on her legs and swishing about her nearly bare calves rose in Sakina Bano's mind again. Like the arrival of an unexpected visitor, a strange question crossed her mind: were Hameeda's legs also skinny like Zeba's?

Drowned in the clamor for the *kheer* which had proven to be a great hit and had been consumed with such rapidity she wished she had made more, the question lost itself.

"*Khalaji*, you must tell Hameeda how you make this," Jamil was saying, and Hameeda hastily interjected, "I think you used a lot of milk."

"Have more," Sakina Bano said.

Tea didn't last long. Within an hour they were on their way to the sea, all of them in Raza's car. Jamil sat in the front with his friend, and Sakina Bano and Hameeda sat in the back, an unfortunate arrangement, Sakina Bano discovered after they had driven for what seemed to her like an hour. It wasn't Hameeda's persistent prattle that vexed her, she realized, it was her perfume. So pungent she could feel it wafting into her nostrils, it irritated the insides of her nose, and then traveled down her throat like the sour aftertaste of an overripe orange. But her discomfort was short-lived; soon she became drowsy and idled into sleep.

To be sure she had heard stories of people who swam in the ocean. She wasn't so foolish as to presume that swimming was undertaken fully clothed. After all, many times as a child she had seen young boys and men from her village swim, dressed in nothing but loincloths as they jumped into the muddy waters of the canal that irrigated their fields. But what was this?

As soon as Raza parked the car in a large, compound-like area fenced in by tall walls of wire mesh, and when her dizziness subsided, Sakina Bano glanced out of the window on her left. Her attention was snagged by what she thought was a naked woman. Certain that she was still a little dazed from the long drive, her vision subsequently befogged, Sakina Bano thought nothing of what she had seen. Then the naked figure moved closer. Disbelief gave way to the sudden, awful realization that the figure was indeed real and if not altogether naked, very nearly so.

A thin strip of colored cloth shaped like a flimsy brassiere loosely held the woman's breasts, or rather a part of her breasts; and below, beneath the level of her belly button, no, even lower than that, Sakina Bano observed in horror, was something that reminded her of the loincloths the men and youths in her village wore when they swam or worked on a construction site in the summer.

The girl was pretty, such fine features, hair that shone like a handful of gold thread, and she was young too, not much older than Hameeda perhaps. But the paleness of her skin was marred by irregular red blotches that seemed in dire need of a cooling balm. No one with such redness should be without a covering in the sun, Sakina Bano offered in silent rebuke.

The woman opened the door of her car, which was parked alongside Raza's, and as she leaned over to retrieve something from the interior of her car, Sakina Bano gasped. When the young female lowered her body, her breasts were not only nearly all bared, but stood in imminent danger of spilling out of their meager coverage. O God! Is there no shame here? Sakina Bano's cheeks burned. Hastily she glanced away. In the very next instant she stole a glimpse at her son from the corners of her eyes, anxiously wondering if he too were experiencing something of what she was going through; no, she noted with a mixture of surprise and relief, he and Jamil were taking things out from the trunk of their car. They did not show any signs of discomfort. Did she see a fleeting look of curiosity on Hameeda's face? There was something else, too, she couldn't quite decipher.

Relieved that her male companions were oblivious to the disturbing view of the woman's breasts, Sakina Bano sighed sadly. She shook her head, adjusted her white, chiffon *dupatta* over her head, and slowly eased her person out of her son's car.

The taste of the sea was upon her lips in an instant. Mingled with an occasional but strong whiff of Hameeda's perfume, the smell of fish filled her nostrils and quickly settled in her nose as if to stay there forever.

Milling around were countless groups of scantily clad people, men, women, and children, coming and going in all directions. Is all of *Amreeka* here? she asked herself uneasily. Feeling guilty for having judged Zeba's contrived imprudence on film a little too harshly, she tightened her *dupatta* about her and wondered why her son had chosen to bring her to this place. Did he not know his mother? She was an old woman, and the mother of a son, but she would not surrender to anger or derision and make her son uncomfortable. His poise and confidence were hers too, were they not?

Certainly he had brought her to the sea for a purpose. She must not appear ungrateful or intolerant.

While Raza and Jamil walked on casually and without any show of awkwardness, laughing and talking as though they might be in their sitting room rather than a place crowded with people in a state of disconcerting undress, she and Hameeda followed closely behind. Her head swam as she turned her eyes from the glare of the sun and attempted to examine the perturbing nakedness around her.

Sakina Bano's memories of nakedness were short and limited, extending to the time when she bathed her younger brother and sister under the water pump in the courtyard of her father's house, followed by the period in which she bathed her own three children until they were old enough to do it themselves. Of her own nakedness she carried an incomplete image; she had always bathed sitting down, on a low wooden stool.

Once, and that too shortly before his stroke, she came upon her husband getting out of his *dhoti* in their bedroom. Standing absently near the foot of his bed as if waiting for something or someone, the *dhoti* a crumpled heap about his ankles, he lifted his face to look at her blankly when she entered, but made no attempt to move or cover himself. Not only did she have to hand him his pajamas, she also had to assist him as he struggled to pull up first one leg and then the other. A week later he suffered a stroke, in another week he was gone. It had been nearly ten years since he died. But for some reason the image of a naked disoriented man in the middle of a room clung to her mind like permanent discolorations on a well-worn copper pot.

And there was the unforgettable sharp and unsullied picture of her mother's body laid out on a rectangular slab of cracked, yellowed wood for a pre-burial bath, her skin, ash-brown, laced with a thousand wrinkles, soft, like wet, rained-on mud.

But nothing could have prepared her for this. Nakedness, like all things in nature, has a purpose, she firmly told herself as the four of them trudged toward the water.

The July sun on this day was not as hot as the July sun in Sialkot, but a certain oily humidity had begun to attach itself to her face and hands. Lifting a corner of her white *dupatta*, she wiped her face with it. Poor Hameeda, no doubt she too longed to divest herself of the *shalwar* and *qamis* she was wearing and don a swimming suit so she could join the rest of the women on the beach, be more like them. But could she swim?

They continued onward, and after some initial plodding through hot, moist sand, Sakina Bano became sure-footed; instead of having to drag her feet through the weighty volume of over-heated sand, she was now able to tread over it with relative ease. They were receiving stares already, a few vaguely curious, others unguardedly inquisitive.

Where the bodies ended she saw the ocean began, stretching to the horizon in the distance. The picture she had carried in her head of the boyish actor Waheed Murad running after Zeba on a sandy Karachi beach quickly diminished and faded away. The immensity of the sea on film was reduced to a mere blue splash of color, its place usurped by a vastness she could scarce hold within the frame of her vision; a window opened in her head, she drew in the wonder of the sea as it touched the hem of the heavens and, despite the heat, Sakina Bano shivered involuntarily. God's touch is upon the world, she silently whispered to herself.

Again and again, as she had made preparations for the journey across what she liked to refer to as the 'seven seas,' she had been told *Amreeka* was so large that many Pakistans could fit into it. The very idea of Pakistan fitting into anything else was cause for bewilderment, and the analogy left her at once befuddled and awed. But had she expected this?

The bodies sprawled before her on the sand and exposed to the sun's unyielding rays seemed unmindful of what the ocean might have to say about God's touch upon the world. Assuming supine positions, flat either on their backs or their bellies, the people on the beach reminded Sakina Bano of whole red chilies spread on a rag discolored from overuse and left in the sun to dry and crackle. As sweat began to form in tiny droplets across her forehead and around her mouth, the unhappy thought presented itself to her that she was among people who had indeed lost their sanity.

In summer, one's first thought is to put as much distance as possible between oneself and the sun. Every effort is made to stay indoors; curtains are drawn and jalousies unfurled in order to shut out the fire the sun exudes. In the uneasy silence of a torrid June or July afternoon, even stray dogs seek shade under a tree or behind a bush, curling up into fitful slumber as the sun beats its fervid path across the sky.

Sakina Bano couldn't understand why these men and women wished to scorch their bodies, and why, if they were here by the shore of an ocean which seemed to reach up to God, they didn't at least gaze wide-eyed at the wonder which lay at their feet. Why did they choose instead to shut their eyes and merely wallow in the heat. Their skins had rebelled, the red and darkly pink blotches spoke for themselves. Perhaps this is a ritual they must, of necessity, follow, she mused. Perhaps they yearn to be brown as we yearn to be white.

She felt an ache insidiously putter behind her eyes. The sun always gave her a headache, even in winter, the only season when sunshine evoked pleasing sensations, when one could look forward to its briskness, its sharp touch. The heat from the sand under the *dari* on which she and Hameeda now sat seeped through the coarse fabric after a while and hugged her thighs. As people in varying shades of pink, white, and red skin ran or walked past them, particles of sand flew in the air and landed on her clothes, her hands, her face. Soon she felt sand in her mouth, scraping between her teeth like the remains of *chalia*, heavy on her tongue.

Ignoring the sand in her mouth and the hot-water-bottle effect of the sand beneath her thighs, Sakina Bano shifted her attention first toward a woman on her left, and then to the man on her right whose stomach fell broadly in loose folds (like dough left out overnight); he lay supine and still, his face shielded by a straw hat. Puzzled by the glitter on their nakedness, she peered closely and with intense concentration—she had to observe if she were to learn anything. The truth came to her like a flash of sudden light in a dark room: both the man and the woman had smeared their bodies with some kind of oil! Just then she remembered the oversized cucumbers she had encountered on her first trip to the Stop and Shop; shiny and slippery, one fell from her hands as she handled them, and she exclaimed in disbelief, "They've been greased!" How amused Raza had been at her reaction.

It's really very simple, Sakina Bano finally decided, sighing again, these people wish to be fried in the sun. But why? Not wishing to appear ignorant, she kept her mouth shut, although if she had addressed the query to Hameeda, she was sure she would not have received a satisfactory reply. The girl was a newcomer like herself. In addition, she was too young to know the answers to questions which warranted profound thought preceded by profound scrutiny. She didn't look very comfortable either; perhaps the heat was getting to her too.

Raza and Jamil, both in swimming trunks, appeared totally at ease as they ran to the water and back, occasionally wading in a wave that gently slapped the beach and sometimes disappearing altogether for a second or two under a high wave. Then Sakina Bano couldn't tell where they were. They certainly seemed to be having a good time.

She and Hameeda must be the only women on the beach fully clothed, she reflected, quite a ridiculous sight if one were being viewed from the vantage point of those who were stretched out on the sand. And while Sakina Bano grappled with this disturbing thought, she saw the other woman approaching.

Attired in a *sari* and accompanied by a short, dark man (who had to be her son for he undoubtedly had her nose and her forehead) and an equally short, dark woman, both of whom wore swimming suits (the girl's as brief as that of the woman Sakina Bano had seen earlier in the parking lot), the woman looked no older than herself. Clutching the front folds of her *sari* as if afraid a sudden wind from the ocean might pull them out unfurling the *sari*, leaving her exposed, she tread upon the sand with a fiercely precarious step, looking only ahead, her eyes shielded with one small, flat palm.

This is how I must appear to the others, Sakina Bano ruminated. Suddenly, she felt a great sadness clutching at her chest and rising into her throat like a sigh as she watched the woman in the *sari* begin to make herself comfortable on a large, multi-colored towel thrown on the sand by her son and his wife; those two hurriedly dashed off in the direction of the water. Why are they in such haste? Sakina Bano wondered.

Her knees drawn up, one arm tensely wrapped around them, the woman appeared to be watching her son and her daughter-in-law. But could Sakina Bano really be sure? The woman's hand against her forehead concealed her eyes. As she continued to observe the woman's slight figure around which the green and orange cotton *sari* had been carelessly draped, she wondered what part of India she might be from. Perhaps the south, which meant she spoke no Hindi, which also meant a conversation would not be at all possible.

Sakina Bano's attention returned to Hameeda who had not said a word all this time. Like a breakthrough during muddled thought, it suddenly occurred to Sakina Bano that there was a distinct possibility Hameeda would be swimming if it weren't for her. In deference to her older companion she was probably foregoing the chance to swim. Will Raza's wife also wear a scant swimming suit and bare her body in the presence of strange men? The question disturbed her; she tried to shrug it aside. But it wouldn't go away. Stubbornly it returned, not alone this time but accompanied by the picture of a young woman who vaguely resembled the actress Zeba and who was clothed, partially, in a swimming suit much like the ones Sakina Bano saw about her. Running behind her was a man, not Waheed Murad, but alas, her own son, her Raza. Was she dreaming, had the sun weakened her brain? Such foolishness. Sakina Bano saw that Hameeda was staring ahead, like the woman on the towel, her eyes squinted because of the glare. Frozen on her full, red lips was a hesitant smile.

Once again Sakina Bano sought her son's figure among the throng near the water's edge. At first the brightness of the sun blinded her and she couldn't see where he was. She strained her eyes, shielding them from the sun with a hand on her forehead. And finally she spotted him. He and Jamil were talking to some people. A dark man and a dark girl. The son and daughter-in-law of the woman in the *sari*. Were they acquaintances then, perhaps friends? The four of them laughed like old friends, the girl standing so close to Raza he must surely be able to see her half-naked breasts. The poor boy!

They had begun to walk toward where she and Hameeda were seated. Raza was going to introduce his friends to his mother. How was she to conceal her discomfort at the woman's mode of dress?

"*Ama*, I want you to meet Ajit and Kamla. Ajit works at Ethan Allen with me. Kamla wants you to come to their house for dinner next Sunday."

Both Ajit and Kamla lifted their hands and said *"Namaste,"* and she nodded and smiled. What does one say in answer to *namaste*, anyway?

Hameeda was also introduced. Kamla made a joke about "the shy new bride," Hameeda showed her pretty teeth in a smile, and then Kamla said, "You have to come, Auntie." Sakina Bano wondered why Raza appeared so comfortable in the presence of a woman who was nearly all naked. Even her loincloth was flimsy. Granted it wasn't as bad as some of the others she had been seeing around her, but it was flimsy nonetheless.

"Yes, it's very nice of you to invite us. It's up to Raza. He's usually so busy. But if he is free . . ."

"Of course I'm free next Sunday. We'd love to come, Kamla."

Kamla said, "Good! I'll introduce you and Auntie to my mother-in-law after a swim. Coming?" She laid a hand on Raza's arm and Sakina Bano glanced away, just in time to catch Hameeda's smile of surprise. Well, one's son can become a stranger too, even a good son like Raza.

"Sure. *Yar*, Ajit, are you and Kamla planning to go to the late show?"

"Yes we are. You? Do you have tickets?" Ajit wasn't a bad looking boy. But he didn't measure up to Raza. No, Raza's nose was straight and to the point, his forehead wide and his eyes well illuminated. But he had changed somehow; she felt she was distanced from him. A son is always a son, she thought and smiled and nodded again as Ajit and Kamla uttered their *namastes* and returned to the water with Raza and Jamil.

"*Khalaji*, why don't we wet our feet before we go?" Hameeda suddenly asked her.

"Wet our feet?"

"Yes, *Khala*. Just dip our feet in sea water. Come on. You're not afraid of the water, are you?"

"No, child." She wasn't afraid. Her mind was playing tricks with her, filling her head with thoughts that had no place there. A change was welcome. "Yes, why not?" she said, as if speaking to herself. When she attempted to get up, she found that her joints had stiffened painfully. "Here, girl, give me your hand." She extended an arm toward Hameeda. Why not, especially since they had come so far and she had suffered the heat for what had seemed like a very long time.

Hameeda had rolled up her *shalwar* almost to the level of her knees. How pretty her legs are, the skin hairless and shiny, like a baby's, and not skinny at all, Sakina Bano mused in surprise, and how quick she is to show them.

She must do the same, she realized. Otherwise Hameeda would think she was afraid. She pulled up one leg of her *shalwar* tentatively, tucked it at the waist with one swift movement of her right hand, then looked about her sheepishly. Hameeda was laughing.

"The other one too, *Khala!*"

Who would want to look at her aged and scrawny legs? And her husband was not around to glare at her in remonstration. Gingerly the other leg of the *shalwar* was also lifted and tucked in. How funny her legs looked, the hair on them all gray now and curly, the calves limp. Now both women giggled like schoolgirls. And Raza would be amused, he would think she was having a good time, Sakina Bano told herself.

Raza and Jamil burst into laughter when they saw the women approach. They waved. Sakina Bano waved back.

Holding the front folds of her *shalwar* protectively, Sakina Bano strode toward the water. As she went past the other woman in the *sari* she smiled at her. The woman gave her a startled look, and then, dropping the hand with which she had been shielding her eyes from the sun, she let her arm fall away from her knees, and following Sakina Bano with her gaze, she returned her smile.

"Wait for me," Sakina Bano called to Hameeda in a loud, happy voice, "wait, girl."

Amy Jones [Sedivy]

SANCTUARY

What has happened down here is that the men have changed. My neighbor Esmeralda attributes the change to some bacteria in the sand. I say no. I say it's because the INS opened an office in our town.

Esmeralda is a *curandera*. She heals with herbs and she knows the earth. She says to me, "Delia, there is something, like a parasite, it is in the sand and the men inhale it. It is what makes them crazy."

She's worried about it too. I hear her chanting in her backyard at night. Looking out my bedroom window, I can see her crouched by a small fire, her face turned up to the sky and I hear, real faint, a chant. Sounds like *"Barriba da da chalala chapala."* It's not Spanish, it's some kind of Indian. I'm not complaining. The chanting is real soothing, makes me feel safe and puts me to sleep after I listen to it for a while. I like living next to Esmeralda. I'm raised Catholic, but there is something natural, right, about her connection to nature and the spirit world. Like my spirit wants to be a part of it too. Like it's only my mind and not my heart that keeps me tied to the Catholic church.

Still, I think I'm right. Here in our small town in the southeast corner of California, most people are farmhands or farmers, a few landowners. There's shopkeepers for us and for the Mexicans who come over during the day to buy stuff. And there's always those who cross over at night and disappear north.

That was happening too much so the INS took over the old Bank of the Desert building in the center of town, and now we see uniformed men all over the place. They're at the 7/11, the TacoBurger stand, the gas station. Once they were in my backyard, standing under my willow tree, the only willow tree in town. My granddad planted it and made it grow in the desert, so my daddy kept it alive and taught me how. It's on the end of my property which backs up to an arroyo that has a barbwire fence and Mexico on the other side. The men were staring across the arroyo at the hard dirt wall below the fence. I went out to talk to them, but they didn't want to ask me anything. I would have answered. I would have lied, but I'd have answered. I'd tell them no one comes through my yard. Sure wouldn't tell them that sometimes they come right through my kitchen and stop for a bite to eat.

But now the men down here are acting oddball. Take Felix on the corner—he's only lived here eight years, moved here from Texas with his god-awful accent and he carries his shotgun with him everywhere.

I asked Felix once, "Are you planning to go hunting?"

He laughed and waved the gun at the border. "Hell yes, ma'am, I'm huntin' them fence jumpers."

I thought, but didn't say aloud, just who is Felix to go shoot some guy sneaking across the border at night?

One night, I was drifting into sleep, eased into it by Esmeralda's chanting. She stopped sudden and I sat up and pulled the curtain to look out my window. Two men stood outside the ring of her firelight, talking to her.

I knew it wasn't INS men; they hold their arms stiff, one straight down, the other cocked at the elbow and with a palm resting on the gun. The two men at the edge of the glow were gesturing a lot, waving their arms around. I knew they were from the other side of the border.

The two men went away, and Esmeralda looked up to my window. I slid it open.

"Es?" I called, hissing her name so no one would know it was a human voice.

She put her hand to her head and nodded.

I made coffee, eggs, bacon, and toast all by moonlight. When the coffee was brewing and the bacon sizzling on the griddle, I put a small votive candle on the table, the only light that would lead them to my kitchen. They came, Esmeralda in the back, keeping an eye on the street, six adults and two little kids. The little boy was about twelve and trying so hard to be grown-up, but he was falling asleep at the table.

The two men stayed outside with Esmeralda. They were the coyotes and Es knew them. I didn't. I never did.

I poured orange juice and watched them eat. Sitting in my kitchen, they were only about a hundred feet across the border. But they had come a long way and they still had a long way to go.

The INS called a meeting open to the entire community, to be held in the lobby of the old bank building. This was one of those old-fashioned banks where the lobby was a wide expanse of marble and you walked like ages to get across it to the teller windows. It had been a nice bank too; we all kept our money there. The tellers knew everybody, and so did the manager, but it closed and now we all have to drive twenty-five miles to the Bank of America.

Me and Esmeralda went to this meeting, but it was mostly men. They were milling around like flies on a new-laid garden, and buzzing just like it too.

Esmeralda said a chant under her breath. I stood right next to her. I could hear the chant, and I could smell on her the deep rich soil that hides below our sand. She'd been working in the arroyo before we came here, working to hide footprints and to keep the shrubs and cactus unharmed by the stream of bodies going past. The scent of the earth calmed me some; the excitement and eagerness of the men around me was unsettling. A young man, blond, tall and husky, got up on a table and waited until we all looked at him.

"Thank you. Now, the reason the INS wanted to speak to you . . ."

I always tune out talking. That's why I did so bad in school—the teacher'd start droning on about something and at the first sentence I'd look out the window and start thinking of things. I thought of Daddy's willow tree, I thought of Mamma's after-school pies, I thought of some boy and if he was going to ask me out. In church, too, I never listen to the priest. No matter if he talks in Latin or Spanish or English, his voice'll put me right into another picture in my head, one that has nothing to do with the man's message. I think that's why I like Esmeralda's religion. When she starts chanting and doing her religious rites, it's *supposed* to put you in a trance. She says she can see God when she's in a trance. But she has lots of gods, one for each bush and tree and animal and all and she sees them and talks to them. Christ, I like that idea. Not talking to trees, but that there's gods in everything. That's much more comforting than one big grey-bearded man looking down on all of us. I worry that he can't really keep track of everybody.

My mind goes like that and I didn't hear a word that INS man said. I was looking at the back of Esmeralda's head, looking at the way her long braid coils around the crown of her head, like a black snake.

Whatever he said sure got to the men; they were excited when we all left the building and went into the street. Esmeralda told me that the INS said everyone should look for illegal aliens and report anything suspicious.

Who are these strangers, I was thinking, who come into our town and tell us to start spying on each other? Snitching is what they want us to do. Esmeralda smiled at me when I told her that.

"It's not all the men, Delia," she said. "The parasite is in some of them, making them crazy. It spins around inside their head and gives them an itch in the center of their brain."

"Es," I said, "all they want to do is be little movie-like deputies and shoot poor old families on the border. Like little boys who got their first BB gun and can't wait to run out and shoot a rabbit."

"Little boys have mothers who stop them," said Esmeralda.

That Esmeralda, she's so smart.

Some summer days are so hot that the scent of cilantro from Esmeralda's herb garden hangs heavy and stifling in the air. It only happens a couple of days a year, but when I smell that and when it's so potent, I remember the day the first fence-jumpers came to my kitchen.

The air was hot then and I was sitting in the kitchen, the back door open, a clunky old fan blowing the hot air and the cilantro scent into my face. I just sat, sipping Kool-Aid and staring out the back door. First there was the dry brown rise on the far side of the arroyo and then, standing on the rise, there was a woman, three teenagers, two younger kids. They were sneaking in at the wire, an older man showing them the place where the fence was weak and easy to push down. That was the coyote, I found out later—the expert—and it turned out that he was leading them to Esmeralda. She was in her herb garden, weeding. I had been idly wondering why the hell she was weeding in this hot weather. I saw her jump up and run to meet the family as they disappeared down into the arroyo and then back up on her side.

The coyote saw me staring at them and he motioned to Esmeralda. She looked at me. From clear across the two yards, mine and hers, I could see her looking right in my eyes like she was assessing me. Next thing I knew, that family passed under my willow tree and was in my kitchen, drinking a fresh batch of Kool-Aid, eating oranges and toast.

I asked the woman, "Where's your husband?"

She shook her head.

"Where are you from?"

Esmeralda said then, "Don't ask, Delia. You don't want to know too much."

They ate four pieces of toast each and I wished I had more to give them. The coyote gave a call and the whole family jumped up and hustled out the door. They followed him, and they disappeared into the low brush of the vacant lot across the street from my house. Esmeralda smiled at me.

"Very good," she said and went to her house.

I went to my living room where I have a large carved crucifix on the wall. The artist carved Jesus out of wood, and painted his eyes blue and the eyes were rolled up, like he was looking at heaven. I prayed for those children. It was summer, hot, and the desert was no place for them.

Esmeralda said she has so many gods that sometimes she doesn't know which one to pray to. We were sitting in lawn chairs in her herb garden, me waiting for her to decide about these prayers. Her garden is huge, and she has herbs I've never heard of and varieties of herbs I've seen before but never in such abundance.

"Is there a god for stupid men?" That was my suggestion.

She stared at her herbs.

"A god against violence?"

"I think it is the owl," she said.

I wanted to ask her, what was the owl, but she had the look on her face, she was thinking and I knew not to interrupt her.

"Maybe I can try the *tomillo, mostaza,* and dried *serpiente* skin," Esmeralda said in a near-chant. "And maybe the god for strangers."

I said, "Be nice to strangers, for they may have entertained angels unaware. Something like that. It's in the Bible."

"We'll pray to protect the strangers and not to change the men . . . that would be better." Esmeralda looked at me. "I know that was from the Bible."

"I'll help but I want to change the men."

"I will pray for strangers. If you want to help, I will be out here tonight." Esmeralda got up, collapsed her lawn chair and went to her kitchen. I picked up mine and went to my kitchen.

This town is so small that when you turn your back it's gone. My father said that. Once he took me to the yard and turned me so my back was to the town. Did I see the town, he asked. No, I said. See how small it is, he said. Then he took me to stand under the willow tree, the pale green fingers of leaves enclosing us. Everywhere you look, he said, do you see the willow? He turned me in a full circle. Yes, I said. The willow tree is big, he explained, and the town is small.

I still haven't figured out what he meant. But I do know that this town is too small. Esmeralda and me, we've gotten five more families through here since the INS had their meeting. One night, I had fed three people, two men and a woman, all very scared and very tired looking. I led them out the front door. I looked both ways. Down at the end of my street, where it dead-ends at an old water pumping station, I saw Felix parading back and forth, carrying his rifle. I pointed to the largest clump of brush directly across from my front door, and told the three to go there as soon as Felix's back was turned. I stood up straight and walked down to the end of the road.

"Evening, Felix. Are you patrolling?"

"INS said they got word that those illegals come in through this arroyo. Tuesdays and Thursdays, that's when I watch."

"Oh. Who watches the other nights?"

"Harold, my brother Frank, and sometimes Gregory or his kid."

I offered Felix a cigarette and he took two from my pack. He put one in his pocket and lit the other one.

"The fence jumpers, they hide over there." He pointed to the dimly lit pumping station. "I want to catch somebody slippin' through. You want my theory?"

I nodded. I was taking small steps around him, so that he was facing the pumping station and not my house. His face glowed red when he took a drag on the cigarette. Over his shoulder I saw three shadows run from my front door to the opposite side of the street.

Felix blew a smoke ring. "I believe we should be visible. Those fence jumpers should get an eyeful of us standing here with guns and change their damn minds about comin' in here."

"Would you shoot them if you saw them coming over?"

Felix looked at me. "Damn right, I'd shoot 'em."

I said goodnight and gave him the rest of my cigarettes. "Help you get through the night, Felix."

When I got back to my kitchen, I saw Esmeralda setting up around her fire to chant. I gave up on the strangers praying after the first few nights. The smell of that dried snakeskin with those herbs was just too much for me. Wasn't as pleasant as the incense they use at the Catholic church. Besides, no matter how hard I concentrated, over Esmeralda's shoulder I'd see the lights of the town and I kept thinking about the men with their guns. The strangers were slipping through okay, but I wanted to change those men.

All summer, it's been hot and dry. I was at church this morning and everybody was fanning their faces with the mimeographed sheets that we picked up at the front door. There was a faint whooshing sound throughout the church as the white papers snapped back and forth. I looked around. Felix was there, with his wife and four kids, and so were his brothers, with their families. The big Jesus on the altar stared at us, not at heaven like mine does. This one used to scare me when I was a kid. Now I wonder about it. What does it see? As soon as the priest started talking, I concentrated on Jesus. I watched to see if the eyes were looking at the men who've been carrying guns. Long time I looked, but the priest finished talking and everybody was getting up. Disappointed, I skipped going to confession and left.

I came home and brought my lawn chair out here to the willow tree. It's almost cool in the shade and I feel better sitting inside the green veil of leaves. The cilantro scent is strong, almost visible in the air, and Esmeralda is in the garden, picking through the dirt around her herbs. She's singing and it seems my willow tree is quivering to the song. Maybe one of her gods is in my willow. I close my eyes and let her song settle me into a trance.

CALYX Journal, Vol. 12:1, 1989

Kathleen Alcalá

THE TRANSFORMING EYE

There were Japanese fishing floats and a dried wreath of grape vines, Persian boxes with enamelled gazelles on the lids, rubber stamps of business addresses, broken coffee mugs, dog leashes, and partially disassembled clocks. Through the window, I could just see either a fur coat or a stuffed animal, several war medals, and some worn leather gloves in a corner; an aviator's cap, drafting tools, and a tied bundle of old fountain pens; tiny dolls with amazed expressions on their faces, accompanied by a straw man on a burro; a saddle with silver trimming, and four matching teacups and saucers. A dried porcupine fish hung from the ceiling, and several transparent, dried seahorses crumbled on the ledge in the late afternoon sunlight. Volumes of books with illegible titles, a lace collar, a scattering of hatpins, and a string of pearls spilled off the shelf below the window.

Each item, I felt sure, had a reason for being there; each had a story of mystery and romance. There, I thought, is what's missing from Los Picos. "The Transforming Eye" was lettered on the glass, and below that "Fine Photography—a Gift to Last Forever" in fancy gold script. It appeared to be more of an antique store than a photographer's studio. A symbol in gold—an eye peering between the legs of a camera tripod—completed the dusty window. Except for the light from the street, all was dark inside and gave the illusion of a half-opened trunk discovered in an attic, filled with lost items from the past. The street remained empty, the shadows long, and I returned home accompanied only by my own footsteps.

I came to Los Picos to help my grandmother to die. My ancient great-aunts, Doña Luisa and Doña Elvira, could no longer care for Abuelita Clara, my grandmother, who lay curled like a mummified doll in her giant mahogany bed. I was between jobs as a television production assistant when they invited me down. Who could refuse an all-expense-paid summer in Mexico, even if it was in a small town? My great-aunts, although well into their seventies, continued with their business of making fine linens. The two no longer did the fine needlework themselves, but hired young women with keen eyesight and strong fingers. The hired women worked in a room which had originally been the parlor, and sometimes one or the other of my great-aunts would sit down at the monstrous sewing machine to hem a finished tablecloth if an order were running late. A renewed interest in fine, handmade items had made my great-aunts well off, and they moved with the grace and assurance of the financially and socially secure.

I fed Abuelita and read to her in the mornings, then tried to feed her again at noon, coaxing a few warm noodles between her slack lips. Her dentures lay on the nightstand, unused. The room smelled of glycerin and rosewater and the stale, sharp smell of old people. Sometimes a tear rolled down my grandmother's cheek, and I didn't know if it was the story I was reading or if she was thinking of something sad. We were said to resemble each other, with our high cheekbones and curly hair, and I watched her palsied hands and trembling lip as though contemplating my own future.

In the afternoons she slept, and I walked slowly up and down the narrow, cobblestoned streets of Los Picos, nodding to the shopkeepers, the flower vendor, and the young woman who cared for the children in the corner house. I saw the same people every day. On the Calle Benito Juarez, which ran all the way around the plaza, was a magazine stand that carried an English language paper; sometimes I read it. The news seemed strange and distant.

In the evenings, we wrapped my grandmother in shawls and carried her out to the front room, where the sewing machine stood in its canvas cover like a horse in its stall, and we sat and read or talked. We thought the change of scene might cheer Abuelita up, and it was easier to talk to her if there were others in the room who could answer. We propped her up in an overstuffed chair, and she stared at us with great brown owl eyes, magnified by her ill-fitting glasses.

"What did you do today?" asked Doña Luisa, rattling a sheaf of papers as she did her accounts for the day.

"I walked way down there," I said, mimicking my aunts in my exaggeration, "and way, way up a steep hill, so steep I thought I would fall off backwards."

"Oh!" said Doña Elvira. "How tiring! I don't like to walk up those hills."

"What was the name of the street you were on?" asked Luisa.

"I don't remember," I said. "I forgot to look. But there was some kind of a shop up there, like a photographer's shop. It was called 'The Transforming Eye.'"

"I don't know what that could be," said Luisa. "I haven't been up that way in ages."

"There used to be that crazy Dutchman," said Elvira. "He had an art studio, or something."

"Oh, him!" said Luisa, dismissing the idea with her hand. "He was always arguing with people and filling their heads with strange ideas . . . Hoove, or Noobes. They ran him out of Europe for being an anarchist or Mason or some such nonsense."

"He sounds interesting," I said.

"No, no. Well, maybe to you," said Luisa, "but he died a long time ago. There used to be people like that all over Mexico, in exile."

"Like Trotsky," said Elvira. "Did Noobes really die?"

"I suppose so," said Luisa. "Who's heard anything of him in ages? Anyway, he was just trouble."

"Too bad," said Elvira, "he was very handsome. He had his eye on your grandmother."

"Yes, but she would have none of it," added Luisa quickly. "She was already engaged to your grandfather."

"Really?" I asked.

"Yes, but enough of that," said Luisa. "Sometimes the past is best forgotten. It's time for bed."

I slept in an enclosed porch off the parlor, surrounded by the spools of colored thread with which the women worked during the day. The vivid magentas and greens and golds seemed to embody the fantastic designs into which they would one day be transformed, and I could sense their glowing presence in the dark.

It rained every day for the next week. The deep gray clouds piled up and piled up until the mountaintops could hold them no longer, then sheets of rain would come crashing down on the town. Each day, the rain came as a relief, the temperature and humidity remaining high until the clouds burst. Our clothes stuck to us, and my aunts carried handkerchiefs soaked in perfume to dab at their brows as they worked. In the courtyard, the doves huddled and cooed, as though mourning their children which were just the right age to be baked into delicious little pies.

On Friday the sky was white and opaque, but it did not rain. I went for my first walk in five days, heading east along the near edge of the plaza, then up into the streets on that side of town. The weather turned suddenly, and it began to rain in fat, wet drops. I headed for a worn green awning, and found myself in front of The Transforming Eye. The front door stood open, so I stepped into the dark, woody-smelling interior.

The shop sagged with dust and neglect. Stacks of old photographs, dismembered frames, and old ends of cardboard lay in the corners. A counter stood opposite the door, but was piled so high with musty books and papers that it was obviously not used for business. A man bending over an old camera looked up at me. He had dark eyes and light, graying hair, and looked somewhere between forty and fifty years old.

"Hello," I said.

"Hello," he grunted, and bent back over the camera. I stood there for several moments before he looked back at me, as though surprised to see a real person in his shop.

"I just came in from the rain," I said, "and was enjoying the things in your shop. Some of them are very old."

"My father's things," he said.

"This is your father's shop?" I asked, and began thumbing through the stacks of old photos. The pictures were striking, and the people seemed very life-like in spite of their stiff poses and formal clothes. Beyond the photos were glass plates covered with dust.

"Was," he answered.

I walked further into the shop and found an area arranged for portraits. There were old hats, sprays of artificial flowers, and what looked like everybody's family Bible. Behind was a painted backdrop. It was in fantastic colors with a checkerboard floor in the foreground.

"This is beautiful!" I exclaimed. The backdrop was Moorish in style, and showed an impossibly lush scene of bright trees and flowers, with mysterious red minarets in the background. Near the center, two lime-green parrots shared a hoop and touched bills affectionately, framed by a full moon. The black and white checkerboard pattern appeared to recede into the trees and buildings above it.

I made my way back to the front of the store and repeated myself: "The backdrop is very beautiful."

"Yes," he said, looking at me. "It came from the cargo of a Portuguese shipwreck. It is very old."

"It looks it," I said, then watched his deft hands as he worked on the camera. I found myself fascinated by his movements and his clothes. He wore a white shirt with the sleeves rolled up, high-waisted trousers, and a vest with a gold chain dangling from the watch pocket. It had stopped raining outside, and was very bright in contrast to the gloomy interior of the shop.

"There," he said, standing back from the camera.

"Do you know how to use it?" I asked.

"My father taught me before I left. But it needs glass plates. It doesn't use film."

"I saw some glass back there," I said, "behind the counter."

He looked at me more carefully as I stood with my hand on the door, ready to leave. "Maybe I'll have the camera working by next week."

That evening I teased my great-aunts. "I found that crazy Dutchman."

"How could you?" asked Elvira. "He's long gone."

"Not really. It was his son. He was trying to fix an old camera. And there's a beautiful backdrop for picture-taking!"

"Really!" said Luisa. "Well, you be careful up there. His father was involved in sorcery, or some such trash. That's why his wife left him."

"Oh, I think I'll be all right," I said. "He doesn't seem to know much about his father's business, much less any sorcery."

Abuelita Clara's face contorted with pain or discomfort, so we carried her back to her room and laid her in the embrace of the great mahogany bed.

I dreamed that night about the backdrop. In it, dusty photos were piled on the checkerboard foreground, and the fountains were running with ice-blue water. When I awoke, it was raining again.

When a week and a day had passed, I returned to The Transforming Eye. The door was open, and a few cobwebs had been cleared away. The photographer was peering at the exotic backdrop through the lens of the old camera.

"I think it's working," he said, "but I'm having trouble adjusting the angle. It seems to slip. There are some prints I've developed," he said, nodding to the counter. "I keep getting things in the frame that don't belong. I've cleared out some of this stuff, so that should help."

One print showed the backdrop with a stuffed pheasant in the foreground. Another showed a large plumed hat on a stone bench, as though left by a distracted lady to be picked up in a moment. I looked around the shop and saw neither of these objects.

"These are in black and white," I said, disappointed. "The colors of the backdrop don't show."

"No," he said, "but they can be colored by hand." He stooped and peered through the camera lens.

"Can you do that?"

"Yes," he said. "My father taught me the craft when I was little. I often colored his prints for him, although he never told the customers."

After another silence, he said, "Come sit over here. I need a human subject. That way I can tell if it really works or not."

I sat in a rickety chair before the backdrop, which glowed with jewel-like colors, while the photographer arranged the lights. When he told me to look up, I did, and sat very still while he exposed the plate.

During that time he said, "Your eyes are very lovely. They remind me of a woman my father used to know."

I could feel my cheeks grow warm under the compliment, although I could not speak. The photographer looked younger than the first time I had seen him.

At last he said, "That's it. You're finished," and I jumped up, almost knocking the chair into the backdrop.

"Now," he said, smiling and placing a hand lightly on my shoulder, "come back next week and I'll have the photo ready. If it's good I'll even color it and give you the print."

"I would like that," I said. "It will give me something by which to remember Los Picos."

He laughed and said, "Why would anyone want to remember Los Picos?"

I smiled and said good-bye. Passing the open door, I noticed that it said in small gold letters, "Hiram Noobes & Son." My feet flew down the cobblestoned streets as I tried to escape the afternoon rainstorm, but I still returned to my aunt's house slightly damp.

"I just had my picture taken," I announced gaily to Elvira when she opened the door for me.

She looked at me slowly and said, "By whom?"

"By Hiram Noobes' son, the photographer."

At the mention of that name, Elvira and Luisa, who had entered the front hall to see who was at the door, stopped where they were.

"You must not go there anymore!" said Luisa finally.

"But why?" I asked, confused by their reaction. I thought they might be pleased by an old-fashioned photograph.

"Some of his father's friends disappeared. No one knows what happened to them," said Luisa.

"Well, you said he was an anarchist," I answered. "Maybe they went to start revolutions in other countries. I don't understand why you're so upset."

"A photograph can possess a person's soul," said Elvira quietly.

I almost burst out laughing. "No one believes that except a few old Indians in the hills!"

"That's enough!" said Luisa, so I went to get my grandmother ready for dinner. I felt sorry for myself, young in a house full of old women, and thought it was just as well that I would be returning to California soon to start a new project.

Dinner was very quiet that night. No one had much of an appetite, and we all retired early to our rooms. My aunts' stories had made me all the more curious about the handsome photographer, but at the same time, I felt that it was time to leave. I tried to book an earlier flight out of Guadalajara the next day, but the airlines couldn't accommodate me. I fed bread crumbs to the doves in the courtyard and shared their mournful mood.

I decided to confide in my grandmother. Although she no longer spoke, I thought that she might have some sympathy. For all I knew, she might have been prevented from marrying Noobes by custom and family politics. As I spoke, her eyes grew rounder and rounder behind her thick glasses.

Finally, she pulled me towards her with a claw-like hand and rasped, with great effort, "Go back. Go back to Los Angeles."

Tears started to my eyes. She, too, had grown tired of me. I ran from her room and spent the rest of the afternoon locked in the little enclosed porch, looking through a book which I had no heart to read.

When I returned to The Transforming Eye, I hurried inside, more anxious to see him than I had realized. The photographer was not there. I paced about nervously, thinking that he must have stepped out for a moment, since the door had been left ajar.

Several new prints lay on a corner of the worn marble counter. They showed a serious young woman holding a bowl of pomegranates in her lap. One of the prints had been tinted. I admired the life-like quality of the photos, until I realized that the woman in the picture was me. The stiff pose and the artificial coloring made me look like someone I recognized, but not like me.

What was even more puzzling was that I had not been holding a bowl of pomegranates when the portrait was taken. He must have drawn it in, although the bowl appeared in all six prints, and he would have had to redraw my hands to make the change.

Impatient, I stepped back into the portrait area to see if the photographer was there. The lights were on, and the backdrop glowed enticingly. On the stone bench in the scene was a wooden bowl full of deliciously red pomegranates. They looked so real that I couldn't restrain myself from reaching to pick one up. The leathery skin and prickly end felt as real to me as any fruit I had ever touched. I turned with the pomegranate in my hand and saw that I stood on the black and white tiles, the bright trees trailing their branches over my head. The photographer's studio appeared vague and dim, as though seen through a gauze curtain. I was inside the backdrop. When I tried to step out, I was restrained by an invisible barrier, which gave slightly and sprang back at my touch.

Convinced that this was some sort of illusion, I sat down on the stone bench and resolved not to panic. I would wait for the photographer to return, enjoy his prank, and free me. Maybe then he would take me out to lunch.

In time, the photographer returned, looking as distant and self-absorbed as ever, and didn't seem to notice that anything was different. He acted as though he didn't see me.

"Hey!" I said finally. "Noobes! Are you through? I'm getting bored in here." And I tried to laugh. He still didn't seem to notice. "Hey!" I yelled, beating my hands against the invisible restraint. "Let me out now!"

Noobes sat by the front window sorting tools. He checked his pocket watch once, then returned to turn off the lights. When he did, it became night in the backdrop.

"No!" I screamed. "Don't leave me here!"

I heard the door shut and lock.

I screamed and clawed at the barrier until I was hoarse and my hands raw and bleeding, but I could not cut my way out. Tears coursed down my face and neck, but I didn't stop to wipe them away until much later. Exhausted, I sank back onto the cold tiles, still sobbing. When I was finally silent, I realized that I could hear the fountain splashing, and a faint breeze stirred the palm trees, bringing the scent of night-blooming jasmine.

It seemed like a long time that I was trapped in the backdrop. The mountains were painted onto another invisible barrier, so there was no more depth in there, at least not for me, than was visible from outside. Sometimes I would see others, men in turbans with swords at their waists, and women in long lace dresses, people from the near past and long ago, but they did not come near. Once, a man seemed to step closer and look at me, but after a minute he went away. Birds sang constantly, and roses and gardenias bloomed in the hidden courtyards. I ate two of the pomegranates.

I found my grandmother's handkerchief in the backdrop, embroidered with her initials in my aunts' distinctive style. I was holding it in one hand and trailing the other in the ice-cold waters of the fountain when a pinpoint of light seemed to open up before me. I stood up and could see my grandmother walking towards me, under her own power. I threw myself in her arms, and she held me in a strong embrace before stepping past me to the fountain, and I saw a man with light hair and dark eyes coming towards her. Just before I found myself back in the shop, I saw that my grandmother looked like the tinted photograph of myself as she reached out her hand to Hiram Noobes.

I returned to the house of my great-aunts to find that my grandmother had died. It was late evening of the same day, and while my aunts had been worried about me, they were too distraught to question me closely. They did not see my tear-streaked face and bloody hands through their own grief.

I don't remember much of what happened during the following days. My aunts were like darkness, pulled into themselves, nursing their grief behind shawls.

Women I had not seen before prepared my grandmother's body for burial, perfuming it and painting her face with cosmetics. I could not help but think that they could never make her look as beautiful as the last glimpse I had of her retreating into that gauze-veiled garden of dreams.

I felt useless. There was no place for me in this atmosphere of ritual grief. I had wept all my tears into the ice-blue fountain, and had none left for my abuela as the coffin was lowered into the grave in the cramped hillside cemetery. I wore a borrowed rebozo over my head and shoulders since I had lacked the foresight to bring mourning clothes to Los Picos.

Immediately after the funeral, I took the bus to Guadalajara from where my airplane would depart that evening. My aunts had been subdued and distant—I could not read their careworn faces as they kissed me good-bye. I knew that I could never ask them the many questions that I had about The Transforming Eye.

As the bus topped the last rise from which the town of Los Picos was visible, I thought I saw a golden glimmer from a distant hillside, afternoon sunlight glinting off a plate glass window with gold lettering, a gift to last forever. . . . Or maybe I just imagined it. I hid my battered fingernails in my grandmother's handkerchief and refused to look back again.

I never went to see my great-aunts again, though I think of them when I spread my embroidered tablecloth for special dinners, and I hope that my grandmother is happy, wherever she is, inside of The Transforming Eye.

CALYX Journal, Vol. 12:2, 1989/90

Ruthann Robson

LIVES OF A LONG-HAIRED LESBIAN: FOUR ELEMENTAL NARRATIONS

Home Fires

It wasn't the fire that killed her, although it could have been. It could have killed me too. It could have killed the woman upstairs with the baby daughter whose hair was just getting long enough to curl. But the fire didn't kill anyone, unless you count the sluggish roaches, which I don't.

There are years before the fire. These years, like all the years of my lifetime, have numbers: 1971 or 1973 or 1974 or 1970. It is after 1967, because Wade is always saying, "Girls, it ain't 1967 anymore." He says this because of how we look. We like to think Wade is a good friend. Wade isn't our friend; he is our pimp.

Wade is always interested in the way we dress, which makes him seem like a friend. I almost always wear a black fitted-bodice leotard, Danskin style 268. I wear it with size 28 Levi jeans or a black and mauve Indian print cotton skirt, depending on the weather. Stacie always wears a green turtle-neck, regardless of the weather. She usually pulls on size 27 jeans, although she also has a jean skirt and a pair of tight-fitting overalls. We wear flat sandals. Wade always nags us about our shoes. He advises, "High heels are hot." We pretend we are naive.

Stacie keeps her hair long and blonde because men like it that way. That's what she says. Wade approves. I don't understand why men like it that way; I've never understood anything about men. My hair is actually longer, but Stacie is shorter, so her hair looks longer. Or maybe my hair looks shorter because it is the color of ashes rather than the color of straw. We are white. We have blue eyes that border on green. We are young. I am always younger.

In summer, we practice being thin. We live on black beauties, water, and bananas. Someone had told Stacie that it was impossible to starve to death if one ingested enough potassium. Bananas are the best source of potassium. Stacie calls bananas "the yellow flames of life." We eat them incessantly. We always eat them sliced.

In winter, we walk the streets past the men who burn fires in trash cans to keep warm. They call out to us. Sometimes we wave. Sometimes we call back. We always keep moving, fast in our flat sandals. We must be cold.

There are several summers and seemingly many more winters. We move around. Wade follows us or finds us places to live. The rooms are the narrowest of hallways or bleed into one another without definition. We have wicker furniture and posters and three ceramic bowls and a hurricane oil lamp given to us by Stacie's sister and some knives. We have candles and incense and a lighter from Pakistan. We have flower pots filled with soil and seed that we move from window sill to window sill. We have one bed, one set of safari animal sheets, two pillows, and a quilt made in Georgia. We have each other.

We are more than lovers. We are mirrors. We are closer than twins. We are two halves craving wholeness. We are lost princesses. We aren't sure what to call ourselves. We say, "Roommates." We say, "Partners." Wade says, "Whatever turns you on, girls."

We want a different life. We sit in the kitchen of Stacie's married sister, Brenda. Brenda says, "Get a straight job." I moan that I can't type. Stacie complains because she doesn't have the right clothes. We decide to become waitresses.

The cocktail lounge is dark. It is hard not to whore. The bartender keeps setting me up with tricks. Men scrape twenty-dollar bills across my fishnet stockings. Stacie works a split shift. The bartender comes home with me, but he is impotent. He gives me a ten-dollar bill and I give it back. Wade comes to the lounge and threatens to break both of Stacie's wrists. We quit.

We start doing Tarot cards, as if to convince ourselves we have a future. Our favorite suit is wands. It seems the most magical and yet the most familiar. We dabble in astrology. Stacie is an Aries with a Leo moon and Sagittarius rising. I have lied about my birthdate for so long, I cannot remember any of the vital information. We begin to talk about moving somewhere very far away. Like Florida. Or New Mexico. Or an island.

A lavender candle tips onto a wicker table. The landlord's insurance agents will try to decipher the shards of a hurricane oil lamp. We will tell them that it never had any oil, but they will not believe us. They will not believe how I pulled Stacie through a flaming window frame. They will not believe that I thought she must be dead. They will not believe how her hair singed to the roots in places, because by the time they see her, I will have chopped it short and defiant.

Wade finds us another place to live. I can't sleep without the safari sheets. Stacie won't eat any bananas. We always think we smell smoke. We try to quit cigarettes. She cries into my shoulder. "Anna, I need to escape from all this shit." I don't describe how the promise of asphyxiation had lulled me. I don't tell her that only when I thought of her also dying had I been able to wake myself up.

Stacie disappears on her seventeenth birthday. It is spring. I finally find her at her sister's house. I knew Brenda and her husband were away for three weeks, so I hadn't looked there earlier. Stacie is hanging from the dining room light fixture. I can see her through the window. I long for the Pakistani lighter. I decide the only thing I could do was set Brenda's house on fire. But I don't.

Instead I change my name to Anastacia, after the mysterious survivor of the execution of the Czar's entire family, after Stacie, after myself.

Instead I hitchhike to Florida. Or New Mexico.

Instead I go to the store and buy a pack of cigarettes and a can of lighter fluid. I take three extra books of matches.

Instead I head for Wade's duplex.

Lavender Oceans

Sometimes a bed seems like an island. It's best if it's raining through an open window, and the surrounding carpet is blue, and if you're sharing a clean quilt with someone who shares your sexual proclivities.

My island had seemed like a desert since Effie had gone back to Athens. I had met her at a rally and fallen in love with her dark and downy mustache. Her two-week tour turned into a nine-month residence at my stark apartment. Three seasons can be a long time. They can also be awfully short.

I missed her so much I couldn't look at another woman.

It is raining and the windows are open. Drops of water stray past my eyebrows, but they could be sweat. The rug is not blue, but lavender. Still, any color ocean will do, especially since I'd landlocked myself into New Mexico.

The quilt is clean. We share it quite nicely, for we are used to sharing. We'd spent years sharing: platforms, funds, derision, dinners, clothes. As coordinators of the Organization for Unity Among Lesbians and Gay Men, we'd fought many battles together. We'd even fought each other. We were confident we could survive together on a desert island.

But we would have sooner thought we'd be stranded in the Aegean than in bed together. We share the same sexual proclivity, in a sense: the sense which guides us away from each other. Our proclivity is toward similarity rather than not; our passion is reserved for our own genders. Side by side, we seem embarrassingly disparate.

I hadn't been in bed with a man since I was fifteen-and-a-half years old. Before then, I'd been with enough men to last me several long lifetimes. But I don't think I'd ever been in bed wearing only one pink sock with a man wrapped in a scarf (mine?). As far as I know, Christopher doesn't make a habit of this sort of thing either.

Here we are. The rain. The lavender ocean. The clean quilt. Our earrings clink against each other. A crisp tongue runs along my fisted knuckles. I scratch an edge of beard and ear. The hairs on our shins ruffle.

"Relax," he says. He begins to massage my back, my neck, my face, and then my head. "Relax your skull," he says, "Is it relaxed? I can't feel it under all that hair. It's weird being so close to someone with all that hair on their head."

"All my lovers say that."

"You know, the first time I saw you, at the Pride March meeting, years ago, I couldn't figure you out because of that hair."

"All my lovers say that."

"Are we lovers?" he asks.

"I don't know."

We float. We sink. I cannot understand what is happening.

If Chris is a man, then I must be a man.

If I am a woman, then Chris must be a woman.

An anthropologist might call this sex. A sociologist might not.

We get up and swim to the shower together. We know better than to argue with either anthropologists or sociologists. Besides, we have a lot of work to do. We must organize a benefit for a Lesbian mother fighting a custody battle.

"Anastacia, Anastacia," he calls from across the room, as if we had not seen each other for seasons instead of having parted that very morning. We abandon a meeting to look for a bottle of wine. We hold hands on the street, both casually and furtively. We go back to the meeting without the wine. I make an inexcusably early exit and walk home. I call Effie in Athens. She is busy and will return my transatlantic call some other time.

I am wearing my hair tucked into a madras hat and watching a softball game when I meet Cora Mae. She is playing first base. She has an infant packed on her back and a cropped Afro. I think she is beautiful. I try to figure if the baby means she isn't a Lesbian.

She is. A wonderful one. But she is just passing through New Mexico on her way to stay with her sister in California, although she decides to pass through a little longer. Her baby, Jasmine, sleeps on the island of a bed with us while Cora Mae and I lick each other nearly senseless. We give each other and Jasmine sweet smelling baths. We powder each other with English lavender which splatters on the rug. She pushes two fingers so deeply into me that my back archs into a circle and I fill the bed with wetness. We talk about our dead parents, about being survivors, about being "natural" Lesbians unwilling to adopt every convention of the life we had chosen. She has her baby. I have my hair.

When she leaves it is raining. I telephone Effie in Athens, but disconnect the line before anyone answers. That night it is still raining. I run into Chris at an AIDS Network meeting. He has shaved his head, his beard. We go out for a bottle of wine. We find a sharp white Bordeaux. I buy a bunch of almost ripe bananas. He buys a bunch of grocery store flowers. We walk back to my place. The windows are open. The rug is still lavender.

He starts to massage my neck, but I ask him to come inside me instead. I am incredulous at my own invitation. He debates, then pulls me on top of him. "Only if it's like this," he says. I nod. My hair falls around his desert-flat chest.

In the morning, he tells me his dreams. He dreamed of a forest, of a woman with long hair who could have been me but wasn't, of someone dancing.

I tell him I dreamed of a pale purple sea. But I had dreamed of his sister. But I had dreamed of Cora Mae and Effie and Stacie. I had dreamed of lighting a fire in the crawl space of a duplex. I dreamed I had been a Lesbian so long I forgot about birth control.

Gaea

Karma lost her shoe. Her mother is standing at the door waiting for me to find it. She comes during lunch to take her child to a doctor's appointment and assumes her child needs both shoes. There are forty cardboard lockers to inspect. Neither Karma nor her mother are helping. The children eat their rice innocently.

I'd been working at Ocala Day School for quite a while, living in a trailer in the woods. There are more woods in Florida than most people think. I take the children on walks and pretend we are a tribe lost in some wonderful wilderness.

While I rub the backs of the children to induce the "nap" in the scheduled "naptime," I daydream of a Greek island. I imagine myself walking through an olive grove on Lesbos. I'd read that the island was called Mytilene now, I guess for the obvious reasons. It is for those same obvious reasons that I want to suck the pits out of olives in those groves.

While I rub the back of Shatki, an un-nappably vibrant four-year-old, I daydream of her mother. Ora has the reddest and shortest hair of any woman I'd ever seen. I can almost see the freckles on her skull. She has freckles everywhere else, or so I imagine. I wonder if she is a Lesbian.

No one else in these woods seems to be. It is hard to live here. I have a crush on Diana, the director of the day school, but she is heartlessly heterosexual. Her husband, Davie, is the school's accountant. He brings her lunch every day. Diana's sister, the assistant director, tells me she thinks Davie is sweet. I think he is sickening. I try not to watch him as he presses his hand between Diana's legs, pulling them apart. I try not to watch him kiss her neck, crumbs of his lunch still on his mustache.

I sit outside and draw my names in the lush dirt with a stick, while the children sleep, each on her or his own mat. The trees beyond the school's clearing look like a green net, like a verdant web. I am sitting on the outermost string, if I am connected at all. It is easy to pity myself because every other woman in the world seems to have a sister.

At six P.M., closing time, on the day that Karma's mother said she would not drop the matter of the unmated shoe, I stand by the gate with ten children. They are all mud-caked and weary. One of them unscrambles himself from the group to pull at my beige camp shorts. For the first time in eight hours, I recognize this creature with blond curls as my son. That leaves nine children waiting for parents.

At twenty minutes past six, the director and assistant director long since departed, only Shatki is left by the gate with Colin and me. I decide to take a risk. I put a note on the door and take Shatki to my trailer. Colin is thrilled. He always loves company, any company, but he is especially impressed with the older girl of auburn hair and green eyes.

I stand in the middle of my bedroom, debating whether or not to put Shatki into the bed where Colin and I usually sleep. We have already eaten, already done Colin's two puzzles several times each, already had baths and snacks. I stand there for a long time, with two confused pre-schoolers, until Ora knocks on the dark door. She'd had truck trouble on a distant road. She is hauling landfill these days. She is appropriately apologetic and grateful. She invites Colin and me for dinner.

I am surprised to find that she is a good cook. It is "just one of her hobbies," she says. For dessert, she makes bananas foster. I wince at the flames. She holds my plate close to my face, thinking she is teasing me. The children laugh.

Later, when the children are snoring in Shatki's bunk beds, we sweat between Ora's jungle-patterned sheets. I blanche when she wants to tie my hands with scarves. Her loving is opulent and virulent. I am shy.

"I suppose with a name like Anastacia, you're afraid of a lot of things," she says softly.

"My real name is Anna," I tell her for no reason. She continues to call me Anastacia.

Her house is cedar. I love the windows with stained glass flowers. She calls me her lover, her sister. I love that too. She has to be on the road, hauling, some nights until late. It seems sensible that I watch Shatki and Colin at a cedar house rather than a rusted trailer. It seems strange to continue to work at the Ocala Day School for minimum wage. I quit.

She likes to drink Rolling Rock beer and she likes to talk. She tells me my hair is too burdensome and she threatens to hack it off. She tells me I am too fat and my muscles are flaccid. She says I am too tame in bed. She tells me I am an earth mother and the children love me. She tells me she will kill me if Shatki ever calls me "mommy." She tells me she is the toughest bulldagger that I will ever know, and if she catches me cheating, she will break my wrists. She tells me when Colin is sixteen, he will be a "man" and will have to move out. She tells me I treat him like a minor god and he will eat me alive.

We are walking in the woods. We are arguing. She walks fast in her expensive sneakers. I skip in my flat sandals to keep her pace. She pushes me harder than she means to. I fall on my face in the path. A branch bends into my neck. I do not try to get up. The earth smells like music. I can feel the vibrations of dancing under the ground.

I spend the seasons growing. I plant bulbs and flowers. I keep an impressive compost pile. I foster enormous cabbages. I tend tomatoes and sweet onions. I have vibrant azaleas. I learn to love color. I wear fuschia blouses and purple pants. I buy the children rainbows of clothes in a thrift shop. I steal a batik cap and stuff my hair into it.

After we harvest the last of the squash, she tells me I have to move. Her husband is returning from Canada.

Aerobics

All the walls are windowless and mirrored. Even the door is mirrored. I stand in front of the room, in my black fitted-bodice leotard and white sweat pants, rolling my neck and then my shoulders. I kick my legs; I squat; I press my elbows together. I breathe through my nose and exhale through my mouth. I shout encouragement. I push the stray hairs from my forehead.

My son brings me lunch on his pink bike. There is cheese and retsina and hard bread. We sit on the rocks outside the studio and talk. He speaks the language like a native. He is teaching himself to read with myths. He asks me hundreds of questions. "Who is Medusa, Momma?" he says. "Who was Antigone? What's a phoenix?" Sometimes I know the answers.

In midsummer, we sleep in our open-windowed house almost on the water and wait for the *Meltemi* winds to wake us. The light from the sea is lavender at dawn. We are warm. We wear open-weave clothes and strapped sandals. I twist my hair and pin it to my head like a pastry.

In winter, there are fewer tourists and the boats run less frequently. The air is sharper and only slightly colder. I sleep later and have dreams of beautiful deserts. My son tells me he dreams of lush forests and eating bananas. If it is especially damp, we share a blanket. I let a braid dangle down my back.

When I first arrived in this tideless part of the world, I turned my passion outward. I feigned love for every woman I touched. I caressed their skins like flames. I even attempted love with two men. The second one tore a fist full of my hair and then tried to pay me for the damage he had done. He never sent me flowers.

But now that I have been here season after season, I do not suffer such distractions. I am as calm as the winds, calmer. I know the women of this island. The women of this island know me.

Most of the women who come to my classes want thinner thighs or flatter stomachs or bodies like young boys. They are tourists or wives of local merchants or waitresses or artists. Some of the women come to these classes for the reasons I teach them: I want women to be strong.

I make the women use weights. I work their biceps, their triceps, their wrists. I make them punch the air. I make them swing and twist and kick and jump. I tell them to pretend the air is water and they are swimming. I teach them resistance. I let them sweat.

I tell my students to call me Anemone. They tell me this means "windflower." I call my studio Aerobics. This means "air," I tell them. Soon, I tell them, we will be as light as air, as fresh as air, as free as air.

I watch my limbs tighten and strengthen. I watch my muscles harden. I watch the women in the room watch themselves in the mirrors. I watch some women more than others.

At first I think the two women are lovers. They have honey hair waved short to their scalps. I learn their names are Crystal and Melissa. Crystal is a sculptor and Melissa is a painter. They say they are English and that since I have an awfully American accent, we must be cousins. They wear sleeveless leotards in identical Capezio pink. I almost envy them. They tell me they are sisters .

Crystal is a Lesbian. The way she stands, the direct gaze of her eyes, her laugh, tell me this. If I were still taking lovers, I would take Crystal. Instead, I work with her on her neck muscles. I massage. I prescribe exercises. She tells me her neck is weak from an adolescent accident.

Melissa is getting married to a Canadian photographer. She wants her stomach flat and unnaturally tight to camouflage any memories of pregnancies. She is letting her hair grow. She is thinking of moving to Athens.

An agent from Athens calls me about selling the business. I have to think a few seconds before I can decipher her English. I am distracted by her voice. I can recognize a former lover, even long distance. I know she will not remember me; I lived in New Mexico then. I am thankful for her fluency because she uses words like "lucrative" and "goodwill." I say I have always been one to consider any offer. Her offer is worth considering.

I announce to the students that I am selling the school. I rent another house. I move outside of the village, higher on a hill, closer to the sky. My son and I discuss whether the air is truly clearer up here or whether it only seems that way.

Melissa sits inside my new whitewashed walls and cries. I look out the window at the pale flowers blooming close to the ground. Sometimes Melissa drifts into sleep, but wakes herself again with sobbing. After two nights, she is able to tell me what is wrong. Her sister and her husband are lovers. She spends a few days deciding which one she hates more, whose betrayal is more heinous. When she says she would like to bury them alive, to set them on fire, to dump them into the sea, I do not believe her.

Instead, I believe we do not know what to do with our love for each other.

Instead, I believe we must learn that we do not have to *do* anything with our love for another.

Instead, I believe we must learn to love and we must learn to do things, to accept connections but not to expect them.

I am thinking of learning herbs. I am thinking of polishing stones. I am thinking of becoming a long-haired Crone. I decide to make feather earrings to sell to tourists. I would like to learn the flute.

The agent comes to my house with final papers. She looks at me and looks at me. Then she looks at my son, shakes her head, but then looks at me again. I inspect her downy mustache. I take off my cotton hat and the ends of my hair follow gravity to my knees. She gasps and coughs to hide her surprise. In her cosmopolitan Greek, she says I seem familiar to her. She says she must have met my sister somewhere in her travels. In my horrid pronunciation and terrible grammar, I say that is impossible; I say I am my only sister.

CALYX Journal, Vol. 12:2, 1989/90

Charlotte Watson Sherman

KILLING COLOR

For Beulah Mae Donald, a Black woman who won a $7 million judgment against the Ku Klux Klan for the murder of her son Michael, who in March 1981, at the age of 19, was strangled, fatally beaten, then had his body hung from a tree. Mrs. Donald was awarded the United Klans of America, Inc., headquarters property in Tuscaloosa, Alabama. She died September 17, 1988.

They say they got trees over seven hundred years old down in that yella swamp where even the water is murky gold. Bet them trees hold all kind of stories, but ain't none of em like the one I'm gonna tell bout Mavis.

Now, I'm not sayin Mavis is her real name. That's just what I took to callin her after seein them eyes and that fancy dress. Mavis had so much yella in her eyes it was like lookin in the sun when you looked right in em, but a funny deep kind of sun, more like a ocean of yella fire. You was lookin on some other world when you looked in Mavis's eyes, some other world sides this one.

I first saw Mavis leanin up against that old alabaster statue of some man my Aunt Myrtice call George Washington, but I don't think so cause it's got this plaque at the bottom bout the Spanish-American War and George Washington didn't have nothin to do with no Spanish-American War.

Anyway, I don't like talkin bout that statue too much cause it just gets Aunt Myrtice to fussin and I was always told it ain't right to talk back to old folks, so I don't. I just let her think she right bout things even though I know better. Still, that statue's where I first seen Mavis, and seem like don't nobody know where she come from. We just look up one day and there she was, leanin against that alabaster statue of not-George Washington.

I ain't no fancy woman or what some might call a hell-raiser, but I know a woman full of fire when I see one, and if somebody hadda struck a match to Mavis, she'da gone up in a puff of smoke.

Mavis got honey-colored skin look like ain't never had nothin rough brush up against her. She had on some kinda blood-red high heel shoes. She the kind wear genuine silk stockins with fancy garters to hold em up, nothin like them old cotton ones I keep up on my leg with a little piece of string tied round my thigh.

Now she was wearin all this right here in Brownville, in the middle of town, in the noonday sun when all you could smell was the heat risin. So naturally I stopped and got me a good look at this woman leanin up against that statue with her eyes lookin straight out at that old magnolia tree front of the courthouse.

Most of us folks in Brownville try our best to look the other way when we walk by that big old barn of a courthouse. In fact, old Thaddeous Fulton, who I likes to call myself keepin company with, won't even walk on the same side of the street as the courthouse, cause most of us know if you brush against the law down here, you sho'nuff gonna get bad luck.

But Mavis was lookin at that old courthouse buildin full on with them yella eyes of hers never even blinkin, and she did it with her back straight like her spine was made outta some long steel pole.

When Tad come round that evenin, I tried tellin him bout Mavis standin up lookin at the courthouse, but he just shook his head and said, "Sounds like trouble to me." He wouldn't talk bout it no more, which got me kinda mad cause I like to share most of my troubles and all of my joys with this man, and I don't like seein his face closin up on me like he's comin outta some bad story in a book. But that's just what he did when I tried tellin him bout Mavis.

That man had somethin else on his mind for that evenin. I could tell by the way his eyebrows was archin clear up in his forehead.

Tad's slew-footed as they come and was born with only half his head covered with hair, so the front of his head's always shinin like a Milk Dud. But can't nobody in all of Brownville match that man for kissin.

Seem like he tries gobblin up most of my soul when he puts them sweet lips of his on mine and sneaks his tongue in my mouth. I nearly fell straight on the porch floor the first time he give me one of them kisses, and it wasn't long fore we got started on one of our favorite pasttimes—debatin bout fornication. We always waited till Aunt Myrtice dozed off in her settin chair fore we slipped out to the porch and started up our discussion.

"Now, Lady (he likes to call me Lady even though it ain't my given name). Lady, I done lived a good part of my life as a travelin man, and you know I lived in Chicago a good while fore I come back home. And things everywhere else ain't like they is in Brownville. People be different. I knowed quite a few women that was good women. Good, decent women. But we wasn't married or nothin. We was just two good people tryin to keep they bodies warm in this cold, cold world. Now what's wrong with that?"

"Well, the Good Book say that them livin in the lusts of the flesh is by nature the children of wrath."

"I done seen more of life and people than ever could be put in a book. And I ain't never met nobody that died from lustin with they flesh. What I did see was folks full of wrath cause they wasn't gettin no sin."

"Well the Good Book say . . ."

"Lady, I don't b'lieve in no such thing as the Good Book cause I know there's lots of ways of lookin at things and you can't put em all in one book and say this be the Good Book."

"Watch out now, Thaddeous Fulton. You can't come round my house blasphemin."

"I still don't b'lieve in no such book. But I do b'lieve in a good life full of love. Now come on over here and give me a kiss."

Right away I started gigglin and actin silly even though I left my girlhood behind fifty years ago. It seems like I never had a chance to be a girl like this and then Tad start up to ticklin me and nobody passin on the road woulda guessed that the muffled snortin lovin sounds was comin from two folks with all kinds of wrinkles all over they bodies.

Tad always ask, "Well, if it's really the Good Book, then shouldn't everything that feel good be in it as a good thing to be doin?"

"That depends on what the good thing is cause everything that feels good ain't good for you," I always say.

"But Lady, look at all the bad that's out there in the world. Folks gotta have some things that make em feel good. Things gotta balance some kinda way, don't they?"

And I always agree there needs to be some kinda balance to what's good and what's bad. Then Tad always starts talkin bout how good he feels just lookin at me and listenin to me talk bout the world.

"I try to show you how much I preciate you with my lips," he say and give me one of them devilish kisses. "Don't that feel good?" he ask and then keep on till we whisperin and kissin and doin pretty near what the Bible calls fornicatin out on the porch.

The next day I went to town and there Mavis was standin in the same spot by that statue, lookin at the courthouse.

Folks was walkin by lookin at her and tryin not to let her see em lookin, but Mavis wasn't payin nobody no mind cause she wasn't studyin nothin but that courthouse and that magnolia tree.

By Sunday, everybody was talkin bout her and wonderin why she kept on standin in the middle of town lookin at the courthouse. Then Reverend Darden started preachin against worryin bout other folks's business and not takin care of your own, so I started feelin shamed. But deep inside I was still wonderin bout Mavis. I decided I was gonna walk up to Mavis and find out what she was up to.

Next day, I got up early, went to town, and walked right up and waited for her to say somethin. But she acted like she didn't even know I was there. So I started talkin bout the weather, bout how that old sun was beatin down on us today, and wasn't it somethin how the grass stayed green in all this heat? Then I commenced to fannin myself, but Mavis still didn't say a word.

I was standin there fannin for bout five minutes when Mavis turned them yella eyes on me. Now, I heard stories bout people talkin with they eyes and never even openin they mouths, but I never met nobody like that before.

Mavis had them kinda eyes and she put em on me and told me with them eyes that she come for somethin she lost, then she turned her head back round and fixed her eyes on that courthouse again. Well, it was plain to me she wasn't gonna say no more, and I was ready to go home and sit in some shade anyway, so I did.

That evenin when Tad come by for a visit, he was all in a uproar.

"Why you messin round with that woman?" he ask after I told him I'd stood up at the statue with Mavis for awhile. "I told you that woman sound like trouble. Folks say she rode off with that old Ned Crowell yesterday evenin and he ain't been heard from since."

"Where she at?" I asked. For some strange reason I was scared for her.

"She still standin up there like she always do. Layin back on that old statue. Somethin wrong with that woman. I told you the first time you told me bout her. Somethin wrong. You best stay away from her fore you get tangled up in some mess you be sorry bout. You know how them folks be."

"Don't go and get so upset your blood goes up, Tad. Ain't nothin gonna happen round here."

I tried to make Tad loosen up and grin a little, but he was too worked up and decided he was goin home to rest. I wasn't gonna tell him bout Mavis and her talkin eyes cause he'da probably thought I was losin my mind.

I let three days pass fore I went to town to see if Mavis was still standin at that statue, and sure enough, there she was.

I went and stood next to her and started talkin bout nothin in particular. I fixed my eyes on the courthouse but couldn't see nothin that hadn't been there for at least fifty years.

"You know they keep that buildin pretty clean and old Wonzell Fitch picks up round the yard every evenin. You might wanna check with him bout findin out somethin you lost," I whispered.

She turned her head and told me with them yella eyes she was lookin for somethin that b'longed to her. She didn't even hear what I said. I didn't say nothin else, just stood with her for awhile, then went on home.

Tad came by later on with his face all wrinkled up like a prune, but I didn't make fun of him cause I could see he was troubled.

"Seem like three more of them Crowells and one of them Fitzhughs is gone."

"Don't nobody know what happened to em?" I asked. "Don't seem possible four grown men could disappear without a trace. What do folks think is happenin?"

"Don't know for sure, but some folks say they saw least two of them Crowells and old Billy Fitzhugh go off with that crazy woman late in the evenin."

"Do the sheriff know bout that?" I asked.

"Naw, and ain't nobody gonna tell him neither. If they do they likely to get locked up."

"Well, sure is mighty strange. Didn't think she even left that spot at the statue to go relieve herself. She just stand there starin, don't ever see her drink no water or nothin, just standin in all that heat."

"Well, look like come evenin she find herself one of them old white men and go off with em and don't nobody see that man no more. You ain't goin round her, is you? I sure hate to see what happen when the sheriff find out bout her bein the last one seen with them missin men, cause you know well as I do what that mean."

Me and Tad just sat together real quiet and still on the porch holdin hands like old folks is supposed to do.

Next day I had to take Aunt Myrtice to evenin prayer service so I decided I was gonna sit outside and watch the statue from the front steps of the church.

"You bout to miss service and then have the nerve to sit on the front steps of Reverend Darden's church?" she fussed.

"I'm gonna do just that and ain't nobody gonna stop me, neither."

"You gonna sit outside when you need to be inside?"

"Yep," I replied. Then I just stopped listenin. I already made up my mind bout what I was gonna do, and even Aunt Myrtice's fussin wasn't gonna change that.

So after all the folks had gone inside, I sat on the porch and watched the sun go down and watched Mavis standin at the statue lookin at that same buildin she'd been lookin at for almost a month now.

When the shadows had stretched and twisted into night, I saw the lights from some kinda car stop in front of the statue. Mavis jumped in the car with what sounded to me like a laugh, and the car eased on down the street.

"No tellin where they goin," I thought out loud as the car moved slowly past the church. I could see the pale face of old Doc Adams at the wheel. Mavis never even turned her head in my direction or anyone else's. Her yella eyes was lookin straight ahead.

"Nuther man gone," Tad mumbled when he stopped by the next day.

"Was it old Doc Adams?" I asked, scared to hear the answer.

"How'd you know? I done told you you better stay way from that woman. God knows what she's up to and I sure don't want no parts of it. You askin for trouble, Lady, foolin round that woman. Best go on in the house and read some of that Good Book you always talkin bout. I know it don't say nothin good bout killin folks!"

"Now how you know anybody been killed, Tad? How you know that? Some folks is just missin, right? Don't nobody know where they at, right?"

"You don't have to be no schoolteacher to see what's happenin! Them men be dead. Just as sure as we sittin here, they dead! Now you better stick round home with Miss Myrtice cause this town gonna turn upside down when they go after that woman!"

That night I turned over in my mind what Tad had said. Could Mavis have killed all them men? How could she do it? She ain't even a big woman. How could she kill even one grown man, even if he was old? And why wasn't the sheriff doin somethin bout it? Couldn't he see Mavis standin right in the middle of town leanin on that statue, like we see her every day?

I could feel pressure buildin up in my stomach, a kinda tight boilin feelin I always got when somethin big was bout to happen. So I decided I best go up to town and tell Mavis to be careful cause folks was sayin and thinkin some pretty nasty things bout her. Not cause of the way she was dressed, but cause of her bein seen ridin off with all them white men and ain't nobody seen em since.

Well, there she was standin in her usual spot with her eyes burnin holes in the courthouse. I didn't have time to mince words, so I didn't.

"Folks is talkin, Mavis. Talkin real bad bout you. Sayin crazy things like you tied up with the missin of some men round here and how you up to no good here in Brownville."

Mavis didn't say a word, just kept on lookin.

"This town'll surprise you. You might be thinkin we ain't nothin but backwoods, country-talkin folks, but we got as much sense as anybody else walkin round on two legs. And don't too many people sit up and talk this bad bout somebody they'd never even laid eyes on a month ago without some kinda reason and some pretty strong thinkin on it. Now I don't wanna meddle in your business none, but I think you got a right to know folks is callin you a murderer."

Mavis turned them yella eyes on me for so long I thought I might start smokin and catch afire. I mean, she burned me with them eyes: "I come for what is mine, somethin that belong to me, and don't none of y'all got a right to get in my way."

I stepped back from her cause she was lookin pretty fierce with them eyes of hers alight, but I still reached out to touch her arm.

"I just hate to see bad things happen to folks is all. I don't mean no harm."

And I turned to walk away. But it felt like a steel band grabbed my arm and turned me back round to look at them yella eyes: "Now you listen, listen real good cause I want all of y'all to know why I was here after I'm gone and I'm not leavin till my work is done.

"Way back when, I lived on what was called Old Robinson Road. Wasn't much to look at, but we had us a little place, a little land, some chickens and hogs. We growed most of our own food right there on our land and didn't hafta go off sellin ourselves to nobody. Not nobody, you hear me? We was free people: livin our lives, not botherin nobody, not messin in nobody's business, didn't even leave the place to go to church. We just lived on our land and was happy.

"Now some folks right here in this town got the notion in they heads that colored folk don't need to be livin on they own land, specially if it was land any white man wanted.

"Old Andy Crowell, who looks like the devil musta spit him out, got it in his head he was gonna take our land. Well, I don't know if they still makin men like they made mine, but my man knew and I knew wasn't nobody gonna get this land, not while we was standin and drawin breath.

"So we took to sleepin with a shotgun next to the bed and one by the front door, and my man even carried a little gun in his belt when he was out in the fields. I kept one strapped to my leg up under my dress.

"We went into the courthouse right here, and tried to find out bout the law, cause we knew had to be a law to protect us, one for the protection of colored folks seein as how slavery had been over and wasn't no more slaves we knew bout.

"We went up to that buildin and s'plained to a man what call hisself a clerk that we had a paper tellin us to clear off our land. My man had the deed to that land cause he got it from his daddy who got it some kinda way durin slavery time, and nobody bothered him bout it cause he didn't let nobody know he had it.

"But it was his and we had the paper to show it, and that ratfaced gopher callin hisself a clerk looked at the deed to our land—our land I'm tellin you—and that clerk took the deed to our land and crumbled it up and threw it on the floor and told us to get outta his office.

"My man was just lookin right in that clerk's face. Wasn't flinchin. Wasn't blinkin. Just lookin. But his eyes, oh his eyes was tellin that man a story, a story that old fool didn't even know he knew. And my man told that clerk all about it, and I picked up the deed to our land and we left.

"Well, it wasn't long after we'd gone to the courthouse fore they come for him.

"You know how they do.

"Sit up and drink a buncha liquor to give em guts they don't have, then they posse up and come ridin for you soon as the sun go down.

"You know who it is when you hear all them horses on the road. Then you look through the window and see them little flickers of light comin closer and closer, growin bigger and bigger till it looks like the sun's come gallopin down the road. Then they all in your yard holdin up they torches till the yard's lit up like daylight, but you know it's the devil's own night. You can smell him out in the yard all tangled up with flint and sweat and liquor. I know the stink of evil anywhere. Then my man picks up his gun and steps out into that red night and tells em to get off his land or he'll shoot. I could see the claws of the devil pullin on my man and I tried to pull him back to the house, but he pushed me back inside and his eyes told me how he loved me like he did his own life. Then the devil's fingers snatched him and his tongue wrapped round my man's arms and drug him out into the middle of satan's circle, where they all had white handkerchiefs knotted round they faces from they red eyes to they pointed chins. Then they knocked my man down with his own shotgun and they kicked him, each one takin a turn. I picked up the shotgun standin near our bed and ran out the house screamin and fired a shot. Two of em fell to the ground, but some of em grabbed me from behind and beat me in the head. By the time I opened my eyes, my man was gone. It was Edith Rattray who come round and found me layin in the yard and cleaned me up and nursed me. I musta laid in bed for over a month fore I could get up and go to town and find out what happened to my man.

"And what I found out was this: Evil can grow up outta the ground just like a tree filled with bad sap and turn every livin thing to somethin rottin in the sun like an old carcass.

Now, you tell them folks what's wonderin why I'm here and what I'm doin and what I'm up to, you tell em that I'm cleanin that tree right down to the root."

Sayin that seemed to make that cold steel band slip from my arm. Mavis turned her eyes back on the courthouse.

I sat on the porch even though it was in the middle of the noonday sun and thought about what Mavis' eyes had told me.

"I must be losin my mind," I said to the listenin trees.

How in the world could a woman tell me any kinda story with no sound comin outta her mouth? What kinda woman was she? And what kinda woman am I? And what would God say bout all of this? I went inside the house and reached for my Bible. Surely some kind of answer could be found there.

After readin a while, I still hadn't found the answer I was lookin for, so I went into the kitchen and started cookin instead.

"What's for supper, daughter?" Aunt Myrtice asked.

"Oh, I'm fixin some squash, some fried catfish, some salt pork, a pot of blackeye peas, a pan of cornbread, and some peach cobbler for dessert."

"Um um. Tad must be comin by. I know you ain't fixin all that food for just me and you."

"Yeah, Tad did say he was comin round here later this evenin. Maybe I'll take you up to prayer meetin fore he gets here."

"Umhum. Y'all gonna get me outta the way so you can sit in this house kissin while I'm gone. You oughtta be shamed of yourself, old as you is."

"I might be gettin on in years, Aunt Myrtice, but I ain't dead yet." I kept on cookin.

I decided I was gonna get Tad to help me watch and see what Mavis was up to that evenin after we dropped Aunt Myrtice off at the church.

"You want me to do what?" Tad shouted after I told him what I wanted. "I ain't goin nowhere near that woman and you ain't either. You wanna get us both killed?"

I patted his arm and talked to him soft as I could to try to calm him down. No sense in his blood goin up over this foolishness.

"Tad, I just wanta prove to you and everybody else that Mavis ain't killed nobody and she ain't done none of us no harm by standin up by that statue. She can't even talk, how she gonna kill a big, old man?"

Tad gave in even though I could see he didn't wanna. He parked the car bout a block away from the statue. We didn't worry bout whether or not Mavis could see us cause she wasn't lookin at nothin else but that tree in front of the courthouse.

"Now look at her. You know somethin wrong," Tad said.

"Don't go and start workin yourself up. We ain't gonna be here long cause it's already startin to get dark and you said she usually leaves bout this time, didn't you?"

"I don't know when she leaves, cause I ain't been round here to see it. Folks just been sayin she leaves bout this time."

"Well, we'll wait a little while and see."

Sure enough, fore too long, an old red pickup pulled up next to Mavis and she ran around the front of the truck and jumped inside.

Even from where we was parked we could hear the sound she made when she got in the car. It wasn't no laugh, like Tad said, it was more like a high-pitched cryin sound mixed up with a whoop and a holler. It made the hair on the back of my neck stand straight up, and Tad said it made his flesh crawl.

Anyway, the truck pulled off and we followed a ways behind it. Couldn't see who was drivin on accounta that big old rebel flag hangin up in the back window.

We followed em anyway: out past the old poorhouse, past the pea and okra shed, past the old Lee plantation, out past Old Robinson Road.

Tad started gettin mad again cause he wanted to turn round and go back home. "You know we goin too far from home. Ain't no tellin where that crazy woman goin."

"Hush, and keep drivin. We gonna prove somethin once and for all tonight. Put a end to all this talk bout murder."

So we kept on drivin, but it was so dark now, we couldn't really make out what we was passin.

After a while, Tad said, "I don't think we in Brownville no more. You can tell by the shape things make in the dark."

I didn't say nothin. Just kept my eyes on the truck's red lights in front of us. A few minutes later, the truck pulled off the road and went into the trees. When we reached the spot where they turned off, we couldn't see no road, no lights, no nothin. Just trees.

"Well, I guess this is far as we go. Ain't nowhere to go now but back home," Tad said. "They probably went back up in them woods to do they dirty business."

"What dirty business, Tad? What dirty business? First you callin her a murderer, now what you callin her?"

"What kinda woman drive off with men in trucks in the evenin? What you think I'm callin her?"

"Let's just walk a ways in there to see if we can hear somethin."

"I'm not walkin back up in them woods. Now you go on and walk up in there if you want to, I ain't goin nowhere but back home."

While we was fussin, a car pulled off the road next to Tad's car. A skinny-faced man leaned out the window.

"You folks havin trouble?" he asked.

"I musta made a wrong turn somewhere back down the road and we just tryin to figure out the best way to get back home," Tad replied.

"You sure musta made a wrong turn cause ain't nothin out this way but trees and swamp."

"Is that right?" Tad asked.

"Yep, that's right. That big old yella swamp is bout two miles in them trees and it ain't nowhere no human man or woman needs to go. Ain't nothin livin that went in that swamp ever come back out that way. Nothin but the shadows of death back up in there. You step through them trees and it's like you stepped down into a tunnel goin way down into the ground. Down there them old snakes hangin down from them trees like moss is yella. Mosquito bites turn a man's blood yella. Yella flies crawl on the ground where worms come up out the yella mud and twist like broken fingers from a hand. Shadows come up and wrap they arms round you, pullin you down into yella mud where sounds don't come from this world. Nothin down there but yella."

Me and Tad thanked the man and turned the car around and went back home. The skinny-faced man's words burned our ears.

"Now don't you try to get me to run round on no wild goose chase behind that woman no more. I don't care what she's up to, I don't want nothin else to do with her."

Next day first thing, I went to town to talk to Mavis. Sure enough, there she was standin next to that statue.

"I been thinkin bout what you told me bout the evil way back when, and it seems it might be better just to let things lay and forgive the ones that did it like Jesus would."

Well, what did I go and say that for? Mavis whipped her head round and shook me with them eyes.

"Who you to forgive all that blood? Who YOU? Put your head to the ground and listen. Down there's an underground river runnin straight through this town, an underground river of blood runnin straight through. Just listen."

Then her eyes let me go and she turned back round. When I turned to walk back home, I saw some old dried-up mud caked round the bottom of that red dress she was wearin, mud that was yella as mustard, but dried up like old blood.

Not long after Mavis shook me up with them yella eyes of hers, I got sick and Aunt Myrtice, poor thing, had to tend me best she could, bless her heart.

Tad came by and helped when he could, but I'm the type of person don't like folks to see me hurtin and I sure didn't want Tad to keep seein me with my teeth out and my hair all over my head, though he claims I still look good to him.

Aunt Myrtice act like she don't hear him, but I could see her eyes light up.

Once I got to feelin better and was almost back on my feet, Tad started hunchin up his eyebrows, so I knew pretty soon we was gonna go out on the porch and get to arguin bout fornicatin, which to tell the truth, I'd rather be fussin over than that foolishness bout Mavis.

But Tad told me Mavis wasn't standin up at the statue of not-George Washington no more and nobody knows where she went off to. She just disappeared easy as she come.

The sheriff never did find out bout her. It turned out all them old missin men had been tangled up with the Ku Klux years back and had spilt plenty blood in the yard of that courthouse, hangin folks from that magnolia tree.

Sometimes, now, I think bout what Mavis told me how evil grow up outta the ground and how that old underground river flows with blood, and I think about puttin my head to the ground just so's I can listen. But I just go and stand by that statue and look up at that courthouse, feelin Mavis in my eyes.

Maria Luisa Puga
Translated by Julie Albertson

YOUNG MOTHER

The birth? No, the birth went well, or, that is, it seemed to go OK. Sure I was scared since it was the first time, but I had talked to a lot of people, to my Mom, to my friends, to the nurses themselves. It was normal. You don't think you can take it. You think you're going to break. You think no one realizes what it's like, or worse, that they don't believe you. I think I spent most of my time trying to figure out a way to tell them that I really couldn't take it anymore. I wanted to be sure and convince them before I began yelling—seriously yelling, I mean—because I felt myself yelling all the time, or groaning, I'm not sure. But when someone suddenly said, you have been very brave, and I heard her—I heard her crying—it was incredible. I was scared. I thought they had brought her over from the next room. She cried as if they'd spanked her to wake her up. I couldn't fathom it. I began to cry too, because I felt so sad and alone, because I knew they weren't going to understand me. Everyone was walking around a lot and I felt them cleaning me and putting things on me, and when the nurse told me, she's fine now, calm down, it's a girl, don't cry, I didn't believe her, I didn't believe her. I thought I'd died and was dreaming—or living my afterlife. Then I don't know what happened. When I woke up they brought her to me all bundled up and clean so that she could nurse. I did what they told me to do. I felt so clumsy, and I felt her sucking on my breast. It was right. My milk let down and something down there sucked it. And I touched her, I felt her breathing, but no, I still didn't believe it. Then they would take her away and I would fall into a dark, narrow dream, as I had all those months before she was born. An enclosed space. It didn't seem that bad to me, that is, I wasn't afraid and I wasn't in any pain. It was only the fear of getting to the other side. I don't know when it started. One day I noticed it, maybe when I felt her inside me for the first time. It was really strange. Not good or bad. Strange. As if I were two people, but I didn't know the other one. And I began to spy on her. Both of us were in my body—no, I'm not talking about the baby. When I thought about the baby, it was in a different way. I talked to her a lot, all the time, I think. And Mario and I made plans for when she'd be born. But that was different. That was when I didn't have to feel the abyss, that other presence, that absence of body. I didn't have to because no one realized it. Not Mario or anyone. Because it wasn't obvious when I looked at myself in the mirror. Because the doctor said my pregnancy was going well, my health was good. And if I told him I felt strange, he would say, it's normal, it's the first time. I made myself believe him. But I dragged this body around with me with an intensifying panic. Feeling like my voice was farther and farther inside. That only I could hear it. That only by yelling really loudly could others hear it. Something in my head was being closed and becoming dark, and I had to keep on looking for the other way out, a way out, any way out. From where I was I couldn't see anything. I began to be afraid of the dark. When the streets quieted down and Mario turned off the light to go to sleep, I was terrified. And when I woke up I would fix breakfast, go shopping, get clothes ready for the baby, talk with people, all the time knowing that it wasn't right, it wasn't right, that I wasn't there but trapped in an endless abyss, that went on and on and on, until it occurred to me to try to get used to it because it seemed like people accepted me that way. Mario never stopped loving me and the doctor told me that everything was going wonderfully. Sometimes my legs would swell and I would feel nauseous and tired, things that are normal during pregnancy. I was reassured. Those were the only times when my body and I were the same. And I talked to the baby. I knew it was alive in there. I felt like I should protect it from this other one. But I'm young, I'm strong. Those aches and pains don't last. They disappeared soon and only left me with a dark taste in my mouth. I would know immediately when it was back. Detached from everything again. Lost again. I didn't realize that I was getting sad, a smile on my face would feel strange. That laugh wasn't mine. And I think I didn't realize it because I had hope. Or they had it for me, I don't know. Maybe it wasn't even hope. Every time I said I felt depressed, they told me it was normal, that all that would be over when the baby was born. That you're supposed to feel depleted of energy and who knows what else. That I shouldn't worry about it. And I began to count down the days. Living with my eyes glued to this date that was supposed to be the birth. Counting out loud. Closing my eyes every time I felt the abyss. And probably because of that I began to hide it. I faked it every time I was with someone, including myself when I looked in the mirror. It was as if I were holding my breath. Not much left now, not much left. When I get out of here, there will be people out there again. I had to believe that because I had to believe there was an end, a way out to the other side. And I was almost curious to see closely what was happening to me. This being without being. This non-being. This dark dream. Because I yearned for the other. And my impatience got in the way of my sleep. And when they took me to the hospital, I grabbed at the nurses' hands so they wouldn't leave me there, so they would make me go toward this side, whatever the price. During the birth everything was clear to me. Pain, I don't know. Pain was everything. I was supposed to be there with all those people around me, and I was trapped and alone without knowing what to do or how. And seeing the baby being born, that it was a girl just as I had wanted. Then hearing Mario say, yes, we'll call her Alina. That was the name he had picked out, but so had I, with all my hope, with all my desire to live. She would be called Alina. She would be our baby and would teach us how to live with her. Feeling her sucking and alive and knowing that I hadn't yet left the abyss, that it couldn't be, that no one understood me when I said I felt bad. Hearing the new phrase, another distant and useless phrase, another deceitful boundary: postpartum depression. They say it's normal, that it goes away in several days, as would the scream that welled up inside me, that couldn't find a way out. And my baby without knowing, trusting, alone like me, alone.

What made me jump? That. The open window in the bathroom, the bustle of the nurses in the ward, the sound of cars below, the thought of days and days and days. The sky was gray, from the window it was a lead, gray square. I didn't look down. We were alone. I jumped.

—And now?

—When the abyss shattered I felt stronger. My life is in pieces around me. Alina died. I'm broken. Now I'm going to live however I can, from wherever I can, with whatever I can.

(A note from the *London Guardian*, Dec. 28, 1977: *A young mother who suffered from postpartum depression jumped out of the fourth floor window of the training hospital in London with her three-day-old baby. The baby died; the mother, badly wounded, lived. . . .*)

CALYX Journal, Vol. 13:1, 1990/91

Rosa Margot Ochoa
translated by Bertie Acker

HAPPY MOURNING

> *Familiar death, death that is transformed into a jointed cardboard figure that moves when you pull a string.*
> *Carnival death that dances fandangos and accompanies us to weep for the bones in the cemetery, while we eat mole or drink pulque beside the tombs of our dead.*
> — Diego Rivera
> *Artes de Mexico, 21, I & II, 1958*

Their fondness for pantheons and churches, fostered by their mother, was born when they were still very little girls.

The death of the *zocoyota*, their new-born sister, started it when Ticha and Techa had just had their fifth birthday. All of it awoke a sorrow in them that caused them great satisfaction even as it drew tears from their eyes: their sister, in a white coffin, dressed like a baby angel, with a brocade tunic and cloak of silver tissue and a beaded tiara on her head, with her hands crossed on her chest and her eyes closed, as if she were asleep; Mama's cries, her face invisible under the heavy veils that almost covered her. From behind the stairway they sat spying on the adults, they watched the weeping of their relatives who, as each entered the living room, embraced Mama like a flock of black buzzards, and made the twins shiver with pleasurable terror.

The following day they went to the cemetery holding hands with their big sister, suffering and enjoying the spectacle of the burial: the little white coffin, carried on the shoulders of their brother and three of their relatives, and then disappearing under the earth, afterward all covered with white flowers.

Much to their delight, every Saturday they would go to visit her and then they would attend a mass "for the eternal repose of her soul" at the cemetery church. From that time on Mama always wore black, and she never ceased mourning for the little baby daughter she had lost.

They were fourteen when their sister died of appendicitis because she took the saying literally—"Don't worry about a stomachache." This time the coffin was big and they stood beside their mother, crying aloud as they received hugs of condolence, and the masses multiplied for the souls of their "dearly departed."

By the time their brother died, after stepping on the soap in the bathtub and cracking his head open on the faucet, they were already experts. They carried a special suitcase with all the necessary utensils: scissors to cut flower stems, poison for the red ants, a little brush to clean the headstones, a trowel to turn over the soil, and a watering can to fill the two vases that flanked the tomb (after using a rag to soak up the dirty water from the week before), and of course their old cloth gloves.

They kept up with who had died. They bought the *San Cristobal Daily News*, and after reading the obituaries, they were the first to arrive at the wakes and the last to leave the cemetery.

Every first of November, All Saints' Day, they would go to the cemetery: Mama with a veil covering her anguished face, surrounded by relatives and close friends, like thick shadows obscuring the brightness of the morning. Ticha and Techa followed her, and last, grumbling as usual, Papa would come, followed by their brother, carrying the baskets containing the baked *cochito* and the *hoyuelas* that they would offer with honey and the inevitable *taxcalate* to regale their guests on those *días de pantéon*.

"How do you want the crying: plain, medium, or very good?" was the question put by the head of the hired mourners, the *planideras*. And Mama, as always, would reply:

"Very good, but they must scream and faint, do you hear? I hope you've brought the rue and the alcohol to 'bring them to.' Last year you forgot, and they almost never called out the names of my deceased, and remember you must repeat them often."

"Don't worry, ma'am, we'll do just as you say." And the laments would begin, accompanied later by the funeral music of the Chamula Indian band and by the prayers and responses called out by the priest, in spite of the fact that, because of this display, year after year, the rest of the town would accuse them before the Archbishop of monopolizing the religious services.

They were also perfectly organized at all the masses. Ticha, kneeling on the black prayer stools placed in the center of the nave, would dry Mama's tears, while they received condolences for "such an irreparable loss." Techa would station herself strategically at the exit, so no one could escape her.

"Pichi, we hope you will be with us for the *novenario*."

"Oh, too bad, dear, but since I work, I won't have time to come! A shame it's at nine in the morning."

"Don't worry. There'll be another one at eight in the evening, so you really must come." And poor Pichi scurried off, feeling trapped.

"*Doña* Zoila, we're expecting you at the *novenarios*. Services at nine in the morning and eight in the evening."

"Yes, yes, naturally," answered the latter happily, savoring beforehand the wonderful gossip she was going to collect to take to her friends and family who lived in Tuxtla. "And are you going to have the open coffin displayed?"

"Of course, and with three priests! The Archbishop will be there! And we'll have the Mothers of the Cross chorus. They'll be singing a new Requiem Mass."

"Thank you, Honey. I wouldn't miss it."

"*Don* Elpidio. You know now that we expect you at the *novenario*."

"I'm very sorry, Techita, but I'm spending all of May in Mexico City. Unfortunately I won't be back until June first."

"Well, what luck! That's when the Gregorian masses begin."

And while *Doña* Zoila went away delighted, and *Don* Elpidio walked off crestfallen, feeling that somehow they had trapped him, Techa merrily spread her nets to catch another victim.

They put their brother in a big grey coffin, and since they had attended the funeral of everyone who had died for years past, the whole town filed on to say a last farewell to him. Ticha and Techa took turns opening the coffin so everyone could see that "he seemed to be sleeping, with that peaceful expression on his face," while they swooned and were consoled and attended by the guests who were there mainly to eat.

After the burial, Papa disappeared, and they never saw him again, which was a new reason to console the perennial anguish of their mother.

Ticha and Techa never got married because "it would be a sin to abandon Mama in her grief," and so, when their youth was long past, Mama went to join her dearly departed. In order to make do with the tiny inheritance from Mama, they had to go live in the capital in a small house their brother had left them.

They were enormously disconcerted. In the cemetery there were no beloved family members for whom they could lift their prayers, no tombstones to care for. They had left them all behind in San Cristobal.

"Now what are we going to do?" asked Ticha.

"Don't worry, I'll work it out," answered Techa, the more dominant of the two.

And in fact, a week had not gone by when she could give rending screams as she received condolences, at the wake for her twin sister. Ticha had died after drinking ant poison, accidentally mixed into the milk she needed for her insomnia.

CALYX Journal, Vol. 13:2, 1991

Aiyana Trotter

WE HAVE ALWAYS STASHED
OUR BONES IN THE CLOSET

for Linda Christensen

After Grandmother's funeral, the relatives ate dinner at our house. They told Mother that her roast beef was just wonderful. She nodded, and cleared the table. Mashed potatoes and peas became victims of the garbage disposal, but the bones were saved. She washed them with the china, wrapped them in a linen napkin, and laid them to rest in a shoe box. When the relatives were gone, she unlocked the hall closet and hid the box behind the old phone books.

Mother cooked a twelve-pound turkey after the car accident. Father was okay. The car got some bruises. The guy on the motorcycle can't use his legs anymore. But it wasn't really Father's fault. The road was icy. Mother cooked turkey because Father likes to make sandwiches with the leftovers. The flesh was cut off and stored in Tupperware. When the bird made it to the closet, all the bones were intact, except for the wishbone. We closed our eyes and pulled. My brother got the long piece.

I think Brother's wish came true. A few months later the neighbor girl was pregnant. You can't really blame him, though. They were drunk. Father paid for her abortion. Mother made barbecue. More bones for the closet.

When I was old enough, Mother taught me the secrets of cooking. Father said that I could cook better than she. I baked snapper and black cod to complement his alcohol. We accumulated so many bones we had to move to a house with better closet space.

Mother had a fibroid tumor. Before the hysterectomy, I made a special dinner. Seven pheasants for good luck. Mother said that I was too superstitious, but father said the pheasants were perfect, and she shouldn't complain. He ate four of them and drank all the wine. Brother didn't get any though, because he was at a basketball game. Usually, I put the bones in the dishwasher, but for Mother I scrubbed, scraped, and disinfected them by hand. I scented the bones with her perfume and wrapped them in a box from her favorite department store.

As I turned the key to the closet, the door opened, but from the inside. The skeleton took the box from my hands and shut the door. I knocked twice. The door opened again. I asked for the bones back. The skeleton shook its skull. I asked what happened to them.

"This will be a woman," he said, opening the department store box. Inside was a skeletal hand crafted with pieces of Mother-scented pheasant bones. Already he was reproducing.

Mother and Father were against having skeletons in the closet. They installed a dead bolt on the door. They looked in the Yellow Pages under Pest Control—ants, cockroaches, wasps, termites, ticks, moles, skunks, opossums, silverfish, birds, and bats, but no skeletons. Mother and Father considered giving him and his bride-to-be a thirty-day notice. I reminded them that the skeletons had all our bones and were capable of blackmailing us. That was the first time I heard Mother swear. Father made another drink.

The Ms. skeleton was created with six months of meals. Mother wanted us to become vegetarians, but Father said he'd rather starve than eat tofu. Mother told him that he could wash the bones and take them to the closet himself. Whenever she made deliveries, the skeletons would try to have conversations with her. They wanted to discuss their bones. Mother would fire at them with wings and thighs, yelling at them to shut up and leave us alone. After kicking the door shut, she would continue to kick on it, chipping off the white paint. Mother was having nightmares about skeletons coming out during parties and dancing with the guests, nightmares about baby skeletons growing in the hamburger.

I thought it would be a healthy thing to do—talking to the school counselor. She said that if Americans didn't have closets, we wouldn't lose our kids to drugs. I told her I didn't have a drug problem. She said that if I have skeletons I must have some kind of problem. She recommended that we display our bones in the china cabinet, like her family does.

Father yelled at me, saying respectable people didn't talk about their closets. Mother was sure that the school counselor would gossip about our skeleton problem in the teachers' lounge. You couldn't trust a woman who flaunts her bones. Brother heard that in Hollywood, skeletons are sold for thousands of dollars on the black market. All the stars want a bronzed skeleton to pose by the coat rack. Father said that backwoods hicks never had closets. They stored their bones under the bed. If a skeleton occurred, the hicks slept on the floor and gave their bed to the skeleton. But Mother said that only the stupid and the rich could get away with such things.

For the price of a stamp, I got advice from an archaeologist. She had dedicated her life to digging out bones from the closets of America. I read Abby's column for one month and twenty-six days before I saw it.

"Confidential to D.W. in Boston: The best thing to do with skeletons in the closet is to invite them for dinner."

I showed the article to my parents. We made the dinner invitation for 7:30. We slid the envelope under the unlocked door. I helped Mother with the shrimp-parmesan fettucini. Father selected the best wine. Brother called his date and told her he wasn't coming over for dinner because his parents sucked.

We didn't speak at all, except when we offered the skeletons food, but they weren't hungry. We listened to them talk, sing, lecture, and recite poetry, describing the bones of their body. Mother cried, remembering those old meals, like the seven pheasants. Father and Brother kept shoveling in the fettucini. Father finished the wine. I couldn't eat anything. I was more interested in all the meals I had missed out on.

There was actually a meal cooked by Father. Before I was born, Mother had a miscarriage. Father made her a pot roast that was too chewy to eat. I thought he couldn't make anything besides screwdrivers.

All the ribs of the male skeleton were meals devoured privately by Mother when Father was spending late nights at the office. She thought he was having an affair. I wondered why she had gained weight.

Ms. skeleton was covered with Kentucky Fried Chicken bones that were meals eaten on the way to marriage counseling sessions. I thought they went bowling Wednesday nights.

When we ate roast beef after Grandmother's funeral, I remember thinking the meat was unusually juicy and bloody, the bones were thick with marrow. Everyone kept wiping their mouths. No one mentioned Grandmother. I hadn't known she was sick until the day she died. For years she had syphilis, but no one ever told me, not until the skeletons came to dinner.

The skeletons had nothing more to say. I saw how their bones glowed, so polished they seemed wet. Brother had his eyes shut, pretending to be asleep. Father stared at his plate. Mother went to the counter to get the bundt cake. The skeletons said that the dinner was lovely but they had to go. Father told me to escort them back to the closet. The skeletons said they wouldn't be going back. The bundt cake fell out of Mother's hands. They told us that their duty as skeletons was over.

"Don't forget us, or we will come back," was the last thing they said before they flipped on the switch, climbed into the sink, and exited through the garbage disposal.

CALYX Journal, Vol. 13:2, 1991

WALKING AWAY

We were sitting at the kitchen table eating spaghetti, when I dropped the bomb on him. Jerry and I have all our fights in the kitchen. My sister Stephanie says I'm probably extra vulnerable there because I never really learned how to cook. Steffie can't get over the night she was here and Jerry came home yelling, "What's for dinner?" and I rolled a head of lettuce at him down the hall.

Since I got my job, Stephanie hangs around a lot, just to see what I'm gonna do next. Nobody can believe how I'm turning out, not even me. I don't know which one is the real me—the good girl I've been for the last thirty-four years or the loudmouthed broad I've become this last six months.

"It's like goddamned Jekyll and Hyde, Buster," Jerry told Daddy.

Anyway, last night it was about the cheesebread. Jerry hates cheese. It's not like I put cheese on *his*—I was making plain garlic bread for him, but I put mine in the microwave at the same time, which is against the rules, and he said he could smell the cheese on his.

"Garlic bread is so *simple*, Faye. I don't see how even *you* can get it wrong. Goddamned cheese smells like a locker room."

I don't really know why I did it then—for fifteen years, I've just gone behind my wall when he digs at me. I could have just pretended to smile and maybe gotten out the Scrabble game after dinner, which I would have lost as usual, and then Jerry would have been back in a good mood. But for some reason last night I'd just had it, and I didn't want to carry the cheesebread around inside me like I did the lukewarm potatoes for three days last week. So I looked right at him and said, "Listen, Jerry—do you think we're gonna make it, or what."

So then he laughs and says, "Don't worry, Faye. Just because I gripe once in a while doesn't mean I'm gonna divorce you."

I never get mad like Jerry and Daddy. I know what it feels like to have somebody mad at you, and I wouldn't ever do that to anyone. Besides which, I'd probably get killed if I did. Watching what happened to my sister when she talked back to Daddy saved me from ever getting hit. Daddy doesn't give you but one warning, not even his customers. What he does if he's plastered somebody's ceiling with acoustical spray and they don't pay up after his one warning is he goes over with his hose and shoots the rest of their house. When we were kids and Stephanie wouldn't make up her bed, Daddy just up and sold it. We came home from school one day and it was gone, and she had to sleep on the floor until she was old enough to leave home.

So I know how to keep quiet. Make it smooth. Fix it up. But honest to God, when Jerry laughed at me like that, I could have spit. I mean, the nerve—him sitting there eating his spaghetti thinking I was worried *he* might divorce *me*.

So I dropped the bomb right on him. I said, "No—I'm talking about the other way around."

He actually put his fork down. For about thirty seconds, he didn't know what to say, and I could breathe. I sat right there at the table looking at him looking at me and I could actually breathe.

Then he whammied me. "Faye, you couldn't any more make it in the real world on your own than you could fly. You're so goddamned scared you can't even drive a goddamned car. You're just like your mother. You're a carbon *copy* of Enola. Goddamned white-knuckle special."

"I got a job." It was all I could get out before my chest collapsed and I couldn't breathe again.

Jerry always gets to me, probably because I'm so scared he's right. It takes Mom two whole weeks to work herself up to being able to go out of the house to dinner, for instance. I could go that way real easy. You just close the curtains and go inside of the TV. It's gotten a lot easier to do since VCRs came out—now you can pick a real nice place, like the Ponderosa, and go there over and over again. On the Ponderosa, no one drives a car and all the men are reliable and Hop Sing does all the cooking. It's pretty appealing.

I've got every Bonanza show, except one, made between 1965 and 1967— that's when Pernell Roberts left the show, and after that they were no good. It took me three years to get them off the re-runs. That's what I mean when I say I could turn out like Mom real easy. The only one I'm missing is "Woman of Fire," the one where Joan Hackett pushes Adam Cartwright into the lake.

Sometimes I have to push myself a little to get out the door in the mornings. When you have a job, you can't just sit in the corner all day long and press your back up against the solid, familiar walls.

"I know it's not much of a job," I started to explain to Jerry, but he wouldn't cut me any slack.

"Working in a fucking dime store, letting them screw you for five dollars an hour. You couldn't even pay *rent* with five dollars an hour."

Once he starts talking, I start spinning. Jerry is real good with words, real smart. When we play Trivial Pursuit on Christmas over at Stephanie and Dane's house, Jerry always wins. Me, I think the only reason they let me pass in school was they were afraid what Daddy might do if they didn't.

I know I'm dumb. Poor little dumb Faye who didn't even know what a calculator was when she started work, and did the arithmetic test with a ball point pen in the palm of her hand. But I'll tell you something—I'm not dumb enough to believe brains are everything.

That's what I told Mr. B. down at the store last week when he made the new girl cry. She's pregnant and a little touchy, and she can't take it like the other girls right now, so when the old man started yelling at her, she went in the bathroom and cried and said she wasn't coming out until he went home, and then she was gonna quit and never come back to that hellhole. "It's like a concentration camp," she said.

Which was ironic, because Mr. B. has numbers stamped on his arm from the Nazis in the war. I thought to myself, I don't care what Mr. B. went through, it's not right for him to take it out on her. I can see how that could happen to a person, but it's no excuse.

So I went and got him in the office and told him so.

"Harry," I said—I forgot to call him Mr. B., he looked so pitiful, sitting there with his tape measure around his neck, all dried up like an old fig. "You made that girl cry. She's in there in the bathroom crying right now."

"She cuts paper with the fabric scissors," he yelled. "A whole quarter of a yard over, besides. Her register doesn't balance. With help like that, I don't need competition. A smart businessman can't let this happen."

"Harry," I said, "You're the smartest businessman I know. You don't need to be any smarter." That softened him up. "But there's one thing you do need, Harry. You need to go to the Wizard of Oz and get a heart," I said. "Brains aren't everything."

The new girl didn't believe I'd really said that to him, until he apologized to her. Nobody believes what comes out of my mouth since I started working. It blows them away, because I'm so short and I only weigh ninety pounds and I wear Mary Jane shoes. I don't look like the type who would say "Fuck off and die" to a customer, even if she was being a bitch, which I did last week. My sister Steffie says, "By God, you've got the Sorensen mouth after all."

Before I got this job, I never used to say anything to anybody. I just stayed home watching my Bonanza tapes and shopping at yard sales and taking care of my turtle. That's why Mr. B. hired me, I think. He thought I was gonna be a good girl and work like a dog and never raise a stink. And I probably would, if I was the only one there. It's just that I can't stand to see the way they treat the girls who've been there for twenty years and never had a kind word, or a coffee break even. When I made Harry give everybody a lunch hour and a twenty-cent raise, they started calling me Norma Faye.

Last night after Jerry whammied me, I was lying in bed, looking out the window for the Big Dipper. I like to lie there and imagine who the other people are who might be lying in bed looking at the Big Dipper at exactly the same moment I am. When Jerry came in, he said, "God damn it, Faye, my side of the bed's all hot. You've got your arm over on my side."

I'm not going to go into why we don't have sex anymore. It's so complicated, and anyhow, nobody would believe it. It's not all Jerry's fault, I'll say that. He doesn't drink or take drugs or beat me up. If I hadn't been so scared from hearing Daddy rape Mama on the living room floor all the time, it might have been different. I'm not sure. I know I'm fucked up from that. Stephanie used to hold me and sing to me and put her fingers in my ears so I wouldn't hear, but I heard anyway. He'd be drunk and yelling "Goddamn it, Enola, your crazy fear spoils everything." He put his fist through the wall one night, right into my bedroom, and then his Popeye face was in the hole asking "You okay, Baby?" and then he took me out and bought me ice cream and a pair of glitter high heels. It's not all Daddy's fault either.

Stephanie says it doesn't have to hurt. She says she and Dane do it for hours, but I don't believe that. I don't see how a person could stand actually doing it for longer than two or three minutes. Probably Dane kisses her a lot first, or holds her afterwards, like they do in the movies, and that's what she means takes hours. I used to think if Jerry would hold me when he got done I wouldn't mind it so much.

Anyhow, I'm lying there last night trying to get to sleep, and Jerry starts moving his furniture out into the spare room. The nightstand with his portable TV, the dresser, the box with his marble collection, everything.

I said, "Oh for God's sake, Jerry, it's eleven o'clock at night."

But he had to make his point. Finally, after he scraped and banged it all down the hall, I got to go to sleep. Funny, how after a scene like that, I could drift off so easy. Usually when he's mad at me, I end up going into the bathroom and turning on the water so I can cry. But last night, I turned over and went to sleep on my right side for the first time in fifteen years. It felt good.

And then, just when I had gotten to the Ponderosa and Hop Sing was fixing dinner and I was climbing a split-rail fence so's I could see Adam Cartwright riding up on his big black horse, there was a bunch of scraping and banging, and here came the damn furniture back into the room again.

Jerry was crying, but it didn't move me one bit. Sometimes I think I *am* like Mama. I mean, a person ought to feel sorry when another person is crying like that. But last night, I just turned over on my left side and went back to sleep, thinking about how tomorrow was gonna be the twenty-fifth anniversary of the first Bonanza show. The best thing that ever happened to me was when I was eight years old and Daddy took me to the Rose Parade, and the Cartwrights rode by me and I heard Pernell Roberts tell Dan Blocker to wave his hat so the crowd would know who they were, and I said, "I know who you are," and he looked right at me and said, "Thank you, little lady."

So today at work, I'm sitting out by the hedge in the parking lot, eating my apple and thinking about how I ought to straighten out the glitter pom-poms and how I must be just as dumb as Daddy and Jerry always say I am. I mean, here I am a thirty-four-year-old virgin, practically, sitting on the goddamned curb, wearing knee-socks and wondering if there's any more to it than this. And if so, when does it start? "If there's anybody listening," I say, "I'd like to know when it is supposed to start." I look up at the sky, but all I can see is San Fernando Valley smog.

So I go back and it's Craft Sale Day, and there's forty-two thousand spoiled women pawing through the bargain tables, hubba-bubba, hubba-bubba, and the lines are a mile long and I see if somebody doesn't do something, it's gonna get ugly. So I get on the intercom and I say, "Hey—who knows what happened on television twenty-five years ago today? The first one to get the right answer gets a free glitter pom-pom."

So that gets them all going, and pretty soon they're all talking and laughing, except this one big guy in the back, who's waiting to buy a roll of Scotch tape, and Mr. B., who descends from the office in a fury because I'm gonna give away a goddamn thirty-five-cent pom-pom. "Whatchoo doing to me," he yells. "Already everything is thirty percent off, and you got to give it away altogether?"

"Breathe through your nose, Harry. We think it's very generous of you to have this sale, don't we ladies?" I reach over and straighten up his bow tie and put my arm around him. "And you can charge the pom-pom to my account, just as soon as you pay me for the twelve hours of overtime I worked last week."

So then we're all laughing, even Harry, who pinches my cheeks and says, "Such a *little* thing, with such a mouth on her." Good, I figure, this is good. The ladies are all talking to each other, trying to figure out what happened twenty-five years ago, and everybody's happy. All except the guy in the back who keeps complaining about how all he came in for was a roll of Scotch tape, not a sideshow, and I'm calculating we've got to listen to another ten minutes of him before he gets up to the register and everybody's gonna be all tense again. He's about six-four, but I don't care anymore, so I yell "Hey you. Yes, *you*." And I stab at him with my finger and motion him up to the front and tell him I'm gonna get him out of my line right now because he's impatient and rude and making a tough situation worse and give me the goddamn Scotch tape, that'll be one-fifty-nine, now you go on home and think about what really counts in life before you come back in my line.

So everybody cheers and applauds, and this one lady who's wearing this really elegant grey suit and diamond stud earrings says to me, "How do you *do* it?"

"I'm on drugs," I say.

"Honey," she says, laughing, while I'm checking her out, "you don't belong in a place like this. Somebody ought to *know* about you." She hands me her business card and I look at her and her beautiful diamond earrings and I'm thinking oh, this is a real *woman*, and she *likes* me, and I had to look away so I wouldn't start crying right there in front of everybody.

So tonight I get home from work, and it's Friday night and we're supposed to go pick up Mama and Daddy for dinner at the Cave. She's got her hair washed and everything.

"Come on, Faye," Jerry says. "Feed the goddamned turtle later."

Right away, Jerry gets in the left lane behind this lady who's going kind of slow, looking at street signs. He gets about two feet from her bumper and stands on the horn. "*Women*," he says. "Jesus fucking Christ."

I am always ending up stuck in the passenger's seat in some man's car listening to shit like that.

So we go get Daddy, and I get in the back seat with Mama, and Daddy shoves a sack of donuts at me. "Here, Baby. Jelly-filled. Your favorites."

Daddy's worried because I don't eat much.

"You oughta give that girl a baby," he says to Jerry. "Woman's gotta have something to keep her occupied."

"She doesn't need me, Buster. She's getting screwed at work."

Oh, good. That's all I need is for Jerry to get Daddy going on top of everything else. "Thirty-four years old, and she's working for goddamned minimum wage." Daddy starts shifting around in his seat, like his underwear is too tight and his mouth starts working and the little blood vessels in his cheeks turn bright red and I know we're in for it now. "I told her not to work for a fucking Jew. Fucking Jew's so tight if you shoved a hair up his ass it'd dislocate both hips."

Oh great. This is just great. We're pulling into the parking lot at the Cave in goddamned Southgate, the taco capital of Southern California, and Jerry's got Daddy going about the Jews. It's only a matter of time before he starts in on the Mexicans.

The Cave is always crowded on Friday. Daddy's into his second double margarita before we get to order.

"I don't know what I ought to have," Mama says. "I just don't know. That green sauce last week just wasn't as good as that red sauce. But it might have been an off night. Maybe I should try that green sauce again. I just don't know."

"For crying out loud, Enola," Daddy says, "make up your mind. And hey— you with the mustache—bring my little girl some of that Mexican candy. Bring her a couple of enchiladas. You can't make babies eating that goddamned rabbit food she likes. Bring her a goddamned fried ice cream ball. Bring her something that'll put a real ass on her, like that one," he says, pointing at the waitress.

Oh God. Here we go.

Usually I fix it up, smooth it over, make a joke, get Daddy talking about something else. It's like living with the threat of nuclear war—you manage. I just sat there, letting the fried ice cream ball turn into a puddle on my plate, watching Daddy's nose turn purple, watching Mama pick her fingernails and smoke her Dorals.

"It might start raining," she says. "The weatherman said it might rain tonight. You kids had better be driving on the freeway if it starts to rain. Faye, you let Jerry drive if it rains."

So we drop them off and we're driving home up the San Diego freeway, and some guy in a Toyota pickup cuts in front of Jerry and Jerry gets ticked off and decides to get even. Jerry's a little guy and wouldn't dare take anybody on out in the open, but when he's in his car, he goes nuts. So he passes the guy and cuts in front of him by about six inches and slows down to about forty-five.

"Jerry, for God's sake, don't."

"Fucking jerk, thinks he's gonna fuck me around."

So then the guy gets over on our right side and tries to ram us. Oh shit. I've finally got myself caught between two crazy men and they're both going about seventy-five and all of a sudden there's a big truck on the left, blowing his horn and somebody's gonna die and it might be me. The Toyota man is about a foot away from me, and he's rolling down his window and yelling "Pull over, you sonofabitch, pull over," and Jerry shoots him the finger and now I know we're gonna die, so I roll down my window and yell at the man, "I'm sorry. I'm *sorry*. It's not me, it's *him*." And all of a sudden, the guy backs off and drops behind us. Jerry just drives along, pretending nothing happened. I look behind us, and the guy points to me and I can tell he's asking me, "Are you okay," like what do I want him to do about this maniac in the car with me, and I nod and say "I'm okay," and Jerry takes the Balboa exit and as soon as my heart stops flooding in my chest, I reach over and turn off the key.

"Let me out of this goddamned car, Jerry. Stop this goddamned car right now. I am not getting killed with you. This is where it stops."

I get out and slam the door and start walking.

"Come on, Faye, get back in the car. Don't make such a big fucking deal out of everything."

I just keep on walking.

I'm thinking maybe I'll go buy myself a car. I'm looking for a bus stop and feeling the elegant lady's business card in my pocket. Jerry's driving alongside me, leaning out the window yelling at me, and I just turn the corner and keep right on walking and leave him stuck there at the red light, yelling.

"Where do you think you're going, huh? Just answer me that, Faye. Where in goddamned hell do you think you're going?"

CALYX Journal, Vol. 13:3, 1991/92

Beth Bosworth

SHEETS

In a hotel room near Paris my mother lifts from her suit-case a story of mine about a father and a daughter.

I want to know, she says, if this is true.

Mom, I say. It's a story.

I have a right to know, she says.

In the story the father has bright blue eyes like my own father and the daughter also has blue eyes and my sallow skin and some of my own questions about the world, about the unknown country through which the two, father and daughter, are traveling. They travel to Mexico City and home again and the pattern of their trip is determined by his desire for her, a zig-zag of rooms and beds. First there is her disheveled room in New Jersey where he asks her to journey with him, his palm spread between her warm shoulders; then the cool beds in the motel room where he tells her that she looks like her mother and that this stirs him; then the big white room in Mexico City where he says that no, it is not only because she looks like her mother. Her mother, for instance, has big dark nipples. He asks her to lift her shirt then and he points out, gravely, that she does not, that her own are rosy and smaller.

Will they change later, he wants to know? He speaks with the same search for honesty, the same grave voice with which years later (but before my mother lifts the story from her suitcase) my own corporeal parents will announce their separation from twenty-seven years of each other.

You look just like your mother from behind, he says in the story. And I miss her so much. That night or another night he says, I'm so cold. Could you come in my bed and warm me up? And that same night or another night in Mexico City he slides his fingers into her underpants and, sucking in his breath, up into the warm lips so that for many years she dreams about intercourse with a fat man whose penis is deliciously swiveled. In the story she remembers kicking him away. She remembers this while she is folding her clothes into her suitcase. They have been traveling for many days now and her mother's neat piles of shirts and shorts and underclothes have come tumbling down. It is not clear to her when this happened, when they all began to drift. She pats at a sprawl of socks and, standing, says, Daddy, that wasn't very nice, what you did last night.

You didn't seem to mind.

I pushed you away.

You pushed me the first time. You didn't push me away the second time.

I was asleep.

Children often pretend to be asleep when they don't want to accept responsibility for something they do.

The daughter frowns and walks into the other room where his parents are waiting. In the story his parents are playing chess and they lift their old heads and smile above the glinting chess pieces, rook, pawn, king, and queen. In the story I linger too long on the old, reptilian features of the grandmother, and, later, on the great love with which the grandfather lifts his grey head and shouts, Esther, you see, she beats me at chess! The child beats me! He lifts his palm to the white, white ceiling in wonder.

This does not really belong in the story at all.

I want to know if this is true, my mother says. Her face glows pale beneath dark hair.

Mom, I say. I am twenty years old and she has flown to Paris to find me and bring me home because I have written to her that I am pregnant and that I mean to keep the baby. That is why we are together now in this hotel room, because after dinner with Pierre, after she has cried and spilled dark wine across his carpet, she has asked me for five minutes of my time. Alone. Pierre stiffens at this. He cannot understand this need of hers to pull me away from him. He says it is the way lovers behave, not parents.

In this hotel room dark metal *volets* cover the windows. When I can no longer stay there with her I twist hard on the knob and swing the *volets* open and holler down to Pierre, who is waiting, *J'arrive!* He shrugs. What is he thinking down there? I can never know. I will never, ever know what Pierre is thinking as he smokes his Gauloise and watches the smoke curl and remembers the morning that I told him that I was pregnant. I stood in his small bathtub and my face felt hot. I'm going to buy cigarettes, he said, and he walked in after a while to say that he had called his mother.

What did she say? I asked. I was dry and sitting on his bed among the rumpled sheets. He dipped his cigarette into the grey pool of the ashtray.

Maman? She wanted to know if you were upset. I told her no.

So?

So? If you're happy, she's happy. You know her. She's always happy to have another baby in the family.

What about you? I ask. Aren't you happy?

I, in life, want a daughter so badly that I spend the many months of pregnancy looking for the perfect name for a boy. I want the boy to have the Jewish names Abraham or Jacob, but Pierre laughs hard at the sound of Abraham in French. We sit on the cool sand and Pierre cups his palms and drips sand across his bare feet.

He would be ridiculed, the poor boy, he laughs. *Abrahm! Abrahm!*

He throws a burst of sand into the air.

Well, then, I say. What about Isaac?

Isaac! Isaac! Why not Moses? He twists it into the French name, *Moise*. Why not *Moise*? Ha! Ha!

That's a fine name, I say, sniffing. I draw a letter *M* in the sand.

Moise! He gurgles in the back of his throat. I hobble toward the water with the briny air and bright cold sky and I squat down, looking away from him. On this beach I am always writing this story in my head about the pregnant girl who liked, as she grew rounder, to sit near the water that was wrapped around the globe just as she was wrapped around the child who swam inside her. I rub a clear patch in the sand and I draw another *M*. Then I snake the ends of the letter around above its two peaks.

Moise! laughs Pierre from behind. He stands, pressing against my bent back with his thighs. Why not God? Why not *le bon Dieu* himself?

I have a right to know, my mother says. She holds up one palm.

Why now? I ask. Why do you want to know now?

Because. Because he was my husband for twenty-seven years.

What difference can it make now?

Her face splinters and her lips stretch out.

Some of it is true. But it isn't finished. It's a story, Mom.

What about this? she asks. She turns the page.

On the page the father and the daughter ride a bus which rocks and plummets across the continent and north, north to their home where the mother waits for them, and now as the bus rocks around a curve and its coiled springs gasp, he asks the daughter to sit on his lap.

Why? I don't want to, she says.

God, you're becoming such a bitch, he says. I don't even know if I can love you anymore.

She shrugs. A hot tear drips from her cheek to the window pane. She watches it drip and flatten and disappear where air vents stripe the cool sill. Why can't you, she wants to say. Why can't you love me? The words are like stones in her mouth. Finally she climbs onto his knees and sits, leaning into the seat ahead. He pulls her closer.

I want us to know each other better, he says. Can you feel me growing?

What?

Can you feel me growing?

No.

That part is true, I say. Well, almost.

The bastard, she says.

I tried to tell you.

You did? When did you try to tell me?

I said to you, Can't you tell your husband to keep his hands from between my legs.

You said that? Those words?

Yes. Yes.

When I said that, she was standing over the washing machine, her head bent, her hands reaching into its flecked bowl. She turned to look at me. Her eyes were flat and dark. They were not the eyes of my mother at all.

What did I say? she asks.

You said, you said, He wouldn't do it if you didn't fawn on him.

I said that?

I think to explain how a person can use words without understanding but then she says, I would have had to divorce him, and I wasn't prepared to do that yet.

She waves little fists. I want to kill him! she cries. I just want to kill him!

Behind her a dark chair hugs the wall. The bed is narrow. She has slept here one night, two nights, looking for me in Paris while Pierre and I have slept at his mother's house by the sea, walked along beaches, thought about names. In this room she has written notes to me and then walked down the broad boulevard and taped them to our door. Looking for you, been here two days, she writes. Then she returns to her hotel room and she rifles through the pages of my story and she—what does she do? She clutches the skin of her throat. She slides under the stiff grey blanket and warms her hands between her thighs. She shuts her eyes. She wonders how often they wash these bedclothes and whether or not she will catch fleas. She does not like the French with their unwashed bodies. As the days pass and I still don't come for her she begins to feel, she says, as though something is terribly wrong. Then Pierre and I drive up to his door on Sunday afternoon and he hands me the note. We walk quickly to the hotel. Pierre speaks to the dark man behind the desk. I sit on an armchair. There is sand in my shoes and one broken shell in the pocket of my full-bellied dress. I smell of the ocean. My mother spills from the elevator.

My daughter, she says, I have spent two days looking for you. I was about to call the police.

Pierre, this is my mother.

That is what I have thought, he says. When he speaks English his voice is like gravel.

Welcome to France, he says.

What do you want to do? I ask.

I finally found you, she says. I don't care what we do.

Would you like to see the *Tour Eiffel?* Pierre asks.

I don't care what we do.

We can go to Luxembourg, he says.

Fine with me, she says. So we walk along the narrow *trottoir* again to his building, and he opens the car door for her. I sit in the back.

Look, I say, when we pass through the *Porte d'Orleans*. Now we're really in Paris.

I've never found Paris to be a terribly pleasant city, she says. The French in general are not a terribly pleasant people.

Pierre, hunched over the steering wheel, snorts and whips his hair off his face and his brown eyes fill the mirror.

You do not want your daughter to marry a French man?

Are you going to marry her?

No.

Good.

Pierre decides that my mother wants to see the Eiffel Tower after all. It is very popular with tourists, he says with a laugh. So we park the car and walk past the green lawns and we go right up inside the Eiffel Tower and out into the wind. Pierre points monuments out to us: That is Montmartre, where are the artists, he says, and that is Sainte-Chapelle. The wind blows my hair into my face and across Pierre's cheek and he puts his arm around my shoulder and I smile at my mother as if she were taking our photograph.

I think you are doing something very wrong, she says. Both of you. Pierre brushes his cold lips against my cheek. We walk a few times around the steel tower but I cannot possibly, now, describe the city stretched out before us, the red mansards and stovepipe chimneys and white cathedrals. The truth is that in those months and years I only see the rooms and beds of our life and perhaps the view from each of our clouded windows—a parking lot, a goat tethered beyond it. We sleep each night naked on his mattress on the floor, in his rumpled sheets, surrounded by our lives, and behind us rises a mural of ocean and sand and blades of bright grass, a bright, bright beach. That evening my mother says to Pierre, How do you feel about this? How do you feel about having a child now?

How do I feel. Ha ha. It is all right by me.

I have some responsibility, she says. This child would be my grandchild and I have a responsibility, not just to you. Have you thought about what you would be doing to this child?

Will be, I say. Will be your grandchild. She knocks her wine glass over. He leaps to sponge up the spreading red stain. She watches him and she begins to weep. Now she is weeping still through the dim panicked air.

I want to know whether or not you and your father have fornicated, she says.

Mom! No!

Do you promise me?

Of course, I say. God. Then I smile as if she will understand that the verb, fornicate, is a good joke.

Don't you see? You're doing this to get back at me, she says. You're doing this out of anger at me.

No.

Yes, yes. Because I didn't help you, you're ruining your life.

I cross to the window and throw open the curtain and twist up the knob and push out the *volet* and call down to Pierre, *J'arrive.*

I have to go now, I say. He's waiting for me.

He can wait.

I really have to go now.

Why? she cries. Why are you doing this?

We walk home, Pierre walking silently ahead of me on the narrow *trottoir.*

What did she want? he asks.

In the morning we leaf through a book of names. We start at the beginning of the alphabet: Alain, Albert, Alfred, and we laugh at some of the names and some of the names make only Pierre laugh (Clovis) and some of the names make only me laugh (Bertrand, Nathan). We go through many letters of the alphabet and although I will never know what Pierre is thinking, so that when he leaves me in three years I am very surprised, I know nonetheless even now, today, the spry hairs which curl above his brown nipples and the tobacco smell of his skin. I also know that he is growing a beard to match my belly. By the time we have chosen the boy's name, Simon, his father Pierre wears a great dark beard like an anarchist. By this time also I make weekly, hulking visits to the public clinic where I wait with other foreigners for the nurses and the doctor to examine me. They ask me to spread my legs and the doctor, a man, slides his sheathed hand up inside me and with the other hand on my belly he pushes down until I wince. *C'est parfait*, he says. His glove, as he removes it carefully, is coated in white clouds of semen and my own viscous secretions and afterwards, walking home, I feel the warm rush of his lubricants into my underpants. All of my underpants are stained like this now. I wash them out and hang them, still yellowed, from Pierre's shower stall.

When I waddle past the hotel where my mother stayed, I think of her still in her hotel room, where I have left her. And although I have taken the story from her she is still holding it out to me. Why are you doing this? she calls.

What's that? asks Pierre.

It's a story.

Where did you get it?

She gave it to me.

What is it about?

My father.
Can I read it?
It's not finished yet.

In the story, in New Jersey again, the daughter and the father argue at the dinner table and when she heads for the stairs he kicks her hard in the back, so that she falls and scrambles to look at him. Then she walks down the stairs to the bathroom and she cuts the skin of her forehead in two places, like horns. He walks into her room when she is dabbing the trickles of blood with a tissue and his face changes when he sees her. Oh, he says. He takes a step forward.

But I plan to change all this.

When I go into labor I climb the stairs of the hospital. I climb the six long flights of stairs and then I turn around and walk down to the bottom of the stairwell and I turn around and climb again. I climb and climb. Are you sure you aren't tired? Pierre asks.

No, I say, I could not ever be tired.

When they force me to a room and into a bed, I wait until they leave and then I slide my feet to the floor and walk in slow circles around, around. When the pains grow sharp I touch the cool, white wall with one insistent fingertip. I spread my legs and step a bear dance, a kind of bear dance and I hear myself saying through gruff lips, Open, open. Later I pant and pant and the nurse says, Look at her! She is wild!

I'm wild! I cry.

I look up and yank hard on Pierre's beard.

I feel sick, he says.

The doctor tries to slide his hand inside me so I kick him in his soft stomach, hard. I have to push, I have to push, I say. He threatens to put me to sleep and only then do I let him touch me. Finally he nods and I push once; I push a second time and its big wet head pokes through *Ho la la*, croons Pierre, it pokes through. Through the membranes and blood they spy the swollen genital fold and say, It's a girl, and I say Pierre, Pierre, it's a girl, a girl—my mother will be so happy.

Her name is Sarah, I tell them. I name her Sarah after a Dylan song about a man and his wife whom he has left, and the children as he recalls them, playing on the bright beaches of their childhoods. Sarah, Sarah, he sings. Loving you is the one thing I'll never regret.

At the day care center at the end of one year, the teachers say to me: It's better now. She isn't so unhappy. At first we were going to tell you, because it was so sad to watch. But now it's all right. And this seems true to me now: that after Pierre leaves us she is very sad and then she is all right. People give her nicknames and each nickname tells a short, short story. When we are still in France, they call her *Sarouille*. By now we have all left the broad boulevard on the outskirts of Paris although in my mind my mother still waits there for my answer. She is waiting for me even when I walk into the day care center and Sarah, who sits hunched on the low bench around a tree, looks up and her face bursts into life. She ducks her head, smiling gently to herself. I push her stroller down the street in this other city where we live now. I push her the long way around the *centre-ville*, looking away from the cafe windows behind which I think that Pierre and his girlfriend sit and talk. I want them to notice us as we wheel by on our way home.

We live in a series of rooms and beds high up above this last city, Nantes; from our last, round rooms I hold her up to the window and we can see the entire Place Graslin, the Opera and the statues of the Muses on its roof and their mother, Memory. In fiction this won't do at all, I know, but in life there she actually stands, white and solemn and symbolic. And I know something more, already, about metaphor, that first, primitive definition of self. Because at first, in this round room, Sarah will only sleep in my bed. She falls asleep only if I let her shove her feet between my thighs and when she stretches out her toes, I think with despair that she is trying to climb back inside. I pull the sheet between my legs then so that her toes claw rhythmically only at the sheet, cool and bunched. And she comes to love this feel of soft cotton. She makes me tie a knot in a pillow case and she tucks this under the covers, down between her ankles. Then she reaches down and pulls it up and wets it with her lips and slides it down again. Then she names it. She names it her *doh-doh*, after the verb, *dormir*. Sometimes we lose it in a corner of the room and she cries out, *Où est mon doh-doh? Où est mon doh-doh?* Sometimes I make her let me wash it, and then she squats and wraps her hands around her knees and watches as I wring out the pillow case and drape it across the small electric heater that hisses and glows. Then she trails around the room, restless and unpleasant, until I tie the knot again and hand the doh-doh to her, almost dry.

Why are you doing this? my mother calls. She goes on calling to me even after we fly back to New York. She calls to me every time my child cries and she rattles the pages of my story. She has made it her own story, too, in some way that I try not to think about; I notice that the ink has come off on her dark fingers.

On Saturdays, now that Sarah and I live in New York, we load our cart with great black sacks of laundry and we navigate the few blocks to the laundromat. When the weather is fine, like today, I let Sarah balance on the tilted cart and she reaches over and pats our sacks. She is four now and experienced. At the laundromat we breathe in the hot air and listen to the shouts of other mothers and fathers and their children. When a machine is free, I lift Sarah and she places the quarters in the round slots. Then we walk up and down the avenue. We stop at gum ball machines or sometimes in the coffee shop for hot dogs and milk. At the laundromat again, behind the round glass, our clothes begin to slow in their whirring around and around so that Sarah sees first a red shirt that belongs to me, then the yellow, faded flowers of her pillowcase. She is old enough to let me wash it now but we are happy to see its folds crumple and stop. We like to put it in the dryer. Then we load all of our other clothes into the dryer too. We like the sound of buttons slapping on its walls. Sarah kicks her heels against her chair. She watches the other children. I watch the other women and their men and once, one Saturday, a tall man wanders in and tends to his own small load with such careless grace that every Saturday for a while I think that perhaps he will return at that same hour. When our clothes are clean and dry, we fold them together on the long wood table. We are always surprised to find which stains have been removed and which have not. There does not seem to be any logic to it. I am still trying to fold shirt sleeves the way my mother could, and Sarah is learning to fold two socks together. We fold everything. Then we stack our sacks again, carefully, the doh-doh tucked on top of them, and we walk out with our heavy cart and we go home.

At home I sit on my bed and make piles of clothes. Sarah rides by on her red truck. She has loaded the back of her truck with her belongings: a bear, a pillow, a box of raisins. She is on her way somewhere.

Hello, she says, Excuse me. How do I drive to First Street?

Turn left at the table, I say. She scoots around the corner and she looks up at me. Her eyes shine bright blue from this distance. She reaches behind her and pats her bundle.

Is that all? she asks.

No, I say. This is a one-way street. You'll have to drive around the table again. There's no parking over here anymore.

There's no more parking?

Not over here.

So she drives around the table and when she reaches the door to the hall she looks back.

You made it, I say. That's First Street.

Later I fill her drawers. Because she has missed her nap today, she lies down and smells her laundered doh-doh and watches me. If I am lucky today she will fall asleep like this, and I will sit on my bed in the other room and look through the curtains at the street below. Then, although I have always been stronger on character than on plot, I will plan for our future. I will say that in years to come I am a teacher and she is a student in the same school and when we feel like it, we eat our lunch together. My salary will permit me to buy her fresh, bright overalls and even some dresses with lace which she will only occasionally agree to wear. We will meet in the cafeteria and she will slip her hand into mine and I will bend to pull up her white socks from around her ankles and both of her socks will match. At lunch she will stare and smile at a man who resembles the man from the laundromat and he will say, What a pretty little girl you are, and she will say, I'm not allowed to talk to strangers. The man and I will laugh about that. We will also agree to meet for lunch another day and then we will marry. In the luxuriousness of our union we will shower her, Sarah, with gifts, with clean, bright clothing and toys and trips to the sea, and names. We will call her Sarah-Bearah, and Boo, and Molly or Molly-coddle, and even sometimes Louise for no reason at all, so that when she is almost a woman suddenly she will turn around at the water's edge, on this bright beach where we have taken her, and with the wind whipping her hair and her blue eyes flashing, she will say to me, her mother, who chose with such care: Why don't you ever call me by my own name? If you didn't like it, you shouldn't have picked it.

Then perhaps the telephone will ring and my mother will say, Hello daughter. You have a hard life. Are you ever sorry?

Am I ever sorry? That is not a question. Mom, what kind of question is that?

Or I will say nothing and look around this room while silence crosses the telephone wire. In this last room I have a bed and the small, round table where we eat and in the corner an old desk, like a schoolchild's desk, where I have put my typewriter and next to them the black trunk which we brought home with us from France. I remember that I have yet to revise my own story, that old one. But now I have more questions. Such as:

How can it be that this father turns so suddenly into a villain?

Would he really use words like bitch?

Wouldn't he worry, on the bus ride, about the other passengers?

And who is he? I have left out so much. I have left out the fact that he is a physicist who has always tried to teach his daughter about the world. He has struggled for many years to find a new language to describe it. Perhaps he has gotten all tangled up in language, so that when he tells his daughter that he wants to carry her to bed and rock her back and forth, gently, crooning the same song that his own mother once sang to him, when he tells his daughter that he doesn't want her to grow up unloved, it may be that he persuades himself of the truth of these words. He may even persuade himself that they will always sound true.

It may be that in the story, when the father has carried the daughter down to bed and is cradling her, crooning, his arm presses warm against the cotton of her underpants and she lets it. She even inches down so that his fingers touch more of the cotton. His breath catches in his throat and then he begins to hum again, slowly, softly. Again she inches down so that his hand lies, each warm finger spread flat against the cotton, pulsing. Then her mother walks into the alcove with a pile of folded linens, and he jerks his arm away and he stands up and bends down and kissing her gently whispers, You're very brave. But she has understood this sequence of events: the mother's appearance, the father's withdrawal. Because she has understood this and because some stories seem to have inevitable and natural resolutions, she glances up and she whispers, Never again. She whispers: Never again.

In life, when I leave my mother in the hotel room, she sits on the edge of her bed and she weeps. Then after she has wept she begins to pack for her return trip to New York. She folds her clothing very carefully and she talks to herself. A fine business, she says, You ought to be ashamed. She lets her voice trail on like a broom, sweeping: a brave one, you are, she says. That is enough. You should be ashamed, a grown woman. Then she goes downstairs to pay her bill. After that she goes upstairs to her room and she lies down until morning.

When she gets home she unpacks her suitcase. She empties a bag of dirtied clothing into her hamper and she puts her hand beneath each clean, folded blouse and slides it into a white drawer. She wipes her palms. She examines her cuticles. She walks through this cool, white apartment. She turns on and off the television set. She opens the refrigerator door. She sees one can of grapefruit juice and a wrapped cheese. This is the first time that she has left and come back to this new apartment, and the return makes it seem for the first time like home.

So it is only in my own fiction that I have left her in her hotel room, waiting for me. She has cleaned the old house after the years of marriage and she has found the story where I left it for her to find, and now she has so many questions. And these years later I have come back, after all. I have come back to answer her although no word or words will quite suffice.

I want to tell you something, I say.

She is older now. Her face is fuller and her jowls hang loose. Her lips turn down at the corners. Over the years I know that she has taken my story and given it to her friends, out of her own mouth, in restaurants, with tears and vocabulary. Every now and then she calls my father on the telephone and he cries, I'm sorry. I'm sorry. How could I? Was I such a bad man?

Today, in the hotel room, the *volets* are thrown back and we can hear the sounds of a woman who squats on the stairs, scrubbing. She grunts and her big brush hisses. We step into a shaft of light. In those months of pregnancy, I remember now, the sun barely shone at all; I remember also that when spring finally arrived in Paris the rains went on, and the new leaves on the trees sagged wet and sad, everything was grey or dull-colored like wet earth. My mother's face quivers in the dim room. What should she do? What has she done? Her marriage has not been what it seemed and her divorce must now be bitter and total. She is relieved at least to find that my belly is almost flat. There is still time to change this, she thinks. At least this. She tilts her palms to the low ceiling. But why? she asks. I reach to take the story from her hands which are thin and veined. I kiss her cheek, wet and too soft like the pulp of fruit, and I touch the edges of the papers, lightly, to her still-black hair.

But why did you do it? she asks.

Oh Mom, I say, because now it's done.

Alicia Ostriker

ESTHER, OR THE WORLD
TURNED UPSIDE DOWN

*And the letters were sent by posts
into all the king's provinces, to
destroy, to kill, and to cause to
perish, all Jews, both young and
old, little children and women.*
— The Book of Esther, 3:13

So many Hamans, and just one Purim.
— Jewish proverb

They tell the story of Esther to children. It's a folk tale. Horror wrapped up as entertainment, threat of annihilation averted. Once a year we imagine the victory of the powerless as a game. Casting lots? Take a chance on Mordecai. And watch those plot twists. Number One Wife Vashti demoted for discipline problems. Esther wins Miss Persia contest to replace her. Sexy Jewess announces If I perish, I perish, and reveals secret of birth. Beauty queen becomes savior of her people. Evil scheme foiled, wicked Haman impaled on his own scaffold. A poke at the principalities and powers. King Ahasuerus, drunk again, countermands earlier order to kill all Jews. In a startling reverse move, all Jews get to kill their enemies.

The story is good for thousands of years, for we have scrolled forward in history, into the normal life of empires where helpless people are crushed as a matter of course, and divine intervention is in permanent recess. Already it is evident that the Jews, a people proudly apart, are available as scapegoats to the mighty and the many, that the malice of human beings will find us especially delectable. We differ. We do not bow down to gods other than our own. That is reason enough for them to hate us and want us destroyed.

Naturally we celebrate this one day of deliverance, in which everything is turned upside down, by feasting and merrymaking. The buds are bursting on the trees, birds stitch across the earth to mate and nest build, the conventionalities of hope assume physical reality among the juices of spring. There is a time for hilarity. Sticky sap flows. Children don costumes. Men and women disguise themselves in each other's clothing, which is otherwise forbidden. When the story is retold, everyone present yells, hoots, and rattles a noisemaker each time the name of Haman is mentioned. The saying also goes that one should drink, on Purim, until one cannot tell good from evil, blessed be Mordecai from cursed be Haman.

Mordecai changes Esther's life, introduces her to her identity. In a similar way my grandfather changes me. I am in his lap getting close to the smells of pipe tobacco and wool, enthroned where so often I have heard him tell the Story of the Man Who Travelled from Place to Place. I am his shayne maydele, his pretty little girl, his one grandchild. He gives me Life Savers on the sly, he glows at me through his glasses, he makes me show how I can already read, he is teaching me to play checkers.

It is Saturday. All week I have been in kindergarten. We learned right away to salute the Flag, now we are learning about democracy and elections. I ask my grandfather who he will vote for in the next election, knowing he will say Roosevelt, since everyone I know will vote for Roosevelt, so we can finish beating Hitler and the Japs. I rub my cheek against his scratchy cardigan. He says nothing. Then he says he is not going to vote. I am shocked. I sit up tall in his lap to give him a lesson about democracy. My grandfather's arms are around me but he looks away, something changes in the air. For a moment I believe I have won the argument, then he says that he will not vote for any president because no president will save the Jews in Europe. It is the first time I have ever heard that phrase: the Jews in Europe.

A quarter century later my mother describes a game they had when she was a young girl. She would come into the house and rush at her father with her arms wide, laughing as if to embrace him; he would run around the apartment, around the furniture, as if he were afraid. She would chase after him and he would yell Oy! Oy! mih shlughte di Yidn! Help, help, they're killing the Jews.

A quarter century later my husband repeats what his father told him and his brothers: In the old country, you would be soap now.

It would be false to say that I am being shoved forward in a line of human skeletons outside the city of Kiev, embracing to my chest a book of poetry which, although I am only five, I can already read. False to say that I am huddled in a sewer under the city of Warsaw frowning over a map. I am not in the woods checking a rifle. No, it is a Saturday afternoon in September 1944 in Borough Park, Brooklyn, America. I am the most ignorant possible American child in my pinafore, sitting on the knees of my Socialist grandfather just outside the kitchen where my mother and grandmother drink hot tea in glasses, the sugar settled in a sweet dissolving heap at the bottom. It would be correct to say that the air around me has changed, has acquired a greater transparency. It is like stories of time travel, where you find yourself unwarned in some alternative universe with new laws of physics. I have no idea what my grandfather means. At the same time, I understand perfectly. I have instantly acquired awareness of a global grief.

An initiation, a kindness without walls, a bitterness without floor—the familiar Brooklyn apartment seems for that instant to have dissolved—an instant and permanent canker on a child's budding patriotism. He squeezes my shoulder, the terrible danger that he will cry is past, I jump from his lap and go in the kitchen for tea. Now I understand that inside is always different from outside, reality from appearance, depth from surface. Don't expect me to forget.

Orphan: she learns to read. She learns to write. She is a pretty girl. She is a beautiful woman. She has grown up in the penumbra of her cousin's ambitions, which inhabit the air around him like furious red sparks zigzagging from an invisible bonfire, when he is calculating, making plans. At times when he suffers disappointment, it is as if a fleet of swallows careened madly around him, wailing, their wings and tails pointed as darts. When angry, he is stubborn as a bull. There are enemies, he says, everywhere. Around her, however, the aura remains glittering, serene, protective. She is an undemanding woman. And her parents, and theirs, and the past? Nothing, nowhere, all of that, the past, belongs to Mordecai. Esther is a pretty girl, a beautiful woman, to whom everything is pleasing. Like a dream, like the glow of dawn in which pulses the spark of a lonely star. She is a Jew. She is not a Jew.

A royal interlude. In the palace the queen has refused to appear when summoned, to display herself to the feasting princes. Too proud for her own good, a dangerous example, rumors ripple through the capital and out into the woods and hills, and throughout the kingdom. For this deed of the queen will come abroad unto all women, to make their husbands contemptible in their eyes. At the center of the ripples, however, the water has become smooth. The marble palace, like a block of ice, has promulgated an edict written in the king's name and sealed with the king's ring, that all wives should honor their husbands, both great and small. The wives smile narrowly, and look with narrow amusement from the corners of their eyes, and the queen has disappeared, leaving smooth water.

Like the glow of dawn in which a lonely star radiates, she is a beautiful woman. She is the most beautiful woman in Persia. She is a queen. She has the breasts of a queen, like honeydew melons. She has the knees of a queen, like crystal. She has the hair of a queen. She has the red fingernails of a queen, like poppies. She has the scent of a queen. She is a Jew. She is not a Jew. She behaves like a tame animal, a large gilded carp swimming most gracefully and languidly among the fishes of the women's aquarium, the harem. Once an orphan, today Esther wears on her head the royal crown, or turban, or scroll, or megillah, as the king has placed it. Ah, but she can read and write. He made her learn, the clever cousin. Not every queen can read and write. And he walks every day outside the court of the women's house, to find out how she is, and what will become of her. In his opinion, enemies are everywhere.

The party is in full swing. Sequins and cigars. Numerous uncles and aunts, great-uncles, grand-aunts, cousins thrice removed, in-law women and their toddlers, a hurricane of family carrying who knows how many branches with it, sweeps tumultuously past me, celebrating its annual survival. My twig of family being the poor relations invited once or twice a year, I don't know these people but I watch them. The bosoms of the women heave, their ample hips undulate, in turquoise taffeta and yellow-and-black ruffled silk, their stockings with black seams down the calves heading for the buffet.

A groaning buffet of food. Chopped chicken livers with schmaltz, gefilte fish, potato latkes, pot roast, celery, beets, gleaming fats. Enormous challah from which to rip pieces, hamentashen like a small Mount Sinai. Eat, my child, eat. The very walls murmuring eat, my darling, eat. The cheek-kissing followed by rubbing lipstick off the cheek, waves of scent lapping the room, the aunts talk about furs, marriages, illnesses, the children going to college, law school, medical school, reprieve, safety. The male bandying, the brandy they are allowing the children to taste, the gossipy shrieking, the men talk garment district, talk lawyers, deals, racetrack, and the brains of their sons.

Some uncles collect like minnows around a big fish up from Washington. A fat uncle standing on a kitchen chair takes flashbulb pictures mainly of his own three fat daughters, tie loosened, big shoulders, pushes people aside, saying Just one minute, excuse me. Children throwing nuts and raisins, small children already whining and tugging on their mothers. The teenage cousins playing with the dreidels and flirting. Everyone eats as if attempting to fill the bellies of the starved, the long dead, they make noise as if to penetrate the ears of the six million. We've escaped, they are shouting. Look at us, we are alive! We're in one piece!

If the six million could see my family, if they could see all the families coagulated together like balls of food, would they rejoice? Would they be reassured, would they weep?

They say her clever cousin is in sackcloth, bitterly mourning. Word comes to the queen. The queen sends word, Why. The messenger hurries from the grate of an outer courtyard, through secret doors and secret corridors. Men in uniform bow and recede, like potted ferns waving in a wind. The message is that Haman the Agagite, descendant of the Amelekites, has written an edict in the king's name and sealed it with the king's ring, to destroy, to slay, and to cause to perish, all Jews, both young and old, little children and women, in one day. Now Mordecai the Jew, descendant of Saul the Benjaminite, wishes her to save the people.

They say the capital is in an uproar, because it is full of Jews.

They cannot wish to kill her, she is beautiful, she is the most beautiful woman in Persia, she is the queen. Tell him, she says, I am afraid. Tell him I cannot help, tell him I am only a woman. A fish. She floats away, flirting her transparent tail mournfully.

I wish to be invisible. I am invisible. Retracted as a snail, I wander along the walls looking at family photographs in gilt frames. If I play dreidels I always lose because my cousins cheat. If I sit in a chair by myself they'll tell me to go enjoy the party. If I flee to the toilet and stay in there reading a magazine a great-aunt will knock, she'll ask am I sick, do I have a fever, a stomachache, what's the matter, a hand to my brow, her perfume suffocating me. My impulse is to steal to the bedroom where the coats are, fling myself on the pile, crawl in among them. No, I am not Queen Esther, nor was meant to be. Am a bookish adolescent who cannot imagine how anyone can admire those sickening feminine wiles. Am rebel Vashti, too proud to obey that loutish king. The whole story infuriates me, especially the part about touching the tip of the king's sceptre, how crude can you get. And why can't they understand that I really want to save my people, save humanity. A lot they care. A lot Esther herself cared, the selfish thing, Mordecai had to tell her she'd be killed with the rest of her people, before she was willing to lift a finger. That doll, that puppet.

She is a Jew. She is. Yes, she is a Jew, she instructs herself, ashamed, afraid, ready. Sweating through her perfume, shivering in her royal garments. Cedar doors, secret corridors. From her warm inner room to the court, doing exactly what she fears, breaking the law, there she goes. Nobody has called her. She has to do it, walk on her hobbled legs, speak with her throttled voice. To the one who wants to kill her she must be charming. She must make her voice musical and issue an invitation.

She instructs herself not to laugh, not to scream, not to spit in his face, not seize the sceptre from his hand and strike him with it, not to throw up out of pure cold terror. To act, to control her body, to be lovely, to be merry.

She rehearses. If I please the king, and if I have found favor in his sight, and the thing seem right before the king, and I be pleasing in his eyes.

Her predecessor refused, she must not refuse. Her body needs to undo the king's writing, scatter the letters, break the royal seal that they say is unbreakable, retract the royal edict they say is changeless. Does she stand on the shoulders of the old queen, does the dead one encourage her?

Obviously he may kill her. She is breaking and entering. Chilly, lofty, empty, the place of power. Its vacuum streaked with gold, the pavement of green, and white, and shell, and onyx marble, and at its furthest end a throne. She feels as if the throne is infinitely distant. I am a Jew, she instructs herself, willing a blush of beauty onto her cheeks, a pout of pleasure onto her lips. Take a deep breath, magnify the breasts. I will do what I fear. And if I perish, I perish.

The big fish from Washington touches glasses with my prettiest cousin. She flashes her eyes, tosses her auburn mane. My snail self peers forth at them. Years later I will think: we save ourselves as best we can, we use whatever we have. Beauty, friends in high places, a rifle in the woods with the partisans, a fountain pen, whatever works. No, I am not ready to think this way. I am not ready to wonder if Vashti and Esther could be secret allies, ridicule of the king joined to manipulation of the king. Sleek small moles under the ground of tyranny, grain by grain overturning the world. I am thinking how my cousin is beautiful, I am clumsy, she catches men in her net while I crawl sullenly along the wall's baseboard leaving my snail trail.

Who are my enemies, who are my allies, how do I learn to recognize them. In the settlement house camp when I was a junior counselor, the senior counselor was a freckle-faced Irishwoman who made everybody laugh. The kids in our fourth-grade bunk loved her, so did I. She was strict but she made up for it by being funny. She would make us roll with laughter at her jokes. All summer, though I tried and failed to please her, I continued to think she was wonderful. When I would tell the kids to do something and she would yell at them to do something else, I felt ashamed of my failure.

The last week of camp I was in charge one rest hour. My senior counselor's daughter bounced on her bed, acting up. She was a child with blond curly hair and angelic looks but a less than angelic temperament. I told her to be quiet. She kept bouncing. I told her again and she bounced higher. I said she knew what the rules were and she should have some consideration for others. Suddenly the child's peachlike complexion turned beet red and she shook with anger. I don't have to obey you, she shouted at me. I'm a Catholic! Oh, I thought—as the summer rearranged itself—so that was why. Now I watch the big fish say something to my pretty cousin, who puts her hand over her mouth, red fingernails, laughing prettily. Pretending to laugh. She leans back, scans the room, merry eyes, sees me. I am invisible, a snail, but she sees me, winks at me. And now the uncles and aunts are mostly drunk, draped over one another's shoulders, what cacophony, the exhibitionist ones dance, stamp their feet, kick into the air, circling ferociously, unwilling ever to surrender their sexuality, festive to the point of blindness, alive, alive.

So there's the whole story, the gantze megillah, the happy ending. Doesn't that crown everything? Scroll forward. Let's have a drink. But the story is not the story. The beginning is not the beginning. Repeat it. Before words, our bodies. My body. I trick him, I fool him, I make him drunk, I unwrite the writing. Ever-returning spring. When I remember myself. When times fly backward, forward, when I/we make him dizzy with desire. When we punish our enemies. This festival has been celebrated forever. Man and woman doubled, the slayer slain, and a tree growing upside down. So who do we think we are? Hadassah the myrtle tree with her flowers like stars. Esther who is Ishtar (Ashtaroth, Astarte, locked out the door, creeps in the window), morning and evening star. Lady of battles, opener of the womb, forgiver of sins. Ishtar whose song is sweeter than honey and wine, sweeter than sprouts and herbs, superior even to pure cream. Ishtar whom Gilgamesh accuses of slaying her lovers. Half laughter, half killer. Coupled with Mordecai, Marduk, bull calf of the sun, armed and winged. Babylonian Ishtar and Marduk having destroyed their enemies, just like that, a new year destroys the old.* Let's leaf. This festival has been calibrated forever. Fast-forward, fast-backward. Put on your mask and dance.

I am and am not a Jew. We are and are not Babylonian, Assyrian, Canaanite. She is and is not the court favorite, the assimilated one, the hidden Marronite, the one in exile, the weeping Shekhinah. We disguise our bodies. Our old bodies. Like truth budding from lies. Our ever-returning bodies. Dying and being born. Overturning the world.

*The Golden Bough *(James Frazer, 1951) relates Purim to the Babylonian spring festival of Zagmuk, in which the Enuma Elish (of which Marduk is the hero) was recited, and the king renewed his power by grasping the hands of Marduk in the temple; and to the Saceaen Saturnalia in which a condemned prisoner was allowed to play king, making free with the king's courtesans, then executed. Ishtar, a goddess of both sexuality and war, in part derived from the Sumerian Innanna, was worshipped throughout the Near East. Vashti and Haman were an Elamite divine pair, according to Patricia Monaghan,* The Book of Goddesses and Heroines *(1981). Scrolling forward,* The Encyclopedia of Religion *(ed. Mircea Eliada, 1987) observes that Esther in the Middle Ages was identified with the court Jew who risked everything to support fellow-Jews; was a favorite of the Spanish Marronites who saw her disguise as symbolic of their own; and was even at times identified with the Shekhinah, as the absence of God in the Scroll of Esther symbolized the hiddenness of the Shekhinah in the world and in exile.*

CALYX Journal, Vol. 15:1, 1993/94

Viki Radden

A THING ABOUT ITALY

Her name's Cherice Robinson, right? I mean, well hell, what can you say about Cherice? Let me put it this way. She's the only black girl you're ever gonna meet who can fry you up a chicken, all nice and crispy, and quote Shakespeare to you at the same time.

I met Cherice at work. At Woolworth's. That's right. The famous Woolworth's on Union Square. Cherice was the one who hired me. And she hired me on the spot, I might add. Seems like a lifetime ago. But actually it's only been four years. And more than a year since I last saw Cherice. Hell, a year and a half. And here I sit, holding an invitation to her wedding and a plane ticket in my hand. But you know, she used to tell us all the time: "One of these days, I'm just going to take off to Italy and marry me a black-haired Italian man." Take off to Italy: that's just what she did.

Me and the other Woolworth counter girls, see, we didn't think she meant it. I mean, since the day I met Cherice, she was all the time poppin off her mouth about Italy. In fact, when she hired me, she started asking me questions about it. I mean, there she was in her pink and white uniform, some little wisps of hair peeking out from her hair net. She was cuttin up a chicken with a long black knife.

"You know how to fry a chicken, girl?" she asked me. Her wire rim glasses were sliding down her nose. I reached over and gently pushed them up for her. I could tell she was a little flustered cause of my gettin so close to her since I was only there for an interview, but on the other hand, I could tell she liked me. And I couldn't help thinking she looked awful young to be callin me girl. I was only twenty, but she looked about twenty too.

"Sure," I said. "I can fry up a chicken blindfolded with one hand tied behind my back."

"Uh-huh," Cherice said. *Whack* went the knife, chopping off a drumstick from a big thigh. Then she turned and looked at me, real serious like, and said, "Did you see the movie *The Godfather?*"

"Excuse me?"

"The movie. *The Godfather.* You know. Mafia. Don Corleone. Marlon Brando." Then she goes off into this Marlon Brando imitation! I couldn't believe it.

"Uh . . . actually, no. I never saw it. That movie was a little before my time. I'm a little too young to have . . ."

"Honey, that's no excuse for not seeing *The Godfather.* I've seen it sixteen times. How old are you, anyway?"

"Uh, I just turned twenty."

"Well, see, like I said, that ain't no excuse. I'm only about to turn twenty-two myself."

I knew I was right. She was only a year or so older than I was.

"See," she went on, "I'm the youngest manager Woolworth's Take-Out Department ever had."

Then she picked up the knife and looked at me. "I tell you what," she said, "you go on over there to the sink and wash up. Then come back here and finish cuttin up this chicken. Then go on ahead and fry it up. If it's good enough for me to eat for my lunch, then you've got the job."

I got the job. See, my family's from Arkansas. We been fryin up chicken almost as long as the moon's been rising in the sky at night. Then when I was leaving, she said one final thing: "You ever read a book called *The Inferno?*"

"*The Towering Inferno?*" I'd heard of that one. My mom has it.

"No, just *The Inferno.* It's by Dante. An old Italian guy. See, I've got this thing about Italy."

"No, I never read it."

"Don't worry about it." She was smiling at me and wiping up the countertop with a washrag. "But *The Godfather.* You have to see that. It's playing next Thursday at the Strand. Wanna go with me?"

"Sure. That's the day before I start work."

"Good. Meet me here at five, okay?"

I met her that night and we ate take-out egg rolls and Mrs. Field's cookies, right on the square outside the store, with all the tourists and the pigeon poop and the street musicians and the Jesus Freaks. We watched the cable cars turn around, then head down Powell, toward the Bay. Then we saw *The Godfather*. I couldn't believe it, but Cherice knew all the Italian parts by heart.

"You speak Italian too?"

"Yeah," she whispered, munching on her buttered popcorn. "Just a little. My dad bought me a set of those Berlitz tapes and I listen to them every night before I go to sleep."

See, that was the thing about Cherice. You couldn't help but love her. After a while, everybody loved her. At first, you could tell, she made some people feel kinda nervous. You know how it is: you don't expect a black girl who's working as a fry cook at Woolworth's to speak Italian and quote Shakespeare and talk about these dead Italian famous guys like Leonardo da Vinci and Michelangelo. Some people were really shocked at first . . . but then, when they saw that smile—that was what did it—those teeth and those dimples the size of gumdrops—when she smiled, even the most stuck-up businessman in a silk three-piece would melt and start smiling at Cherice, big as life.

I guess it must have been the same way for her in Italy. She must have really charmed the men. Especially this Count Valmontone. Count Bracciano Valmontone. Isn't that a great name? Sounds like it really means something. See, we didn't believe Cherice, me and Carmen and May Ling and the other counter girls. We didn't believe Cherice when she said she was going to Italy cause, hell, we all said we were going somewhere, away from the hot smelly grease and the ugly white shoes and our wet hands all covered with flour. But you know, one day I started to believe Cherice. I remember that day; it was almost three years after I started at Woolworth's— the day when the Big Boss called a meeting and told us that they were closing down the Union Square Woolworth's. Blame it on the recession, he said. We had a year to find other work.

Some of us cried, especially the older people who'd been there for twenty years, but not me. And not Cherice, either. No tears for her. She just said, "This is it. Now's my chance. I'm going to Italy the day after they close down this store."

And that's just what she did. She started working nights at City Lights Books, reading every book about Italy that they had, making her plans, saving every penny. We had our farewell party at the store, then the next day she was gone, on a 7:35 A.M. nonstop flight to Rome.

"Girlfriend," she said as we hugged at the gate before she walked toward the plane, "I'll write to you as soon as I can. But you know, I have a feeling I won't be coming back."

And you know, I might not be coming back either. I'm going to this wedding. Cherice says she and the Count have a private villa outside Rome that's all theirs and that I can have my own room for as long as I want. She says there's plenty of work for people who want to teach English . . . Hell, why not? I can play that part. I've never been out of San Francisco, but maybe it's time to see what's waiting for me on some distant shore. And Italy, even if I don't like it, how bad can it be, when Cherice and I can snap our fingers and get pasta and pizza, cappuccino and gelato? Maybe we'll even fry up a chicken for dinner.

Cherice and me, I can see us in Italy. There we are in dark glasses, in our flowing print dresses and Bandolino flats, wandering among the ruins. Or maybe we're strolling down the piazza on the arms of our black-haired Italian men, doing the Italian two-step. Our laughter goes bubbling up, then cascading down over us, like cool, cool water from one of those old Roman fountains.

CALYX Journal, Vol. 15:1, 1993/94

Carolyn Barbier

NIGHTHAWKS

know I'm in a hospital. I know it's serious and I should be scared. I cannot quite remember what has happened. I feel more excited than alarmed. I feel the adrenaline of the moment pushing me.

A tube presses my tongue flat on the floor of my mouth and bulges it against my teeth. The pipe reaches down my throat. It branches out of my mouth against one corner, pulling my lips down on that side. A young woman secures the tube with tape across my upper lip. I want to fix it like a bulky fold of sock in my shoe. When she's finished she smiles, cocks her head, and pats the tape, her package wrapped, the bow in place. "You're going to be just fine," she says. I want to tell her how sure I am she's right.

I want to tell all these people I will work with them. I smile and nod but they don't notice. Occasionally they look over at me and tell me something they're about to do to me and how it will feel. They speak normally to one another, but when they turn to me they speak loudly and articulate very distinctly. They call me hon or say OK as a question.

Of course it's OK. You go right ahead with what you're doing.

I want to cooperate with them, to show I'm part of the team. The room is bright, all the lights are on, but the window is dark. It is night.

I wake up inside my eyelids. I listen. No voices now except for a woman in the distance. Her tone is kind but business-like, and I imagine her assisting a phone customer with an order for take-out food.

For a moment I think I hear waves. But the whooshing is too constant and marked regularly by a loud pop. I realize these sounds match my own tense breathing. I can't relax. I have to keep time.

I remember lying next to my mother as a child. She is sleeping. I try to match my breath to hers. Hers are longer than mine. I concentrate. I push the air out slowly. The emptiness in my lungs stings. I wait for her to inhale.

Years later, I would lie awake next to Joe as he slept. I resisted, but the old childhood habit would creep back until I noticed I was breathing faster than I liked, to keep up with him. I switched just short of full and just short of empty. I would catch myself working hard to keep his rhythm, and had to move away from him to the other side of the bed.

Now, in this narrow bed, I have no choice. I try, but I can't move. A machine with a rhythm only partially related to my own is breathing for me whether I want it or not. It blasts air into my lungs before I have a chance to completely empty them. I hear it switch, loud and hard. I try to match it. I wait for it. I ache inside with desire for air. I try to be ready but it startles me. It jams air into me.

I open my eyes. The room was bright before. Now it is like a bedroom with a pale reading light. The hall beams a reflection on the shiny floor. A young man sits in the doorway, using a bedside table as a writing desk. He sips from a mug that says, "You want it when?" His baggy green scrubs accentuate the sinew and muscles of his bare arms and neck. I imagine touching his firm skin. He writes and glances up and writes more. He doesn't glance at me but rather past me. I picture a large scoreboard on the wall above me. He sees something which concerns him and moves toward me, adjusts something behind me, and sits to write more.

I try to signal him. I move my fingers and wave—a polite, country-road kind of wave. The effort surprises me. He doesn't see me so I decide to flag him down by waving my arms. I discover my arms are too weak. My hands are tied to the bed. Bound softly with fabric straps in wide loops. I must have done something earlier to deserve being tied now. I hang on to this rationalization to quiet the panic.

"Ms. Paige . . . can you hear me?"

I open my eyes. The room is light now. Light everywhere. Daylight.

A man in his early fifties stands next to my bed. "I'm Dr. Ruskin." He holds a folder open, resting it on the siderail above my face. He looks from the equipment behind me, down at his papers and to the men and women gathered around. He speaks about me.

He looks into my face when he speaks to me.

Flecks of color in his tie pick up the blue of his shirt. His graying blond hair is waved carefully in place. I envision a woman's long fingers with lacquered nails giving it shape. He must have shaved only five minutes ago. His discreet clean scent refreshes me in this room so full of strong odors.

"You were very lucky, young lady. Those Coast Guard guys got you out of the water just in time."

The water. I remember the storm. I had to get off the water.

The doctor talks on in the easy tones of a salesman showing a new line of designer shoes. I am distracted by the ragamuffin band of his followers. Some have red eyes. Some look two or three days past bathing. One has buttoned his shirt in the wrong buttonholes. Another has lipstick smeared past the perimeter of her lips.

I hear Dr. Ruskin's voice summing up, ". . . so, your job is to get through this present crisis. After that, we'll begin to discuss the possibilities for the future. But, let's not worry about that now. You're going to be just fine." He smiles but none of his students smile. Each face in the room is trained on mine. What do all these people know about me?

After they leave, I try to remember what he said. I try to relax. I try to shut off my mind. What possibilities for the future?

The light is bright in the room and the noise in the hallway is constant. I hear hard footsteps coming closer, like leather pumps, not the comfortable rubberized soles worn by the people who work here. I hear the even teaching voice of a nurse moving closer with the click of the pumps. My shoulders stiffen.

The sound of the heels stops outside my door but the voice continues, ". . . her face is quite swollen. Prepare yourself because she won't look like Margaret to you. She can't talk and can only feel and move her hands a little. But remember, she's fully conscious and can hear and communicate. If you'll try to be patient."

My mother walks in the door wearing a charcoal gray skirt and lighter gray sweater. Her turquoise scarf and silver hair lift the monochrome. She smiles as though caught in an embarrassing moment of recognizing a face but not remembering the name. She stands in the doorway, giving herself a moment to adjust.

"Margaret . . . sweetheart, I'm so glad to see you." She crosses to the bedside. "I just got here and took a taxi right over from the airport." She takes my hand and considers it. "You look . . ." She closes her eyes and bends down to kiss my cheek. Her face has softened when she moves back to look at me again and she smiles. "It's so good to see you. I couldn't wait to get here. I was desperate to see . . . for myself."

My mother is the first person who knew me before the accident to see me now. I had not looked in a mirror until she walked in the door.

I tell time by the level of light in the room. I know there is a clock on the wall to my left but I can't turn far enough to see it. I know it's there because a nurse will occasionally glance toward it and tell me what time it is. I no longer tell time by my usual six A.M. shower, round of lectures and appointments in my office, or a relaxing martini before dinner.

Now, when I am being bathed, I know it is sometime around three in the morning. It is about five in the morning when my blood is drawn. If it's daylight outside and my blood is drawn, I know my numbers are wrong. A new nurse comes on duty and I know it is seven in the evening if it's dark outside the window, seven in the morning if it's light. There are never any meals.

I tell myself every few moments, you can do this.

I wonder what floor of the hospital I am on. The large window gives me a view of the building next door. A view of one brown brick wall. The building must be very tall because I can't see the sky above it. I try to remember the layout of this part of the city and what building it is. Light changes the color of the bricks and they entertain me. When they are a dark, an organic chocolate brown, I assume it is cloudy outside. I can't see the sun but it shines in the flecks of mica in the brick. Once, I was thrilled to see the bricks sparkling, but also dappled with deep chocolate as raindrops fell.

I think of my studio. My hands yearn to mold clay, to capture the stippled quality of the brick, and to glaze it with flecked brown.

I can see the window, the door into the hallway, and the supply cabinet on the far wall of the room. Each person who works over me makes trip after trip to the cabinet and back. At one time I began counting the trips required to complete one procedure. My intention was to count, then average them. I lost count somewhere.

Oftentimes, the cabinet door hangs open with a half-folded sheet tumbling out toward the floor. I lie here imagining myself folding the sheet. Putting it back on the shelf. When I try to ask the nurse to close the door with small pointing motions toward it, she always tries to guess what I want inside. The guessing frustrates both of us.

The nurses and doctors laugh and joke in the hall right up to the threshold of my room where they suddenly become solemn and professional. I imagine a transformation shield stands in the doorway. I want to ask them to bring their funny stories into my room with them. I hope there is light in my eyes when they look at me, but I can't tell.

It is dark. I can tell dark and light through my eyelids. I can hear the nighthawks calling as they dart between the buildings snatching insects from the air. Their cry is loud and nasal, an unattractive buzz. And yet, it is wild and alluring.

The first two years I lived in this city I loved the sound but never knew what bird made it. I heard it late at night while driving home from dinner with friends. I knew it was not safe to drive alone with all the windows rolled down, but the city was quiet, the air was cool, and the streets almost empty. I drove fast to feel my hair blown across my face. At that hour, the city belonged to me. It didn't threaten me with all its unknown. It belonged to the nighthawks and they flew, freewheeling in the air between the buildings.

I feel that exhilaration now, in this bed, when I hear them call outside. I want to reach over and push the window open, to feel the air on my face.

I am lying on my side, propped by pillows. I am facing the window and the brown bricks beyond it. The dull lack of color in the wall tells me it is just before dawn. I have been bathed, and for just this one moment, I feel neat between my cool clean sheets. Tonight, Angela is my nurse. She takes care of me often. When I first saw the name on her badge I was sure it had to be a joke, a nurse called "angel." We have become accustomed to one another, and I feel ease when she walks into my room.

Angela comes in now and I hear her behind me, "Oh, no, Margaret, not again." I notice the familiar sweet concentrated smell and immediately feel ashamed. She keeps assuring me it will only take a moment to clean up, that everything's just fine. I see the way she will not look at me. I see the tears she can't wipe away because her gloves are smeared dark brown.

It's not just fine, Angela.

She tells me not to pay any attention to her and explains it has been a tough night and she's ready to go home.

Later, I see her walking down the hall with her coat over her arm. She usually says good-bye to me before she leaves. She wants to get away from here as fast as she can. So do I.

The room is barely light but Dr. Ruskin's arrival with his colleagues means it is eight in the morning. I assume the sky is cloudy, and the spatters on the window please me when they begin.

The rain started. My hands were wet. The wind ripped at the mainsail and the waves tore at the rudder in my grip.

"We haven't been able to wean you off that ventilator, Margaret, and you can't breathe on your own. It looks like you're going to be on the machine a long time, and the tube's been in your mouth for three weeks now. Way, way too long." He speaks to me in a light tone, but when he asks one of the students for an interpretation of my numbers, his voice deepens and his wording is complex.

"So, we're going to make a hole in your throat for the breathing tube. You'll be much more comfortable this way. We'll all try to read your lips so you can complain about the way we're treating you."

I expect him to take a knife out of his pocket and cut my throat. I won't complain, I promise. He laughs and pats my hand. Several of the students smile on their way out the door.

I'm confused. Then I realize they will take me to the operating room and put me to sleep.

Wean. A child learning to feed herself after a life of drinking only from her mother's breast. An addict giving up a beloved drug slowly, to make the pain of withdrawal more tolerable.

I wait for the machine-driven blast of air. I need it. I am relieved when it enters me.

"Margaret? Wake up, honey. It's me, it's your momma."

I open my eyes to the brightness of the room and my mother's smile. She wears deep brown slacks and a blue knit blouse that looks soft to the touch.

"Good morning, sweetheart. You look all nice and clean and ready for a new day. It's a beautiful day too. Look, the sun's shining bright, not a cloud in the sky." She goes to the window and cranes her head upward near the glass. As she turns back to me she looks stricken, wishing she'd said something different. I smile but the tube pulls one side of my mouth down. I want to make her comfortable. "Well, at least it's nice and bright in here." She pulls a chair up to the side of the bed.

"I've been busy this morning. Let's see . . . I made a couple phone calls. I called Lori, of course. We decided to rent one hotel room nearby. She said she'd make reservations to come down right away."

Stop.

"She has to shop around a little to get the best fare, and I said I'd help her out with that, so she'll be here as soon as she can. Before you know it. And with a room nearby, one of us can be here with you and the other can get some rest."

Stop.

"Your house is just too far away to keep shuttling back and forth like I've been doing for the last week. I think it'll work out just fine."

Stop. Please. I don't know what you're saying.

"And, honey, I called Joe."

Stop. Stop and explain. I can only roll my eyes and feel silly doing it.

"I know. It felt a little awkward calling him, I can tell you that. He was terribly upset, but he was glad I called."

Stop.

"I think he still misses you. Did I do the right thing, honey?"

I just stare at her.

"I thought he at least deserved to know about the accident and what a rough time you've had bouncing back." She stops a moment and looks at me. "I feel so clumsy sitting here talking to you like this. Tomorrow after the surgery you can tell me all about it. I'll learn to lip read, I promise. Anyway, Joe said to give you his best and to let him know if there was anything he could do."

I don't need anything Joe could do.

"I think maybe he feels a little guilty. He was the one who got you interested in that damn boat."

That's true, but he hated my love for it.

She pulls her lips in over her teeth and bites them until they are white edges. "He said to tell you he still loves you."

Don't.

She stands and moves to the window, then turns to me the way she would with a great new idea. "Margaret, you've got to be strong, you know. Dr. Ruskin says we've got to get your lungs cleared out or they'll scar even more. And then you'll never breathe on your own again. You don't want that, do you, sweetie?"

And if you don't wipe that ugly look off your face, young lady, it's going to freeze that way.

"He says when you're better they can start therapy to help you use your arms some. You've got to come out of this. You've got to fight."

I was fighting to hold the rudder. My hands were wet.

"You have all these folks pulling for you, people who care about you."

I was reaching for the halyard to reef the mainsail.

She laughs. Her hands are in fists. "See, I almost forgot. Dr. Jaynes calls almost every day, even though he knows you won't be back to the university."

Stop.

"He just wants to check on you. He says to tell you how very much you'll be missed. Do you understand me, hon?"

No, I don't understand. I want my studio. I want my art. I want my students.

"What, honey? What are you trying to say?"

I reached for the halyard and the rudder pulled out of my hands. Then it slammed back into my side. The boat pitched.

"Now just relax. Everything's going to be just fine." She looks over my head and behind me. People often look at the equipment there when talking to me is difficult. "Do you want me to get the nurse? Are you OK? I just don't know how to communicate with you right now."

She turns to the window and I see her hand go to her eye but when she shifts back toward me she is defiantly perky. "You listen to me. You pull yourself out of this little crisis and we'll fly you back up to Denver in a special plane. You know, ever since your Daddy died I've been so lonesome. Then you left Joe and I started thinking. It'd be fun for both of us to live together."

Stop.

"Now we have our chance. This way I can take care of you. I know you like your independence but you're still my little girl. You need me now."

Stop.

"I know that's not the right thing to say, but it's true. We can get one of those nurses who come right to the house. We'll be good company for each other. I know I could use some company. I can make it up to you for always being too busy. I remember times when I'd buy you a new dress and wouldn't get it hemmed before you grew out of it. After all these years, I wish I could've balanced things out better. What do you think?" She leans forward and takes my hand. "I know. We don't have to decide anything right now. You rest and I'll just sit here with you for a while."

She pulls her knitting out of her bag and starts to work. I watch her steady hands hold the needles and make quick repetitive movements wrapping the yarn around again and again. She notices me watching her and smiles at me.

I think of being in the same room with her for days on end, listening to her. Unable to say a word. The way it used to feel years and years ago.

I remember the joy I felt living alone after ten years of marriage to Joe. Deciding when I would eat, working in my studio as late as I wanted, going for days without turning on the television. I liked sailing more than he did. The boat allowed me to escape his constant evaluation of me. On the water I was free of his critique. When I first left, I thought I felt no grief and would never cry.

Then, I walked into the studio and accidentally shut the door on the tips of my fingers. I howled with pain and knelt down over my stool and held myself while I wept. All the pain and grief I felt collected there in my fingertips. I knew it was right to finally feel my loss through the part of me I used to touch the world, to mold clay.

I try to feel my fingers now. I know they are there but they are unavailable. I don't recognize them. My body is like a concealed identity on TV. The face is camouflaged by flashing colored squares but occasionally the outline of the jaw or the hair bleeds out over the edge.

I think of living with Momma, with her as my hands and eyes and speech. Her interpretation of the world, her evaluation and critique. Reclaimed by the womb.

I want to hold a book, to read, and to turn the pages myself.

Someone is in the room with me. Someone is sitting by the bed. I can hear the squeaky suck of chewing gum, and the rough rub of denim as legs in blue jeans are crossed. I can hear the page of a book flip up at the corner and slide slowly through fingers as it is turned over. I decide to open my eyes. It used to be an automatic movement.

Lori sits in an orange molded plastic chair. Her jeans are designer but her blouse is rumpled. She wears her long blonde hair swept back from her face and her makeup is perfect. I want to throw my arms around her, to tell her how happy I am to see her. Or, at least, to scream at her. Her fingers slide down the page of the book in her hand. She slowly turns her head to the left as she turns the page and glances at me in passing.

"Hey, cutey! We were wondering when you were going to check back in." She unfolds her tall body, unloads her book, and comes over to me. She leans down to hug me. Her perfume feels like a dull blade in my nostrils. Damn, it's good to see you in there. They did the surgery three days ago. I guess you needed some time to sleep it off."

Sleep is the great escape, Lori. You know that.

She strokes my forehead and holds my hand. I am so used to the probing intimate touch of strangers, the sweetness of this touch from a friend stuns me. I miss it so much it hurts.

My nurse enters the room to tend to my tubes and bottles and adjust my equipment. Lori proudly presents me in my newly conscious state, as though it were something she and I accomplished together. The nurse seems very pleased to see me and says they've all been worried about me. She introduces herself as Debbie to Lori. "Dora told me all about you—how you and Margaret have been best friends for years and all."

It's odd to hear my mother referred to as Dora. The conversation we had. Not a conversation. When? Dora, in her brown slacks and blue blouse, telling me how she's picked up my life where I left off. Lori, get me out of here.

"Well, I couldn't stay away, could I?" Lori says. "Margaret and I have been best friends for almost twenty years."

"Boy, that's a long time." Debbie hardly looks twenty herself.

"We've been through everything together. Every new style, every new project, and every new man. I bet if you added up all the husbands and boyfriends and lovers we've had between us, and you laid them end to end, they'd stretch for at least three city blocks."

She squeezes my hand harder and I look to the nurse to check her reaction. Lori follows and sees the younger woman's wide eyes and solid plaster smile. I want her to stop this performance but she rushes on.

"And what do we have left after all that? Just each other." She looks down at me. "I know I sure couldn't ask for anything more." Lori grins the same lewd way she did when we were twenty-two and comparing fish stories about our current men.

Don't, Lori.

"To tell you the truth, I wouldn't mind getting laid a little more often." Debbie shares Lori's laugh, but her hand covers her mouth and her face is down. The laugh in my chest battles with the machine-driven burst of air and loses to a cough. I see Debbie pat my foot on her way out, but cannot feel it.

Lori shakes her head, "Well, I guess I really impressed her, didn't I? I always say the stupidest things when I'm nervous."

Talk to me, Lori. I'm scared.

She walks over to the window and says, "They sure gave you a crappy view." Her shirt is taut across her hunched shoulders, her fingernail in her mouth.

Talk to me, Lori. Tell me why you're so scared.

"Well, I promise you one thing, girl." She turns around to me and smiles, "When you get out of here, I'm coming down for that visit you keep asking me to make."

No. Get me out of here now.

"What is it, Marg? Don't you want me to come?"

Yes. You're the only one who can get me out of here.

"It'd be great. You always make me so much more adventurous. We'd have a great time. What are you trying to say? I know, I've been a real poop. You must be totally disgusted with me. I don't know why I've been putting it off so long. Life just never lets up with these little lessons, like you always say."

What little lessons? Like make hay while the sun shines? Or maybe, you don't miss your water till your well runs dry?

I am shaking my head as far to each side as I can. My neck hurts like hands are around it squeezing tight. My mouth is dry and feels full of my tongue without the tube to hold it flat. I begin to mouth the words. NO. NO. OFF. OFF.

To look at the bowl sitting on the table is like looking at a photograph of me. Me before. Its surface is smooth and crimson and as the lip curves inward at the mouth, the creamy underglaze shines through. I have always refused to sell it, no matter what the offer. I kept it, so I could see my own ability to create. Now it doesn't matter.

Angela is washing my legs. I can see her lift each foot and rotate it, lift each leg and bend it at the knee. "Gotta keep these joints moving," she says. She spreads lotion on my legs. "Sorry my hands are cold, Margaret." She looks up at me, narrowing her eyes. "God that was a stupid thing to say." I can feel a cool pressure when she holds my hand and looks me in the face.

"So, Dora brought this bowl in. I think she wanted to make you feel better." Angela's fingers run along the curving lip of the bowl with the same tenderness I can see when she touches my legs. "You must be really good. I mean, I don't know anything about art, but this is wonderful."

Angela who is full of wonder.

She holds the bowl up toward the light and touches the glaze. She watches me while she says, "I don't know, I guess, I might be all wet, but, it just seems a little teensy bit mean to me, to bring this." She puts the bowl down. "But I'm sure her intentions are good."

Take it. I mouth the words slowly. I want you to have the bowl, Angela.

"Here, let me roll you over so I can do your back."

I shake my head no. Take it.

She resists. She says she can't. She says it would be unprofessional. Then, "Do you really mean it? You really, really want me to?"

She's behind me. I can hear the water splash lightly and drip off the washcloth as she lathers soap. I see her bend while she washes my back. The sound of the wet cloth and slippery soap almost convinces me I can feel it.

"Lori stopped me when I came on tonight. She's really shook. I guess she's scared, but I know she wants what's best for you, Margaret. I'm just going to clean down here between your legs. You have to be sure, really sure. Lori'll stand up for you, and I will too. Here, let's roll you back and I'll fix your hair. It's getting long. Lori says she thinks you want the ventilator taken off."

The window is dark and the movement in the hallway outside my door has slowed. It's evening. My friend, my doctor of refreshing smells, is leaning against the doorway of my room.

I hear my mother's voice demanding, "Don't I have any say so in this?"

"Yes, as next of kin you certainly do. But, ultimately it is Margaret's decision," he explains, leaning down to her.

"I'm trying to understand. Every inch of me is her mother and wants to keep her alive. I want her alive, don't you understand?"

"I understand. I'm a physician. I want to keep her alive."

I can see Lori, tall and blonde, pacing just beyond.

"She's all I have left in the world."

Dr. Ruskin stands straight. "The chances of her ever breathing on her own again are very remote. She thought this all through when she signed a living will years ago." He glances back toward me and notices me watching, listening. "It's her decision." He reaches inside the room and pulls the door closed.

I hear Dr. Ruskin's quiet shoes creak in the hallway. His hair is still in a perfect finger wave and his shave is close, but now he wears the same exhausted look of his ragamuffin compatriots. Angela is his partner now. He asks if I'm sure this is what I want and I can only signal with impatient nodding. He asks if I'm sure I understand. I hope he understands. He explains about the sedative and the removal of the breathing tube.

Angela holds my hand, and this time does not hide her wet eyes. Lori holds my other hand, her body erect, elegant in her courage. When the tube slides out, my throat closes and I feel I will choke. My body insists I breathe, but I cannot. I remember the water over my face becoming deeper and deeper. My lungs curse me, and for a moment I doubt I can stand the pain. Then I hear the nighthawks. They call to me as they fly.

CALYX Journal, Vol. 15:2, 1994

Kim Silveira Wolterbeek

SARAH'S T-BIRD

for Courtney

After Sarah plowed her T-Bird into a fire hydrant, our father buried the car in the hole he'd been digging for a fallout shelter.

"I guess we've got Castro to thank for this," Sarah said, watching from our bedroom window as the first shovels of dirt thumped onto the roof of her T-Bird.

I remember wanting to say something appropriate that would articulate our loss—because even though it was Sarah's car, I was the one who rode shotgun.

My father tossed aside the shovel, slapped his pockets, and walked next door to get Al's tractor. While he was maneuvering the John Deere through the gap in the privet hedge, I imagined a language that would reinvent the good times—the sound of tires rubbering against wet pavement, the loose ping of gravel ricocheting off hubcaps. At fourteen I had an adequate vocabulary for relaying facts, but even in my limited experience, I knew that facts had a way of obscuring magic, so I said nothing. Not that Sarah expected any more from me. She was, as I remember, looking past me, out the window at our father.

"Goddamned Fidel Castro," she said.

Twenty years later, after both our parents have died—he of an aneurysm, she of a deep cancerous sorrow—I remind Sarah of the old T-Bird and the fallout shelter.

"My accident was just an excuse," Sarah says. "He did it because of her." She pauses—a caesura of suspense—and then continues. "Just because he loved her doesn't mean Mom didn't drive him crazy." When I don't immediately respond, she grows exasperated. "The accident just gave him the excuse he needed. He said he couldn't afford to finance my hit-and-run driving, but that's not why he buried the T-Bird. He did it to get back at her for the abortion."

Although Sarah's conclusions often confuse me, I've always admired the way her ideas turn on each other in perfect arabesques of reasoned sentiment. It seems to me she speaks with deep courage, even if she does sometimes leave out important details. For instance, in analyzing my father's action she forgets the part about fear, fear of anything beyond his control: the missile crisis, errant daughters, disobedient wives. There's a similarity of effect, on a purely personal level, if you see what I mean.

"I still don't get your drift," I say to Sarah. "I don't see the connection."

"It's simple," Sarah says. "He hated the fallout shelter—her idea—and he hated the idea of my driving—also her idea. Burying the T-Bird was a double whammy—he got his way and he got his revenge. Tit for tat and he never had to say a word because she understood."

I feel awkward discussing our mother's abortion while nursing my sister through her third miscarriage in just as many years. Also, I am beginning to recognize the direction this conversation is taking. I see now that our mother's abortion is what we will talk about instead of Sarah's miscarriage, and quite suddenly I'm afraid. Maybe we're getting ready to bury Sarah's loss the same way our father buried the T-Bird—with well-muscled and devious intent—never even commenting when flowers sprouted in the yard where they'd never grown before: hubcap daisies and dandelion fenders.

I take a breath, wait for something to happen, half believing that if only I can find the most appropriate phrases, adjust my syntax and assume a sharp-edged inflection, my words will perform the same magic as a midwife's kitchen knife slipped under a mattress to cut the pain of labor.

That afternoon I go straight home and I call Leo. He picks up the phone and the first thing he says to me is, "Baby, when are you going to make an honest man of me?" I forget how my stomach sags against hipbones that once jutted, and for a moment I see myself as Leo claims to see me—firm-bodied, physically passionate, if emotionally reticent.

Leo is my post-divorce lover. After meeting him for the first time, Sarah asked, "Why him?" I wasn't sure how to answer, but I gave it a try. I pointed out that Leo was an artist, had a two-inch pony tail and a mustache that flared across his face in a way that was undeniably sexy. "And then," I said, "there's the obvious. He's not my ex-husband. He's not Ron." But Sarah was not satisfied. "Surely it's more complicated than that," she said. "If it is," I said, "I don't want to know."

"Leo," I say, "I can't see you tonight. I need to be with Sarah. She lost the baby." I don't cry or show any emotion. After hanging up I realize that I called Leo because I needed practice for when I have to tell my daughter.

Janine is thirteen years old and has artistic aspirations. She speaks with the voice and conviction of the young Sarah. "My medium is pen and ink," she says. Her drawings are intricate, busy. She admires M.C. Escher and has papered her walls with prints of his woodcuts, engravings, and lithographs. I don't understand her fascination. I'm disturbed by stairways that traverse doorways at odd angles, silver globes that reflect an infinity of curved and curving realities: *Relativiteit, Relativity, Relativität, Relativité.* The only Escher I find the least bit interesting is the woodcut over her bed: *Day and Night.* I love the angular silhouettes of flying birds—white on black.

Since the divorce, Janine seldom talks to me, and when she does she uses artsy phrases that I'm unfamiliar with. Most of the time I have trouble following her train of thought. Except for when she told me about negative space. That I understood.

Negative space—it's how I felt lying alone in bed after Ron left, wondering if I still existed without his shaded presence to define me.

When Janine comes home from school I tell her about Sarah's miscarriage. She drops her books on the kitchen table. "Shit," she says, "not again. Oh shit. Sarah's all right?" she asks. When I nod she walks into her bedroom, closes her door, and puts on music she likes to sketch to.

I picture Janine chasing a vision across the page with a shard of charcoal, satisfied when what she imagines begins to emerge.

"Dinner," I say aloud, and walk into the pantry where I scan the cluttered shelves for possibilities. Reaching for a can of chili, I remember two unrelated events.

The doctor who examined Sarah in the E.R. was young, harried, and didn't even make eye contact when he told her that she had "spontaneously aborted the fetus." He looked shocked when Sarah rose up on her elbows and confronted him. "Three days of cramping and bleeding—you call that spontaneous?"

The second is something I heard my father tell my mother when she got pregnant with the "change of life baby" she aborted. "How could you do this to me?" he said. "How could you let this happen?"

After dinner Janine goes with me to take Sarah oatmeal muffins.

"Shouldn't we be bringing her food rich in iron?" Janine asks me on the drive over. "I mean, don't you lose a lot of blood when you have a miscarriage? Amy Buchanan's older sister had a miscarriage at home, right in her own bed. Amy said they had to cart the mattress to the dump afterward."

I am always startled by the bluntness of Janine's infrequent conversations, although I try not to show it. "Actually," I say, "in the first trimester, it's like a heavy period." As soon as the words are out of my mouth I wish I could take them back. Janine, who has just started menstruating, doesn't need this kind of association. But when I glance over at her, I begin to wonder if she even heard me. She's looking into the sky, squinting, tilting her head, considering. "From a certain distance," she says, "birds in flight look like angles." When I look confused, she lifts her hand and makes a "V" with two fingers. "You know," she says, "like in geometry."

When I pull into Sarah's driveway, Janine opens the car door, leaving the oatmeal muffins on the seat for me to carry in. Sarah meets us at the door. "Hey, gorgeous," she says, and Janine, who shrugs away physical contact with me, walks into her aunt's embrace.

Inside, Janine looks around for her uncle. "Where's Danny?" she asks.

"Out of town until Wednesday," Sarah says.

Sarah has decided to wait until he returns to tell him about the miscarriage. "It's not the kind of thing anyone should hear over the phone," she told me in the emergency room when I offered to make the call.

"Sit down, sit down," Sarah says and points to the family room where I notice she has the heating pad plugged in. When she sees me looking, she says, "I'm alright, really."

Janine speaks more to me when Sarah is around than at any other time. She pretends to be talking only to Sarah, but when I ask questions she answers, sometimes without glancing my way. My daughter sits in a low-riding slant of winter sun that sets off the amber streaks in her wavy hair and engages in a breathless monologue about tetrahedrons and octahedrons, explaining the way an artist can stack geometric shapes in combinations to fill up space.

This talk of space makes me think of my mother sitting in the tiny corner of the windowless porch she called her "sewing room." After the abortion she sat mute, staring at the willowy mulch of wood fiber in the Chinese lacquer screen that separated her from the rest of us. I began to understand the implications of my mother's action near the end of my own marriage when Ron grabbed me by the arm and spat his anger into my face. "Your silence," he said, "is more lethal than any words I'm capable of using against you."

But it's only now, listening to Janine, that I see the corrosive link between the negative space of what's left unsaid and the angular pain of what gets buried.

"Will you try again?" Janine says.

I am shocked by the audacity of her question, frightened by the effect it might have on Sarah.

Sarah shrugs. "If I do, I'm on my own. Danny says if I have another miscarriage we should take it as a message from God that we weren't meant to be parents and get on with our lives."

Janine frowns, tosses her hair over her shoulder. "That's stupid," she says. "Since when has Danny been getting messages from God?"

Sarah laughs, the first time since the miscarriage.

"Sarah," I try, "what do you mean you'd be on your own?"

"I wouldn't have to tell him I was trying. After the fact, what's he going to do?" Sarah adjusts the heating pad against the small of her back. "On the other hand," she says, "maybe Danny's right. I'm beginning to think having a baby would take nothing short of a miracle."

I don't know what to say, but Janine does. She leans forward in her chair and says something she seems to have been saving up. "Escher," she says, "once gave this lecture in Hilversum where he talked about the impossible, spent the entire lecture going on and on about the impossible."

"Well," Sarah says, "I know all about the impossible."

Janine then flicks her hand in the air, a flick of dismissal, of that's-not-what-I-meant, and then she continues. "Escher said that the thing about human nature is that it's always yearning for the miraculous. . . ." She shrugs her shoulders and Sarah turns to me and smiles.

"This kid of yours is something else," Sarah says. She reaches out and touches Janine and Janine does not tilt her head and pull away. She lets Sarah's fingers glide the length of her glorious hair. "I always thought that my babies would have hair this color," Sarah says and drops her hand reluctantly. "Enough of this maudlin stuff. Did your mother ever tell you about the T-Bird your grandfather buried in the backyard?"

Janine shakes her head. She looks at me briefly, but turns to Sarah and asks the year of the car, the color of the interior. "I don't even know for sure how Dad got a hold of it. I know it wasn't registered. I think it was given in trade for some work he did." Sarah shrugs. "The good part was riding with your mother. Remember?" Sarah asks me. "Remember?"

I do, and in our telling Sarah's memories mesh with my own: I'm Sarah smashing into a fire hydrant, I'm the mother defying her husband, I'm me, silently inciting Ron's anger, and in this way, in this collage of rememory, I begin to understand Janine's fascination with form.

When Sarah gets to the part about burying the car, I interrupt her. "It was about this time I started having the dream about the end of the world," I say, only I don't know how to describe the complete absence of sound that preceded the flesh-melting flash of light. For the first time, it occurs to me that the dream, my mother's abortion, and the quick and unceremonious burial of the T-Bird might be interconnected. I'm tempted also to see in the dream some frightening foreshadowing of my failed marriage. I stop, turn to Sarah.

"Here's something even your mother doesn't know," Sarah says and smiles at Janine. Then she tells a story about our father. When it was clear that he was serious about burying the T-Bird, Sarah waited until night. After he fell asleep, she sneaked into his bedroom and stole the pocket watch from deep inside his discarded pants. Next morning before anyone was up, she threw the watch in the backyard hole and kicked dirt over it so that the sun would not produce a glint of suspicion.

"The way I figure it," she says and laughs, "he had it coming. Tit for tat."

Janine turns on me. "How come you never told me any of this stuff before? How come you keep things hidden from me?" She looks right at me.

"Hidden?" I say. "There aren't any secrets between us."

I'm lying—there are any number of things we will never tell each other—but the lie gives me time to consider my response to the question she isn't asking, the one that doesn't have anything to do with Sarah's buried T-Bird. What Janine really wants to know is how to step behind my Chinese lacquer screen and touch the silent hollow of my pain.

I close my eyes and rest my head against the couch, remembering an earlier time. My mother is holding a glass of flat ginger ale to my lips. I must have had a high fever, the kind that filters sound into tinny reverberations, because my mother's words get lost. The next thing I recall, maybe the following day or week, Sarah has her T-Bird, I'm sitting beside her, she's turning the key. . . .

"Mom," Janine says and jostles my arm. "Are you sleeping or what? How could you go to sleep in the middle of our conversation?"

Suddenly I'm laughing. "You should have seen him," I say. "You should have seen the look on your grandfather's face when he started shoveling dirt. From the window I could see his lips moving, talking to that hole like it was going to answer. He kept slapping his pockets, looking for his watch, never imagining what Sarah had done."

Janine wants to know what happened when her grandfather's pocket watch failed to turn up, whether the neighbors thought burying a car wasn't a little strange. She wants to know what else I haven't told her.

I understand it's my turn to speak, and I'm more than a little afraid. Once I get started, once I shift decades, accelerate out of this slippery memory curve and speed clear of my mother's legacy of silence, there's no telling where we'll end up. Sarah smiles and nods. "Go on," she says, "answer your daughter."

In this way I begin speaking words that dovetail our lives, make our stories soar with the magic of Escher birds winging through space.

CALYX Journal, Vol.15:3, 1994/95

Terese   Martineau

SISTER ZITA

I am dying. I am in a room at St. Margaret's Hospice. My husband brought me here. The hospice is kept by nuns. These nuns know nothing of interior decoration. Every room has a plastic crucifix and a Claude Monet print left over from some museum fire sale. I can see how the prints were almost destroyed, their crinkly brown edges licked by fire. The Monet print is directly across from the headboard of my metal bed and I look at it every morning when I wake and every night before I sleep. The nuns think it's important to subdue the dying with fine art. I have always hated the work of Claude Monet. I hate all the impressionists and now impressionism is the last detail in my last bedroom on earth. I could ask to have it removed but I like hating art. It gives me something to do in the hospice.

My diagnosis was grim from the beginning. No one ever held out any hope to me. But at first I was infatuated with my death. It was like falling in love and having sex all the time and how in the beginning sex can make you feel so important. I liked to daydream about people crying over me. I especially liked how death freed me to say anything. Anything I said was important to everyone. Even when I told them I preferred oatmeal for breakfast. In the beginning it was like being some kind of saint with stars at my throat and a tongue blessed to drip honey. People wanted to touch me. People prepared my oatmeal like a ritual offering. It was powerful and exciting. It was like being a movie star.

Until just recently I thought maybe I'd have a mock death. A long time ago when I used to cook I'd tell my girls we were having mock meatloaf for dinner because it wasn't really meat, it was tofu. My girls gag on tofu. When I thought about that tofu scam, it was like I wasn't really dying. I liked the idea of dying if I was only dying a little. I've always had a sense of doom about myself and never had a vivacious or enthusiastic or cheerful personality. I was never fun at parties. When I first heard my diagnosis I thought, I've finally arrived. I am a born tragedienne. I've been described as a quiet woman but now it's obvious I am quiet and stoic, not quiet and dull. I liked such available drama. I liked to see the look of horror I excited in people. I maybe was like the Loch Ness monster to them or Bigfoot or that woman with snakes for hair. I felt nice and mythical. People think you know certain things when you are in a dying condition.

My photograph was even in the newspaper. I sent an old photograph to the editor, from the time before I was sick. In the photograph I am on a ferry and the wind is blowing my hair straight up to the sky. I am grinning and holding a drink in a plastic cup. That day I was drinking a double gin with limes. You can't tell from the picture that I am drinking alcohol. Some group of people were organizing a craft and bake sale to raise money for my family. I think they were going to sell funny refrigerator magnets and clothespin dolls and brownies. Everybody was sweet to me and in the article I said, "I'm overwhelmed—I want to thank everybody." I talked just like a movie star. I remember the way I held my breath when I said the word "overwhelmed" and spoke with my fingers touching my throat. I was trying to be theatrical. I was having fun. They raised $750 in the end and I had to act grateful.

I tried to be gung-ho about my dying. I pretended to be fascinated by science when all my hair fell out. "Isn't this amazing," I'd say, and I would reach into my skull as if it were a sand dune and pull a clump of my roots loose. My hair would fall like dirt. I bought velvet hats and feather hats and hats with cloth roses puckered like kisses and one purple turban clasped with a rhinestone pin. I'd put all these beautiful hats on my bald head and laugh a lot, like I am a lucky woman to have no hair and no breasts and cancer and all these beautiful hats for disguises. I don't even have pubic hair or eyelashes or eyebrows left. For a while I penciled my eyebrows in with brown liner, but I didn't bring my make-up bag to the hospice. My Grandma Judy and Lana Turner both lost their eyebrows in 1937 and had to draw them on forever after. Grandma Judy shaved hers off on a dare and I read somewhere that Lana's were sacrificed for her film career.

A friend visited me in the hospice and before she left I said, "I never wanted to be surprised by death." That's part of the truth. This friend knew I hated surprises, even surprise parties. I listed to myself all the people I knew who had died surprise deaths. It was a form of meditation. An ancestor of mine was shot dead by a bounty hunter for fifty dollars. My grandfather died while driving a car. He had a heart attack and the weight of his corpse drove his Pontiac through the side of a house. The family who owned the house had been in the kitchen, making pancakes and watching TV. Luckily my grandfather crashed through the master bedroom. That evening the family was on the news and they had to visit a relative's house to see the broadcast. You could see my grandfather on the news too. His body was covered with plaster and he looked like white alabaster. Then my only sister was walking downtown on a Tuesday after work carrying a birthday cake when she fell to the sidewalk in a crumble of heat. Something exploded in her brain. We were never close.

Things are different in this hospice room with the Monet prints. That dramatic stage seems like a long time ago, like it happened in my childhood. My husband brought me photos I never put in an album to remind me of home. There's a picture of my husband with a neighbor's dog and my two girls in tap dancing costumes. But I'm not at home and this room is not my home and this earth is not even my home for long. I want this room bare, like a nun's room. I don't want any reminders of what has been. I must look to the future, even if the future is nothing.

I still try to put on the act for my two girls. One daughter is seventeen and the other is sixteen. After they were born, I discovered the joys of birth control. I eventually called my cousin Nancy who worked for Planned Parenthood in South America because I was too bashful and dumb to go to strangers. Cousin Nancy wears sandals all the time, even in winter. In the winter she wears woolen socks underneath her sandals. I ask my girls to bring me caramel corn when they visit, even though I can no longer chew. Caramel corn used to be my favorite food and I would eat it all the time. I didn't like to eat regular meals.

I don't want the girls to bring me any flowers in here. I can't tolerate flowers anymore. They smell strange. Flowers smell like food and food smells like plastic. The smell of my girls disturbs me. They smell like sulfurous flowers. I noticed distortion in smells the day after I entered the hospice. I am now able to smell all the different variations of odors that make up one smell. I smell like I see a disgusting Claude Monet. The smell is a glob up close but at a distant view the glob can take a familiar and monstrous form. I can see the figure of each smell, rising in oily shapes to smear the air.

When the girls visit I wear the red and black striped robe, a gift from the oldest one. I put a kernel of caramel corn on the tip of my tongue and suck and pretend I am transported by some heavenly taste. I do not tell the girls how my pain blazes me to ashes. The pain is clean and shiny and incorruptible. My bones have changed into blades. The blade severs my body in two and the split cracks all the way through the floorboards of St. Margaret's and divides the earth. The pain is as autonomous and violent as the sun.

Instead I cultivate a fatal charm for my girls. I speak of old loves. I tell them when I was their age I worked at the drugstore candy counter and wore my hair back in a barrette. I licked my finger and made little spit curls fall over my ears. I sold chocolates to a man in the Marines and once we slept together. He wore his uniform to bed and I was naked. He went away and wrote me letters for a year. One year later I almost married a Jewish man but didn't because of religious complications. He thought I lacked spirituality. Someone told me he became a Sikh and went to live in an ashram. Then there was a man named Larry and sometimes he still visits me. Larry has one bulging eye as a result of a childhood accident. He could have been a model if not for that eye. I used to lick his bug-eyed eyelid and drive him crazy. He raises Doberman Pinschers even though one of his dogs almost killed his own son. The dog bit into the baby's head. When Larry used to visit me at home he'd bring some Dobermans and they'd pee everywhere. They peed on my kitchen table and my clean laundry and my fancy woolen rug with the swastikas. The swastikas aren't the symbols of Nazism but the Greek cross. It's an antique rug and it was woven one hundred years before the Nazis. My mother wanted me to marry Larry. Larry always smells of dog piss.

"It's the kissing and the lovemaking I remember most," I tell my girls and they giggle in a graceless way and the youngest one says, "Geez mom." It's the pathetic truth. Lovemaking was the most significantly active thing I ever did in my life. Nothing in life ever angered me too much. I supported no one else's ideas or causes, I barely supported my own. I was too timid to ask questions of a bus driver, even the bus driver I used to see every morning and every evening for five years in a row. I always wanted to ask which number bus went down Meany Street and I never did.

I had small dreams, cheap as coins. I didn't ever dream of being anyone special but I did dream of sensations. I wanted to live in the southernmost part of Georgia where my face would always shine with a delicate sweat like a fine veil and every day I would wear a fragrant flower in my hair. When I looked out the window, Spanish moss would drift like vagabond ghosts. I could eat a bag of peanuts on the front porch until my mouth was dried with peanut skins. Then I could pick a peach from my own backyard and suck out all the juice. No one would think I was quiet. I would be mysterious. I failed at even those puny dreams.

Now I am failing the act for my girls. My girls and I are having less and less of good times. I am thinking of telling my husband that they shouldn't come here anymore. Death makes me cruel. One day my oldest came in and I didn't like what she was wearing. I don't know which day anymore because I don't have days in the hospice, just darkness and light. She was wearing typical teenage clothes. She was like any other teenager. She was anonymous to me. Anonymity is frightening to someone in my condition. "You're a fuck-up," I said. "Don't wear that outfit to my funeral," I said. Then I laughed like some sicko, "I wouldn't be caught dead in that outfit." Morbid jokes made by the dying are all the same. They're like the racist jokes when you can substitute Polish for Indian for Jew for Blonde Female. And when she cried like she was drowning, I said, "Why are you crying? I'm the one who's dying."

I yelled at my favorite nun too. Sister Zita always has a story to tell and usually she brings me morphine. Sister Zita knows all about the saints and sometimes when I'm bored here and not contemplating on my demise I ask for the lives of the saints. Saints had such interesting lives. I like the saints because they did not recognize pain or death. I like to hear about the gory saints like St. Simon Stylites, who bound himself with ropes of palm and twisted stinking sores into his flesh. Sometimes Sister Zita will tell me about the sexy saints, although she doesn't tell me much. There is St. Theoctista, the girl from Lesbos, and St. Theodora, sentenced to life in a brothel. The other day Sister Zita wouldn't allow me my morphine until I answered correctly, "Who is the Saint of Deliverance of Women from Their Unwanted and Troublesome Husbands?" I knew that was St. Wilgefortis, the girl who grew a beard as protection against suitors. Happily I accepted the prize.

Sister Zita had promised me the story of St. Rose of Lima, the girl who liked to rub pepper into her cheeks. She came to see me and keep her promise. My room was full of sunbeams that dazzled the plastic Jesus with light. I was calm and watching the light move and waiting for Sister Zita and her morphine and the life of Rose of Lima. When Sister Zita smiled at me, I could see the thick plates of gold flashing behind her teeth like riches. Sister Zita has beautiful eyes. Her eyes are more purple than Elizabeth Taylor's and her eyelashes are long like a cat's whiskers. Sister Zita sniffled. I thought, Sister Zita must have a cold and then an eclipse seemed to pass and I shouted "Get out get out get out" over and over like that. When she left I cried and I thought I had given up on crying. If I caught cold now maybe my life would shorten by a week or a day or even a quarter of an hour. And even that piece of an hour is priceless to me. The rest of the day I had no personality and didn't want any visitors.

Before I got sick my husband and I went to dinner at a restaurant that floated on a barge in the middle of Lake Deep Rock. You had to walk out across a long dock to get there. We had a table underneath a green striped awning. "Don't you love to eat al fresco?" my husband asked. The wind moved my hair, like a hand pushing it aside. We ordered champagne and everyone in the restaurant said "ooh" when the waiter popped our champagne and the cork flew across the lake like a Roman candle. The waiter looked ashamed and said, "I'm not supposed to do that." The woman at the table next to ours said, "Now you've ruined perfectly good champagne." She had a sturdy and sensible face. Later in the evening I heard her discussing tapeworms during dinner. I watched the lake to see where the cork would land and I don't know why I thought I'd like to kill myself. I was a few months away from being sick then. I didn't know anything was wrong with my cells. Maybe even that night my cells were dividing faster and faster until there was no room for anything else and they choked out anything good and massed together with insane, military discipline. I was staring into the lake. I wanted to jump in that water so black the blackness had a thickness and a texture like it was dark oil on fire or a woman's deep and kinky hair or a blackbird's wing. I would jump down and down and die before I reached bottom. The black water would enter into me like a heavenly drug, like instant morphine.

I wait for those moments in the hospice when the fears uncurl and I hold on to the allure of black water. Even in this room I can feel it come over me, despite the Monet print stuck to the wall with yellowing tape and the yellowed plastic Jesus, his face the color of horse teeth. The allure is like a miracle. My skin hardens into a tight stony shell but inside I am floating in the deep black water and I can hold the blackness to me like a velvet cape, and there is nothing but the allure of the blackness.

The nuns think my death will come soon. I overheard Sister Zita say to my youngest, "I want you to know hearing is one of the last things to go." I thought I'd die all at once but Sister Zita seems to think it will happen in parts. Meanwhile I will be able to hear everything, in case my daughter wants to confess one last dirty act. I don't trust these nuns' knowledge of the physical realities. That's not their strong subject, necessarily. Sister Zita and my daughter tiptoe into my room as if I were asleep. At least I know I can still hear. "Can I help you with anything?" Sister Zita asks. I want to say that no one can help me now but that is too dramatic even for my taste. My daughter won't look at me, she looks only at the clock. Maybe she has an appointment.

I hear a lot of things in here when the nuns think I am sleeping or maybe too drugged to listen. It is like being dead already. It is like listening in on my funeral. The other day Sister Felicity and Sister Rosalie were in my room near the small closet with the toilet. I use a bedpan, so I call the toilet the guest room. Sister Felicity's skin is bumpy with big red pores, like the flesh of a freshly plucked chicken. She had been hanging a plastic holly wreath on my door. The nuns like to decorate the hospice at Christmastime. Now she was tacking Christmas cards on the toilet door. There was a Santa Claus card and a baby Jesus card and one card picturing bunnies with holly hanging around their little necks. It is only the beginning of November but I guess my friends and acquaintances from all over the world want to give me Christmas early this year. They want me to note I am still on their fucking Christmas card lists. I tolerate the decorations and the cards although their calendar means nothing to me now.

Sister Rosalie was adjusting the blinds in my room. I had been watching snow fall thick as leaves against the window for a long time. Maybe Sister Rosalie was afraid I would be struck snow blind so she closed the blinds. After a while she moved over to Sister Felicity who was still messing with her Christmas cards near the toilet. I could smell Sister Rosalie's chewing gum when she walked by my bed. Sister Rosalie is always chewing strong peppermint gum. Joan Crawford used to chew a lot of gum too. She chewed to keep her facial muscles firm. Sister Rosalie has a very muscular face and her jawline is taut. I am constantly amazed at all the garbage in my head. When I imagine the inside of my head I see Lana Turner's eyebrows twisting like snakes in a mound of Joan Crawford's chewing gum. "She's giving up now," Sister Rosalie said to Sister Felicity, obviously referring to me. "It's only a matter of days. She's stopped fighting."

I would love to be alive to visit your deathbed, Sister Rosalie. It will probably be in a room just like this one. It might be in this hospice, with all your sister nuns in attendance. I wish I could be there when you die, Sister Rosalie, you bitch. I would join all the sisters ringing around your bed, all of us dressed in black like witches. We'd circle you like the planets and their sister moons. I'd say, "Let's play ring around the rosy," and we'd dance in ecstasy until our black clothes closed in like water. We'd hold hands and we'd chant, "It's all your fault, it's all your fault." Because you're going to give up the fight too. You're going to lose in the contest of the immortals. "Cunts," I said out loud. They were two hairy caved cunts stuffing pebbles at the mouths of them to keep them closed. That gave the sisters a scare. Maybe they thought I was a ghost speaking. I am a ghost of my former self, as they say in the clichés. I wouldn't speak of cunts when I had my good health and fine manners.

I could be overreacting. That's just the way I feel. I'm a bit irritable.

It has been a while since I insulted Sister Felicity and Sister Rosalie in my room. I hear dozens of footsteps hissing through the hall. Then there is an unearthly silence. I try to hear anything. I am a little desperate. I can hear the clock in my room. Every room in St. Margaret's has a giant industrial clock with a big blank face and heavy black hands. We had clocks like that in grade school. When I was in fourth grade a bat flew into the classroom and banged its head into the clock above the blackboard. The teacher had written "i before e except after c" on the blackboard. The bat banged again and again. Everyone in the classroom screamed except me. Even the teacher screamed for the janitor to bring a broom. I thought the bat was beautiful but foolish. The bat's wings were lacy and rose-petaled. The janitor ran in with his broom like he would bring the bat down in a shower of arrows. This clock at St. Margaret's looks exactly like the school clock with the same clock hands hovering like the hands of a strangler.

I can hear but I can't speak. Words dissolve before I can say them. I want to cry for a nun. Something like a bird is plucking at my chest but it is my own two hands. I read somewhere that people always pick at themselves like vultures prior to their death. If that's true then I'm in trouble. My veins will open up and the unrestrained blood will carry me away in a flash flood, my stunned body swept away like a matchstick, with my hands folding helplessly over my head.

I think it is good that I can still hear. I am reconsidering Sister Zita's ideas on death and hearing loss. I listen to all the sounds I can hear. I hear the clock, I hear my blood rush. Now I hear my door open, and the dull fluttering thud when the plastic holly wreath slaps against the plywood. I hear my husband speak to me. He is speaking to me of love and promising me heaven. I wish he'd shut up so I could think. I'm sorry I was such a bad mother. I didn't want any children. I didn't breast-feed. I would take long naps and ignore my two girls. I let them run wild and chew sticks. Only rarely would I wake up to make them lunch. I would open the cabinet and look for a can of tomato soup. I could easily fall into the canned goods and cereal boxes and I would be lost to this world. I would live in a forest of dried spaghetti and pillow my head on jet-puffed marshmallows like they were clouds of the heavens. I thought maybe I would like to walk across the country, away from everything. My husband used to shake me in anger but he didn't know anything about me. "Girls, girls," I would scream to my daughters, "your father is trying to strangle me."

Other faces are flattening against me. My girls have wide and stretched out mouths like they are laughing in a carnival mirror. My family is here but they are as otherworldly to me as a rank of angels. They are space aliens with their identical wide foreheads and huge, demanding, hungry eyes and they have come to take me on a journey where they will poke me full of extraterrestrial fluids. They will stick a needle up my nose and probe my brain. Maybe they will poke into my rectum. I am surprised to see my father among them. My father never visits me. He has his hand on his heart, like he is going to pledge allegiance to the flag of the United States of America. His face looks crunchy. When I was a little girl my father told me about space aliens. He told me that anyone could have an encounter with aliens, even a respected man of the church or an officer of the law. But aliens especially liked to kidnap women and make them pregnant, and someday it might happen to me.

My husband's mouth is stained red with tomato sauce. He had taken the girls to Rocco's Italian restaurant and they were midway through their ravioli when the nuns called. For weeks my husband has been leaving all forwarding phone numbers for the nuns. My husband is saying he loves me. Goodbye husband, I have forgotten your name.

I guess I'm going back into eternity, back into the time before I was born. I didn't worry about the eternity I've missed so I guess I won't worry now. Eternity is flowing out of my mouth. It pushes me out of this bed and into the street. I am lost in the street. At first the streets are named for numbers and alphabets but I keep walking and the streets change. Now they are named for poets and then for war generals and then for kings and queens and then there are no streets. The searchlights are out but that probably doesn't mean much. It's maybe beaming from the top of a potato chip factory or a used car lot, trying to attract a crowd.

I can't believe this but I am actually walking next to one of Sister Zita's saints. This saint is wearing an iron collar and grinning at me. Then the saint disappears and I think I must be in a time before language when fish-birds ate meals of chalk and wing-fingered birds walked but never flew. I am visiting the world before fire. I am underwater, drifting through seaweed. Animals float past me like globs of jelly. The animals look like vegetables because they have no backbones.

I am sinking deeper now. I wonder if I'll see the Titanic. That would be something to see. The Titanic sunk in a far distant time from here but maybe I am at the spot where all time converges. The Titanic carried everything you'd ever want, beautiful jewelry and clothes and money and wonderful foods. The eggs that sank in the Titanic's pantry are edible forever. There's really no mystery to preserving things for a hundred years or more. Eggshells are so porous they can drink up the brine in the sea and preserve themselves for all eternity. I wish I could reach out now and peel one and eat the egg whole.

And Sister Zita, I can't hear a word.

CALYX Journal, Vol. 16:1, 1995

M. E v e l i n a   G a l a n g

HER WILD AMERICAN SELF

t's like my family's stuck somewhere on the Philippine
Islands. My grandmother, Lola Mona, says that I'm as
wild as Tita Augustina. That I have that same look in my eye. A stubborn-
ness. And if I'm not careful, I will be more trouble than she ever was. She
says her daughter was a hard-headed Americana who never learned how to
obey, never listened. Like me, she says. My family believes that telling her
story will act as some kind of warning, that I might learn from her mis-
takes.

When she was young, Augustina wanted to be chosen. Maybe it was all
those movies about Teresa and Bernadette, flying off to heaven, but she
imagined she would be a modern-day saint from Chicago's north side. Sit-
ting at her window before bedtime, she'd divide the night into decades and
mysteries. The moon was a candle offering and she surrendered prayers to
Mary by that light.

When she was eleven, Augustina wanted to be an altar girl. In a red robe
and white gown, she dreamed of carrying the Crucifix down the aisle. Her
mother wouldn't hear of it. "God loves your devotion, hija," she'd say. "He
loves you whether or not you carry Him down the aisle at church."

To rebel, Augustina stopped going to Mass with the family. "God loves
me," she'd tell her mom, "whether or not I show up on Sundays."

Augustina's dad, Ricardo, clenched his jaw tight, spitting words through
the space of his gold-capped teeth. "How can you do this to your mother?"
he demanded. He gestured a bony brown finger at his wife who was col-
lapsed on the living room sofa sobbing.

"How will this look?" she cried. "My own daughter missing Sunday Mass.
People will talk."

Augustina tried bargaining with them. "Let me be an altar girl, let me keep playing baseball with the neighborhood kids, and I'll keep going."

Mona let out a little scream. "Even worse!" she said. "Your reputation, anak!" Mona dramatically curled her palm into a tight little fist and pounded her chest, keeping time with the painful beat of her heart.

Ricardo placed Augustina into the back seat of the car, threatening to send her to the Philippines for lessons in obedience. The threats meant nothing to her. She sat in the car all during Mass, making faces at the people who'd stare into the windshield. Next Sunday, her parents let her stay home alone.

This did not sit well with the family. When Mona and Ricardo moved to America, they brought with them a trunk full of ideas—land of opportunity, home of democracy, and equality—but God forbid we should ever be like those Americans—loose, loud-mouth, disrespectful children. Augustina was already acting wild and stubborn, opinionated too. To tame her, they sent Augustina to all-girl Catholic schools.

On her first day at Holy Angels, she walked into the cafeteria with her cold lunch—a Tupperware of leftover rice and fish. There was a long table of girls sitting near the window. Recognizing some of them from class that morning, Augustina walked over to a space at the end of the table and as she got nearer, their voices grew silent. She greeted the girls and they smiled at her, they nodded. "Mind if I sit here?" she asked. They stared at her as if Mary Mother of God had swiped their voices. They just stared. Augustina sat with them anyway. Then Colleen Donahue said, "This school's getting cramped." She was talking to the girl across from her.

"Yeah," the girl answered. "What *is* that smell?"

Augustina scanned the table—the girls were eating oranges and apples. Some sat with nothing in front of them. She was the only one with a Tupperware of food. Then she said to the girl sitting next to her, "What kind of lipstick is that? It's wild." But the girl turned her back on Augustina as if Our Lady had plagued her.

"I think it's coming from her," said the girl as she held her nose.

Augustina looked down the row of milk-white faces, faces so pure and fresh, it was hard to tell if they were born that way or if they'd simply scrubbed the color out of them. She looked down at her hands, at the red nail polish peeling, at her fingers stretched out stiff in front of her. She had never noticed how brown her skin was until then. She would never have a single girlfriend among them. In fact, they say that Augustina's only real friend was her cousin Gabriel.

When Augustina got home that first day, she begged her mother to let her transfer to the neighborhood school, but her mother wouldn't listen. Instead she sat Augustina down on her bed, brushing the hair away from her face, and told her, "Your father and I work very hard to keep you in that school. It's the best, hija," she told her. "You'll see."

So she started hanging out with her cousin Gabriel in places they'd find disturbing. We have pictures that Gabriel took of Augustina dancing among tombs and statues of beautiful women saints at Grace Cemetery. In many of the photos, her image is like a ghost's. There's the snow-covered hills and Augustina's shock of black hair, her elephant-leg hip-huggers, moccasin-fringed vests and midriff tops, the scarves that sailed from the top of her head, the loose beads and bangle earrings flipping in the wind. They say her cousin Gabriel was in love with her, that he was what made her wild.

Mona used to complain to her husband, "Why does she always have to go to that place? Play among those dead people? Maybe we should have sent her to public school after all, Ricardo, or maybe we should have encouraged her friendships with those children, those boys next door." Her father, a hardworking surgeon, denied there was anything wrong. "Nonsense," he'd say. "She's a girl and she should act like one."

One night, when Augustina was sixteen, she locked the door to her bedroom and hid away from everyone. Her room was a sanctuary where Gabriel's photos plastered the walls, a row of votive candles lined her window ledge, and postcards of Lourdes and Fatima decorated her bedpost. She had built an altar of rocks from the beach up on Montrose, a tiny indoor grotto where she burned incense. She put on an old 45. Years later, Augustina would sing that song about Mother Mary and troubled times and letting it go—or was it be? Whatever—at parties and weddings and funerals and any event where she could bring her twelve-string guitar.

Lighting a cigarette, Augustina waved a match in the air. Then she slipped a hand underneath her pillow, pulling out a fine silver chain. At the end of the chain was a small medallion, oval like a misshapen moon and blue like the sky. From the center of the pendant rose a statue of the Virgin Mary, intricate and smooth like an ivory cameo. Augustina had taken the necklace out of her mother's jewelry box and kept it for herself. She believed it was her lucky charm.

She held the necklace between her fingers, rubbing its coolness into her skin, begging the Virgin to hear her. "You were young," she whispered. "You know what it's like to love a boy." She imagined her mother's swollen heart bursting and water spilling out, cascading down her tired body, mourning as though her daughter were dead. Her mother would never forgive her. After all the trouble her parents went through to keep her away from the bad crowd, the boys, and lust in general, Augustina still managed to fall in love.

Her mom stood at the door, knocking loudly, but Augustina pretended not to hear. She took another drag of her cigarette, then snuffed it out in the cradle of a votive candle. Reaching to the side of the table, she lit a stick of incense, disguised the smoke with the scent of roses. She slipped the pendant under her pillow and held a picture of herself sitting on the rocks at Montrose Harbor. She was wrapped in the cave of Gabriel's chest, curling her body tightly into his. The waves were high and one could see a spray of water falling onto them. Her mother would die if she saw that picture. "Augustina," her mother said, "open up, hija, I want to know what's bothering you."

"Nothing, Mama," she answered. "I'm just tired."

Her mother jiggled the door. "Open up. Let me look at you, you were pale at dinner." She waited another moment and then asked, "Why don't you talk to me, Ina? Let me know what's wrong."

Talking to her mother was like talking to the house plants. With good intentions, she would sit, gladly nodding, smiling, but she wouldn't hear. Like the time Augustina tried to tell her mother about the nuns, how they pointed her out in class, saying things like, "Thanks be to God, Augustina, the Church risked life and limb to save your people, civilize them. Thank God, there were the Spanish and later the Americans." All her mother said was, "She meant well, hija. Try to be more patient."

The next morning Sister Nora gave her annual lecture to the sophomore class. Standing in front of a screen, a giant projection of the world splattered across her face and the gym at large, she waved a long pointer in the air, gestured at the map. "There are cultures," she said, "that go to great lengths to keep their daughters chaste." Augustina envisioned a large needle and thread stitching its way around the world, gathering young girls' innocence into the caves of their bodies, holding it there like the stuffing in a Thanksgiving turkey. She had to excuse herself.

The heat in the building was too much, too suffocating. Every time she closed her eyes she saw her mother's image on the screen before her or she'd picture the girls in Africa, their stitches bursting wide open. Augustina ran out. She sat on the curb, cupping her hands against the wind, her thin legs sprawled out in front of her. She slipped a cigarette between her lips and listened to the girls' voices wafting out of the building. She hated everyone at that school.

A low riding vehicle, brown and rusted, snaked its way along Holy Angels' driveway. Augustina took another drag from her cigarette. As she moved away from them, she could hear the girls howling.

"It's her sexy cousin," yelled one girl, "the Filipino house boy."

"You'll get caught," Colleen said plainly.

As she climbed into Gabriel's Mustang, Augustina swore under her breath, asked, "Yeah, so what's it to you?"

He drove uptown, taking side streets, weaving the car around pedestrians. His camera, a thirty-five millimeter he had inherited from his grandfather, was carefully placed next to him on the seat. It was his lolo's first possession in the States. Reaching for it, Augustina played with the zoom, slipping it back and forth, in and out like a toy.

"Don't break that," Gabriel warned.

The light from outside framed his profile. She could see the angle of his cheekbones, how they jutted from his face, the slope of his nose and the dimples that were set in his half-smile. She snapped a picture of him, click, wind, click. Snapped another. She pointed the camera out the window and watched the streets through an orange filter. They rode most of the way in silence and then he finally said, "So did you think about it?"

"Yep," she sighed, "it's all I can think about."

"Me too," he said.

"Maybe we should stop hanging out so much," she said. "Maybe that would help."

But Gabriel shook his head. "That's not right either."

The window was splattered with slush from the streets. Through the viewfinder, she caught a girl carrying a baby. The infant, dressed in a light blue snowsuit, draped its body across the girl, curled its head into the crook of her neck, slept comfortably amid the winter traffic. Click, she snapped another picture.

Augustina thought the girl carrying the child looked like Emmy Nolando, the daughter of her parents' tennis partners. Apparently, Dr. Nolando refused to give his daughter birth control and when she came home pregnant, the Nolandos sent her to a foster home in town. Disowned her. Augustina's parents milked the story for almost an entire year.

"Can you imagine," her mother whispered as she leaned over her bowl of soup. "The shame of it."

When Augustina asked why Emmy was sent away, her father shook his head and muttered, "Disgraceful."

Ricardo leapt into a long lecture concerning those loose American girls and their immorality. "She's lucky she's not in the Philippines," he said. "There she'd have that baby and her parents would raise that child as their own."

"That's stupid," Augustina said.

"Oh yes," Mona said. "That baby would never know who his real mommy was. That's how it's done back home. That's how they save the family's reputation."

Even though Emmy had spent her pregnancy in a foster home, and even though she gave her baby up for adoption, Augustina was still told not to speak to Emmy. No one did. The Filipino community ignored her. "Better not be wild, better not embarrass the family like that girl. Better not, better not, better not."

Of all their hangouts, Grace Cemetery was their favorite. At Grace, the sun shattered into a thousand bright icicles, splintering branches into shadows, casting intricate patterns on hills of white. New-fallen snow draped the statues of saints and beautiful ladies like white linen robes. The statues stood at the doors of tombs and prayed for souls. They stood guard no matter what—storms or drought. Once a twister ripped across Grace Cemetery and trees broke in half—a couple of tombstones even uprooted. But these women stood strong.

Augustina sat at the foot of St. Bernadette's statue, gathering snow into little heaps. When Bernadette was visited by the Blessed Virgin back in Lourdes, they thought she was crazy. They didn't believe her. But Bernadette didn't give a fuck what they thought. She just kept going up that hill, praying, talking to Holy Mary like it was nobody's business. Augustina ran her hands along the statue's feet, tracing the finely etched toes with the edge of her finger. She listened to the wind winding its voice through the trees like a cool blue ribbon.

Gabriel fiddled with his camera, flipping through filters and lenses. She watched him sitting on a hill, his long body bent over the camera, his hair falling to either side of his face, shining midnight under the hot winter sun. Augustina believed Gabriel was an angel in another life. She could tell by his pictures, black and white photos of the city and its people. He once told her that truth cannot possibly hide in black and white the way it does in color. Colors distort truth, make the ugly something beautiful. She considered him brilliant.

"Bless Gabriel," she told the statue. Augustina looked up at the saint's full cheeks, which were round and smooth like the sun. Her eyes were carved into perfectly shaped hazelnuts—so lifelike that from here Augustina could see the definition of her eyelashes.

"Augustina!" Gabriel yelled. "Look up." He jumped up onto someone's tombstone. The light from behind him glared at Augustina, forming a haze of white around his black mane. "This light's great," he said. "Your eyes are magnificent."

"I'm squinting," she said. He leapt from the side of the tomb, and leaning over her, he tugged at the ends of her hair.

Augustina placed a cold hand on the side of his face and he shivered. "What would your parents say?" she asked. "What should we do?"

He stared at the graves. The sun slipped behind a crowd of clouds and suddenly it was cold out. Augustina lit a cigarette and offered him a drag. He buried his face in one hand as he pushed her away with the other.

Getting up, she slipped away, walked underneath the rocks that formed an archway where Mary stood serenely veiled in paint—sky blue and gold. Tossing her cigarette to the ground, Augustina walked past the bench, pushed up against the iron rail, leaned her pelvis into the gate and pulled at one of the rods. She stared at the thick wooden rosary that draped Mary's white hands. Augustina told the Lady, "It feels natural. Why not?"

She had not meant for any of it to happen. A few weeks before, *The Chicago Tribune* awarded ten prizes to the best high school photographers. A manila envelope came to Gabriel's house thick with a piece of cardboard, his prize-winning photo of the Rastafari woman on Maxwell Street, and a check for two hundred dollars. Second prize. The letter that came with the announcement talked about Gabriel's use of light, texture, and composition. The judge said Gabriel's intuitive eye was not only a gift but a way to see the world. Gabriel should develop his potential.

When Gabriel showed his father the letter and winning photo, Uncle Hector blew up. Told Gabriel he was wasting his time again, taking risks with his life, traveling into dangerous neighborhoods and for what? A picture? "Don't be stupid," Hector told him. What if something would have happened there on the Southside? He could have been mugged or knifed or beaten. He could have been shot from the gun of a passing car. Was he crazy, Hector wanted to know. Grabbing Gabriel's camera, Hector shook it over his head like a preacher with a Bible, its strap casting shadows on his face. "Enough of this," he said. "Stop wasting your time." As he threw the camera across the kitchen, the lens popped open, crashed on Tita Belina's marble floor, and shattered.

That night, Augustina sat on the rocks at Montrose Harbor, holding Gabriel's head on her lap, brushing the hair from his face, wiping the tears as they rolled from the corners of his eyes. "Count the stars," Augustina whispered. "Forget him." Augustina felt so bad for him, so angry at her uncle. And when Gabriel glanced up at her, she leaned down to meet him and kissed. She let her lips rest there, held onto him, and something in her stirred, some feeling she was not accustomed to. She let go a long sigh, let go that little bit of loneliness.

Augustina thought she saw the Lady smiling at her, looking right through her. Okay, she whispered, I can't stop thinking about him. Am I bad? At night she imagined the weight of his body pushing down on her, covering her like a giant quilt. She saw his eyes slipping into her, his beautiful face washing over her in the dark. She tried to remember the feel of his hair, how the strands came together, locked around each other. Sometimes she thought she could smell the scent of him, there at the lake, a fragrance of sandalwood, a breeze from Lake Michigan. I'm crazy, okay, she thought. A tramp, if you will. But he loves me, Mary, doesn't that count?

She thought of Sister Nora and the girls whose parents made sure of their virginity. How they'd mutilate them in the name of chastity. And does that operation keep those girls from love, she wondered. Does it keep them from wanting boys? Sister Nora would find out and tell everyone. Use her for an example. No, she'd rather die. She imagined her body floating, swelling in the depth of the lake. She imagined herself swimming eternally. Augustina closed her eyes, putting her face to the sky. The sun came out every few seconds, ducking out of the clouds so that Mary appeared hazy and kind of aglow—but only for seconds at a time. "Hail Mary," she said. "Hail Mary, full of grace, the Lord is with thee, so please, please, please, put in a word for me, Hail Mary." She was so deep in prayer, she didn't even hear Gabriel sneak up behind her.

"Are you worried?" he asked.

"A little," she said. He put his arm around her and they embraced. Kissed. Slowly fell into that long black funnel, slipping across borders they had never crossed till now. They spent the rest of the day lying under the branches of the grotto, watching the changing sky and waiting for the sun to sleep. Neither one of them wanted to go home.

The house was locked when she got there, so Augustina fumbled for the key she wore around her neck. When she opened the door, the symphony from her father's speakers rushed out to her like waves on Montrose beach. Music filled the house so that when she called out to her mother, her voice was lost and small.

Mona stood at the stove, her feet planted firmly apart, one hand on her hip and the other stirring vegetables. Augustina snuck up behind her and kissed her softly on the cheek. "Hi, Mommy," she whispered. Mona continued to mix the stir fry, beating the sides of the frying pan with quick movements. Beads of sweat formed at her temples as she worked. "Do you want me to set the table?" Augustina asked. Turning, she saw the table was already set. Four large plates, a spoon and fork at each setting, a napkin, a water glass. "Okay," Augustina sang, "well, maybe I'll wash up and I'll help you put the food out."

The music was blasting in her father's room. She popped her head in and waved at him. "Hi, Dad!" she called. He was reading the paper and when he didn't look up she tapped him on the knee. Leaning over, she kissed him.

"Sweetheart," he said, "is dinner almost ready?"

"Yeah, Dad. In a minute."

She felt as though she had been up all night. Her body ached, was covered with dirt from the cemetery. Gabriel's cologne had seeped into her skin, and she was afraid that her mother had sensed it. So instead of simply washing her hands, she bathed.

The cool water, rushing down her body, washed away the cigarette smoke, the cologne, the dirt. She could almost feel the water coursing through her, washing over her mind, cleaning out her tummy, circling about her heart.

When she got back to the kitchen, she found she was too late. Her mother had placed a huge bowl of rice on the table, a plate of beef and vegetables, and a tureen of soup. "Sorry, Ma," she said, as she grabbed a cold pitcher of water. "I just needed a shower."

"Is that all, Augustina?" her mother asked as she looked up from the sink. "What did you do today? Ha? Where were you?"

She felt her face burning bright red. "At school," she answered, "where else? Then Gabriel and I went to the mall."

"School?" her mother whispered. "They were looking for you at school."

Augustina stared at the table, ran her fingers around the edge of the water pitcher. It was cold and moisture shivered from the pitcher's mouth and ran down its sides. Her mother's voice was low and angry. "How many times do we have to go through this, hija? Why can't you just stay in school?"

"But I was feeling sick," Augustina said.

"So you had Gabriel pick you up and the both of you were absent?" Her mother threw a dish rag on the counter. "You were at the cemetery again?" She pulled Augustina close to her. "Do you want your father to send you to the Philippines? Maybe that would teach you how to behave." Her parents often threatened to send her there, to all-girl convent schools, where nuns pretended to be mothers. "If you think the rules are strict here, wait till you have to live there."

"Sorry, Mom," Augustina whispered. "But the truth is that Gabriel had another fight with Uncle Hector and he was upset. He came to get me so we could talk."

"Still, hija, that's no reason to be absent from school." As Mona brushed the hair out of her face and kissed the top of her forehead, Augustina's father stepped into the kitchen.

"Ano ba," he asked. "What's going on?"

Mona tucked her hair behind her ears and told him, "Nothing, nothing, Ricardo. Dinner is ready. Come sit. Ina, call your brother."

Augustina spent the next two days locked up in her room, blasting her record. The needle slipped over that old 45, bumped along the grooves and scratches, whispering a mantra. "Mother Mary," she sang along, "comes to me." An old church organ cranked a sacrilegious funk, a honky tonk, that seemed to fade into the slow rise of the electric guitar's bridge. She played around with Gabriel's photos. She mounted them on cardboard and painted borders around them—daisies and rainbows and splotches of love and peace and kisses drawn in giant bubble letters. Her mother stood at the door, knocking, forever knocking, but she pretended to not hear. "I'm not feeling well," she had told her mother. "I don't want to go to school." Bile rose up in her throat, churned in her stomach, swamped up against the cavern in her chest.

Her family came to the door one by one. First her mother, then Dad. Even Auntie Belina, her cousin Ofelia, and Uncle Hector came knocking, but the door was locked and there was no opening it. When Gabriel stood at the door, she whispered through a crack, "I'm sorry, I can't let you in. They can't know."

When she finally went to school, Sister Nora stood in front of the classroom, whacking her giant pointer stick across the blackboard. "There has been disgraceful conduct. Sin, sin, sin. Apparently, the story of the young girls and their experience with genital mutilation has not taught you anything. You girls must be punished."

Augustina thought the nun knew, was about to expose her when Sister ordered the girls who attended Kat O'Donel's slumber party to step forward. Apparently the sisters found a video tape of "Marlin the Magnificent" dancing in his elephant mask—and that was all he wore—a mask. The tape was found lying in the Cathedral—second to the last pew, across from the confessional. Fran Guncheon, class librarian, and Augustina were the only ones not in attendance, so they were given permission to leave. Augustina took this opportunity to run to Grace Cemetery.

The clouds drifted north, slipped by fast like the second hand in her grandmother's wristwatch. Her body was numb, frozen like the ladies in he court. She thought they had grown sad. Her constellation of saints, like everyone else in her life, had stopped listening to her. Snow melted around St. Bernadette, the sun burning holes in the ice underneath her. Augustina smelled the earth seeping through the slush. It was sweet and fertile. A rickle, a tear, maybe the melting snow, slipped down Bernadette's face. Inside Augustina, something grumbled, roared. She had stopped praying weeks ago. God confused her.

Augustina looked up from the statue and saw her mother climbing over the hill. The sun shrouded her in light. She wore her off-white cashmere coat, the one that fell to her ankles because she was so short. She wrapped her black hair in a white chiffon scarf that trailed past her shoulders, followed the wind. There was a cloud of white smoke trailing from her breath, rising up and floating away from her. When she came near, her mother said, "She's beautiful."

"She's strong," Augustina answered.

"So this is where you go." She tugged at Augustina's braids, examined her face, kissed the top of her forehead. Then, pulling the chain from Augustina's neck, she said, "Where did you get this, hija?"

"Isn't it my baby necklace? I found it in your jewelry box."

Her mother shook her head. "I got this from my godmother. You shouldn't have taken it without asking."

Slipping her head onto her mother's shoulder, Augustina felt her body soften, the energy draining from her. She considered telling her mom about Gabriel. Would she understand? She closed her eyes and fell in time to her mother's breathing. Maybe, she thought. Her mother embraced her, told her, "Whatever is troubling you, hija, don't worry. Family is family."

Of course, Lola Mona never tells me that part of it. The story goes, Tita Augustina went to the Philippines six months later. Some of the relatives say it was to have a baby, others say it was to discipline her wild American self. Still stuck back on the islands, they tell me, "You're next. Watch out." Even my mother thinks her older sister was a bad girl.

"How do you know?" I ask her. "You weren't even born when she left. You hardly knew her." My mother always shrugs her shoulders, says she just knows.

Last time I went to see Tita Ina, she held out her tiny fist, wrinkled and lined with blue veins, and slipped me the Blessed Virgin dangling from the end of a fine silver chain. "Here, hija," she said, "take this." I placed the necklace up to the light. The paint was fading and chipping from its sky blue center, but still there was something about Her. The way Her skirts seemed to flow, the way Her body was sculpted into miniature curves, the way the tiny rosary was etched onto the metal plate.

CALYX Journal, Vol. 16:2, 1995/96

Hollis Seamon

GYPSIES IN THE PLACE OF PAIN

W hen the gypsies came and camped in the hospital
waiting room, anything seemed possible, for a
while. Our little world of 9-South widened for that week, and something of
the strange and magical was let in. After they left, carrying their healed
daughter away in their arms, I stood in the empty waiting room and just
breathed their air. It still smelled different from ordinary hospital air—
spicy and sweaty, smoky and free. I miss the gypsies. But that's the whole
point, I guess: gypsies go and we stay.

The gypsies had come suddenly, as all the old stories warn us they will.
One minute the hospital halls were full of us ordinary parents and our ordi-
nary sick or wounded children and the next they were full of men in tight
black pants and loose white shirts and women in full skirts of many colors.
The gypsies spoke fast and loud in a language no one else knew, and its
strange cadences silenced our usual hum of Spanish and English as we all
stopped to listen. In one afternoon, the gypsy women took over and trans-
formed the parents' lounge, spreading bright blankets on the floor and over
the vinyl couches and drawing out packages of food from their deep bags
and bundles. The gypsy men leaned against the walls of the lounge, smok-
ing dark cigarettes and eating from plates of food carried to them by the
women.

Up and down the hall, ordinary parents drew their children, those who
could walk or wheel about the corridors, in close. The old stories say that
gypsies steal children, but when the gypsies had gone, no children from 9-
South were missing and no changelings had appeared. Of course, our chil-
dren were poor candidates for stealing—some would have died by nightfall
without their IVs, their respirators, their transfusions. Our children were

quite safe from gypsies. In fact, before she left, the gypsy grandmother made charms for many of the children to protect them. My son Ted still has his taped to his latest dressing—a small triangle of different-colored threads woven together with pieces of straw.

I wasn't exactly surprised when the gypsies arrived on our floor but I was still amazed. Delighted, actually, to see that gypsies really do exist, just as we've been told—a tribe, a people entirely foreign but here among us, after all. Not legends but flesh. I wasn't surprised because, early on the day they came, my son's surgeon had pulled me into the 9-South supply closet to tell me they were here. He'd done a classic "Psst," crooked finger invitation as I walked by the closet on my way to face a terrible cafeteria breakfast. It was pretty laughable, the great and handsome surgeon huddled in the closet, sitting on a giant institutional-size box of Pampers, waving me in.

I went in and leaned against the shelves stacked with boxes of syringes and sterile tubing and tried to look perfectly normal. "Yes, Doctor?" I said.

"Close the door," he said.

"Wow. Is this a proposition, Alex?" I asked, wishing it were and knowing it wasn't.

"Just shut the door, OK?"

I reached over and swung it shut. "Damn. No lock," I said.

He put his head in his hands, half laughing, half moaning. "You won't believe this," he muttered. "This is too weird to believe."

He was wrong about that, of course. I believe anything. You can't spend years hanging around Babies Hospital in New York City and maintain a normal sense of incredulity. Really, as the bumper stickers say, "Shit happens," and unbelievable shit happens to our kids all the time. But I didn't want to answer him right away; I was just enjoying looking at him in close closet range. He is a golden man, blond and tan as only the rich and privileged seem to be. And he was wearing his surgical greens and white sneakers, my favorite outfit. He looked young and rumpled, as vulnerable as any guy caught in his pajamas.

OK, so it's not hard to tell that I'm half in love with him—the classic mother-falls-for-her-kid's-doctor routine. But it's exactly that: half in love. I am emphatically not in love with Dr. Alexander Harvey, the chief pediatric surgeon who marshals his troops and marches them around the halls in the mornings, pointing at the kids in their rooms like they're cases in some ever-changing file cabinet and making little jokes to entertain the interns: "This is Ted, who got the worst of both worlds. Nature screwed him up and lousy early medical care made him worse." This is Ted, I think back at them a polite smile on my face, my beloved, intelligent, funny, wounded eight-year-old son: look in his eyes, you pompous bastards, and weep. But I *am* in love with Alex, who often shows up alone, at odd hours, looking weary, and who sits on the end of Ted's bed and trades sports stories. This Alex sends Ted tickets to Giants and West Point football games, and this Alex once took Ted out of the hospital, removing all the tubes he would later have to replace himself, and transported him to Yankee Stadium by subway. So, sure, I'm half in love with my son's surgeon, and why not? He loves my son, I know that, and he loves him because he cannot cure him, not because he can. Give the man credit: it's real easy for big-ego surgeons to feel fondness, almost gratitude, for their successes and real, real hard for them to love the failures—the patched-up, cob-job kids we hold together with tape and spit and guts, walking reminders that medicine is not magic. On 9-South, we call these kids repeat offenders, and we laugh.

He lifted his head and looked up.

I smiled and sat down on a box, knee-to-knee with Alex. "OK. So what is too weird to believe?"

"Gypsies," he said. "There is a whole pack of gypsies in my office downstairs."

I'll admit that was unexpected, "Gypsies? Like real gypsies? Gold hoop earrings, shawls, crystal balls?" I was harking back to my favorite Halloween version of gypsies, the costume we could always whip up at the last minute. "Gypsies? In New York?"

He nodded. "Not only that. The princess of the gypsies is lying on the couch in my office, right now, with a fever of 105. Lois is trying to find her an endowed bed."

Lois is Alex's secretary—a hero in any time and place. She lets me use her typewriter to type papers for my correspondence classes, and she once let Ted sneak an X-ray of a Mickey Mouse toy, posed so that Mickey was giving everyone the finger, into a pile of films Dr. Harvey was presenting at a fancy medical conference. It was a big hit and now they keep it in the files all the time.

"They have no insurance, of course," he was saying.

"Wait—the princess of the gypsies?"

"Yeah. The honest-to-God princess of Romany, I swear—or one of them, anyway; she may not be the first in line for the throne—is in my office." He rubbed his face with his hands, "She's six years old. She's pretty sick. And they brought her to me, because they asked at other hospitals for the best pediatric surgeon in town. So, of course, someone mentioned me." He said this with not a stitch of false modesty; one of the things I love about him is his absolute hubris. "Now they won't let anyone else touch her. I understand that her father waved a pretty big knife at an intern who tried to divert them to the emergency room instead of my office." He grinned. "Her father carried her right into my office, put her into my arms and said, 'You will fix my daughter's kidney.'"

I laughed. "Or else?"

He nodded. "That was the implication. They have her films from another hospital, and he is right about the diagnosis. She's got an obstruction and one kidney is a mess."

I looked over his head at the piles of clean white sheets. "Can you save it?"

He touched my knee. "Sure. It's not as far gone as Ted's was. And her obstruction isn't bilateral and she doesn't have all the other complicating factors. Sure. It's really pretty simple; they're lucky they came here first, before somebody else screwed around with her. But she is a sick kid right now." He stood up and stretched. "And I better fix her. I have a feeling that if I don't, my first-born son is a goner."

I tried to laugh. Alex's first-born son is named Chad. He's a chubby kid who comes in with his father on weekends sometimes and plays video games with Ted. He's a nice kid.

Alex tapped my head on his way out. "She's coming to this floor, the princess. And the whole gypsy encampment, I bet, will follow her. Keep watch."

I smiled. "Good. It will make a change around here. And I want my fortune told."

He left the door open and I sat back on the box, looking at the floor. I didn't want my fortune told, not really. What if we all had knives, I thought, and what if we all threatened to take their first-born if they couldn't save our own? What if it were that simple—one day we all just stopped smiling and being polite and keeping our lips stiff? What if we wailed and rent our breasts and demanded justice? It was worth thinking about.

Because when the gypsy parents came on the floor, that's what they did. Or at least they let their anger and their fear show as their little girl was put in the bed in the single room at the end of the hall. Her father wouldn't let the orderlies put her on a stretcher; he carried her in his arms, her little dark head tight against his chest, all the way up in the elevator, the nurses told us later. The nurses had a very hard time getting near her to take her temp and start her IV, her father hovered so close. Her mother stood a little aside but her eyes were fierce and she watched them so closely that it made them nervous, the nurses said, and they had to stick her twice. They were sweating, they said, when they left the room, and they drew straws to choose her night nurses. No one wanted to work under the pressure of gypsy parents' eyes—royal gypsy parents, at that.

By that afternoon, the gypsies had taken over the lounge, and the security men had been sent up, again and again, to explain that it was only for parents and to explain the rules about smoking and how many visitors the children could have at any one time, and so on. There was a lot of shouting and then I guess a compromise of sorts: her parents could sleep on cots in her room, as we all did, and her grandparents and a few other close relatives could stay in the lounge. The few others amounted to about twenty-five people and they all roamed our hall in bands of bright color and strange talk. They stuck their heads right into our rooms, pointing at our children and waving their hands toward our TVs and video games. They observed none of the usual dictates of hospital etiquette, the rules of proper parental behavior that say, basically, "Don't stare at other people's pain."

An old woman dressed all in black, the princess's grandmother, it turned out, came all the way into our room. I was reading and Ted was sitting up playing with his guys—small action figures he keeps spread across his bed table, arranged into elaborate warring factions. His big stuffed cat, a round black scowling thing that he loves, sat at the foot of his bed. Sometimes at night Ted tells me stories he's made up about this cat, whose name is Fuzzle. He leans down from his high bed over my cot and says, "Hey, Mom. Want to hear an exploit of Fuzzle?" And he goes on to tell one, some outrageously wicked adventure of Fuzzle, a cat with no scruples whatsoever—bad-tempered, foul-mouthed, vengeful, and gleefully mean. They're a riot, those stories.

The woman came right in and touched the cat. She looked at me and said, in oddly accented English, "For luck?"

I nodded. "For luck."

She shook her head and touched Ted's foot under the sheet. "Is there luck, in this place?" She waved her hand to indicate the whole hospital.

Ted looked up at her and grinned. "Sure," he said. "Bad luck."

She nodded and tapped his foot. "This is a smart boy," she said. She looked over at me. "A smart strong boy." She turned and left our room. Behind her she left a scent. It smelled to me like cloves, a warm dry smell. Comforting.

I felt sudden tears on my cheeks and I walked to the window to keep them from Ted. I looked out into the graying afternoon. There is a small rocky park just across Broadway from the hospital; its few trees were bare.

I'd almost forgotten it was November, nearing Thanksgiving. In here, time is all the same. The temperature in the halls remains steady, summer and winter. The windows don't open.

I looked into the street, where everyday people were walking home from work under the low sky. In the park bunches of people were gathering. I could only see a funny, foreshortened view of them from up here on the ninth floor, but I realized who they were—gypsies, hundreds of them. They had come from somewhere, from everywhere, to camp outside the hospital in the cold. I felt a little hiccup of hope in my chest: if gypsies still existed and if they came like this, rising out of the streets of New York like mist, when and where they were needed, wasn't anything possible? Anything at all?

For days the gypsies stayed in the little park and they actually had real campfires. Ted and I sat on the wide windowsill in the evenings and looked down on the spots of orange flame nine stories below. Ted began to make up a whole new series of Fuzzle exploits—Fuzzle and the Gypsies. In these adventures, Fuzzle learns a lot from the gypsies about knives and horses and crossing palms with silver. As I recall, Fuzzle also teaches the gypsies a thing or two about pure, unadulterated meanness and spite.

While the fires burned outside, the princess was feeling better inside, the antibiotics working on her infection. She got out of bed and walked the halls with her parents or her grandmother and she smiled shyly at the other kids. She was a pretty little girl, all eyes and shining teeth and black curls. Someone, I think it was Nicole, the four-year-old with leukemia, showed her how to ride on her IV pole, standing on its base while her parents rolled it down the hall. Someone else, probably Richy Nikovic, who'd just awakened from a two-year coma and was anxious for action, showed her how to ride the IV pole all by herself, handling it like a scooter, pushing one foot along the floor for acceleration and then lifting both feet onto the base and just sailing. The nurses smiled at her as she cruised along, her IV bags rustling in the wind her passage created. They're good like that here. They let the kids be kids, whenever they're able.

I noticed that Dr. Alexander Harvey stayed off the floor most of the time because as soon as he showed his face, he was surrounded by gypsies, waving their hands and asking questions, looking at him with burning eyes. Even the supply closet wasn't safe anymore because the gypsies had become used to going there for their supplies, as we all did. Some parents hinted that the gypsies were stealing boxes of diapers and stacks of sheets, but never saw them take anything but what they needed, day to day, like anyone else. We all make our kids' beds ourselves and most of us even change their bloody dressings. I've gotten real good with the complicated sterile dress-ings on Ted's central line; I wear the whole get-up—gown and mask and gloves—and I've got the procedure down. That line goes into the vena cava, just above his heart, and it feeds him. If I want to take him home someday soon, I have to know how to take care of that line. If you've got a kid who can't eat enough on his own to keep himself from starving, you learn. All of us learn. I bet that if the gypsies had had to, they'd have learned too.

But Alex did come up one night, late, and he sat down on the end of my cot. I was half asleep and I just curled my feet up to make room for him. It was nice—cozy and homey, in a way—to have him sitting there.

Ted, who was supposed to be asleep, rolled over and looked down at us through the high steel sides of his bed. "Hey, Alex," he said. "Want to hear an exploit of Fuzzle?"

Alex had heard these before. He told me once that Ted entertains the whole operating room with Fuzzle exploits just before they put him under. He grinned and put his head back against the wall. He was wearing his green surgical cap and it was all sweaty around the forehead. He must have had emergency surgery, this late, and from the look of his face, it hadn't gone well. Most of the time, late-night surgeries at Babies are on kids from neighborhood streets, kids with gunshot wounds sometimes. Alex closed his eyes to listen. "Sure," he said. "Tell me the one about Fuzzle's uncle."

Ted nodded and settled back onto his pillows, his arms bent beneath his head. He loves to tell the same exploit, over and over, expanding it each time. "One day," he began, "Fuzzle went to visit his rich old uncle."

I should have tried to stay awake to listen but I was so warm and so content that I couldn't. I drifted into sleep with Ted's voice spinning in my ears and the good solid weight of a man on my cot. I think that Alex also fell asleep for a while and eventually Ted slept too. It's funny how soothing hospital sounds can be, if you're used to them: the steady counting of the machine that measured the drops of liquid nutrition into Ted's line; the beeping of his roommate's heart monitor; the almost but not quite silent humming of all the devices that keep our kids living; the quiet rubber noise of the nurses' shoes, always there, keeping watch. It's like a lullaby for these kids. Sometimes Ted can't sleep at home without it. I often can't sleep at home where there is only me to guard him.

Alex probably never went home that night, because the next morning, early, he performed the princess's surgery. Even the security men couldn't keep the gypsies off the floor that morning. The campers from the park came in and halls were packed with smoky, dark people, holding vigil.

I took my morning shower and wheeled Ted off to the tenth floor school-room. He always complains about the injustice of having to attend school in the hospital but I always make him go. We waited for the elevator surrounded by gypsies. It was a strange gathering, like being at a fair, the air buzzing with energy.

When I came back to 9-South I couldn't stay in Ted's room. I was restless and hungry, somehow, for the company of gypsies. So I found myself a small corner in the hall and sat down with them and waited. Most of the women sat on couches, rolling beads through their fingers, saying a kind of rosary, I guess. The men did nothing, just leaned against the walls, their arms crossed over their chests. There were even babies and small children with them—strictly against hospital rules—crawling over the women's knees and running around the men's legs. I found myself staring at the children, strong healthy children whose faces were unmarked by pain. I wanted to hold one; I wanted to feel the body of a healthy child in my arms. I wanted to run my hands along chubby legs and to press my face into a soft, laughing, unscarred belly. I wanted to steal a gypsy child and keep it for my own.

But I'm a polite and ordinary parent, and I just sat quietly until Alex came out of the surgical wing and walked over to the gypsy parents. He was smiling. He took hold of the father's hand and shook it, as if the child had just been born. "She's just fine," he said. "She'll be fine," he said. "She'll be fine. Perfect. No problems." A noise went up from the crowded hall, a noise I'd never heard before—the rushing sigh of collective answered prayers.

I slipped away into the parents' bathroom, the only room on the floor with a lock on the door, the only room where you get left alone, and I pressed my face against the cool tile on the wall.

That night the gypsies celebrated. The princess was back in her room, and in pain, but essentially healed. Her grandmother sat with her, while her parents laughed and danced in the lounge. Whenever I passed her room, going back and forth on my errands around the floor, the grandmother was rocking in her chair, smiling to herself, weaving together bits of colored string and straw. She was a small woman, all in black. I thought about her—she, too, must have the royal blood of the ancient race of Romany and some of their special powers.

After Ted was asleep, I went to the princess's room and stepped inside. The little girl was asleep and I stood at the foot of her high bed and looked at her. She was lovely. Her grandmother nodded at me. "I'm glad she'll be OK," I said.

The grandmother sighed. "She will have a scar," she said. "A big scar, right across her belly. They put big ugly metal staples in her skin. Can you imagine that, stapling a baby?"

I looked down at the child's face. "It will fade," I said. "It will be just a thin white line in a few months."

She sighed again.

I tried to keep quiet, tried not to be a self-righteous, my-kid's-suffered-more-than-your-kid jerk of a parent, but I couldn't help it. It just comes out sometimes. "My little boy has had fourteen operations," I said. "Some of his scars have been opened and re-stapled three or four times."

She looked at me, her face dark and foreign, a net of deep lines. "How can you keep from screaming?" she said. "How can you keep from cutting up these doctors with their own knives?"

I looked at the little princess, sucking her thumb in her sleep. "I don't know how to scream. No one ever taught me how to scream, and now I can't learn, I guess," I said. "And then sometimes I see kids get better. Like her." I looked at the grandmother.

She made a rough sound in her throat. "Thank God, she will be better. But yours? Not yours?"

"No. Not mine." I walked toward the door and she rose and touched my arm.

"Your boy will live, though. I see it in his face. He is still curious, interested. He will live."

I felt both my hands reaching out and clasping hers. I felt the lifting of a great weight, my fortune finally told. "He will?"

She squeezed my hands. "Yes, of course he will." She smiled. "He has that cat, that fat black cat. That cat is so fat and so mean because he's swallowed so much pain." She laughed and shook her head. "What is that cat's name?"

"Fuzzle?" I said.

"Yes, yes, Fuzzle. He's a one, that Fuzzle." She dropped my hands and reached up to touch my face. "I've heard those stories he tells, your boy. Oh yes, that boy will live."

I nodded. Really, I've always known it, but it's easy to fall into doubt.

The grandmother gathered up the little triangles she'd been weaving and said, "Come on. I'm giving these to the children. For luck."

We walked along the hall and she went in and out of rooms, slipping her charms under most of the kids' pillows. I tried not to notice which children she skipped over because I knew why: only the children who are going to live will need luck, after all. But I am curious, like my son, and so I kept track. She left a charm for Richy but not for Nicole. She slipped her last charm under Ted's pillow and so there was none left for his roommate, Robby, whose mother sleeps on her cot beside her son's bed just as I do.

That whole night I lay awake listening to the songs and the laughter from the lounge. I knew that even gypsies would not light campfires inside a hospital, but I imagined that they did. I imagined violin music and wild dancing around tall, leaping flames. I imagined that the fires grew, higher and higher, until they set this place ablaze. I imagined that fire, growing huge and white hot, consuming all of this and setting the children, all the children, free.

CALYX Journal, Vol. 16:2, 1995/96

Dee Axelrod

RIVER

'm parked on the bed in our motel room. That's where I've been for a week, waiting for Tim. I haven't stuck my head out of doors. It's just a nowhere desert town like the rest, anyway.

We get to stay in a motel for once because Tim sold the tools he borrowed from this guy in Albuquerque. Tim said I might as well be comfortable because his business would take a day or two. I was real curious, but all he said was that if things worked out we'd never sleep in the van again. Then he left and I haven't heard from him since.

I am kind of tempted to call my mom. She's been on my mind a lot lately. We haven't spoken since I left with Tim six months ago. I'll be seventeen in two weeks and that was the age she had me. If I make it until my due date, I'll be seventeen when my daughter is born.

My name is Stacey Karr and I live in a car.

I like the way that sounds, even though it's not a car, it's a van. Karr is not my real last name—it's Tim's. I use his name because shelters won't let you stay together if you're not married. Tim thinks shelters are better than the van when it's real cold. He had a friend that froze to death in an old Buick.

I should also mention that Stacey's not my real first name—not the one I started out with, which was River. That name was a holdover from my ma's hippie artist days. I took on "Stacey" in self-defense in the fifth grade. My mom was sad when I did that because she said the name fit me. "You are like a river," she said, "always on the move."

I inherited my traveling shoes from her and I also grew up that way, riding in Stepdad's big rig.

The other thing she gave me, she taught me to see things. She'd take me outside just to look at clouds. She was big on sunsets, too, and just afterwards when the sky is darkening up. She'd point out pine trees on the ridge, black against that greeny-blue sky so you could see every needle, just about. She'd hug me and say, "This world can break your heart in six places, but it sure is a beauty, baby girl."

My mom was beautiful, in a hippie way. I saw a picture of her at a rock concert in cut-off blue jeans with lots of beads. The braless look, they used to call it.

I once asked my mom did she sleep with a lot of guys in the sixties. She said, "Don't ask nosy questions, things were different then." I try to imagine her long legs spread wide for some hippie boy, but my mind snaps shut, like books she'd slam closed in mid-air with one hand when she got tired of reading to me.

I've only slept with two men that I wanted to, including Tim and the baby's dad.

Sirens are coming this way, getting louder. That don't worry me. The cops are around a lot to bust up fights in the bar next door. They fight all the time over there.

I turn up the TV so I can hear "General Hospital" and go back to playing with Little Cat. Tim hung a sock from the ceiling on rubber bands tied together. I pull on the end so it bounces all over the room and Little goes crazy. We found her scratching in the dirt outside our motel room. She's just a skinny old scrawny thing. Tim says I looked like her when we got together. I didn't know I was pregnant and of course Tim didn't.

When we make love now, he wedges pillows around me and under my legs to make me comfortable, and then he arches like the cat when she's got her back up so he won't put any weight on me, doesn't touch my stomach at all. When we do it, the baby rocks in there and I think, that's like the baby being rocked in Tim's arms, and I wish all over again that Tim was the father.

My mom was mad when I went on the road with Tim because he's thirty and been in prison. She also didn't like that he was a biker. Even when Tim was a Hell's Angel, he was a gentleman, though. When the bikers had their orgy parties, he'd stand at the door to make sure the girls knew that they belonged to everyone if they came in.

I never could make Mom understand how being with Tim made me feel like I was asleep the rest of the time. Like when we'd drive in the old convertible he used to have. He'd say, "Tie your head on," and flip the top back. The wind would whip my hair like to pull it off—like a red flag, Tim would say—and he'd scoop me next to him. I'd want to die from being happy. Just like that and with nothing added.

I went down on him once while we were driving. I don't know, it just occurred to me, so I put my head in his lap. He drove off the road and into a field. Afterwards I thought about how we could have been bad hurt. I asked him if that's why he looked so pale and shaky, but he just smiled and traced my lips with a fingertip, nice like he always is.

The way I met Tim, it was a few weeks after I found out about Danny being married. Danny and I had gone to a big Fourth of July party, but we were fighting about his wife. A friend of mine, Eulah, was there so she and I went off to a bedroom to talk. This guy who turned out to be Tim was there, drinking a Coke. He offered us some and Eulah took a drink but I said no thanks.

Later he came up behind me and put his hands on my shoulders. He pulled me back against him, and I could feel the heat from his skin right through my blouse.

He whispered in my ear, "Why wouldn't you take a swallow off my Coke?"

"I didn't know you."

"Know me any better now?"

So I took his Coke. This was before he stopped drinking hard liquor, so I could smell the whiskey. I put my head back and took a long swallow.

"What about this guy Danny?" he said, so I knew he'd been asking about me.

"To hell with Danny."

"Just like that, 'To hell with Danny'?"

"Just like that."

But we didn't make love. We lay on a blanket under a shade tree and told each other things about ourselves. He held my hand, and that meant more to me than everything I'd done in bed with Danny.

After that I told Mom I was moving out.

TV has the five o'clock news on. Every time I see the local news I'm afraid they'll report on some crime and I'll just know Tim did it. They'll say he's dead or on the run. I know he's not in jail or the hospital because I called. When the weatherman comes on, I turn off the tube and make dinner.

I cook my meal on a propane camper stove. That's against motel rules, but I sure can't afford to eat out. The room came with a little refrigerator, and Tim put a bunch of food in it before he left. Of course he got junk like hot dogs.

I'm educated about food from my mom. She once worked in a health food store in Denver. I used to try to get Tim to eat right. It was one fight we had. He told me to mind my own business and shut up about my mom. Later he apologized and said maybe I should call her since it was obvious I missed her big-time. I almost did it, I wanted to real bad.

My mom wasn't really an artist. She was an artist's model at a school in Kansas City. That's how she got to be a hippie, she said, because all the rich kids at art school were hippies pretending to be poor. Her joke is that she was better at it than them because she really was poor.

Modeling is a harder job than people think. Not just anyone can do it. It's not easy to hold still, and you have to mark with chalk around your feet so you can get back into the same exact position. You have to be almost like a dancer and think up interesting poses because the teachers can't always think of them.

It's not like being nude, like in *Playboy*.

It's a real job.

My mom liked listening to the teachers criticize the student drawings. She learned quite a lot, and once when she sneaked into a drawing class with her sketch pad, the teacher picked out her drawing as the best one. He said, "This drawing shows understanding of the human body from the inside out." She always remembered he said that.

My mom didn't like the way some teachers had of talking about her like she wasn't there. Once a teacher jumped right up on the model stand, pointed to her breasts, and said what great shapes they were to draw because they were so saggy!

But if she hadn't been a model, I wouldn't be here.

When my mom and dad got together, it wasn't anything like love at first sight. It was something that just happened. A student had asked her to model for him. He was making a sculpture, and one part of it was a woman lying on her stomach on the sand in a bathing suit.

Everyone liked this guy, he was just a real likeable character. Mom liked him too. From the way she smiles when she says it, I can tell she had a lot of feelings for him.

She lay on her stomach while the student stood over her and sketched. He straddled her with his feet touching her sides. She said that she could feel his eyes moving up and down her body like two laser beams, while the charcoal scratched on the pad. One thing led to another.

And that was my real dad, except he never knew she was pregnant. She left Kansas with a group of students going to India. One of them bought her the ticket because it would be good karma. They would all work for this Maharishi guy.

Mom said she didn't know where they were going. She couldn't find India on the map. But she lived there for two years, on an island called Goa.

So I was born in a place pretty different from where I grew up in Montana.

I was too young to remember Goa—the pictures in my head must be her stories. A beach of white sand. Children running around naked. In the dark, animal sounds.

Mom told me that Goa was kind of a low point for her—she was doing a lot of drugs at the time and she couldn't think too straight. Some of the details escaped her. For instance, she can't remember how we got back to the States.

She does remember hanging around Taos for a while. Then she wandered up to Montana with me tied to her back like a papoose. We blew into Miles City and got caught there, two tumbleweeds blown against cyclone fencing.

She met my stepfather and we moved into his trailer. She calmed down some, but she didn't entirely lose her traveling ways. She still rode with Stepdad in his rig. She says it was a good thing when we moved in because everyone has to be somewhere. She couldn't take living on the road anymore.

I always liked hearing her stories, but sometimes it's hard to imagine her traveling alone and having adventures because since I've known her she's been on the quiet side.

When I was thirteen, Mom's brother Ray moved to Miles City and lived with us. That was a big surprise because I never knew she had a brother. So I asked about her family, but she didn't have much to say, except that the man she thought was her dad turned out not to be.

I guess I hung onto the stories I knew about even more after that.

I used to stare in the bathroom mirror at my red hair and freckles and wonder, is that an Irish face, a Scotch face?

It's funny not to know who you come from. It's like my family began with my mom and me.

And now there's my daughter.

It's two in the morning and all the guys from the bar are whooping it up in the parking lot. Next thing the police'll be back here. I can't sleep and there's nothing decent on the tube. Just an old musical about people in World War II. The faces are orange, but I can't adjust it since the control panel is locked. The TV is chained to the table, which is bolted to the floor. When we first checked in and saw that everything was nailed down, I thought it was kind of disgusting, but Tim just laughed and said, "Looks like they were expecting me."

The acidy colors are making me nauseated so I flip through the channels. I guess I could always eat something to settle my stomach. Look like even more of a blimp.

I don't know why anyone would get pregnant on purpose. A doctor I went to said my stomach muscles have stretched about all they can. My feet are all swollen up. I wish it was Danny sitting here all uncomfortable. Serve him right for telling me he's sterile. Come to find out he's married with two kids.

But it's not your fault, little baby. You didn't choose Danny to be your dad.

Since Tim's been gone, I talk to the baby. I tell her I understand how she must feel squished in there, now she's too big to turn around. I know she can see light and hear music. I wonder what she likes to listen to on MTV. I'm thinking about what it will feel like to hold her.

I wonder if she'll be sad, like I am, not to know her real father. At least Tim will love her.

I miss him so bad. I know Tim probably did something he shouldn't of, but right now I don't care about that.

It was months before I realized I was pregnant. Tim had to tell me. He sat me down one day and said, "Girl, you're pregnant." He knew it wasn't his because of the timing. He wasn't angry for long. We were on the road, traveling all over the Southwest, and there I was, pregnant. We were in bars all the time, but Tim convinced me I shouldn't smoke or drink, so I'd be watching everyone else get ripped.

When you're traveling, you meet other people who are on the road too. We saw this one guy in Phoenix. Then we ran into him again in Parker. Then we were sitting in a bar in Santa Fe and there he was. Tim went up to him and said, "Are you following us?" He said, "No, but if you want to give me a ride, I could use the company." His name was Jack and he rode with us for a while. He'd been a smoke jumper. He told us about jumping out of airplanes and fighting forest fires. He'd work for twelve hours straight. He took the glamour out of that life, all right. But he seemed to miss it all the same.

We drove all the back roads through New Mexico and Arizona. We drove through these Indian reservations. There would be nothing, not a fence or a cow, not any kind of yard—just little shacks with tin roofs plunked down on the desert.

We stopped at a jewelry stand by the roadside. There wasn't another building for miles, just flatness all the way to the pink bluffs on the horizon. There was an Indian woman asleep in a car and one asleep on the counter in the middle of all the jewelry, wrapped in a blanket with every color in it. She woke up and smiled at us. I wished I had a little money so I could buy something and make her happy.

Jack said, "Well, they're just desert niggers."

Tim said, "You shut up with that shit."

When Tim was in prison he had to join the Aryan Brotherhood. In prison, white sticks with white, black with black, red with red. It's a strict inmate rule. Whites have to join the Aryan Brotherhood, but Tim hated it. He has different colored friends on the outside, so he thought it was just stupid.

After I knew Tim for a while, I asked him if he was ever raped in prison. He got real stern and said, no, he'd kill anyone who tried.

Every guy I know who's been in the joint, if you ask them were they raped, they'll say no.

I decided Tim was telling the truth about prison after he told me how he got tough. His dad used to beat him every day of his life and cuss him like a dog until he learned to fight back. He was knocked unconscious so many times it's amazing he survived. I wasn't beat until I turned thirteen, so I was fortunate that way.

There was something about my growing up that my stepdad just couldn't stand, I guess. There I was, thirteen, my body popping out in a new place every week, it seemed. I didn't know which end was up.

Thirteen was a big year, all right. That was the year my life fell apart. I had to know Tim really well before I finally told him about it.

We were staying in a log cabin for a month in exchange for Tim's doing some carpentry for this guy. Jack had gone his own way, and I was glad to be alone with Tim again. The cabin had an outhouse and no TV. It was cozy though.

I'd cook big dinners when Tim came home from work. After dinner he would teach me new and fancy games of solitaire. He knows about a hundred variations from being in the joint. We'd talk about the future. Tim would say, "We'll do this for real, I'll build a cabin in the mountains. You'll go back to school. I'll stay sober and we'll raise our kids the right way."

One night when we were in the loft making love, Tim fell asleep with his full weight on me and I got that panicky feeling. I shoved him off, but he kept hold of my hand.

He said, "Are you ready to talk about it?"

"About what?"

He said, real gentle, "I can feel that something is missing for you, and I'm sorry about that."

Tim always knows just the right way to unlock what's inside me, it seems. But I always try to be so tough, so I said, "Well, it wasn't no big deal."

Tim said, "Right." Sarcastic, but not really. I could see Tim's face by the firelight, quiet and worn-looking. Not a face to judge me, so I told him what I hadn't talked about in the two years since the trial.

The trailer was cramped after Uncle Ray moved in. I noticed it especially because I wanted some privacy to be a teenager.

In one way, how we lived was very private. There wasn't another house for a mile. But inside the trailer it was tight. I had to give Uncle Ray my room and sleep in the living room. I didn't have anyplace to put my things. Not that I had a lot, but I had started to do some oil paintings with this paint my mom got me for Christmas. Those paintings were for me and no one else.

Partly I was thinking about my dad and how he was an artist. I would meet him later in life and we would both be artists. I was also looking real close at stuff. I could see how a rock or even a lump of dirt was something you might want to paint. Something you'd pass by as having no interest had its own life.

Well, Uncle Ray thought those paintings were a real laugh riot. There wasn't anyplace around the trailer I could hide them that he wouldn't find them. He'd wait for my mom to go somewhere and then he'd sniff them out.

"Well, what do we have here, another masterpiece? Hey, honey, you don't have to go painting no rocks, you already got plenty in your head." He and Stepdad would laugh so hard they'd shrill their beer down their bellies.

So after a while I didn't do any paintings. It was like too much of me was sticking out and I had to pull it back in.

After that I ignored Uncle Ray, but it wasn't that easy to avoid a 225-pound guy in a trailer. Seemed like every time I turned around, there he was.

The week before my fourteenth birthday, my mom and Stepdad went off in the truck. They left me with creepy old Uncle Ray. I told Mom I was scared, but Stepdad wanted her to drive so she had to go.

I ran into my mom's room and locked the door. I usually locked the bathroom door too, but this one time I forgot. I was in the shower and I heard something behind me and it was him. He took me by the neck and slung me down. I fought him but he done it anyway. Next thing I was running naked three miles to the sheriff and I was bad tore up so they believed me all right.

It's funny. I don't remember much from the weeks right after being raped, but I remember the exact pain, the part everyone says you're supposed to forget. It felt like someone had filled me up with blackberry brambles in both places and then tore them out.

I took my uncle to court. I got him put away for ten years. All the time in court he stared at me with his yellow eyes. He wrote me a letter from prison threatening my life so I got him put away for three more. This one policeman said he couldn't believe a kid could be so brave. That's something I'll always remember, like Mom remembers what that teacher said about her drawing.

While I'm telling Tim this, he's stroking my hand so lightly. I think it's the gentlest anyone's ever touched me.

The worst part, I tell him, was that my mom didn't stand up for me. It was worse than being raped, in a way. When I told her and Stepdad what happened he said, "You lying little slut, he never did." Mom didn't say a word. My beautiful, artistic mom just faded on me. When I tried to talk to her after, she only said, "You're going to find out some things aren't that easy." So I could see that when it came down to me or her husband and brother, I had to lose.

You can miss someone who's gone, and you can miss someone you've never even met—and that's my real dad—but I never knew until then that you could miss someone who's still with you.

And Tim made me realize about missing pieces of yourself.

So what I did after that, I got tough and I got a mouth on me and I gave them all the trouble I could. My stepdad beat me up one side and down the other and my mother never said "Boo."

She and I never did take in any more sunsets.

Everything in the motel and everything outside is perfectly quiet. It's the high desert before dawn, that slippery cool. I'm too tired to sleep, so I drag a chair outside. I let the sweet night fill me easy. Let my sore body be a shadow in the dark. Minutes pass or could be hours.

Then there's one bird and the outline of a tree. A little lurch and everything starts up again, carried forward into day. Pulled toward the sunrise and no turning back, that's the feeling.

It's weird having been up all night, but I do feel good. I think it's because I know what I have to do. Yesterday I couldn't think about leaving but today I understand I have to go. Like something in me that couldn't move came unstuck.

I run a bath and lower myself into the tub, which is a pretty big project. The warm water swirls around me, until my belly sticks up like an island with stretch marks.

It's not easy, that's not what I'm saying. It's hard, all right. Leaving the motel will be admitting that something bad has happened, that he's really gone.

The thing is, every time I turn around in my head, I bump into some happy thought of him and me. There's lots of people live their whole lives without finding someone they love that much. You can feel that deep-down sadness in them. When I get old, I won't be sad for having missed it, and that's something.

I towel off and lie down. Tim put all his posters and things up so we'd get the best view of them from the bed. That's why there's nothing up over the headboard, because that's a waste, Tim used to say. He hung an American flag, a photo of a kitty that looks like Little Cat, and some other stuff. The only one I didn't like was of a biker mama sticking her butt out. Tim wanted a picture of me to hang; he wanted me to do those glamour shots where they make you up, but I wanted to wait until I wasn't pregnant. Now I wish I'd done it.

This motel might be our last home together, so I hate peeling those posters off the walls. I need to leave some things behind too. Basically whatever won't fit in the duffle bag. When I'm packed I write a letter to Tim, telling him the places to look for me. I give my letter to the woman at the office to hold for him. Also she keeps Little, which is better for a cat than hitchhiking.

Too bad because now I'm stuck having to check out and use up the money Tim left me. But it's worth it to have her hold the letter. To have some hope he'll find me.

Maybe Tim's OK and he's just staying away until the coast is clear. Like what animals do, lead the hunter away from the nest. Thing is, I can't wait around to find out, unless I want to get stuck having my baby here.

The lady offers me the phone to make a call if I want. I think about calling my mom, but I pass. This time it's not because I'm mad at her. I'll let her know when the baby comes, but now I have business to take care of that I need to do for myself. I have to get to Albuquerque, where there's a good hospital for my baby to be born in. Tim would understand. I think he'd say, "Go for it, girl!" but that's not why. It's the thing I can do for my daughter, and you could say it's for myself too. A different choice from my mom's.

A pregnant woman toting a duffle bag doesn't have to stick her thumb out to get a ride. Soon I am floating over the state line in some trucker's rig. I feel light and heavy at the same time, knowing where I'm headed for a change.

CALYX Journal, Vol. 16:2, 1995/96

R e b e c c a   L a v i n e

AFTERWARD

S ometimes I blame you. Most often the blaming starts at night, when you are sleeping and I lie awake, caught inside your breathing. As your body slopes against mine in the dark, your hand feels skinny and childish clutching my breasts. Your lips feel flaccid against my neck, and I feel trapped in your sleep-embrace.

Once I begin blaming you, it becomes easier and easier. You send me a suggestive kiss while I lie in the bathtub, unhappy in the cooling water— how could you look at me that way? You forget to feed the cats, who then worm under my feet, insistent and angry. You leave the ashtray next to the bed where I can't help but knock it over in a silver-grey shower. *How could you,* I keep asking silently, bitter when you eat the leftover curry or finish the tampons without buying a new box. *How could you let something like that happen to me?*

Of course I know it wasn't your fault. I'm not stupid. I know who to blame: him. Sure, that's easy. I could blame him if his face showed up in my dreams or if I thought about him late at night. But I don't. It's easier to think about you, because you were there then. You're still here.

Actually you and I had fought that night. Remember? I don't know about what. Maybe the chick with the shaved head you had flirted with at the party the weekend before.

We were enclosed in a booth at one of the dense, smoky pubs you liked to take me to, and you had ordered black and tans for both of us. We could barely hear each other because of the football game roaring from TV sets on either end of the bar. All around us, red-faced men would suddenly jam themselves into the air when something happened in the game, yowl at one another before they'd subside, and you'd glance away from our conversation to the TV for a moment, not quite long enough for me to complain. It was the kind of place I never would have walked into without you. I never would have looked twice at the green and yellow storefront with the neon shamrocks and lit-up pit bull in the window, but I've been back since, when it wasn't football season. I liked the varnished, oily look of the tables and the beer-on-tap and the way nobody said anything to us at all.

You stared into your half-pint and licked at the corners of your mouth while I talked, and I remember the angry buzz of my own voice, but not my words. I remember your face: freckled, blunt, and a little confused. What seems sad to me now is how angry your confusion made me. You'd apologize and I'd fling myself back in my seat. *What for?* I'd ask you.

You'd turn away, shrug so that the chains on your leather jacket would wring against each other. *I don't know,* you kept saying.

Then I don't want your apology, I'd say, with extra, angry spit in my mouth, consciously twisting my eyes away from your ruddy face. I told you, *Don't say it if you don't know what you're sorry for.*

We left the bar, pushing through the excited crowd of men who never met our eyes. Outside, the stars were slung low and the streets were slushy. Tears scraped their way out of my eyes, slow and leaky. Before the fight, before we'd gone into the pub, we had been shoving each other playfully, slamming up against each other's bodies. You had lifted me up onto your shoulders while I wriggled, screaming, and passersby had watched us, stunned. But after the fight, we walked in silence. Disoriented by the tears I was trying to blink back, I skidded on some ice. You held my arm but I jerked myself away, so you walked ahead of me, indifferent.

I blame you for it because nothing like that ever happened to me when I was alone. Men tried to pick me up or asked me annoying questions—but nothing like that. Together, duplicated, twinned, in our leather jackets and spiky hair, it happened to us all the time. One early summer evening, we stood downtown, me kissing you earnestly on your forehead and you pressing against my kisses in that mute, endearing way you had. You were holding onto my waist. We had only been dating a few months, so we considered running into each other that night one of those marvelous surprises that meant we were destined to be together.

The man who screamed at us wore a Red Sox cap and jeans; he was white with a fleshy, mottled face. He yelled something about perverts and killing us and hell. Here's where it gets blurry for me, because I don't remember him. I remember us. I remember you. I remember how he moved closer to me with a threatening fist and how I moved closer to him, unafraid, sure I couldn't be hurt with a crowd of people watching. I remember taunting him, *You're just jealous, 'cause for sure no woman would look twice at you,* and I remember my satisfaction at watching his face double up with rage and his skin shiver and his offer to shut my mouth for good.

You stepped between us and you were quiet, talking to him in a language I didn't entirely understand, the language of someone who had grown up pretty close to where he had grown up. You leaned against the slight air between him and us—you were angular and threatening and I watched your strong back, your ironed white T-shirt, feeling proud and safe. He stepped away from you, sweating, and loud still. People behind us applauded and I swung around to see a semicircle of young men and women in the shimmer of lights from a record store. One gave us the thumbs-up sign.

Babe, I told you, *let's get out of here.*

Another time we were walking back from a Fred & Ginger movie fest, in slender rain, holding hands. From time to time you swung me around and I tried to be graceful for you, even in combat boots. When three frat boys passed us, splashing mud from puddles, I ignored them, but you slammed your feet against the pavement and turned around. From the expression on your face I knew something was wrong. I pulled my skirt down lower and tried to look mean, ready to back you up.

You pinched me on the butt, you told one man. Your blonde hair was flattened by the rain and your face looked soft, angelic. The rain curled down your cheek companionably.

Oh please, he said. He had stopped with his friends. His shiny green jacket was halfway zipped and he wore chunky rings. *I did not touch your dyke butt,* he said.

You shook your head and moved closer to him, looking fearless. *You pinched me on the ass and I'm going to kick your ass,* you said to him. All three looked at us and pulled their young faces into sneers. One jutted out his lower lip and shoved me on the shoulder, and my body jolted back, but I refused to fall. I began hitting at him—ineffectual slaps on his arm. But you, you sent the boy with the rings sprawling onto the pavement, his face scraped against the sludgy ground. He staggered up and they ran away, leaping over puddles, while we watched and jeered. When they were out of sight, you wrapped your arm around my shoulders, calm and triumphant.

And there were other times, I could go into them all: the time you took the pamphlets out of a young skinhead's hands on the train, tore them up and then blocked him as he tried to punch me; or the time we were walking to a club and a man in a car wagged his tongue suggestively at me, and I, maddened, ran up to his car and kicked it until the light turned green— you pointing at the driver and telling him, *You're going to die;* or how you taught me to find a stick or a rock to carry on my walk home from work and how I used one once, against a car of teenagers—breaking their windshield before I ran like hell.

But—I must admit it—those aren't the times I think about. I think about the swollen silence between us that night on the subway, how the train screamed and shook and dragged itself along from stop to stop, noisily expressing everything we couldn't, or wouldn't. I think about how everything lodged itself in my eyes: dust, anger, tears. From time to time I could feel you looking at me and then away, but I, sitting by the door as it hissed open and shut, wouldn't look at you. Instead I watched a man across from me, who was idly playing with a bottle, shredding first the paper bag, then the bottle's label. I saw him without seeing—his shiny, porous skin, how his long hair didn't cover his scalp, how his mustache curled inside his mouth. When he looked back at me, I shifted my gaze automatically, staring at the advertisement above his head for a sad-eyed lawyer, with a telephone number stamped across his forehead in purple ink.

He got up and stood, swaying against the train's rhythm, close to me, close to the exit. I pulled myself tighter into myself, but only a little. I didn't want to seem scared. I didn't want to cuddle next to you, sitting so comforting and solid and infuriating next to me.

He said to me, menacing, *Whatchu looking at?*
You looked up. I stared at my boots, at the strips of damp newspaper on the floor, flattening my tongue inside my mouth.
He said again, *Whatchu looking at,* and then, wrapping his hand around the pole next to me so that I could see his neatly trimmed fingernails, *Dyke bitch?* He asked this in a singsong voice and leaned closer to me.
I wouldn't shrink away. (Not from him, not near you.) I looked up into his sunken face, into his bland, blue eyes, and I smelled adrenaline, that sweet-salt smell deep inside my nose. I told him, *Nothing.* I flicked my eyes over him and away, and repeated, *Nothing at all.*

You didn't say anything, though I was waiting for your arm to rise up, protective. No, you sat as still as a stranger. I bent my neck and examined my folded hands, listening to the doors swish open. I thought you were watching him, and that made me feel safe. I heard him get off—but no, you said later—you saw him stop. You told me later how he held the door open with his foot, how he turned and lunged toward me. You saw the bottle sliding over my head with that sudden splintering crash and you heard him screaming and you saw his lips turn back. You showed me later, and I saw it in your face. I saw it there.

Once a friend mimed a monster for me. She was an actress and she was doing it to further some other point in the conversation, to tell a story that I don't remember now. She pulled her hands in front of her face, making it seem as though her hands were pulling her features down into a contorted droop, a snarl of skin and teeth and eyes. Then, one moment later, she pulled her hand back up and was herself again. I felt such relief to see her old face back. I hadn't even known how disturbed I'd been, until I saw her regular self, smooth and upright and easy. When she resumed her conversation, I had to sit on my hands, resisting an urge to kiss her and hold her in my arms like a child and never let the monster come back.

Before you leave in the morning for work, so early, you part my sleep with questions—*Do you need anything?* you ask me.

I shove a hand into the air. *I don't need you, I don't want you,* my hands say, urgently, but neither of us knows that language.

When I come home at night you dance up from the TV set, your bright hair bent in wild angles from lying down so long, and squeeze me into your circle of light and I tell myself I'm where I want to be.

It's only when we get to bed and we peel off our clothes and shiver against each other and press our lips, like silent compliments, against each other's chests, that I begin again to blame you. Did I blame you right after it happened? Did I wonder as I lay toppled on the floor, drooling and bleeding against a gritty newspaper, why you left me for an elongated moment to scream, frenzied, after him? Did I wonder why you didn't ask anyone for help instead of holding me to you, fiercely picking glass from my head, and wiping roughly at my face; did I wonder, when we got to our stop, why you forced me to get up, to walk home in the dark, lurching inside my sobs and holding onto you?

I was scared, you told me later. You trusted no one. You left me alone only to call my best friend, who hung up the phone and called an ambulance. You didn't want to let the driver in, but at last pried open the door and let them clean and bandage me, right there in the bed, before they took me to the hospital, refusing you passage because you weren't family. To come see me, you had to go back to that same subway stop and wait again for that same train.

At the time, I didn't know where you were. All my thoughts shook as I lay in the jostling ambulance. The cheerful technician bent over me, gold teeth gleaming, breath garlicky in my face, and asked me jocular questions, laughing at my sloppy replies. The world became too shiny and slippery to hold onto. The technician's face was too close and, as he began to wrinkle and dip, he leaned even closer, looking anxious. The light was too sharp, the thick disinfectant smell too stinging—and then the technician disappeared from view. He was replaced with you, your difficult face. I knew you'd be there when I woke up, and you were. You looked rinsed out, but I didn't look at you much. I just stared, loosely, at the white hospital sheets.

It was my own private theater, replaying that breath of time you watched him stop the train doors and then turn. What, I wanted to know, were you thinking when you watched him slam that bottle on the top of my head? Did you feel a curious detachment, watching someone hit me in a way that you knew you never could? *Just tell me,* I thought, *I want to know.* Did you feel any envy watching him haul out that hate inside of him and shatter it on top of me?

Before he released the train door he spat—once at you and once at me. You, returning from your near pursuit, put your arms around me and held me against your body—while I scratched over and over at my face where his spit had landed. No one else on the train would come near us. You rocked me in your arms, crying small, bare tears. With one hand you picked off the glass and wiped the spit and blood from my face. You let the tears dry like a sheet of clear plastic on your cheeks. You said, *I'm sorry, I'm sorry,* and I mumbled, thickly, *Baby, it's not your fault, stop,* and at the time, I meant it. But afterward, when I opened my eyes and looked at you, I saw only a stranger—the same stranger my friend had become right as the monster was leaving her—right before she became herself again. Lying in your arms, the only thing I wanted, as though I'd never wanted anything before, was to have all of you back.

CALYX Journal, Vol. 16:3, 1996

K r i s t i n   K i n g

THE WINGS

When they were married in the Salt Lake Temple, she saw how it would be after she died, in the resurrection. Marriage was a dry run for immortality, a message from God telling them what it would be like. Wing-back chairs, crystal-and-gold chandeliers, oak, marble, stained glass letting in the daylight, beige walls with paintings of Christ beckoning his rag-clad followers, ceilings so high she could hardly see them. She thought of God in the spaces between the walls, airy, just beyond what she could see, so big He filled the entire place, or standing just behind her, vanishing when she turned. When she and her husband were married, they were covered in white up to their necks, and all their guests were covered in white. The temple was even covered in white. Her husband stood in the inmost room, the holiest, loveliest, right there next to God's heart, she thought, separated from her by a curtain, and then he pulled her in. This is how it would be.

On Sunday morning, oh, it was always so hard to get everyone in order. The boys wouldn't be dressed, or they would dress in nice shirts and pajama bottoms, or they would not have remembered to brush their teeth until they were almost out the door. She had to find the right dress, remember what she'd worn all those last Sundays, find some pantyhose that matched. Her husband, though, was always there, right on time, perfect. Once they got to church, they sat in the fifth row. There were always the same number of songs before the Sacrament, two. The bishop told them what was going on in the ward, like a holy news reporter. Then they took the Sacrament, then different people (it didn't matter who) talked about the Lord. There at church everyone knew what to do. The little one was even old enough not to bang his legs against the seat.

On Sunday night, this particular Sunday night, she was satisfied. Things went as planned. The chicken dinner—chicken baked in mushroom sauce and potatoes whipped in her blue mixing bowl—went as planned. The children behaved. On nights like this, she didn't go up on the rooftop. She offered herself up to her husband just like she offered up her sins to God, and then she slept the whole night long. She never woke up once, not even to go to the bathroom.

On Monday morning after everyone had left, she sat on the living room couch with a cup of honey tea. Everyone was where they were supposed to be: at school, at work. The boys would come home for lunch and she would make them split pea soup and tuna fish sandwiches. For dinner it would be lasagna; she'd have to start that early.

In between the lunch and dinner, though, she wasn't sure what would happen. That was bad, three hours where anything might happen. But it would be fine; she'd read her scriptures, the Book of Mormon, the part where Alma says to his people that Christ can never vary from what's right, that Christ's course is one eternal round. Yes, everything would be all right.

That night she turned on the electric heater and waited for her soft husband to come to bed. She hoped he wouldn't want anything and when he kissed her she turned away. When he lay back down, she put her arm around his body and kissed his shoulder. Good night, she said.

Sometimes, like tonight, when she couldn't sleep, she would open the window and go out to the roof. Part of the roof, just for decoration, slanted just past her window; she would climb up that part like a cat, with her bare feet and her hands. She would go up partway to the top, where the roof narrowed to a point, staying on just by using the friction between her body and the red roof tile. Or she might climb toward the back of the house, where the roof flattened out. There, it was covered with sticky black tar. Afterward, when she came back, her hands and feet would be gritty with bits of red roof tile and sometimes sticky with black tar, and she'd get bits of tar or red tile on her white sheets. But before that happened she could feel the cool air and look at the darkness; she could feel how nighttime felt without her husband.

In the morning she had things to do. After breakfast there were spots of blackberry jam on the table that she had to wipe off, hope they wouldn't stain. A drawer that could be organized. In a few days she would have to make cookies for the ward party because it was her turn. She could go to the grocery store today, especially since her husband was out of shaving cream and they were a little low on catsup.

At night he asked her, Why don't you want to do it, and she said, I won't mind, really. It was just not important for her. Not interesting. She would rather feel the wisps of his chest hair with her fingers, have his arm protecting her back. She was willing enough, though, and when they finished she reached for a roll of toilet paper to clean it all up, then she went into the bathroom and sat on the toilet, letting it drip away from her. This had to be better than douches, because douches just push it up farther. Not that she didn't want any more babies, oh no, because she did. Really she did.

When she came back to bed she watched him sleep, because he was beautiful. She smelled the sweet smell of Drakkar on his neck. She wondered what she would smell like wearing Rose Petal, and would it clash with his cologne? She put her head down on the pillow and tried to relax, breathing in and out with her chest, then her abdomen, then her sides. She stared at the wall. Then she saw a puff of white out the window.

Who are you? she called, and when nothing answered she got up and opened the window, and the puff flew away to a tree in the neighbor's yard. She climbed out onto the roof for a better look, and the puff of white flew behind her house, so she had to climb all the way to the top of the roof, standing up and holding onto the pointed edge with her hands. She saw long red hair, softly clawed feet, wings that folded perfectly into the body. Come back, she said, and she almost lost her balance trying to see the angel's face. But the angel didn't pay any attention, just lifted its clawed foot to its mouth and nibbled on it. Then it unfurled its wings, each of them six feet long, and flew off toward the south.

In the morning she didn't want a bubble bath but she wanted her honey tea. She wanted to call Sister Mortensen but she didn't. She thought she might want to make the cookies that day instead of the day after, so she got out the butter and nutmeg and milk and eggs and sugar and flour and put it all in a mixing bowl, but then she looked closely and noticed there were bugs crawling around in the flour, and she had to take everything outside and dump it in the garbage. She hosed the bowl down before she brought it back in the house, but even so she was a little worried that the bugs might have crawled someplace, so she got out the bleach and disinfected the floor and then the cabinet. By the time that was done the boys were home, so she didn't have any time to go to the store and get more flour. Butter too, she'd used up most of the butter.

At dinner she made up for not baking cookies like she should have by getting a pound cake out of the freezer and serving it after the spaghetti casserole. Really, they didn't go together, but no one seemed to mind. I bed her husband seemed happier than ever, so she lay there and thought about the scriptures. Her body was a temple, not to be defiled by passionate thoughts or actions or anything else—dirty words, coffee, wine. In real life you had to have a slip of paper, signed by your bishop, in order to go into the temple. Everyone protected the temple. But your body had nobody to protect it but you.

After he was asleep she had an idea, and she went downstairs to get a bit of leftover pound cake. She went back upstairs to the bedroom window, opened it, held the pound cake out at arm's reach. The angel had been hovering in the next yard, and it circled close, closer, and looked at the pound cake with its small black eyes, but would not take it. She put the pound cake on the roof and shut the window and watched. The angel flew closer and closer until she could see its body, saw that it had tattoos on its legs, pink flowers circling green dragons the way the tattoos circled the angel's legs. Then the angel grabbed the pound cake with its clawed foot and flew away.

Night after night it was like that. The angel would fly closer and closer, until the woman could sit on top of the roof and hold the food (a bit of apple, a piece of bread, who knows what angels like best?) away from her body, and the angel would come. She could see parts of the naked angel, enough to know it was a woman, but she would look away from those parts, ashamed, down to the tattooed legs or up at the dirty white wings. She grabbed at the wings once, not knowing why, but the angel backed off the edge of the roof and rose high above her. The angel did not come back that night.

Days the woman could not seem to do anything after everyone had left, so she went back to bed and watched the red digits on her alarm clock shift. Things went undone: crumbs of toast sat on the carpet and were taken away by ants, lunches didn't get ready in time, the toy Count from Sesame Street lay on the kitchen floor for two days before she noticed him and put him back in his Sesame Street house. Her husband pretended not to notice, figuring, she thought, it was that time of the month. But all that time, she was planning. She would catch the angel by its tattooed legs and *make* her carry her to where the angels go. Yes, and she would carry a bag of rice, dyed green, and drop it on the way so she could find the angel's home again in the morning, after everyone had left.

One night she stood on the tarred part of the roof and offered the angel, who was crouching in a tree, some raisins. The angel moved toward the woman and opened her wings, looking as if she would take hold of the woman with them and pull her toward her chest. Then the woman saw the tattoos weren't just on the angel's legs, but climbed up the sides of her body and spread out toward her wings. The woman touched the angel on her soft stomach, in the safe place between the pubic hair and the breasts, and the angel folded in on herself like a little piece of origami. Then the woman stroked the soft wings, smoothing the feathers that were sticking out awkwardly, flicking away the white dandruffy bits of dead skin. The angel opened her wings a little and made a soft bird cry. The woman offered the angel raisins again, but she didn't take them. She just watched the woman for a while, smelling sweaty and creamy and nicely sour, then moved her head back and forth the way birds do when they are about to fly, and beat her wide wings at the air until she lifted up.

The woman wanted to do that too. She spread her arms but they were not wings, and they did not lift her up. She walked to the side of her roof and wondered for a minute what would happen if she walked right off the edge. Then she thought, in the morning they would find me and what would they think? Possessed by demons. Yes, that was it. There was once a bishop who wanted to know more about the occult, who studied Church books and then academic books and finally the books written by people who loved the devil, until one day he lifted three feet off the floor of the dining room and started banging his head on the ceiling. His wife called a man in the Stake Presidency who called a man in the Quorum of the Twelve, who came over and prayed softly to the Lord for an hour until the man fell to the floor, having learned his lesson. Who sells eternity to get a toy?

She scooted down the roof and climbed back in the window. The grains of roof tile fell off her feet onto the floor, and she left them there when she got back into bed. She rolled her husband's body over onto hers, and he said, Huh? She tried to pray but how could she, there was nothing to say if she wasn't going to say she was sorry. Then she went to sleep. She dreamed of dark holes that make you disappear if you touch them. She dreamed she was disappearing.

In the morning the can opener didn't work; every time she tried to use it the detachable attachment came off, and she couldn't make any tuna fish. The boys had to have peanut butter for lunch instead. When she walked by the broom closet, the little whoosh of wind she made caught the broom and it fell down, clackety-clack-bang. A candle fell out of her hand and rolled into the fireplace, got covered with ashes. The dishwasher leaked and when she pulled out the lower rack to take a look she found a lump of seaweed in it: how did seaweed get in her house? It was the house, yes, it had to be the house against her. It didn't like her on its roof? She didn't know. Or maybe it was what she knew in the back of her head, that she couldn't have both things, the angel and the perfect house. She could only have one or the other.

Saturday night she lay in bed and tried to sleep. When she shut her eyes, a voice like the man on television earlier that night told her about the New World snowy egret, its long neck and long legs, the way male and female together cared for the young, how millinery had nearly wiped it out. She could feel her husband pawing at her with fuzzy bear hands and she turned toward him, but in her half-sleep she was still there, with the snowy egret. Afterward she got up and sat on the toilet while the semen leaked out, and then she went back to bed and tried to sleep, tried to sleep, until she couldn't stand it and she *had* to go out onto the roof with the peeled orange she had by the bedside (so yes, she had planned it, she had to say that, she was guilty of meaning to do it) and wait for the angel. When the angel finally came, she fed her the way she would feed a lover, the way her husband fed her cream puffs once until she laughed and turned her head away. She fed her slice by slice, not pulling her hand away until the angel's wet lips touched her fingers. Then she stroked the feathers on the angel's wings, and she touched the inky tattoo on her thigh to feel whether the skin was smooth or rough. She could feel (oh so lightly) the outline of leaves on the angel's legs, and she could smell (only just barely) flowers, like lilies.

When she went back to bed she stroked her husband's leg to see if it felt like the angel's, but it was just hairy. She rubbed the hairs on his thigh and felt them with her finger pads. Then she had to feel his penis; that would be softer, smoother, and it was. When she cupped it in her hand, she felt it start to grow, and she started rubbing and squeezing it the way she saw him do when he thought she was asleep. She felt tremendous, ticklish, as if she were as big as an airplane or rolling through dandelions. Her whole body itched. By the time he woke up she was already on top of him, and by the time they were done she had licked, bitten just as much as he.

On Sunday morning she panicked when she woke up, as if someone were dying. Her heart beat fast, it must have been a hundred and forty beats a minute, until she checked to see that her husband and boys were all there. Then she opened her closet door and the bar that held all the clothes hangers fell, everything crashing to the ground. She shut the door, quick, but nobody came to yell at her and she opened it again and picked out a dress. Her husband could fix the bar on Monday but until then all her clothes would have to be on the floor. Dust would settle on them, bugs would crawl over them.

Later, when she cracked open an egg to make breakfast, a chick popped out, said Cheep, and fell onto the counter, dead. She wanted to sit down then, quit, cry, but she couldn't let the boys see the chick. She took it outside to give it a proper burial, and when she got back in the house her dress had somehow gotten dirt on it.

But the husband and the boys, they were spotless. After breakfast they all got in the car and drove to church. They sat down and then Sister Mortensen sat down with her five little girls, all of them wearing the dresses Sister Mortensen had sewn, lavender floral prints with puffy sleeves. She'd have sewn dresses for her girls too, only she didn't have girls, she had boys. She brushed another bit of dirt off her own dress, bought at a store in the mall. And then the other thing was, how would she have found the time for all that sewing? She noticed a bit of slime near the hem of her dress, probably from the chick. She didn't know why she hadn't changed into another dress.

When they passed the Sacrament around, she didn't take it, even though Sister Mortensen was watching. Next week she would take it; she'd shut the blind and not go near the angel, not once.

After church she asked the bishop if they could talk, and they went into his office. She didn't know how she could say to him, I have been, night after night, going up to my roof for love of an angel. In the end she said, I desire a woman. He wanted to know, Who, does she reciprocate, and she couldn't say. Have you acted on it, he said, and she said, No. Keep your scriptures nearby, he said, hold them close to your heart. This is grave but with the help of the Lord we will prevail. The bishop's forehead wrinkled and she left the room, embarrassed.

That evening her husband came back from going to the temple (or so he said), and something wasn't right; he had a funny glow like he'd had his face near a fire. He grinned with all his teeth and held the oldest boy upside down by his legs, to shake out all the yellow, he said laughing, and the oldest boy laughed too. The boy struggled and then fell on the ground with a bang, but then he sat up again and untied her husband's shoelaces. I have a present, her husband said, and he took saltwater taffy out of his pockets to give to them.

I have a present for you too, he said to her later, when they were in the bedroom, and he gave it to her: a purple nylon leotard with a hole between the legs, black panties, and a black dress that looked as though it had been shrunk. Oh, she said. Put them on, he said. Oh, she said. Do I take off the garments? she said. And he rubbed his hand all through her hair and down her neck, so it tingled and she had to pull away. She could put the leotard on, and the panties, but the dress was so tight he had to help her pull it over her shoulders, and he had to zip up the zipper. It was long and sleek and dark.

Turn around for me, he said, smiling. Should I? she said. Sure, he said. She spun around in her stocking feet. She didn't feel holy enough. When he pulled her toward the bed she said, Let's sleep with the blind shut, I can't sleep with it open. She pulled the covers up over her body like a turtle and shut her eyes. She thought holy thoughts, and half fell asleep. After he had finished and put her black panties back on, she woke up a little and watched the ceiling, which spinned. Spun. She was not going to open the blinds, she was not going to go out there, that was that. Final. She'd wake him up first, tell him she wanted it, before she would go out there again. If she went out, would it all spin, the stars, the moon, or would it be the house spinning under her? She was not going to go out. In the morning, at six-fifty, she would wake up, make lunches, make orange juice from concentrate. Little glasses for her and the children, a big glass for her husband. By seven-thirty they would all be gone. Not going out. Then she would sit around reading her scriptures. She was not going out. Or maybe there wouldn't be time for that; she'd have to take a shower and clean the house before ten, when she had to meet with Sister Jensen to plan out the songs for the next Sunday. Then she remembered what she was wearing, and she meant to take it all off and put her garments back on, but instead, feeling the way the black panties pushed into her skin, she moved her legs a little to make the panties push even better. She fell asleep and woke up once, when she thought she heard the sad sound of claws at the window.

In the morning the alarm didn't go off. Her husband had to go to work without shaving, dirty-chinned, and then the younger boy hit the older boy on the cheek, hard, and how could she send him to school with a bruise? What would they think? Then she went back to bed, forgot all about Sister Jensen and when Sister Jensen came all she could find to wear was a cotton dress with a rip down the side, held closed by a safety pin. Tattered. The day was tattered. Wouldn't it be getting better, though? Wouldn't the house calm down, now that she had given up the angel?

That night she had no mushroom sauce, so she tried to use tomato sauce instead. The chicken came out looking bloody, with loose clumps of tomato looking like raw bits of skin. Poor carcass, her son said. Her husband ate, maybe to be kind, maybe thinking he would be rewarded later, ha! As soon as she thought that, she thought, I should not be thinking that about him, poor thing.

All the men in her life fidgeted after dinner. The younger boy ran his train around the living room carpet, saying vrr-r-rr, and the older boy switched the television set on and off. Her husband unbuttoned his pants and walked from room to room, Looking for something, he said every time she asked. She went upstairs and took off everything for him, even the garments, and put on a T-shirt nightgown, but by the time he finally sent the boys to bed and came upstairs she was asleep, the blankets wrapped tightly against her body. In her dreams, giant headless chickens flew at her, enraged. Then she thought she felt her husband reaching for her in the dark, and after that, when she thought perhaps he was still working at it, she thought she heard the pitter-patter of her son's footsteps. Laughing in whispers, just outside the door, listening to them. She started awake; she rolled over to touch her husband and he was not there. Where was he? In the bathroom? She waited but she didn't hear anything. She got up and then she thought, the roof.

She opened the window and climbed up the grainy red tile, but no one was there. Then she heard sounds, like soft breathing and touching. She climbed toward the back of the house, where the black tar was, and no one was there. It was cold, and she tried to cover herself better with her T-shirt nightgown, but a bit of wind came and exposed her pubic hair. Suddenly she thought—and why hadn't she ever thought this before?—that someone could see her, out there on the roof! She hurried back toward the tile, nearly falling off the roof, and clambered up it, then down again toward the bedroom window. But in her way, blocking the window, there was the angel, half-sitting, half-lying, and facing her husband, who was touching her between her legs with his hand. He couldn't! They couldn't! Oh, but didn't she deserve it, such a bad wife, not staying in the house like an ordinary woman but having to come out to the roof every night and, she had to admit, she wanted to do what her husband was doing. It was her fault. She sat down on the roof and the angel looked up at her (probably seeing, like all the neighbors might have seen, those vile pubic hairs), but the woman had to look away so she wouldn't see the places her husband was touching. She would just wait until they were done; that was all.

But she couldn't. The wind snuck in through the holes in the fabric of the T-shirt nightgown, licking her nipples, no matter how tightly she crossed her arms in front of them, and she knew the Lord was looking down on her, shaking his head. And something was coming inside of her, slow like a steamroller, but coming steadily, until she knew what it was. It was what Jesus did when he saw the money-changers. She stood up and ran toward the angel, shouting, Shoo! so that the angel lost her balance and toppled off the roof. She opened her wings just before she reached the ground, and then made a lonely wail and flew away. She flew south without looking back, until she was just a dot in the sky.

Then the woman climbed back in through the window, put on her garments, and went straight to bed, lying stiff and still when her husband followed. In the morning it would be all right again; yes, it had to be. She'd have sheets to wash, breakfasts and lunches to make. In the morning she'd get up, she'd have her honey tea, she'd take her bubble bath, she'd go to the store and buy some more light bulbs to replace the ones that had burned out in the kitchen.

CALYX Journal, Vol. 16:3, 1996

Margaret Willey

SCISSORS GIRL

B ecause she'd had no previous experience as a sales-
girl, Alice suspected she'd landed the job for being so
poised and direct during the brief job interview. She had, by then, perfected
a few techniques for impressing adults—unwavering eye contact, enthusi-
astic nodding, earnest questions. She'd stared, nodded, and queried all
through the interview—ten minutes with the Personnel Director—and then
walked the two miles back to her own neighborhood, smiling to herself,
swinging her book-filled backpack by one strap, basking in a premonition
of triumph.

Her two-story house was easy to see from a few blocks away; it was planted
at the dead end of the street, like a schoolhouse or a church, a narrow
driveway on one side. From a distance, it looked stately and inviting, white
with black shutters, a pillared porch centered by the front door. Up close it
showed the wear and neglect that came from enclosing so many people—
the fading paint, the battered window trim, the sagging porch. One railing
was cracked clear through from a recent fight—two of her six brothers had
battled over the porch swing. Still, Alice always felt a wave of relief as she
approached her house, her safe harbor, the place where her mother waited
for news of her latest victory.

"What kind of questions did he ask?" Mrs. Peterson wondered fretfully.
She became unmanageably nervous whenever Alice was on the verge of a
new accomplishment.

"He asked if I had any experience working in a store," Alice admitted. "I
told him no, but that I get straight *A*'s in math."

Mrs. Peterson nodded approvingly. "That's good, that's right. And did
you look him right in the eye when you said that?"

They were preparing meatloaf for nine in a Pyrex bowl the size of a washtub—Mrs. Peterson chopping celery and onions, Alice, up to her elbows in meat, folding vegetables into a football-sized wedge.

"Right smack in the eye, Mom."

"And were you extra-extra polite?"

"Mom, I called him *sir*. I don't think he was used to being called *sir* like that, I could tell he liked it." Alice grinned at her mother knowingly, wiping her hands on a dish towel. "I just know I'm going to get the job."

"You sure are something else," Mrs. Peterson said fiercely, smacking the beef into two huge loaves. "That fool would be crazy not to hire you tomorrow." She shook her head angrily, upset in advance at the possibility that anyone might overlook or underestimate Alice.

Two days later, when the call from Personnel came, Mrs. Peterson agreed without hesitation to drive Alice to Steketees at 4:30 each weekday—a huge suppertime inconvenience, but worth it if her oldest child was "going places." She called Alice's father at his piano store to tell him that his contribution would be to bring Alice home after her shift ended at nine. When he didn't respond to this news with enough enthusiasm, Mrs. Peterson hung up on him and turned back to Alice. "He'll do it," she said grimly. "Don't worry, he'll do it."

When Mr. Peterson came home from work at 5:30 and had settled tiredly into his recliner, Alice explained to him that she had been hired to demonstrate an exciting new holiday product.

"Selling is no Sunday picnic, Alice," Mr. Peterson sighed, pushing his hair back, elevating feet cased in threadbare argyle. "It's completely unpredictable, even at Christmas."

"Listen to the big expert!" Mrs. Peterson called from the kitchen.

"They hired regular salesgirls too," Alice pointed out proudly. "But they thought I would be especially good at explaining the electric scissors concept to the holiday shoppers."

"Don't get commission," Mr. Peterson warned. "Go for straight salary."

"Thank you, Salesman of the Year!" Alice's mother hollered.

Alice rolled her eyes at her weary father, acknowledging her mother's unnecessary bitterness. "It's minimum wage," she whispered. "A small holiday commission if it goes well."

"All you can do is try," he replied, rubbing his temples.

The job required Alice to stand each evening behind a spotlighted and tinsel-framed table on the main aisle in Fabrics, wearing a coaster-sized button that said: *Holiday Gift Expert—Just Ask Me!* At the table she buzzed the electric scissors through swaths of remnants, using the more sleek and expensive model to get the customer's attention, always quick to point out the affordability of the larger economy model, which vibrated more drastically, but cut through fabrics just as well. This she stressed with particular sincerity to the shabbier shoppers, the factory-workers and farmers from the townships. As she spoke she would display various cutting tricks—circles and zig-zags and sharp angles, pointing out that the scissors were both powerful enough for denim and accurate enough for fine fabrics. Lastly, she emphasized the holidays-only price—twenty percent off with a rebate. She looked each customer right in the eye, communicating her eagerness to save them money. Her first week, one customer out of three, she made a sale.

She was, her supervisor pronounced, *the best little salesgirl they'd ever hired, especially with the men.* Connie Ryder winked as she said this, one purple eyelid drooping suggestively, a congratulation from one good-looker to another. "Maybe I'll take a few lessons from you."

Alice responded with a prim smile, put off by the compliment, because Connie Ryder was a notorious flirt and Alice never flirted. She preferred to be taken seriously. She avoided short skirts and spandex and loud colors and wore only the sheerest lipstick and no eye makeup, although she did curl her eyelashes because she was proud of how long they were, long and pale, like her hair. She knew she had a tidy attractiveness; she relied on it. She always made an effort to be pleasant and speak grammatically. Boys ignored her, her girlfriends often forgot to include her, but adults recognized and rewarded her gifts. Alice believed she was successful at selling because people trusted her. They believed in her and accepted her assurance that a pair of electric scissors might really make their Christmases more memorable.

But after Connie's congratulatory teasing, Alice began to notice that it was mostly men who stopped to watch her well-manicured, vibrating hands. The women who stopped were mostly older, heavy-set types, in tent coats and orthopedic shoes, women apparently too tired to care anymore about saving time. Women who would study the scissors mistrustfully through the divided world of bifocals and then move along, occasionally throwing back a humorless cackle. The laughter was particularly unsettling; Alice felt accused of selling something frivolous. She didn't actually sew herself, but she had no doubt that a pair of electric scissors would be a genuine timesaver—anyone could see it. And the sale price, combined with the rebate, was a significant savings. Still, she began to draw back and glance away whenever an older woman approached her table. It was easier just to wait for the nice men. Sooner or later, one would shuffle along, behind or separated from his scowling wife, perhaps shopping furtively for her. Alice would turn on the luxury scissors and prepare for eye contact. She felt herself change as she did this, her cells realigning themselves in the narrow space behind the table as she channeled all her positive energy into her face and hands. If she could get a man to stop, she could get him to try the scissors. If he was hesitating, she could put the scissors into his hand and guide his hand across the fabric with her own. If he had questions, she could try to answer them honestly. If he agreed to buy a pair, she would smile at him as though he was doing the right thing at last. It was a process, both mysterious and familiar, and she felt at home with it.

Her mother was thrilled and righteous. Her father was surprised. The Fabrics Department had to order a new shipment of electric scissors two weeks early. It was her first taste of career success.

The third week of the job, a middle-aged man in a hunting jacket stopped, listened carefully to her sales pitch, and bought a luxury model. "My wife sews like nobody's business," he told Alice, shaking his head, as though he couldn't imagine why.

"Oh, this will save her so much time!" Alice assured him.

"You sew yourself?" he asked.

Alice hesitated, not wanting to lose face, and at that moment Connie Ryder came up behind the two of them and interrupted brightly. "Our little Alice just loves to sew!"

The man turned around, met Connie's big-toothed, red-lipped smile. She added coyly, "Poor old me, I can't sew a stitch."

The man grinned, flustered by the sudden close range of Connie's neon make-up and earrings.

"Only one pair?" she asked him, taking the boxed scissors. "Sure you don't have another woman in your life who could use one of these babies?"

The man looked away, blinking, half-smiling, deciding how to respond. Then he said, "I got a sister."

Connie laughed her girlish laugh and picked up another boxed pair of scissors, holding it out, tempting him. "I'll bet that sister of yours wants one too."

"Maybe," he said, cornered but grinning about it. "Okay, better give me one of them cheaper ones. I don't want to start a feud."

Connie's laugh rose and peaked. Alice, angry at the interruption, watched Connie leading the man away. It was the third time in a week that she had come up to the table and talked a customer into buying two scissors instead of one. The man shuffled to Connie's register, pulling bills out of a battered wallet. He called back, over his shoulder, in Alice's direction, "That's one fine little salesgirl you got there."

"We know it," Connie agreed. "We're all in line to take lessons from her!"

In the employee lounge there were three older salesgirls; they eyed Alice suspiciously over their cigarettes, knowing that she had been hired to perform a special, possibly less tedious holiday task than theirs. "How's it going with those electric what's-its?" one asked gruffly. "People actually buy them?"

"They're moving along," Alice said vaguely. It was what her father always said about pianos.

Another of the three leaned forward and asked more boldly, "How can you stand working with that flaming bitch Connie?"

Alice, relieved at the invitation to complain, blurted, "She keeps butting in at my table every time I turn around."

"Did you see she got December Top Salesmanship?" the first asked the other two, picking up the Personnel newsletter from an end table and waving it. "They even put her doggy face right on the cover."

The tallest of the three responded, "Wonder how many guys she had to screw in Personnel."

The others hooted. Alice laughed with them, but weakly; she was shocked. After they left the lounge, she put her feet up upon the plastic sofa, stalling and fidgeting, not wanting to go back to the display table. Finally, Connie herself came looking for her. She stood, hands on hips, in the haze of smoke that her detractors had left behind. "Come on, girl," she teased. "Your fans are waiting."

Alice followed her listlessly. The evening had started out slow and she wasn't in the right mood to turn the tide. She stood at the display table for the remaining hour and a half, plucking lint from remnants, avoiding the eyes of the customers, wanting only to go home.

When she climbed into the front seat of her father's van, she told him that she'd sold only nine scissors that night and that she had never been so tired, ever, in her entire life. She put her head against the seat and closed her eyes. "And I still have all my homework to do!" she groaned.

"Maybe you need a night off from that job," her father suggested. Early on he'd said that he thought it was too many hours of work for a high-school girl, after which Mrs. Peterson had accused him of caring only about his precious drinking schedule. This silenced him—it was true that picking Alice up interrupted his after-dinner beers at the Pine Pub, although most nights he dropped Alice off in the narrow driveway beside the house, waited until she had gone inside, and then headed back downtown to the bar.

Alice liked having her father pick her up after work, liked the unfamiliar arrangement of sitting in the front seat with him, liked the mixed scents of tobacco, alcohol, and his limey cologne. It made her think about a future with men—being driven around in a car without grubby brothers fighting over candy in the back seat. Her father seemed also to appreciate this uncategorizable time with her; he always seemed amazed at how well she was doing selling scissors, amazed and happy for her. Those first few weeks the numbers had climbed and climbed—now they were going back down, but still, he seemed impressed. "Selling runs hot and cold," he explained. "Be glad you got an early taste of the hot. You've definitely earned yourself a night off, Alice. Go out with your girlfriends tomorrow night, have some fun."

"There's no one else trained to do this, Daddy," Alice explained patiently. "I'm the only scissors girl."

"You're a *kid,* Alice," he reminded her. "It's not like you're supporting a family."

He grinned across the seat at her—a clandestine moment because they both knew that Alice's mother would have a fit if she could hear him, encouraging her to skip out on work. He was challenging Alice to see the world his way, a way that included occasionally letting people down, risking the contempt of the more responsible. Alice smiled back at him, but more in sympathy than conspiracy. She was too much her mother's daughter to take his advice. "It's a foot in the door, Alice," Mrs. Peterson had insisted that very morning, she who had never quite gotten her own foot in. If the department store was a "going-places" kind of place, Alice would keep going; she would not blow this chance to be a winner in life; she would keep her foot in the door. She was lucky, she was different, she was "something else."

But by mid-December, it was becoming more difficult to feel like there was anything promising about demonstrating electric scissors. The continuous standing exhausted Alice; by evening's end, her back and neck were full of a new, adult tension. She had never been in a store for so many hours at a stretch, never realized how many people shop resentfully and desperately and consider salesgirls a nuisance. And she genuinely despised Connie, cringing every time she came near the display table. How the woman had ever become the supervisor of the Fabrics Department, Alice couldn't imagine. She seemed to have nothing but contempt for all her customers. She would shake her head at departing shoppers, rolling her eyes and wondering aloud, "Why would anyone *want* to spend their time sewing? Who has *time?*"

In the final week before Christmas, the store was particularly clogged, the shoppers frantic. Connie decided to make her own contribution to the chaos by putting all Christmas fabrics at fifty percent off—all the red and green calico, the velvet, the red flannel. To Alice, it seemed a final carrot held out to the weak. The Fabrics Department was mobbed, and because of this, the husband shoppers were frightened away. Alice's sales dwindled— sometimes an entire hour would pass without anyone to even give a demonstration to.

So when she spotted an unattached man coming down the aisle with a dogged gait and a lowered head, she wondered hopefully if he might be a scissors man. She turned on the luxury model and lifted her chin. Only when he was a few yards away did she realize it was her own father, a man who rarely entered a department store unless forced to. "I came a little early tonight," he explained uneasily.

"Is Mom with you?" Alice asked.

He shook his head. "I thought maybe I'd take a look at those famous power scissors of yours."

Alice shrugged and lifted a pair. "They're just scissors, Daddy."

"Electric scissors," he corrected her. "Scissors of the future." He was teasing, but she didn't smile. He picked up the more expensive model and turned it over in his hand, cupping it gingerly, like it was a hand grenade.

"You're holding it wrong," Alice complained. "It works like this. See? Here's how you make it go faster. Here's how you slow it down."

"What about one of these for your mother?" he asked hopefully.

Connie had come up behind him, grinning her predatory grin, poking her head around his shoulder. "Have you asked our little sewing expert about—"

"He's my dad," Alice cut her off. "He knows I don't sew."

Connie drew back, clucking at this unprecedented rudeness. Her father also seemed surprised; he coughed nervously, picked up the economy model, and turned it on as Connie slipped away.

"Dad," Alice chided. "Mom hates to sew. Electric scissors are for people who sew all the time. Make their own clothes and curtains and stuff."

She was scolding him, aggravated that he would pick out a present for his wife that she would surely add to her list of grievances against him.

He insisted defensively, "Hey, your mother's not the easiest person in the world to buy presents for!"

They looked away from each other. Then he mumbled, "So when can you get out of here?"

"I won't be finished for another half-hour."

"I'll let you get back to your customers," he said.

"I don't have any customers," she grumbled, but he had already shuffled away.

Almost as soon as he was out of sight, Alice felt sorry for being so harsh. *It's this job,* she decided. *It's giving me a bad attitude.* She looked around the corner, saw that Connie was caught in a snarl of women fighting over the last bolt of red velvet, and sneaked away from the display table to help her father find a present for her mother. She searched for him for ten minutes, in the Women's Department, Perfume, Millinery, until she had a sudden, appalling thought—that her father might wander back to the scissors table and without her to protect him, Connie would talk him into buying a pair of scissors. The thought enraged her; she headed back to the display table at a half-run.

But he wasn't there. Alice saw with alarm that the economy model her father had turned on had vibrated its way off the table and was hanging, still buzzing, by its cord. She turned it off and put it back in the box, thanking her lucky stars that no one had noticed it. *I hate this job,* she thought. When she got out to the van, she said it aloud to her father: "I really hate this job!"

"Hell, I couldn't work in a store like that," her father agreed, shaking his head. "Too many people. Too much junk nobody needs. And I'm not exactly the world's greatest salesman, as you know."

It made her feel worse to hear him bringing up his own failures. She frowned and looked away.

"Everybody has a bad night now and then," he assured her. "We won't tell your mother. Look, how about I buy her electric scissors, give you an easy sale, and we'll kill two birds with one stone?"

Now she felt a wave of deeper anger rise within her. "Daddy," she repeated slowly, "Mom hates to sew. She doesn't have *time.*"

"I can't think of anything else to buy her," he admitted.

Alice looked at him; his expression was pleading. She sighed. "She wants a beaded cardigan. They have them on sale in Women's." She had already bought one. It was stashed, gift-wrapped, on the floor of her bedroom closet with her other carefully selected Christmas gifts.

"How much?" her father asked.

She had paid forty dollars for it; she told him twenty-five.

He thought it over. "Agreed," he said. "I'll give you the money tomorrow, and you can pick out a nice one for her, okay?"

"Okay." Alice stared out the window again.

Her father gave her shoulder a punch. "See?" he said. "You just made a sale, Alice. You still got the touch."

Alice got out of the van without looking at him. He waved to her; she lifted her hand. When the van was out of sight, she stood on the snow-crusted curb a long moment, wondering where in the world she'd find the time to track down a Christmas present for her mother as perfect as that beaded sweater had been, stuck as she was behind the scissors table until January. From the curb she could hear a chorus of voices from within the house—the staccato commands of her younger brothers, her mother's voice climbing in anger, the baby howling. An hour ago, she'd wanted only to come home, to be free of the colored lights, the numbing holiday music. Home, where her mother would lift a plate of still-warm dinner from the oven and ask her how the evening had gone, eager for details, numbers, information about the world. A freezing drizzle had started, soaking her hair and her collar, but still she stalled, pacing the curb in front of her house, trying to shake a drained, cornered feeling before she went inside.

CALYX Journal, Vol.17:2, 1997

Rita Marie Nibasa

A LINE OF CUTTING WOMEN

This story is dedicated to those who've seen
everything but a way out.

I come from a line of cutting women, so it was only natu-
ral that I took up the knife. My mother's mother cut six
men, my mother cut four. At seventeen I had cut only one, but it was enough
to make me lay down my knife. Men who see their own blood bond too
easily for me.

Now, my grandmother cut one of her husbands to the bone and dared
him to talk about it. At the hospital, he reported that he'd been cut in a card
game. Seven years later when she next saw him, he stopped his car in the
middle of the street and yelled as she paused on the sidewalk: "Katie, you
the meanest thang in Memphis." Even my mother didn't have any prob-
lems with the men she cut—one of whom was my father, who, afterward,
brought his check home more regularly. But me, well, I had to cut a man
who took it as an act of love—tough love, as it were.

It happened on a Friday afternoon in April and I was just beginning my
long walk from school. I lived with my eldest sister, Mary, about four miles
from my high school. Mary was ten years older than me, and although she
left home when I was just a child, she would visit me frequently at home
and, to my chagrin, at school. Recently I'd started skipping classes and
hanging out in one of the nearby hamburger stops. Mary would find me
and walk me back to class. After several days of this, I arrived home early
one day to see Mary's car. As I opened the door, I heard my mother shout
my name, not to me but to Mary.

"Hello," I called out as I walked toward the kitchen and into the middle
of a standoff. Neither my mother nor Mary spoke. The triangular emblems

on the kitchen curtains hung above their heads like daggers. I stood nervously in the doorway, glancing first at my mother and then at Mary.

"I've decided you should live with Mary for a while," my mother said, with hands-in-the-air defeat.

I gasped. "What? Live with Mary? No!" I folded my arms and dug my feet into the threshold. Having Mary show up at school was one thing—bad enough, yes—but living *with* her every day was a different matter. Up until five months ago, I had spent time with my grandmother, cleaning for her, caring for her. If she were still living, I'd have turned my back on both my mother and Mary and walked, but instead I turned slowly toward my mother, my eyes and silence demanding an explanation. Mary stood up, smoothed the creases from her dress, and put her arms around me.

"Listen, Darlene, I can see where you're headed, and I can't pull you back. That only you can do. It's a shame, Darlene, when the first light is dim and the first faces you see are those you have to struggle the most against." Mary drew her anguished face close to mine. "It's a damn hard fight when you're born in the middle of it."

"Yeah, whatever," I muttered.

"Go and pack, Darlene." Mary pried me from the doorway and pointed me toward my room.

Hoping my mother would call me back, I started into the living room at half speed, almost tripping over her surrender.

Three years later I was still living with Mary and attending private school. I would be graduating in two months and was considering my next move, which Mary hoped would be to somewhere far away. Each day I received stacks of mail—from this college, from that one, from the Army, the Navy, and the Air Force—all places Mary had written. I even got an offer from a college on a ship that sailed the Pacific. After three years with Mary, I could swim the Pacific.

And so, it was because I lived four miles from school that I was glad when James, a friend of ours, pulled up beside me to ask if I wanted a ride home—although Ricky also sat in the car. Everyone thought Ricky was to be avoided. A few years ago, he was a great ball player in high school, but now everyone said he stole from his mother, and not just small change from her purse but rent money and money she needed for food. This was the worst thing a son could do, and it was enough to mark Ricky for life.

As I walked toward the car to talk to James, Ricky opened his door and motioned for me to sit between them. An open bottle of beer cradled between Ricky's knees tipped forward slightly, spilling beer onto his shoes:

his prelude to the evening. I told him he couldn't pee on my head and make me think it's rain, and, carrying my mother's and sisters' reputations, I opened the back door and climbed in.

Before we could even test zero to sixty, Ricky wanted to know when he and I would get together. Now mind you, this was only loose talk. I just chuckled. Then he asked me if I knew that in the realm of sexual endeavors he was king. I leaned forward in my seat and said close to his ear that I knew it, but I'd heard his throne was shaky and that all his subjects were imbeciles. Now, I admit, I liked the sound of my own voice; I had always considered myself witty, a wit I thought to be beyond Ricky. I was wrong.

Ricky drew back his arm and slammed his fist into my chest, knocking me back. I bounced against the seat a few times and fell against the door. "Man, I can't believe you hit her like that," James mumbled, turning to Ricky and shaking his head. Ricky sat sullen and silent.

I closed my eyes and saw, smiling meekly at me, the faces of the men my mother and sisters had fought. And there too was Ricky's father and my own, among the woman-beaters and womanizers I knew. And James—who often visited Mary and me, who sat in our home and ate our food—now stood out among the weak. I wondered whether all men were mere walls with cracks.

What would my mother think? What would she say if she knew I had let the son of a wife-beater hit me? Ricky's father often beat Ricky's mother so badly that she would have to be hospitalized for days. Once, after he heard she had the police looking for him, he went to the hospital and tried to choke her.

The popping sound of gravel spewing from beneath the tires reverberated in my head like the feet of displaced women and children running. James had turned his car into my driveway. I got out and slammed the door. And I, who often wore light clothing because I didn't want more pressure on my skin, swayed under the added weight of Ricky's blow.

I walked into my house, put down my bookbag, and changed from my school uniform into a pair of jeans and a loose shirt. I went into the kitchen, opened a drawer, and took out a steak knife. Of my mother's four daughters, it seemed that I, the youngest, would be the one to take up the knife. Charlene never fulfilled that potential, although her ex-husband says she sleeps with a pistol near her head. Linda has a fondness for threatening errant boyfriends with a baseball bat. Several times she could have gone home instead of spending the night in jail if only she'd heeded the policeman's warning to put the bat down.

Standing before the drawer, I slowly replaced the knife. I went to a cabinet and climbed onto a chair to reach the cabinet's top shelf. I removed the heavy cutlery block and examined each knife, from the long saw-like blade for cutting bread to the razor-thin knife for filets. I shuddered as I imagined the wound made with a serrated edge. I thought for a moment and then chose one from the middle, sharp but neither too long nor too thin, an all-purpose utility knife. This would teach Ricky a lesson. He had hit me for no reason. People would have to hear that I defended myself. We lived in a very small town. I would run into Ricky often, and if I didn't go out now to find him, every time we saw each other he'd see himself hitting me.

I placed the knife in a brown paper bag and walked out the door. I had no idea where I was going, but evil lying by the wayside joined in and led me across town in a direct line to Ricky. After about a mile and a half, still clutching the bag, I spotted James' car in front of a liquor store. Ricky sat in the car with his elbow resting on the door and his fingers tapping the hood. I tiptoed up to the car, took the knife from the bag, and drew it back. As Ricky saw the knife coming down, his arms flew up and he gasped. I ignored the little boy I saw in his eyes and plunged the blade into his upper arm.

I dropped the bloody knife back into the bag and raced toward home, scenes from old shows flashing in my mind as I ran like The Fugitive. A mother runs down the street in the night, a baby pressed tightly in her arms, small children trailing. Why can't they go home? Why can't they sleep in their own beds? In a street in the middle of the night, compromises are made, and years of fight fade bitterly into submission.

As I slowed down, I realized that I was in the street. I looked around me, letting a car pass, and then stepped onto the sidewalk. I turned the final corner toward home, and the car that had just passed was idling next to the curb. Through the back window, I saw some girls I knew: Gloria, who would be graduating with me but dropped out of school at sixteen with her first child, at seventeen she had her second. Pat, who was also my age, had so many men that she turned into one. And Teresa, sweet Teresa, in and out of jail, lost custody of her children. There was room enough on that junk heap for my dreams too.

I pushed my key into the door and rested my hand on the knob, hesitating to turn it, ashamed to walk in and face Mary. "Of course," I whispered aloud, "why didn't I go to Mother's?" At last an intelligent thought separated itself from the sludge in my head. I pulled at my key, ready to run again, but Mary had heard my fumblings and opened the door.

I tried to brush past her. I felt her eyes piercing me as she placed her hands on my shoulders and led me to the mirror in the hallway. My thick hair hung about my face like Medusa's, and a large drop of dried blood ran down the front of my shirt, like a tear on a cheek. The words to describe what I'd done trembled haltingly out of me.

"Girl, I'm scared for you. You poor mother's child."

A heavy weight fell from my throat down to my legs. I dragged myself into the bathroom and cleaned the blood off my hand. When I returned to the living room, Mary motioned for me to sit down.

"Listen, Darlene, you've always idolized Mother, and not to take anything away from her, I must say life was much different for me. It hurts me that you're so enamored of her reputation. Mother has come far. But, Darlene, the object is not to learn to fight men, but to choose better—to choose men you don't have to fight."

I wondered whether as a baby Mary had been dropped off at our door. She did look like us, but the difference in lifestyle was just so fundamental. Were I sitting across from my mother, from Charlene or Linda, I would have been welcomed into the inner circle of accomplished women. And now here was Mary, telling me there are men I don't have to fight—contrary to what I had been taught since birth. "That's all very interesting, Mary. So you say we can choose better. And just what have you chosen, Mary—I mean, for yourself?"

"I've chosen not to live Mother's life."

"No, Mary, you've chosen not to live, period—not Mother's life, not your own life. . . . At least Mother had a life. So you're telling me that your dreams are only what Mother discarded."

"I had dreams, Darlene, but I put things for myself aside because I wanted to help my sisters. I couldn't reach Charlene and Linda, but it's not too late for you." Mary sighed, seemingly exhausted.

I felt the weight of Mary's net around my shoulders, and I flinched. "Not too late for what, Mary? Not too late for me to be you? I can't be you. I don't want to be you. You're not even you. You're just a vague assortment of could-have-beens, a pile of losses heaped onto others." The heat of my words singed my own apathy and I wanted to chase after them, to retrieve them before they burned Mary, but anger runs wild and too fast.

Still, they had only rushed past Mary, who sat motionless, her gaze fixed on the blank wall above my head. "I can still remember the many times I had to bundle up Charlene, Linda, and you and run with Mother in the middle of the night to Aunt Lena's. I can still see Father stopping us in the street. Sometimes we returned home, Darlene, sometimes we kept running. Of course, you probably don't remember these things." Mary fell silent and retreated inward.

I saw again my own flashbacks and wondered how much of my life had become a movie to me and what role I was now playing. In some way—maybe even a bit perversely—I liked the distinction my mother carried in our town. My head was full and heavy; I wanted to get away from Mary. Hers had been a long, unfolding sadness, but sitting there I seemed to have witnessed it all at once. "I need to sleep, Sis. We'll talk, we'll talk again in the morning."

I awoke exhausted, bewildered, gasping. I had dreamt that I was beaten very badly. A man had kicked me about the chest and face so severely that my insides fell out, so severely that I vomited up parts of my own lungs. Somehow, I was able to wrest a knife from him and stab him in the temple. Then, cradling parts of my stomach and intestines in my hands, I stood up and began to walk. With each step I took, my body grew stronger; I was able to ease my insides back into me. I walked to my mother's home, where she and Charlene sat talking at the kitchen table. I tried to speak, to tell them what had happened to me, but I couldn't yet. Congealed blood and lungs, filling my throat, jutting from my mouth, let only a hoarse, raspy sound escape. Neither my mother nor Charlene came to my aid. Charlene said only that she was pleased I had made it on my own.

Did I wake up? Or did I fall out of bed? I don't know. I just know that I was up, dressed, and in no hurry to go out and talk to Mary. She might want to put me on that ship this morning.

I piddled about in my room until Mary answered a loud knock on the door and I heard Ricky's voice. Running out, I stood behind the door, to the right of Mary, and watched Ricky through the slight opening. His upper right arm was bandaged, and he held two old, beaten-up tennis rackets in his left hand.

"Can I speak to Darlene?" I slashed the air sharply with my arm and mouthed No.

"I don't think Darlene wants to see you, Ricky. She's sorry for what she did, but—"

At that nonsense, I reached for Mary's arm. She represented me so poorly. I wouldn't cut someone and be sorry for it. Mary swung the door open a bit wider, hoping to step out and talk with Ricky and keep me inside. I moved from behind the door and walked out to meet Ricky.

"What are you doing here, Ricky?" He searched my face and slowly raised his left eyebrow, like a question mark that had fallen over, awaiting the proper question to lift it again.

"I wanted to know if, if you'd like to play tennis."

"Are you crazy? My mother didn't have any fools. Do you want me outside so I can fix your other arm? Anyway, if I wanted to play, why would I want to play with you? And how can you play—with your arm and all?"

"Oh, it's not too bad, just a nick."

"What?" I shouted. Such would be my luck: to show how tough I was by nicking someone with a six-inch blade. After all, I had a legacy to uphold.

"Yeah, I only needed a few stitches."

I felt a little better that he had required medical attention. "You had no business hitting me, Ricky," I said, belligerently.

"I know I didn't, Darlene, and I came to say I'm sorry."

The boy who stole from his mother wiped away tears from his eyes. Mary invited him into the house for breakfast, and he and I sat in the living room.

Ricky sat with his back straight against the couch and his fingers intertwined. As I looked into his eyes, the little boy there pleaded once more. Perhaps, I thought, not all men are walls with cracks.

Ricky said that while James was driving him to the hospital, they'd passed his father on the road. His father, like him, a little bit high, a little bit drunk, riding around aimlessly—Ricky in a few years.

"I have to find what you have, Darlene," Ricky said, turning toward the kitchen, where Mary prepared breakfast. Ricky looked back at me and smiled, the image of Mary cradled in his eyes. I am not Mary, I wanted to tell him, but instead I sat there silently, the film of last night playing in my head. I was the bored, ungrateful one, and there was Mary trying to complain of a headache to me, someone whose entire mind was in a sling.

"I'm going to work all summer and then move to Milwaukee to live with my uncle." Ricky inhaled deeply and exhaled so forcefully that his body shook. Oxygen is such a lonely air, I thought; every now and then one must inhale the exhalations of another. I wanted to move closer to him. But what would I do but cup my hands in hunger, for at that moment, as I watched him seek direction, it seemed that he had so much more than I.

I wondered whether I really wanted to be known as a woman who cut men. Men hoping to conquer my reputation would certainly seek me out, and women who wanted to prove how tough they were would surely try to challenge me. I'd have no peace. I thought of Charlene and Linda. At one time, they were very pretty women, but now their struggle could clearly be seen in their hard faces. Charlene has a small scar on her upper lip, and Linda, poor Linda, has a sleepy eye, from a ring on a finger.

Mary floated in and sat near us. Tears streamed down Ricky's face like a trail. To where, I wondered. Sitting there with bone-dry eyes, I too wanted release, but I didn't know how or where to begin. Then, compounding my self-pity with downright shame, Ricky said, "I want you to know, Darlene, I never stole from my mother."

I wished he had said anything but that. In my mind I could justify cutting him because a boy who steals from his mother needs to be slapped down. But now I didn't even have this deed of his to fall back on.

I stood up and walked toward the door. I pushed it open, stepped out, and began walking, not so much to a place but rather past—past my mother's house, past Charlene calling to me from her car, past friends I'd hung out with. I passed my grade school and the school where Mary had put me. I walked on to the Wanderer's Rest Baptist Church, where as a child, more hopeful then, perhaps, than now, I sat as a penitent on the Mourner's Bench. I thought of the deacon and the countless times he'd asked, "Are you saved?"

I continued walking past things, people, places. I stopped and stood before the house where I'd cared for my grandmother and where she died. And then just like Lot's wife, I turned and looked back at life, but unlike her, I felt some perspective of distance. In that glance I saw a world, my world, sagging from the weight of defeat. I sat there on my grandmother's porch, missing her, thinking of lives lived and unlived—Mother's, Charlene's, Linda's, and Mary's . . . especially Mary's.

Suddenly I was crying so hard I was heaving. What years on the Mourner's Bench had failed to release, thrashed about there in my storm. My tears though were not only flesh and blood. A body, you see, is really just a small thing to bury.

A dream, now that's something else.

CALYX Journal, Vol. 17:1, 1997

Contributors' Notes

These notes serve as an index. The story title, page number, and CALYX *Journal volume and publication date follow each biography.*

KATHLEEN ALCALÁ'S publications include *Mrs. Vargas and the Dead Naturalist* (CALYX Books), winner of a King County Publication Award; *Spirits of the Ordinary* (Chronicle Books/Harvest), which received a 1998 Pacific Northwest Booksellers Association Award; and *The Flower in the Skull* (Chronicle Books). She is an assistant editor of *Seattle Review*, a co-founder of *The Raven Chronicles*, and the Distinguished Northwest Writer-in-Residence at Seattle University. ("The Transforming Eye," p. 114, 12:2, 1989/90)

CLARIBEL ALEGRÍA was born in Estelí, Nicaragua, and grew up in El Salvador. A major voice in the struggle for liberation in El Salvador and Central America, she is one of Central America's most eminent poets. She has published over forty books, including fifteen collections of poetry, and received the Casa de las Américas Prize of Cuba for her book of poetry, *Sobrevivo*. Some of her other works in English include *Ashes of Izalco, Luisa in Realityland, Family Album,* and *Fugues,* all published by Curbstone Press. ("Luisa in Realityland (excerpts)," p. 54, 11:1, 1987/88)

JULIA ALVAREZ is a poet, essayist, and novelist born in the Dominican Republic. Her novel *How the Garcia Girls Lost Their Accents* (Algonquin Books/Plume) won a PEN Oakland Award and was named a Notable Book by both the *New York Times* and the American Library Association. Her second novel, *In the Time of Butterflies* (Algonquin Books/Plume), was a finalist for the 1995 National Book Critics Circle Award in fiction. She has two books of poetry, *The Other Side/El Otro Lado* (Dutton/Plume) and *Homecoming: New and Collected Poems* (Plume). She has a third novel, *¡YO!* (Algonquin Books/Plume), and an essay collection, *Something to Declare.* She lives in Vermont. ("New World," p. 24, 8:2, 1984)

DEE AXELROD earned her MFA from Washington University in St. Louis (MO). She received an NEA Emerging Artist Fellowship, the New York State Arts Council grant, and three McDowell colony residencies. Her short stories are published in many journals, including *Nimrod, Bomb, Catalyst,* and *Sou'wester.* She lives in Washington State. ("River," p. 243, 16:2, 1995/96)

CAROLYN BARBIER lives in New Mexico with her husband, cat, and two parrots. She writes and continues her career as a registered nurse. She has taught at the Duke University Summer Academy Creative Writing Workshop for Health Professionals. ("Nighthawks," p. 191, 15:2, 1994)

BETH BOSWORTH is published in *The Kenyon Review, The New Virginia Review, Hanging Loose,* the annual *Side Show,* and the Bench Press anthology, *The Whole Story: Editors on Fiction.* She is the author of a collection of linked stories, *A Burden of Earth* (Hanging Loose Press). She is a graduate of the University of Paris and the NYU graduate fiction program and has taught English and writing at Saint Ann's School, the New School for Social Research, and the City University of New York. She lives in Brooklyn with her three children. ("Sheets," p. 165, 14:3, 1993)

BARBARA BRANSCOMB lives in Eugene (OR) and is currently working on a novel, *Father and Daughter,* which won the first Heekin Foundation award for best novel-in-progress. She is published in *Writers' Forum* and received a Centrum residency. ("Walking Away," p. 157, 13:3, 1991/92)

BETH BRANT is a Bay of Quinte Mohawk from Tyendinga Valley in Ontario, Canada. She is the recipient of an NEA fellowship, a Canada Council grant, and an Ontario Arts Council award. She is the author of *Mohawk Trail* (Firebrand/Women's Press), *Food & Spirits* (Firebrand/Press Gang), and *Writing as Witness* (Women's Press). She is the editor of *A Gathering of Spirit* (Firebrand) and *I'll Sing Till the Day I Die: Conversations with Tyendinaga Elders* (McGilligan). ("The Fifth Floor—1967," p. 33, 8:2, 1984)

MARISHA CHAMBERLAIN is a playwright, poet, and fiction writer. Her stage adaptation of *Little Women* played at the 1997 Stratford, Ontario, Theater Festival. Her original play, *Scheherazade,* won the FDG/CBS regional and national awards. Chamberlain has recently returned to fiction and just finished her first novel. ("Firewood," p. 6, 5:1, 1980)

M. EVELINA GALANG is the author of *Her Wild American Self* (Coffee House Press). She has been the John Gardner Scholar in Fiction at Bread Loaf Writers' Conference and the recipient of the Colorado State University Graduate Diversity Educational Fellowship and a Lannan Fellowship. She teaches in the MFA program at the School of the Art Institute in Chicago and Goddard College (VT). Currently, she is at work on a novel, *What I Call Tribe,* and a screenplay, *Dalaga.* "Her Wild American Self" was named one of the 100 Distinguished Stories of 1996. ("Her Wild American Self," p. 221, 16:2, 1995/96)

MOLLY GLOSS is a fourth-generation Oregonian. Her novel, *The Jump-Off Creek* (Houghton-Mifflin), received both the Pacific Northwest Booksellers Award and the H.L. Davis Book Award of the Oregon Institute of Literary Arts and was a finalist for the PEN/Faulkner Award. *The Dazzle of Day* (St. Martin's Press) was named a *New York Times* Notable Book and was nominated for the PEN/West Fiction Prize. She has recently finished work on a novel titled *In a Wild Wood.* She received a 1997 Whiting Award. "The Doe" was her first publication. ("The Doe," p. 12, 6:1, 1981)

LINDA HOGAN is a Chickasaw writer. Her novel *Solar Storms* (Scribner) received the Colorado Book Award. Her novel *Mean Spirit* (Atheneum) was a finalist for the 1991 Pulitzer Prize. *Seeing Through the Sun* (University of Massachusetts) received an American Book Award. *The Book of Medicines* (Coffee House Press) received a Colorado Book Award and was a finalist for the National Book Critics Circle Award. She is a co-editor of the anthology *Intimate Nature: The Bond between Animals and Women.* She is the recipient of an NEA grant, a Guggenheim Fellowship, a Minnesota Arts Board Grant, a Colorado Writers Fellowship, a Lannan Fellowship in Poetry, and the Five Civilized Tribes Museum Playwriting Award. ("Crow," p. 38, 8:2, 1984)

AMY JONES [SEDIVY] lives in Los Angeles with her husband, Richard, and their son, Rylan. She is published in the *Louisville Review* and *Kalliope.* She has written one unpublished novel and is at work on another. She is self-employed, writing and designing newsletters and brochures. ("Sanctuary," p. 107, 12:1, 1989)

KRISTIN KING earned an MFA from the University of Washington and lives in Seattle. Her story "The Wings" received a 1998 Pushcart Prize. She has published short stories in various literary journals and won recognition for her work from the Writers at Work program and the Utah Arts Council. ("The Wings," p. 260, 16:3, 1996)

REBECCA LAVINE is an American Jew living in Cambridge (MA) and attending graduate school in theology at Harvard University. She is writing a novel about her experiences in Israel and about renewing a relationship to the sacred. Her work is published in *Sojourner: The Women's Forum, The Boston Phoenix, Otherwise, The Virginia Review,* and many other periodicals. ("Afterward," p. 254, 16:3, 1996)

SHIRLEY GEOK-LIN LIM is a professor of English and Women's Studies at the University of California, Santa Barbara. She is a two-time recipient of the American Book Award, for her memoir, *Among the White Moon Faces* (The Feminist Press), and for the anthology *The Forbidden Stitch: An Asian American Women's Anthology* (CALYX Books), which she co-edited. She has published four books of poetry, three collections of stories, and two critical books. Her most recent book of poetry, *What the Fortune Teller Didn't Say,* was released in 1998 (West End Press). ("Native Daughter," p. 86, 11:2&3, 1988)

TERESE MARTINEAU received a BA in English from the University of Minnesota and lives in Massachusetts. She is published in literary journals such as *Quarterly West, The Denver Quarterly,* and *Quimby.* Her story "Sister Zita" was selected as one of "100 Other Distinguished Stories of 1995" in *Best American Short Stories 1996* (Houghton Mifflin). ("Sister Zita," p. 211, 16:1, 1995)

VALERIE MATSUMOTO teaches U.S. history and Asian American Studies at the University of California, Los Angeles. She is the author of *Farming the Home Place: A Japanese American Community in California, 1919-1982* (Cornell University Press) and co-editor of *Over the Edge: Remapping the American West* (University of California Press, forthcoming). She is presently researching Nisei women and urban youth culture in the 1930s. ("Two Deserts," p. 67, 11:2&3, 1988)

CHERRÍE MORAGA is a poet, playwright, essayist, and teacher. She is a co-editor of the anthology *This Bridge Called My Back: Writings by Radical Women of Color* (Kitchen Table Press), which won the American Book Award. She is a co-founder of Kitchen Table: Women of Color Press. She has published two books of poetry and prose: *Loving in the War Years: Lo Que Nunca Pasó por Sus Labios* (South End Press) and *The Last Generation* (South End/Women's Press). Her play *Heroes and Saints* won every major West Coast award, including the Will Glickman Prize, the PEN/West Award, the Drama-logue Award, and the Critics Circle Award. She received an NEA Playwright's Fellowship and continues to write plays, as well as teach classes and workshops in creative writing in the Bay Area. ("It Is You, My Sister, Who Must Be Protected," p. 27, 8:2, 1984)

TAHIRA NAQVI, originally from Pakistan, lives in the U.S. with her husband and three sons. She wrote two collection of short stories, *Attar of Roses and Other Stories of Pakistan* (Lynne Rienner Publishers) and *Beyond the Walls, Amreeka* (Toronto South Asian Review Press, forthcoming). She has translated Sadat Hasan

Manto and Ismatr Chughtai. She teaches English at Westchester Community College and Urdu and Hindi at Columbia University and NYU. She is working on her first novel. ("Paths upon Water," p. 96, 11:2&3, 1988)

RITA MARIE NIBASA holds an MA in German literature from the University of Illinois and has studied at universities in Regensburg and Tubingen, Germany. She has published poetry, essays, and translations. Her first play, *Stories like Ours,* was produced at Parkland College in 1995 and a monologue from it is included in Heinemann's *More Monologues for Women, by Women, 1996.* She is a member of the Chicago Dramatists Playwrights' Network and three of her plays—*I Know You Don't Know Me, Adam and Dawn in a Garden,* and *Healthy Primates*—have been performed at various venues. Her short story "A Line of Cutting Women" was selected for an Illinois Arts Council Finalist Award. ("A Line of Cutting Women," p. 279, 17:1, 1997)

ROSA MARGOT OCHOA is known for her poetry, plays, fiction, and essays. She was anthologized in *Mexican Women Writers as Seen by Other Mexican Women Writers* (University of Nebraska Press). Her three collections of essays, originally published in the Mexican newspaper *Ovaciones,* are especially renowned. In 1997, she was chosen by UNESCO to represent Mexico at an international symposium on ancient Greek drama. BERTIE ACKER (translator) earned an MA from Southern Methodist University and a PhD from the University of Texas at Austin. She has taught at the University of Texas, Austin, the Universidad del Valle in Calí, Colombia, and the University of Texas, Arlington. She is the author of two books of literary criticism and translator of a novel by Teresa de la Parra, *Iphigenia: The diary of a young lady who wrote because she was bored* (University of Texas Press). ("Happy Mourning," p. 149, 13:2, 1991)

CAROL ORLOCK teaches writing and serves as faculty advisor for *Spindrift* art and literary magazine at Shoreline Community College in Seattle (WA). Her two novels, *The Goddess Letters* (St. Martin's Press) and *The Hedge, The Ribbon* (Broken Moon Press), have received numerous awards, including the Pacific Northwest Booksellers Association Award, the Washington State Governor's Award, and the WESTAF Book Award for fiction. Her stories and poems are published in *Ms., Women of Darkness* (Tor Books), and *Fine Madness.* ("There Are Colors," p. 19, 7:3, 1983)

ALICIA OSTRIKER is a professor of English at Rutgers University. Her most recent book of poems, *The Crack in Everything* (University of Pittsburgh Press), was a National Book Award finalist and received the San Francisco State Poetry Center Award. Her obsession with the Bible has resulted in two books, *Feminist Revision and the Bible* and *The Nakedness of the Fathers: Biblical Visions and Revisions* (Rutgers University Press). ("Esther, or The World Turned Upside Down," p. 178, 15:1, 1993/94)

MARIA LUISA PUGA won Mexico's Villaurrutia Award in 1983 for *Accidentes* (Martin Cassillas Ediciones), which contains "Joven Madre." She teaches at the National Autonomous University of Mexico (Mexico City). JULIE ALBERTSON (translator) has an MA from SUNY, Binghamton. She lives in rural, upstate New York, where she is a research analyst at Cornell University, and dreams of someday having time to translate again. ("Young Mother," p. 146, 13:1, 1990/91)

VIKI RADDEN is a poet, essayist, and fiction writer who lives in Northern California. Her fiction is published in *You Go Girl: Travel Writings by Black Women* (Eighth Mountain Press) and *Sisterfire* (HarperCollins). ("A Thing about Italy," p. 187, 15:1, 1993/94)

RUTHANN ROBSON is the author of two collections of short fiction, *Eye of a Hurricane* (Firebrand) and *Cecile* (Firebrand), two novels, *Another Mother* (St. Martin's Press) and *a/k/a* (St. Martin's Press), and a volume of lesbian legal theory, *Sappho Goes to Law School* (Columbia University Press). Her volume of poetry, *Masks,* is forthcoming from Leapfrog Press in 1999. ("Lives of a Long-Haired Lesbian: Four Elemental Narrations," p. 124, 12:2, 1989/90)

SANDRA SCOFIELD is the author of seven novels, most recently *Plain Seeing* (HarperCollins) and *A Chance to See Egypt* (Harper Perennial). Her work has received wide critical praise, including an American Book Award, the Texas Institute of Letters Award for Fiction, and nominations for the National Book Award and the Oregon Book Award. She is a regular contributor of book reviews to the *Oregonian,* the *Chicago Tribune,* and *Newsday.* ("Loving Leo," p. 47, 9:2&3, 1986)

HOLLIS SEAMON teaches writing and literature at the College of Saint Rose in Albany (NY). Her fiction is published in *Chicago Review, The American Voice, 13th Moon, The Creative Woman, The Hudson Review,* and several anthologies, including *Sacred Ground: Writings about Home* (Milkweed Editions). ("Gypsies in the Place of Pain," p. 233, 16:2, 1995/96)

CHARLOTTE WATSON SHERMAN was raised in Seattle (WA). She received a BA in Social Sciences from Seattle University and has worked as a domestic violence and sexual abuse counselor and a mental health specialist. Her writing has been published in *Ms., Essence, American Visions,* and *Parenting,* as well as numerous anthologies. She has received many awards and grants including the Washington Governor's Writers Award, the GLCA Fiction Award, a Black Women's Gathering Woman of Achievement Award, and the Seattle University Award for Professional Achievement. She is the author of the short story collection *Killing Color* (CALYX Books), two novels, *One Dark Body* (HarperCollins) and *Touch* (HarperCollins), and is the editor of *Sisterfire: A Black Womanist Anthology* (Harper Collins). ("Killing Color," p. 134, 12:3, 1990)

SHIRLEY SIKES has published articles on banking, travel, and short stories in a variety of journals. She received an O. Henry award, five commendations from Best American Short Stories, and a nomination for a Pushcart Prize from Anne Tyler. She is working on a book about traveling in Switzerland. ("Falling off the Matterhorn," p. 59, 11:1, 1987/88)

KATHERINE STURTEVANT is published in *Sinister Wisdom* and the San Francisco State literary magazine. She is the author of a lesbian historical novel, *A Mistress Moderately Fair* (Alyson), and a travel book, *Our Sisters' London: Feminist Walking Tours* (Chicago Review Press). She is a San Franciscan who now lives in Berkeley, where she is working on an historical novel for children. She is a (dissenting) Roman Catholic and the mother of seven-year-old twin boys. "Apple and Stone" was her first publication. ("Apple and Stone," p. 1, 4:2, 1979)

AIYANA TROTTER has recently settled in Oakland (CA) after seven years of moving around. She dedicates much of her time to designing scenery and costumes for local theater companies, as well as teaching theater arts to youth. Now that she has graduated from Hampshire College, she might consider trying to publish some of the poems she has been hoarding in notebooks. ("We Have Always Stashed Our Bones in the Closet," p. 153, 13:2, 1991)

MARIANNE VILLANUEVA is the author of *Ginseng and Other Tales from Manila* (CALYX Books), a finalist in the Manila Critics' Circle National Book Awards. She has been a California Arts Council Literary Fellow and a Bread Loaf Fiction Scholar. She is widely published and anthologized in books such as *Flippin: Filipinos in America* (Asian American Writers' Workshop), *Into the Fire* (Greenfield Review Press), *Charlie Chan is Dead* (Viking), *The Forbidden Stitch* (CALYX Books). ("Siko," p. 76, 11:2&3, 1988)

MARGARET WILLEY lives in Grand Haven (MI). Her short stories are published in *Confrontation, Passages North,* and *Redbook.* Her most recent young adult novel, *Facing the Music,* was a 1997 American Library Association Quick Pick and was also awarded the Patterson Prize for Books for Young People. ("Scissors Girl," p. 270, 17:2, 1997)

PHYLLIS WOLF was born at the Ft. Peck Reservation in Montana. She works developing entrepreneurship in indigenous communities—in the past with the World Bank in sub-Saharan Africa and most recently within American Indian communities. Her poetry and prose is published in *Clouds Threw This Light* (American Indian Arts Institute) and *Talking Leaves* (Dell). She lives in Wisconsin. ("White-Out," p. 31, 8:2, 1984)

KIM SILVEIRA WOLTERBEEK lives in the San Francisco Bay Area, where she teaches writing and women's literature at Foothill Community College and is co-director of the annual writers' conference. Her fiction is published in numerous periodicals including *Other Voices, Buffalo Spree, West Wind Review, Santa Clara Review,* and *City Primeval: Narratives of Urban Reality* and has twice been nominated for a Pushcart Prize. Her short story collection, *The Glass Museum,* is forthcoming from Bellowing Ark Press. ("Sarah's T-Bird," p. 204, 15:3, 1994/95)

About the Editors

BEVERLY MCFARLAND became a CALYX volunteer in 1988, a member of the *CALYX Journal* editorial collective in 1989, and a half-time staff member in 1991. She is CALYX's senior editor. She is the recipient of the University of Oregon's Center for the Study of Women in Society 1993 Women of Achievement Award. Her major avocation has always been reading, so it was marvelous finding work that rewarded her passion. She earned a Bachelor's of Journalism and a BA in English from the University of Texas, Austin, and an MAIS in English, Journalism, and Education from Oregon State University (Corvallis). She is married to a fellow ex-Texan, and they have three grown children.

MARGARITA DONNELLY, a founding editor of CALYX, is currently the director. She edited (with Shirley Geok-lin Lim and Mayumi Tsutakawa) *The Forbidden Stitch: An Asian American Women's Anthology* (CALYX Books) for which she received a 1990 American Book Award. She also co-edited *Women and Aging* and *Florilegia* (CALYX Books). When she finds time she writes and received one of the first Fishtrap Writing Fellowships for her short fiction. Her writing is published in *The American Book Awards Poetry Anthology* (Norton), *Small Press Magazine, CALYX Journal, Women and Aging, Feminist Bookstore News*, and *Women's Press*. She was a founding editor of *Women's Press* (Eugene, OR). She is a recipient of the inaugural Distinguished Achievement Award from the Oregon State University Friends of the Library (1994). She was born and raised in Venezuela.

MICKI REAMAN moved to Corvallis, Oregon, for a CALYX internship in 1992 and became a staff member soon after. She is currently CALYX's managing editor and is a member of the *CALYX Journal* and CALYX Books Editorial Collectives. She edited *Present Tense: Writing and Art by Young Women* (CALYX Books, 1997) with the other members of the young women's editorial collective. She is published in the Bench Press anthology *The Whole Story: Editors on Fiction*. She is the recipient of the University of Oregon's Center for the Study of Women in Society 1993 Women of Achievement Award. She earned a BA in contemporary literature and feminist theory from The Evergreen State College (Olympia, WA).

TERI MAE RUTLEDGE began working at CALYX as a summer intern in 1993. She earned a B-Phil from Miami University's School of Interdisciplinary Studies (Oxford, OH) and returned to CALYX in 1994. She was a member of the *CALYX Journal* Editorial Collective from 1995 to 1998. She joined the CALYX Books collective in 1997 and was also a member of the special young women's editorial board for CALYX's *Present Tense: Writing and Art by Young Women* anthology. She was the promotions coordinator at CALYX and is now assistant editor at *Feminist Bookstore News*.

Selected Titles from Award-Winning CALYX Books

NONFICTION

Natalie on the Street by Ann Nietzke. A day-by-day account of the author's relationship with an elderly homeless woman who lived on the streets of Nietzke's central Los Angeles neighborhood. *PEN West Finalist.*
ISBN 0-934971-41-2, $14.95, paper; ISBN 0-934971-42-0, $24.95, cloth.

The Violet Shyness of Their Eyes: Notes from Nepal by Barbara J. Scot. A moving account of a western woman's transformative sojourn in Nepal as she reaches mid-life. *PNBA Book Award.*
ISBN 0-934971-35-8, $15.95, paper; ISBN 0-934971-36-6, $24.95, cloth.

In China with Harpo and Karl by Sibyl James. Essays revealing a feminist poet's experiences while teaching in Shanghai, China.
ISBN 0-934971-15-3, $9.95, paper; ISBN 0-934971-16-1, $17.95, cloth.

FICTION

Switch by Carol Guess. Quirky and charming as *Fried Green Tomatoes.* Cartwheel, Indiana, seems normal enough. But through Guess' seemless narrative, a mystical town full of unexpected secrets is exposed.
ISBN 0-934971-60-9, $14.95, paper; ISBN 0-934971-61-7, $28.95, cloth.

Four Figures in Time by Patricia Grossman. This novel tracks the lives of four characters in a New York City art school. Grossman reveals the struggles of these very different individuals whose lives coincidentally and irretrievably intersect.
ISBN 0-934971-47-1, $13.95, paper; ISBN 0-934971-48-X, $25.95, cloth.

The Adventures of Mona Pinsky by Harriet Ziskin. In this fantastical novel, a 65-year-old Jewish woman, facing alienation and ridicule, comes of age and ultimately is reborn on a heroine's journey.
ISBN 0-934971-43-9, $12.95, paper; ISBN 0-934971-44-7, $24.95, cloth.

Killing Color by Charlotte Watson Sherman. These mythical short stories by a gifted storyteller explore the African-American experience. *Washington Governor's Writers Award.*
ISBN 0-934971-17-X, $9.95, paper; ISBN 0-934971-18-8, $19.95, cloth.

Mrs. Vargas and the Dead Naturalist by Kathleen Alcalá. Fourteen stories set in Mexico and the Southwestern U.S., written in the tradition of magical realism.
ISBN 0-934971-25-0, $9.95, paper; ISBN 0-934971-26-9, $19.95, cloth.

Ginseng and Other Tales from Manila by Marianne Villanueva. Poignant short stories set in the Philippines. *Manila Critic's Circle National Literary Award Nominee.*
ISBN 0-934971-19-6, $9.95, paper; ISBN 0-934971-20-X, $19.95, cloth.

POETRY

Indian Singing by Gail Tremblay. A brilliant work of hope by a Native American poet. Revised edition, expanded to include new poems and new artwork and an introduction by Joy Harjo. *Indian Singing* is a visionary quest, a work of hope that presents enduring lessons to accommodate change in troubled times.
ISBN 0-934971-64-1, $11.95 paper; ISBN 0-934971-65-x, $23.95 cloth.

Details of Flesh by Cortney Davis. Nurse-practitioner Cortney Davis conducts a frank exploration of caregiving in its many guises: a nurse tending to her patients, a woman tending to parents, children, lovers.
ISBN 0-934971-57-9, $11.95 paper; ISBN 0-934971-58-7, $23.95, cloth.

Another Spring, Darkness: Selected Poems of Anuradha Mahapatra translated by Carolyne Wright et.al. The first English translation of poetry by this working-class woman from West Bengal. "These are burning poems, giving off a spell of light...."—Linda Hogan
ISBN 0-934971-51-X, $12.95 paper; ISBN 0-934971-52-8, $23.95, cloth.

The Country of Women by Sandra Kohler. A collection of poetry that explores woman's experience as sexual being, as mother, as artist. Kohler finds art in the mundane, the sacred, and the profane.
ISBN 0-934971-45-5, $11.95, paper; ISBN 0-934971-46-3, $21.95, cloth.

Light in the Crevice Never Seen by Haunani-Kay Trask. This first book of poetry by an indigenous Hawaiian to be published in North America is about a Native woman's love for her land, and the inconsolable grief and rage that come from its destruction.
ISBN 0-934971-37-4, $11.95, paper; ISBN 0-934971-38-2, $21.95, cloth.

Open Heart by Judith Mickel Sornberger. An elegant collection of poetry rooted in a woman's relationships with family, ancestors, and the world.
ISBN 0-934971-31-5, $9.95, paper; ISBN 0-934971-32-3, $19.95, cloth.

Raising the Tents by Frances Payne Adler. A personal and political volume of poetry, documenting a Jewish woman's discovery of her voice.
ISBN 0-934971-33-1, $9.95, paper; ISBN 0-934971-34-X, $19.95, cloth.

Black Candle: Poems about Women from India, Pakistan, and Bangladesh by Chitra Divakaruni. Lyrical and honest poems that chronicle significant moments in the lives of South Asian women. *Gerbode Award.*
ISBN 0-934971-23-4, $9.95, paper; ISBN 0-934971-24-2, $19.95 cloth.

Idleness Is the Root of All Love by Christa Reinig, translated by Ilze Mueller. These poems by the prize-winning German poet accompany two older lesbians through a year together in love and struggle.
ISBN 0-934971-21-8, $10, paper; ISBN 0-934971-22-6, $18.95, cloth.

ANTHOLOGIES

Present Tense: Writing and Art by Young Women edited by Micki Reaman, et al. Show-cases the original art and literature of women linked by their youth, women of different sexual orientations, ethnicities, socio-eonomic backgrounds. Contributor Kristin King's story, "The Wings," received a 1998 Pushcart Prize.
ISBN 0-934971-53-6, $14.95, paper; ISBN 0-934971-54-4, $26.95, cloth.

The Forbidden Stitch: An Asian American Women's Anthology edited by Shirley Geok-lin Lim, et al. The first Asian American women's anthology. *American Book Award.*
ISBN 0-934971-04-8, $16.95, paper; ISBN 0-934971-10-2, $32, cloth.

Women and Aging, An Anthology by Women edited by Jo Alexander, et al. The only anthology that addresses ageism from a feminist perspective. A rich collection of older women's voices.
ISBN 0-934971-00-5, $15.95, paper; ISBN 0-934971-07-2, $28.95, cloth.

CALYX Books are available to the trade from Consortium and other major distributors and jobbers. CALYX Journal *is available to the trade from Ingram Periodicals and other major distributors.*

Individuals may order direct from CALYX Books, P.O. Box B, Corvallis, OR 97339. Send check or money order in U.S. currency; add $3.00 postage for first book, $1.00 each additional book. Credit card orders only: FAX to 541-753-0515 or call toll-free 1-888-FEM BOOK

c o l o p h o n

The text of this book was composed in Clearface
with titles in Optima.
Page layout and composition provided by
ImPrint Services, Corvallis, Oregon.